Dave,
you're an awesome
servant of God. I'm
so glad we've come to
know one another.
Best regards,
Robert

Odd Man Out

A Novel

By

Robert J. Sutter

WWW.ROBERTSUTTER.COM

ISBN: 1-4033-4000-5 (e-book)
ISBN: 1-4033-4001-3 (Paperback)
ISBN: 1-4033-4002-1 (Dustjacket)

This book is printed on acid free paper.

Cover design and illustration by Rick Lovell
http://www.ricklovell.com
Author photograph by Deb and David Clymer

1stBooks – rev. 08/08/02

Dedication

This book is dedicated to all who served their country in a time when her people were either unable, or unwilling, to appreciate their sacrifice.

Washington DC – November 1998

Washington's air held the promise of change. Fiery autumn leaves danced on the Potomac's shimmering mirror, and frost covered ground suggested winter was on its way. The fall breeze was cleansing the city of the corruptive stain self serving men had left upon her clothes.

From the road below, the steady drone of weekday traffic was noticeably absent, and only an intermittent stream of joggers kept the streets from resembling a ghost town. In the nation's capitol, Sunday mornings are reserved for drinking expensive coffee while reading the *Post* or *The New York Times*.

Washington's elite believe themselves to be gods, and Capitol Hill is their Mount Olympus. In this town, the mighty and the merely influential sweat six days a week to grease the wheels of government and commerce. Playing God is hard work, and they deserve their day of rest. Toil on Sunday is reserved for *lesser* mortals.

On this hillside above the river, two of these lesser mortals stood silently as the casket was lowered into the grave. A third man closed his eyes and clearly pictured a rolling sea of white markers in long neat rows, converging at the base of the hill. Guarding the soldiers interred there, the tombstones of Arlington National Cemetery forever stand at attention. The man stood as rigid as the stones, and though dressed in civilian clothes, he was unmistakably a Marine. His massive fingers, locked together in a military salute, veiled the moisture welling in the corner of his eye. He cut his hand away sharply, bringing it to his side, as the last note of "Taps" hung in his mind like a child's balloon in the sky.

Opening his eyes, Arlington's stones of white vanished...replaced by the granite and marble markers of this secluded cemetery on the north side of the Potomac. Arlington is located on the other side of the river, miles to the south. Her hallowed womb doesn't receive our nation's heroes on Sundays, and like a doting mother, she vigilantly protects her sleeping warriors by carefully screening those who are welcome to join them.

The soldier being buried today had betrayed all that he'd once revered, and had forfeited his right to rest in Arlington. This funeral was devoid of the usual customs and courtesies extended to fallen soldiers. No honor guard...No twenty-one-gun salute...No flag draped casket. "Taps" wouldn't sound from a lone bugler on a hill, and no white tombstone would watch over him through the ages. He would never be read about in the paper, or talked about on *CNN*.

A week ago, as the gods of Washington rested, this soldier tried to kill his Commander-in-Chief.

Chapter One

CHANGES

"It's like a heatwave...burnin' in my heart."

Martha and the Vandellas

Khe Sanh, Republic of Vietnam - Early September 1967

August was in the books for the Marines of "Mike" Company, and had been a month of light casualties. No one had been killed in several weeks, and those wounded received only minor shrapnel wounds. The Asian sun had been up for less than an hour, and it was already very hot.

Corporal Mark Reilly was hungry and bone tired. He wanted something to eat, and some shade to grab a little sleep. Last night had been spent lying in ambush. Nothing had happened, which suited him fine, but he always felt drained after a night of lying awake, motionless...waiting. The heightened state of his senses and the adrenaline crash that followed always left him with a pounding headache.

Mark began rummaging through his pack, looking for a can of C-Ration peaches he'd been saving for a couple of days. He rubbed the sweat from his face with his towel and dropped it into his lap. He opened the peaches and took a bite. Their thick, sweet syrup had a tendency to stick to the tongue and the roof of the mouth. Even though they made him thirsty, they were among the few things available that tasted good any time of day. Since he didn't smoke, he had a practice of trading his C-Rat cigarettes for canned fruit, so he always had something to eat that didn't require cooking.

C-Rats came in limited varieties, such as meat with potatoes in sauce, canned tuna or boned chicken in oil (which could never be told apart) or ham and lima beans, affectionately known by all as "Ham and Mothers." Like most Marines, he got used to them, and some weren't bad if he had the time and security to heat them. When he was humping the hills, like the past week, he ate in a hurry, which meant everything was eaten cold, straight from the can. Tabasco had a way of making them palatable.

The meals were short on taste and high on calories. Two per day could provide a Marine with several thousand calories, depending how much and which items he ate. Mark had lost a lot of weight carrying 80 pounds of gear every day in the extreme heat, but as tasteless as the food was, it kept him functioning. All in all, he'd have preferred a cheeseburger and a cold Coke from the soda fountain at Northside Pharmacy back in Atlanta. It would taste one helluva lot better than canned peaches. Even better, no one would shoot at him when he finished eating.

He'd get that chance soon. Sixty-five days and a wake-up, and he'd be out of Vietnam. The "Freedom Bird" would swoop him off the planet and fly him back home, as he'd sit back in that comfortable, air-conditioned airplane seat and stare at the long-legged stewardesses with the pretty smiles. He had saved nearly every dime of his pay since boot camp, and he was going to buy a GTO or a Vette when he got home. Then, he planned to drive all over town with the best looking girl he could find, riding with him in the front seat.

That was his favorite dream, and he tried to conjure it in his head every morning while he ate. He'd savor the thought for a few minutes each day, then quickly put it from his mind. Daydreaming in Vietnam got guys killed. He'd seen it happen too many times. That being true, he made his men stay focused on patrol, and he demanded no less of himself.

For the next two months plus five, he was in for a ton of heat, serious discomfort, and a whole bunch of locals who wanted to send him home in a box. Mark's plan was different than his enemy's. He planned to go home with two of everything he brought with him to Vietnam: two arms, two legs, two eyes, and a pair of intact balls. He was a little nervous about his time getting short. Lots of guys got killed in their last month of combat. They forgot where they were, and let their minds wander.

Mark was determined to stay focused. His thirteen-month tour of hell was nearly over. When he was safe at home, there'd be plenty of time for cheeseburgers, fast cars, and pretty blondes. Right now, he needed some sleep. For him, a couple of hours at a time usually did the trick. With his towel draped over his eyes, he dozed in the shade of a poncho suspended between two stacks of old ammo crates.

He'd been sleeping less than an hour when he woke abruptly to someone shouting, "Hit the deck, Marine!" accompanied by a hard kick to the sole of his boot. Only a new guy could be dumb enough to wake a man who'd been out on ambush all night. Snatching the towel from his eyes, Mark could only see the Marine from the waist down, standing there in faded camo trousers, capped by boots that had been in-country a long time. They had the dingy, off-white, salty look that boots get after lots of sweat, dirt, and exposure to the weather. Mark thought they'd better belong to an officer, or someone was going to get his ass kicked for waking him this way.

Crawling out of his makeshift hooch, he was about to rip the moron's head off…until he saw his face. It was the mirror image of his own. He rubbed his eyes and stared for several seconds. Recognition swept over him as he processed his own reflection and realized what he was seeing. Standing before him was his 20-year-old brother, Matthew, his senior by all of three minutes. What really stunned him was how much older he looked. His face was weathered and tan, and his eyes were deeper in their sockets than they'd been before. These eyes had seen more than their fair share of death. Death that was up close…personal…and frequent. As he looked at his brother, Mark thought, *if Matthew looks this awful, I must be a Godawful sight, too.*

"Close your mouth," Matthew said, "or the mosquitoes'll fly in."

They both broke into smiles and embraced each other with the bear hug reserved for a brother who's been long away at war. Mark said, "It's great to see you, Matt!" As he slapped his brother's shoulder he added, "Where the hell have *you* been?"

"We've been workin' out of DaNang for a while," Matt replied. "I met a couple of guys from your unit gettin' patched up at the hospital.

They said they were waitin' on a resupply hop to take 'em back to Khe Sanh. I thumbed a ride to come visit my little brother. The boss says I can stay 24 hours, then I need to head back. I break in a new partner next week."

"Take a load off and grab some shade," Mark said, inviting Matt to join him under the poncho. "You gotta' tell me where you been, and what you've been doin'. Want somethin' to eat?"

"No, thanks. I ate before the ride up," Matt said, leaning his rifle against the ammo crates. "You heard anything from Luke?"

"Nothing lately," Mark replied, "but Mom's last letter said he's doing fine. The little prick gets hot chow and clean sheets every night, then plays war for a few hours every day. Some guys have all the luck."

"Horseshit," Matt barked. "He just picked smarter than we did." With a grin and a wink he added, "If you didn't want to sleep in the dirt, you shoulda' joined the Air Force, too."

Luke Reilly was brother number three. Not just Matt and Mark's younger brother, but their younger brother by less than eight minutes. These boys weren't twins. Matthew, Mark, *and* Luke were identical triplets, born to John Francis and Mary Quinn Reilly on April Fools Day, 1947. The family was as Catholic as an Irish family could be, and when the boys were born, John Francis thought it a real hoot to name his three sons for the authors of the Gospels. Growing up, the humor was lost on the boys, but it scored them some points with the nuns who taught them in school. After the first few days each year, the novelty wore off and no one gave it another thought. The three boys looked identical in every way, yet were as different as the names they'd been given.

Luke was also serving in Vietnam, but by comparison to their living conditions, his brothers thought he had it made in the shade. As a crewman on an Air Force B-52 bomber, Luke would leave Anderson Air Force Base in Guam in the early hours of the morning, fly over the northernmost reaches of South Vietnam, bomb the crap out of it, and return to Guam. There were worse ways to fight— assuming his plane didn't get shot down, which would either get him killed or taken prisoner for the duration of the war.

Mark envied him the clean sheets and the hot chow, but didn't relish the idea of being taken captive by the enemy. He'd heard stories about flyers becoming POWs, but he'd never known of an infantryman being captured. In the long run, he'd forego Luke's creature comforts for the reasonable chance to go home when his tour of duty ended. The key was to stay alive and in one piece.

The long odds of being born a triplet collided with the vagaries of politics to send Matthew, Mark and Luke Reilly to war at the same place and time. Three Christian boys serving their country, just as their father had done during "The Big One." Like many, they wrestled with the conflicting demands of their country and their faith. God commanded, "Thou Shalt Not Kill." Lyndon Johnson commanded, "Pack Your Bags for Vietnam."

They'd answer to God later. For now…LBJ had won the debate.

Returning his focus to Matthew, Mark said, "God, it's good to see you, man! It seems like forever since we've been together."

"Yeah it does," Matt replied. With a mischievous smile, he added, "I bet you'd like to kick my butt for talking you into coming here."

"One day I may, brother, one day I may." Mark thought about the last eleven months and sarcastically asked the rhetorical question, "Is Vietnam a good deal, or what?"

Matt laughed and nodded. "Well, you could be listening to some pointy-headed professor at Tech tell ya' how to build a damned bridge."

"Yeah, but when class was over I'd go across the street and get a chilidog and some onion rings from The Varsity," Mark said. "You know, Matt...I think I miss good food as bad as I miss fast cars and good-looking women."

"You'd better believe it," Matt said, recalling their mother's cooking. "I'd give anything for one of Mom's Sunday dinners. Right about now, I could put a huge dent in a plate of her fried chicken or pot roast."

"Me too," Mark said.

"Speaking of Mom, whadya' hear from the folks?" Matt asked.

"They're fine, last I heard. Mom writes a lot...Dad writes once a week or so." He glanced at Matt. "You hearing' from 'em about the same?"

"Yeah. Lots of letters...mostly made up of small talk. Mom doesn't want to admit to herself we're all over here, and Dad knows only too well what it's like." Matt thought to himself how odd it must be for his parents to have all three of their sons in combat. "There's no point in making' 'em worry more, so I don't say much. Hell…lately I don't write 'em much at all."

Mark changed the subject by saying, "The guys over in 9th Marines talk about you a lot." With a touch of pride in his voice, he added, "They say you're kickin' ass and takin' names with that sniper rifle."

"You bet," Matt answered, grinning ear to ear. "They say I'm a legend in my own time."

"That's not what they're saying by a long shot," Mark replied. "They say you're a legend in *your own mind!*" Pointing at Matt's sniper rifle with the large telescopic sight on its barrel, Mark's tone changed. "Matt…" he asked in a somber voice, "how many men have you killed with that thing?"

"Every one I've ever placed in the crosshairs, little brother." The statement was made as fact…without the slightest trace of bragging. "The Scout-Sniper School motto is 'One Shot - One Kill!' I make damn sure I'll hit my target, or the trigger doesn't get squeezed."

Mark was a little put off by the remark, but he let it slide, then said, "I know I've hit a few dinks since I've been here, but when there's so many outgoing rounds, it's hard to tell who actually dropped 'em." He stared off into the distance as though he were trying to recall, then realized he didn't want to. "I've had just about enough of this shit, Matt. It gets to me sometimes, man. Two more months and this place can *kiss my ass goodbye.*"

"My first five months here, I felt the same way," Matt said. "Too much noise, too much confusion, and *waaay* too much blood...an awful lot of it mine."

Matt filled Mark in on the firefight early in his tour, where he'd been wounded by an enemy grenade. He'd taken a tremendous amount of shrapnel to the left side of his upper body. His flack jacket had saved him, but the flesh that was exposed had been cut up badly. A buddy of his, a black kid from the streets of Philly, had come to see him in the hospital. When Matt told him how many stitches it had taken to close his wounds, the kid let out a low whistle and said, "Dude...you look like a guy I knew back home that came out on the bad end of a knife fight. Man...that dude was cut fo' ways:...long...wide...deep...and *again*!"

Matt and Mark both laughed at the thought of a guy being cut four ways.

Matthew showed him the 18-inch scar that ran the length of his bicep. It stopped at his shoulder where the flack jacket had been, then continued as a six-inch long gash up the side of his neck. The scars were still angry looking, and had turned a purplish hue from constant exposure to the harsh Vietnamese sun. Mark thought they looked pretty awful, but figured long sleeves and a shirt collar would hide all but about an inch or so of the neck scar.

Matt had chosen to extend his tour after his thirteen months ended. For the first time in his life, he was the best at something. In high school he'd earned a reputation for being a badass. His attitude and his penchant for fighting had always gotten him into trouble back home. Here, those qualities were considered an asset. He'd been in-country for seventeen months and eight days. He had no plans to go home until the war ended or somebody sent him home in a box.

He picked up his rifle and laid it across his knees. Pulling a cloth from his breast pocket, he began wiping it slowly. "You know Mark, this war's gonna go on for quite a while."

"Could be," Mark echoed. "What makes you think so?"

Matt looked him in the eyes and said, "Because a whole lot of folks are having *much* too good a time to let it end. You and I are just fighting one of the wars going on over here. The CIA has their own little fight…the Russians are here helping the other side…and there's a bunch of spook outfits over here that don't even have names. There hasn't been a good shooting war since Korea, and everybody wants a piece of the action."

"How do you know all that?" Mark asked.

Matt answered, "A couple of months ago I was having a beer in Thailand while I was on R & R. I met a guy who was one of the *real live shadow people*. He seemed to know a lot about me. Since I'd never laid eyes on *him* before, that sorta' made my skin crawl. He had a hard as nails look, and wasn't the kinda guy you'd want to mess with. The first time I asked his name, he dodged the question. The second time he just gave me a nickname he said his friends called him. He said his outfit could use a guy like me, and offered me a chance to come work for him."

"What'd you say?" Mark asked.

"I told him to take a hike! I like what I'm doing now *just fine*. No more shootin' at ghosts for me." Matt propped the butt of his rifle on his knee and elevated the muzzle. He wiped down the scope with the cloth. "Mark," he said, "right through this scope I've seen the face of nearly every guy I've popped over here. I've looked some of them right in the eyes before I squeezed the trigger. Once that round leaves the barrel, I *know* they're dead. There's no policing the area after the shootin' stops to collect the body parts. There's no exaggerated body count to please the headquarters pukes. It's one shot...one kill...end of story."

Mark was stunned by the malevolence in Matt's voice. His tone was cold and callous. It seemed Vietnam changed everybody, but it had *really* affected his brother. All his life he'd enjoyed a good fight, but it appeared now that he'd come to enjoy the killing.

Matt could see the concern on Mark's face. He dismissed it with a knowing look and a wave of his hand, saying, "Don't sweat it, Mark. There's no hate involved...it's just the nature of the business."

Matt had plenty to keep him busy. For the past few months, business had been *very good*.

Chapter Two
OVER THE RAINBOW

And the Good Witch of the East said to Dorothy,
"Follow the yellow brick road to the land of the Little People."

From *The Wizard of Oz*

Each had come from the same place, by a different path, but Vietnam was the common destination.

Atlanta in the fifties and sixties was not the sprawling supercity it would become later, but a collection of small communities that might as well have been separate towns. Ansley Park and Druid Hills were close to the downtown business district and were old, established sections with stately homes.

The area of town the Reilly boys grew up in was known as Buckhead. When the Reilly boys lived there, Buckhead was nothing but houses, small shops, a bunch of schools, and more trees than you'd find in most forests. It was a great place to live. Buckhead had all kinds of folks, from the very wealthy, to average, to dirt poor. Their fathers might have known which category they occupied, but only the kids of the snobs and the dirt poor really cared. The rest didn't give it much thought. The whole area was contained in about five square miles.

There were no official boundaries around Buckhead, but Peachtree Road ran north to south, right through the middle.

Peachtree Creek marked the south end, and when you got to Brookhaven you'd gone a half-mile too far. Westminster High School was as far west as anyone ever went, and there wasn't any need to go further east than Buford Highway.

Buckhead was a little like the TV town of Mayberry, minus Barney, Aunt Bea, and Gomer Pyle. It had the same kind of innocence. There were plenty of places to hang out: the Piedmont Drive-In on weekend nights, and the Cue Room to shoot pool if you liked hanging out with the toughs. Northside Pharmacy, the Zesto, and Garden Hills Drugstore were good places to eat after school. There were three public high schools in Buckhead: Northside, North Fulton, and in the early sixties they built a new school named for the retired school superintendent, W.F. Dykes.

By mid-November of 1965, Matt decided that being a freshman at Georgia State was a drag and Buckhead's five square miles was just too damned small. Over two six-packs of beer, he tried to persuade his brothers they were the Three Musketeers and adventure awaited them in the far away land of Vietnam. His brothers didn't see it quite that way, so the next morning at 8:25 a.m., he was waiting by himself at the recruiting station downtown. The Marine gunnery sergeant unlocked the door at 8:30 sharp, and invited him to be the first member of the Reilly clan to join the Corps.

His parents nearly had a stroke, but he was 18 years old, and his signature was binding. He left for boot camp at Parris Island, South Carolina two weeks later. Matt had always been tough, and he had a bit of a mean streak in him. He took to Marine training like a duck to

13

water, and graduated number one in his recruit platoon. He also achieved a perfect score with the M-14 rifle, which, combined with years of outdoor skills from hunting the North Georgia mountains, made him a natural when he arrived in Vietnam. The day was April Fools Day, 1966...his 19th birthday...and the irony wasn't lost on him.

After five months in an infantry company, his deadly aim with a rifle, his keen senses, and his ability to move with little noise earned him a spot in the newly formed Scout/Sniper Program at 3rd Marine Division Headquarters in DaNang. The school was supposed to last a week, but due to limited range facilities, it turned out to be a three-day course. Anything they hadn't taught him would have to be learned on the job. That suited him just fine. He was a fast learner, and had already learned a lot about combat. Matt liked the work, and he was in no hurry to go home.

While Matt was learning to kill, Mark, who liked math and science, enrolled at Georgia Tech. It was a lot harder than he thought it would be, and he worked hard to earn an "A" average by the end of his freshman year. Over the summer he worked construction during the day, and drank beer and chased girls at night. He and Luke, who had enrolled in nearby Emory University, loved each other in the way common to multiple birth siblings, but their interests were different as night and day. Mark and Luke had never seemed to spend as much time together as Mark had with Matt. They had always had more in common, and for years they had looked out for each other. If one got into a fix, the other was close by to cover his back, even though it was usually Matt that caused the trouble, and Mark that did most of the covering. In addition to just missing Matt, Mark felt as though he'd been disloyal and had let him down by not going with him to Vietnam.

On July Fourth evening, while perched cross-legged on the hood of his dad's Impala at the Piedmont Drive-In, Mark came to a decision. Georgia Tech would be there long after he was dead and gone. Matt was in Vietnam now. He went to the recruiting station the following Tuesday, and asked the recruiter if he could sign up and join his brother in Vietnam.

The gunny said "No sweat, son."

Now, Mark's question had meant: "Can I join *my own* brother in *my brother's* unit?"

Unfortunately for Mark, the gunny's answer meant that once he signed up, he'd most certainly join his brother, *and all the other Marines—in Vietnam.* Two guys talking about the same thing, with emphasis on different words.

This was the first of many misunderstandings Mark would have with Marine gunnery sergeants. Their answers to questions weren't necessarily lies, but were usually framed in whatever context it took to get the job done. Invariably, their answers were prefaced with "No sweat, son."

On July fifteenth, Mark passed through the gates of Parris Island to begin his recruit training. After eight weeks of boot camp and another month of infantry training at Camp Lejeune, North Carolina, Mark had learned that nothing in the Marines comes easy but being tired, hungry, and miserable. Soon, he would learn about being scared. None of these lessons came without a lot of sweat.

So long, Buckhead…Hello, Vietnam.

Luke was the odd man out more often than he liked to admit. He was smarter than the other two. He knew it, and they knew it. They just wouldn't admit it. All three boys were adept at schoolwork, but unlike the others, Luke thrived on it. The world needed smart people, and he planned to make his mark by being one of the smartest.

In January 1961, Luke hung on every word of John F. Kennedy's inaugural speech, where the new president had talked of going to the moon in this decade, and of the good government can do when the best and the brightest put their minds toward the task. When Luke heard him challenge all Americans, young and old, to ask not what their country could do for them, but what they could do for their country, Luke bought the whole story hook, line, and sinker.

Most 14-year-old guys in his freshman class were focused on football, girls and trying to act cool. Listening to the president talk made government work sound like the coolest thing he could imagine. Let the other kids concentrate on the trivial. He had a mission. He was going to grow up and change the world. What could be cooler than that?

After graduation in '65, Luke enrolled in Emory University. For him, it was the perfect school. Unlike Mark, Luke's mind was more geared toward words and ideas than formulas. He loved to read and debate. Emory was an excellent liberal arts college, with heavy emphasis on the liberal. He liked the professors, and he liked the intelligent students. With the academic crowd, America's involvement in Vietnam wasn't popular, but in the fall of '66 it hadn't yet reached the volatile point it would reach in just a few more years.

No one else in his circle of friends had a family member or close friend in Vietnam. Luke had one brother already there, and another training to go. Staying behind would've been hard enough if they were older by several years, but they weren't. They were his alter egos, and with them gone, it was as though he were missing limbs. Mark had felt guilty when Matt left for the war, but Luke now felt utterly lost since both brothers had gone. Other than what could happen to *them*, he could care less about what happened in Vietnam. He had no passion to join the fight. According to everyone he hung out with, the fight wasn't even a "just one," whatever the hell that meant. Still, the war was eating at him. Choosing to sit it out at Emory, while his brothers went to combat, was going to drive an even deeper wedge than had always been between them. He couldn't stand the thought of that. He cared for his brothers, and hoped they cared for him, but what he really needed more than their love was their respect. Emory would still be there when he returned. Even better, being a war hero hadn't hurt the political careers of Teddy Roosevelt, Dwight Eisenhower, or JFK.

Luke's better sense kicked in before he did something really stupid. Being a *living war veteran* was better than being a *dead war hero*. He'd made his decision to join the fight, but he'd be damned if he was going to do it on the ground. Luke was no Spartan. He liked being comfortable, and all he'd heard from both brothers was that comfort was hard to come by in the Marines. He briefly thought about the Navy, but he'd been saltwater fishing twice and puked his guts out both times. Once might be a fluke, but twice was the start of a pattern. The Air Force was the place for him. They attracted smart people, they never went to sea, and they placed a high value on air-conditioning. He had also observed that the guys in the Air Force ROTC didn't seem nearly as serious about all the military crap as the Army and Marines. For Luke, the Air Force was the ticket.

Months later, as a tail gunner on a B-52, he was on his first mission, dropping bombs over Quang Tri Province and the Demilitarized Zone. From 50,000 feet he couldn't see the results, but he could see the shock wave from each bomb as it radiated from the center in an ever-enlarging circle. BOOM! BOOM! BOOM! BOOM! Day after day, for weeks at a time, he continued to do the same thing. He had no idea who he was killing, but with the size of the bombs and the number they dropped, he was certain death wasn't being overly selective. America was at war with the North Vietnamese Communists, though he didn't feel as though he was bombing an ideology…he felt like he was bombing the ideology's people.

Luke's brothers thought he had a cushy job. His parents' letters said that Matt and Mark envied his ability to enter and leave the arena every day. Matt and Mark were sure that his missions were stressful, but they'd have given anything to get a good night's sleep without keeping one eye open for a deadly enemy. *What did Matt and Mark know?* The safety of Guam simply afforded him the time to think about what he was doing...and think he did. That's all he did. He thought on his way to the target, and all the way home again. He thought in his room. He thought in bars. Even with plenty of air-conditioning, clean sheets, and hot chow, he found it difficult to get the good night's sleep his brothers thought he was getting.

Some men were made for war. Matt was. Some men could deal with war. Mark could. Some men let war destroy them, even if their bodies survived to go home. All Luke had to show for his months of thinking was the conclusion that coming here had been the biggest mistake he'd ever made. Once again, he had allowed his need for his brothers' approval to overrule his good sense. He was smarter than the other two. He should've known better. He wasn't going to let this war destroy him. He had more important work ahead. He would find a way to make it right. He'd have to.

Chapter Three

THE ROAD NOT TAKEN

"We gotta' get out of this place…If it's the last thing we ever do!"

Eric Burden and the Animals

Laotian Border, near the DMZ,

Republic of Vietnam – Early September 1967

Matt crouched low in the tall grass just below the crest of the ridge. From this vantage point, he had a commanding view of the valley below. He swept the valley floor with his binoculars. Kneeling next to him was his partner, Lance Corporal James Ashcroft, known to one and all as "Ash." For weeks, the valley had been the route for movement of large numbers of enemy troops and supplies. Patrols had seen the telltale signs for several days. Matt was told to take Ash and set an ambush for the next group that moved through. They would operate from this hillside for a couple of days, and keep an eye on the valley.

Hollywood is fond of portraying snipers as lone wolves who operate independently, always deep behind enemy lines. In Vietnam, nothing was further from the truth. For one thing, scout-snipers worked in two-man teams. The shooter was usually the senior man. The spotter was the assistant gunner, target locator for the shooter, and security for the team. They were attached to larger infantry units in a supporting role. The "behind enemy lines" was another fallacy. Other than the Demilitarized Zone and the Laotian and Cambodian borders, this war had no enemy lines to be behind. If you were outside of a base camp, you were in "Indian Country."

This isn't to say that snipers didn't cross the borders for selected missions. They did, but their primary mission wasn't to assassinate big shots in safe havens. It was to strike terror into the heart of the ordinary foot soldier. There's nothing more demoralizing than eating your chow in an area you think is secure, only to see your buddy's head explode before you even hear the crack of the rifle. With a touch of fatalistic sarcasm, any Marine will tell you, "A bullet in the head will flat *ruin* your whole day."

Matt was measuring Ash on this mission. The kid appeared sharp and competent, but the verdict was still out. Distrustful of new troops, it would take him a while to rely upon his new spotter. A scout/sniper team is more than two experts with a long-range rifle. It is a deadly weapon system, only as effective as the teamwork displayed by its members. Matt was a sergeant and by far the better shooter of the two. With more time in-country, he was senior, and was the team leader. Ash was a 19-year-old kid from the Kentucky hills, new to the team in the last week. Matt's previous partner had rotated back home when his tour ended, and his timing turned out well. While waiting for Ashcroft, Matt got to stand down for a few days of R & R and a quick visit with Mark over at Khe Sanh.

Matt carried an M-40 sniper rifle, capped off with a 3 x 9 variable power Redfield Accu-Range scope. This rifle fired the same 7.62mm

21

round as the M-14 rifle that had been carried in Korea and the early stages of Vietnam, before the introduction of the lightweight M-16. The M-40, a modified Remington Model 700 hunting rifle, was a bolt-action weapon with a five round capacity and an effective range of 800 meters. Fully loaded and with its scope in place, it weighed a little more than 14 pounds. It was a mother to haul, especially when combined with the rest of their load.

A scoped sniper rifle is of little use in a sustained firefight, so the team carried additional weapons to protect themselves should they be detected, or fall prey to an ambush while moving. Both men carried government issue .45 automatic pistols, an assortment of grenades, and Ash had an M-14 for more firepower. He was free to carry the lighter-weight M-16, but the M-14 had several advantages. When first introduced in 1966, M-16's were susceptible to jamming problems. This was a definite drawback for a two-man team with no other buddies to back them up. Another advantage was the -40 and the -14 fired the same size and type bullets. Other than for the pistols, there was no need to pack different caliber rounds. The third advantage was that their "starlight" scope, which enhanced night vision, could be mounted on the M-14. This made the team effective night or day.

The extra weapons made them feel more secure, but for self-preservation, their best weapon was stealth. If they were ever detected, they'd likely get their butts handed to them.

About fifteen minutes after sunset, Ash saw the first one. He'd been moving in a stooped position to keep a low profile, stopping every few steps to look and listen. Each time he paused, he would drop even lower and remain still. Behind him and to the left, he saw another man moving in the same manner.

Ash placed a hand on Matt's shoulder to draw his attention. Without a word, he followed the direction of Ash's binoculars toward the valley floor and saw what he was watching. He could've taken both of them in an instant, but he recognized the dance below for what it was. This was just the recon team. They'd check out the open area to see if it was safe to cross. If Matt were patient, he'd have a much greater prize. Eighteen months in combat had taught him to be *very patient.*

Matt and Ash remained motionless while the recon team searched the area. Ash's blood ran cold when one of the enemy soldiers looked their way for what seemed a little too long. Matt knew they hadn't been seen; the soldiers were simply looking in the places that were likely locations for a sniper team to hide.

The men proceeded with their search and satisfied themselves that no one was in the area. One of them crouched by a large fallen tree, then stood to full height, exposing himself as if to tempt a sniper to fire if he was lying in wait. Matt didn't take the bait. The recon team returned to the treeline from where they'd come, and disappeared. It would take them a few minutes to report to their commander. Matt and Ash put those minutes to good use.

Earlier in the day, Ash had used his rangefinder to determine the distance to the fallen tree. He had it fixed at 500 meters, which is about five football fields plus fifty yards. After laying out ten extra rounds within easy reach of Matt's right hand, he double-checked his own M-14 and made sure his extra magazines were accessible. Matt tightened the rifle sling to his bicep, wrapped his left arm through it, and locked the rifle into a secure firing position. He aimed at the tree and moved the scope slightly to his left. This provided a clear view of where the trail ended and the clearing began. Smart soldiers usually try to stay off trails. They're too easy to ambush, and frequently booby-trapped. That being said, if they were moving supplies, these guys would be using the trail. They'd come into view any moment, and that was just fine. Matt and Ash were open for business.

A few minutes passed, and the same two soldiers appeared at the trail's mouth. They turned their heads slowly, looking for any sign that the area had changed since moments before. Nothing alarmed them, and they signaled for the caravan to move forward. A motley supply train, comprised of farm animals and light-wheeled vehicles, emerged from the tree line. Men in their sixties and boys ranging from twelve to fifteen were manning carts laden with weapons and ammunition. Two bicycles were loaded with food and medical supplies that towered over the young boys walking on each side of the bikes to keep them upright. A water bull pulled a large cart containing mortars and mortar shells.

Matt had seen supplies moved this way before, and figured he'd see ten to twelve potential targets. When they entered the clearing, there were a total of just eight Viet Cong in the group. Matt waited until the entire supply caravan was exposed before sighting his first target. He knew precisely in which order he planned to shoot them.

What happened next was a lesson Ash hadn't received in Sniper School.

If Ash had been the shooter, he would've chosen to start shooting from the back of the column and march his rounds forward for as long as he could before they realized they were under fire. With that strategy, he could drop two, perhaps three, before they heard the shots and began to run. Half or more would probably escape.

Instead, Matthew employed a lesson he learned on his first dove shoot when he was just eleven years old. The scenario below was actually quite similar. When doves fly over a field, only a rookie shoots the lead bird before he's led in the rest of the flight. Once they're all in range, they get shot from both ends of the field by several hunters. This causes the birds to make banking turns and fly in the opposite direction. Instead of fleeing the field to safety, the birds remain in the killing zone. Matt planned to turn the valley floor below into a one-man dove shoot.

The old man driving the large cart was the last man in the column. Matt squeezed the trigger and caught him just above his right ear. The force of impact launched him off the side of the cart. The second man was pulling a handcart, and never heard Matt's first shot; his head was gone by the time the sound reached the valley below. The two reports caused the third soldier from the end to stop and turn toward the noise, as Matt knew he would. His rifle was trained on that spot, and as the young boy turned, the bullet drilled him in the chest. He slammed into and over the bicycle he was steadying, knocking over his partner on the blind side, and pinning him under the weight of the supplies. Matt would come back to him in a few seconds.

By now the cat was out of the bag, and the two men who'd performed the recon were running for cover. Like doves breaking for freedom, Matt focused on the lead soldier and hammered his right thigh. The man's partner made the fatal mistake of breaking stride, as if to help him, then thought better of the idea. That brief hesitation cost him his life as the next bullet smashed into his neck.

Seeing the carnage ahead of them, the younger boys balancing the other bike dropped it and turned back toward the trees from where they'd come. As they ran for the trees, Matthew loaded three more bullets into his rifle and selected his next target, the boy who'd been pinned earlier by the toppling bicycle. He'd managed to push it off, scramble to his feet, and was now running away from the caravan. Matthew placed him in the crosshairs and put a round between his shoulder blades. His body crumpled to the ground fifteen feet ahead of the bike boys running toward the trees.

They were running one behind the other, about three feet apart, and reacted just as the Georgia doves had so many years before. Seeing their friend killed right in front of them, the lead runner stopped abruptly and turned, colliding headlong into the boy behind him. It knocked the wind out of both of them, and they fell to the ground. Trying to crawl out of danger while still gasping for breath…Matthew killed them both. The whole ambush had taken less than ninety seconds.

Ash stared in disbelief. In his entire life he'd never seen anything like this...and doubted he ever would again.

The only man still alive rose to his feet and limped toward the opposite tree line as fast as his mangled leg would take him. Matt's bullet had been a through-and-through, meaning it had torn muscle and flesh but hadn't struck bone. Falling down after a few feet, his body tensed and shook as he waited for the bullet that would end his life. It never came. Matt let him go as the echoes of his last two shots faded from the air.

Matt remained motionless for several seconds, surveying the area for signs of bad guys coming to the rescue. Satisfied that there were none, he ordered Ash, "Get on the horn and call the artillery for a fire mission. Let's blast those supplies off the map."

"What about him?" Ash said, pointing to the enemy soldier making his way into the treeline. "Why didn't you put him away?"

"Somebody's gotta' be alive to tell the VC what happened here tonight," Matt said, barely containing his pride. "I'll be damned if the artillery's gonna get credit for what I just did. That guy's pals are gonna know I'm out here...in their backyard, taking care of business."

The first artillery round to hit the valley floor was long by 30 meters. Ash radioed the correction. The second round was right on target. "Fire for effect!" he ordered, and within seconds a half dozen rounds impacted on the enemy supplies. They watched to make sure they'd been destroyed, and then Ash and Matt low-crawled their way over the ridgeline.

As they set in for the night, Ash had never felt more alone. Until a few hours ago he thought he was part of a team, but his partner had just put on the display of a lifetime, and had made it clear that it was all *his* show. The fact of the matter was...*it had been*. Ash hadn't said a word from beginning to end. He wasn't the only one being measured today. His partner had shown what he was made of, and the image he'd portrayed scared the crap out of Ash. Matthew Reilly was a man to keep an eye on.

The next morning, about twenty miles away, Mark's battalion was moving out. He didn't know the reason, but he'd heard they were moving over to Con Thien. This was a big move, and it bore all the signs of being a really bad time. They went to the airfield to catch the choppers that would take them there. The CH-53 Sea Stallions, called "53's" for short, began packing troops on as tight as sardines. The Marines love to make you walk, so when they decide to let you fly, no one complains about being packed in close.

From the air, Mark could see most of the territory he'd been humping for several months. When he wasn't in or around Khe Sanh, he had been all over Quang Tri Province. The northeastern part was called "Leatherneck Square" because of the four main bases at its corners. Cam Lo occupied the southwest corner, and Dong Ha was at the southeast. Gio Linh was at the northeast corner, and Con Thien lay to the northwest. Cam Lo was located along Highway 9, which ran east and west. Dong Ha was near the intersection of Highway 9 and Highway 1, which ran north and south.

Calling these roads highways was a stretch. By American standards, they weren't even wide enough to let two large American cars drag race. Even so, Con Thien was a valuable artillery base with unobstructed views of Dong Ha and Cam Lo. From there you could also observe the Ben Hai River, which officially separated North and South Vietnam. Con Thien was the best vantage point in Quang Tri, and it looked as though the North Vietnamese Army had set their hearts on having it. Mark's unit was being sent there to see that it didn't change hands.

The North Vietnamese were turning up the heat. For months, Mark had been fighting the Viet Cong, who his former company commander often referred to as the Pitchfork and Farmer brigade. There had been lots of booby traps, sniping, and ambushes, but for the most part it had been hit-and-run type action. The activity going on around here was of a different stripe entirely. The fulltime North Vietnamese Army troops were a more formidable foe than their cousins, the VC. They were well trained, well supplied, and this was *their* country. Mark's battalion was embarking on a whole new war.

He stood on the perimeter of the artillery base at Camp Carroll with Corporal Mike Thomas, a friend from boot camp days. Mike, who'd been at Camp Carroll for quite a while, had been a "cannon cocker" with the 12th Marines since he arrived in Vietnam. Mike pointed into the distance at the highest piece of ground to the north

29

and said, "See that?" Without pausing for an answer he continued, "That's Con Thien."

Mark could see a large hill with a flat top. To the right of it, several miles to the east, he could see the South China Sea. On the other side of the hill was the Ben Hai River. The area on either side of the river was the Demilitarized Zone, or DMZ as it was called. It seemed a silly name for it, because there was plenty of military from both sides, and enough hostility to last a lifetime. On the horizon across the river, well past the DMZ, Mark could see an Air Force B-52 making its bombing run. Even this far away, he could feel the explosions as the bombs shook the ground, and stood in awe at the destructive power emanating from the plane. He wondered to himself if it was his brother's B-52. It made him feel good to think that it was. He'd just seen Matt for the first time in months, but had not heard directly from Luke in several months.

Mark hadn't seen Luke since the night he left Atlanta for California, on his way here. He hoped he was safe and doing well, just as he looked forward to the day they would all be away from here. Realizing he was daydreaming, he quickly pushed the thought from his mind. Focus was the key to staying alive.

Mark wanted to learn everything he could about the area before they began patrolling. The 9th Marines had been all over this area for months, and knew it like the back of their hands. His unit would be relieving them, and he hated the idea of being in terrain he didn't know. He was a quick study, though some lessons had been learned the hard way. In the past nine months, his body had been cut up and bruised, but nothing life-threatening. In his third month in-country, he'd been wounded when another Marine tripped a booby trap. It was the simple kind: a grenade with a pulled pin, stuffed inside a C-Ration can that had been secured to the base of a tree. Attached to the grenade was a wire that had been strung across the trail to another tree. A Marine with his mind on something other than the trail he was walking tripped the wire and pulled the grenade from the can. Yeah, it was the simple kind...the kind that killed you, along with anyone else near you. With all the careless dumb-asses around, it was a wonder anybody ever went home in one piece.

With that thought in mind, Mark said goodbye to Mike Thomas, who left him with the admonition to watch his ass.

Later that evening Mark made his rounds, checking the defensive positions of his squad. They were assigned to two-man fighting holes on the perimeter of the firebase. Most of his men were seasoned troops, but he had serious concerns about two new guys. Private First Class Bill Nichols was a nice kid from Omaha, who had been in the squad for less than three weeks and didn't have a clue about what a world of shit he'd just stepped into. PFC Don Jansen, a blond haired, blue-eyed bodybuilder from Southern California, had arrived six weeks before they moved from Khe Sanh to Camp Carroll. Jansen had spent the first 19 years of his life focused on himself, pumping iron, and admiring his form in a mirror. Mark could already tell he was going to be a problem. He pegged him as the kind of guy who looked powerful on the outside, but who didn't have the stomach to squash a roach. He was the kind who'd get you killed, and then spend days telling everybody how sorry he was for his mistake. His type was always sorry for their mistakes...but sorry didn't bring good Marines back from the dead. Sorry was for a lifetime, and more often than not, it was someone else's. The special attention Mark had been showing Jansen for the last few weeks would continue until he got with the program.

As Mark approached the new guys' hole he could hear them talking in voices much too loud. It was a clear night, with enough ambient light to clearly see someone's silhouette. Mark knelt and listened to determine which guy was which, and what they were doing. It didn't take long to figure it out. Unlike your living room, a two-man fighting hole is cramped, and makes you long for the comfort of your favorite easy chair.

The two men were facing each other as they talked. Nichols was sitting exposed on the upper edge of the fighting hole, his feet dangling down inside. Jansen was sitting in the hole, no doubt with his legs outstretched as far as he could. Each guy was just trying to get a little more comfortable. To make matters worse, Nichols was holding a lit cigarette in his right hand. Neither man was being alert.

Mark approached quietly from Nichols' blind side, and announced his presence with a swift kick from the sole of his boot. The blow caught Nichols squarely in the middle of his back and caused him to let out a loud gasp as he crumpled into the hole, landing on top of Jansen. Before either man could react, Mark was on top of them. He grabbed Nichols by the forehead and yanked his head back sharply. With a quick stroke of a sheathed K-Bar knife he made a swipe across

Nichols' throat and said, "You're dead, asshole!" He jammed the knife butt into Jansen's neck and said, "If I'd been the enemy, you'd be dead too!"

The shock and fear on both men's faces turned to embarrassment, then quickly to anger. Nichols said, "What's up with sneaking up on us like that, Reilly?"

"Shut your mouth!" Mark said in a hoarse whisper. "And I'm *Corporal* Reilly to you shitheads! Put that cigarette out, keep you mouths closed and your ears open. Do your damn job! In the morning, I want to talk to both of you."

There wasn't enough light to see the color drain from their faces, but Mark knew the rebuke made the red flush of indignation disappear in a hurry. He turned and was gone as quietly as he'd appeared.

The next morning, both men reported to Mark. Nichols spoke first, and began to apologize. It came as no surprise when Private Jansen chimed in with the fact that *he* hadn't been smoking. Mark waved his hand to cut them both off in mid-sentence.

"Both of you shut up!" Mark said as he spit in the dirt. "*I* talk... *You* listen!" He proceeded to fire them up. "I don't know either of you guys, and to be honest I don't care if I ever do. I got all the friends I need in this world, and you two aren't people I plan to add to my list. Some of these other guys, however, *are my friends*, and it's my job to keep them, *and you*, alive. That stunt you pulled on perimeter duty last night can get you killed. Worse than that, if *you* get killed, others will too. Like I said, I won't miss you 'cause I don't know you. You will, however, piss me off *royally* if you get any of my real friends killed. *Am I understood*?"

"Yes, Corporal Reilly!" they both barked in unison.

Mark told them to sit down, and changed his tone to an almost fatherly one. Then he began to instruct them in some basics of doing their jobs…and living to go home:

"Private Nichols, you can smoke at night if you shield the lit end with the palm of your hand. It's a stupid thing to do when you're in a fighting hole, or on a listening post. If the enemy doesn't see it, he'll sure as hell *smell* it. My personal opinion is, you should only smoke if your ass is on fire. Until that happens, I'd kick the habit. I trade cigarettes from my C-Rats for cans of peaches and pears. You'd do well to do the same."

"Corporal Reilly," Nichols said, "I've been smoking since I was thirteen. I don't think I can quit…especially in this place. I've been nervous as a cat ever since I got here."

"You'd better give it a try. My brother is one of the top snipers in Vietnam. I saw him about a week ago and we had a chance to talk. He told me a story about 'three on a match.' Ever heard of it?"

Both men shook their heads.

"It's an old expression from World War I, when the troops were fighting in the trenches of France. It seems the fighting would cease at night, and guys would let their guard down. One soldier would light a cigarette. He'd hold the match to the end of his buddy's and light it for him. The third guy would lean in to light his, and a German sniper would blow his head off. It became a real superstition with the troops.

34

If you were the third guy on the match, it was as though you'd broken a mirror, or had a black cat cross your path. It didn't matter whether you got shot right then or not. You were considered a marked man for the future."

"Matt said he had stalked a small group of gooks a couple of months ago. While they were fixin' chow at dark, they decided to have a smoke. *Sure as shit,* three of 'em lit their cigarettes off the same match. Matt blew the third one's brains all over the other two. He let those two go so they could tell their pals the three on a match story. He figured the gooks hadn't read much about World War I, and they could start the superstition over here, with *their* buddies." He fixed the young men with a stare, hoping his next words would sink in: "I shit you not, fellas. You play with fire over here, and a sniper will put your lights out. *He'll flat ruin your whole day!*"

The sun hung low over the South China Sea as Luke's B-52 began its bombing mission just north of the DMZ. As the plane approached the target area, he stole a glance out the starboard window to the distant hills of Con Thien and Camp Carroll. He had no idea where his brothers were, but he knew these were Marine hills, and it caused him to smile for a second, knowing wherever they were, they had buddies watching their backs.

After nearly six months in his squadron, Luke was getting a reputation for being a malcontent. He kept to himself most of the time, and had little use for socializing with the rest of the crew. Even though the others didn't care for his attitude, they respected his competence. Luke didn't like what he was doing, but he did his job to the best of his ability. He just seemed to let it *get to him* more than the others. As usual, he believed himself to be the smartest member of the crew. The only one he had anything in common with was the copilot, Lieutenant Steve Driscoll.

Driscoll was like Luke in many ways. At heart he was a pacifist who found himself in hostile circumstances of someone else's creation. He was a true believer that wars could be prevented if one understood what other nations thought and believed. When he returned to the States, he planned to look into employment with the CIA or the State Department. Luke and Steve had a number of discussions about the war, and America's involvement in the internal disputes of a tiny Asian nation. Theirs was a friendship based on mutual respect for intelligence and idealism. Like many friendships formed in wartime, it was also based on shared misery. It was the kind of friendship that would last the rest of their lives.

As the bomb doors closed, Luke scanned the skies for enemy planes. Twenty minutes south of the DMZ, he settled in for the ride back to Guam as the huge plane banked over the sea and made a gentle turn to the south. Luke had no way to turn off his conscience, and the thoughts that constantly plagued him returned once more. The words of an old Animals song crept into his thoughts, and he began singing in a low voice:

"We gotta' get outa' this place...If it's the last thing we evvver do.

We gotta' get outa' this place...Girl there's a better life for me and you!"

Chapter Four
CHECKOUT TIME

"Gimme a ticket for an airoplane…
Ain't got time to take a fast train.
Lonely days are gone…I'm a goin' home
…My baby, she wrote me a letter."

The Box Tops

The Churchyard, Na Tho An Hoa – Mid-September 1967

During WWII, the Marines fielded five divisions. By the early sixties they had only three active duty divisions, with a fourth comprised of reservists. Rather than call up the reserves for service in Vietnam, which might not sit well with the American public, Congress authorized the re-commissioning of the 5th Division. At Camp Pendleton, California, the 26th Marine Regiment was re-formed over a period of several months. As each battalion was assembled and ready, it embarked for Vietnam. Upon arrival in-country, the new battalion was "chopped operationally" to the 3rd Marine Division to reinforce its units. Early September of '67 was the first time the regiment had combined to operate together since the end of WWII.

Mark belonged to the 3rd Battalion, 26th Marines, known as "3/26" for short. The four rifle companies that made up the battalion were India, Kilo, Lima, and Mike, which is the company Mark belonged to.

On the morning of September 7th the battalion, minus Lima Company, moved toward Con Thien, just north of the Cua Viet River above Cam Lo. Its mission was to flush out the headquarters of an enemy battalion thought to be operating just south of Con Thien.

Out of the blue, small arms fire and mortars opened up from three sides on India Company, who was a little west and north of the destroyed village of Nha Tho An Hoa. By midday, the entire battalion found itself in the middle of the biggest fight it had encountered since arriving in Vietnam. The fighting was heavy the rest of the day on the 7th, lightened up some for the next two days, and all hell broke loose on September 10th. Years later Mark would learn they'd locked horns with the 812th regiment of the North Vietnamese Army, not the battalion headquarters they'd been sent to find. While in the middle of the fight, all he knew was that his unit was in a shit-storm of epic proportions.

The fighting was horrific, and close. Early in his tour Mark had seldom seen the enemy, since they would hit fast, then disappear. This morning he could see enemy soldiers everywhere, and they weren't wearing black pajamas. The tan uniforms and pith helmets of highly motivated NVA soldiers swarmed through the dried-up rice paddies. The distance to the enemy was measured in feet, not meters. Grenades were being flung in both directions.

Lance Corporal Dan Kelley was using his M-79 grenade launcher as though it was a mortar. The M-79 resembles a sawed-off shotgun, with a short stock and a barrel big enough to fire a racquetball-sized grenade. He was holding it nearly vertical as he knelt in a shallow ravine, and was firing rounds as fast as he could break it open and load another one. Mark had never seen the weapon used this way, but it was working very effectively.

The rest of his squad was laying down fire while trying to stay low enough to dodge incoming rounds and grenades. The Marines believe in "peace through fire superiority." At the moment, the incoming and outgoing rounds were pretty even. Mark had already exposed himself several times to pass out ammunition and direct the fire of his squad. He'd taken a small amount of shrapnel earlier in the day, but had been patched up by Doc Peters, a Navy corpsman from San Diego. On any other day, his wounds would've been not only painful, but sufficient reason for evacuation. Today, the adrenaline was pumping so hard the pain was minimal, and he wasn't leaving his men until the fight was finished—or he was.

A few yards to his right a grenade hit the ground and one-hopped into the depression occupied by PFC Nichols. With a deafening *whumph* it exploded at the private's feet, lifting him off the ground and throwing him into an exposed position. The concussion bowled Mark over onto his back. He shook his head and rolled back to his stomach, suddenly realizing all sound had disappeared except for a loud ringing in his ears.

Nichols was flailing on the ground, and though Mark couldn't hear him, he could see that he was screaming in agony. Jumping up from the relative safety of his own position, he ran toward Nichols, diving on top of him to keep him down. Bullets impacted around them, sending spits of dirt and rocks into Mark's face. He dragged

Nichols' body with one arm while using his other arm and his legs like bulldozer tracks to move across the ground. Falling back into the ravine, he looked closely at Nichols for the first time. What he saw sickened him. Shrapnel had been driven up through the man's groin into his lower intestines. His flak jacket had protected his torso, but the grenade had done serious damage from the waist down. Nichols coughed up blood so dark it was nearly black. His eyes rolled back in his skull, and he was gone.

It seemed a crazy thought at that moment, but Mark conjured up the ass-chewing he'd so recently given Nichols about his cigarette habit, and thought, *he can smoke all he wants without worry now.*

Mark's hearing returned slowly, bringing the sounds of battle back as though someone were turning up the volume on a car radio. At first there was nothing, and then it was so loud Mark wanted to yell at someone to turn off the damn noise. He looked to his left to find Private Jansen putting out rounds with deadly accuracy, making Mark think he might have misjudged him earlier. As he looked over the ravine, it appeared as though the whole rice paddy below him got up and moved. He'd never seen so many enemy soldiers before. Looking at the shredded remains that a moment ago had been a kid from Nebraska, his fear drained away. It was clear he was going to die today. There'd be no fast cars. No pretty blondes. Just a funeral in Arlington.

It didn't make him sad. It just pissed him off. He grabbed all the grenades he could from Nichols' lifeless body and added them to what he already had. Holding one in each hand, he pulled the pins

41

from both, and ran from his protective cover toward the approaching enemy. With all his might, he threw them both and fell headlong into the dirt. As soon as they exploded, he rose up and repeated the drill. Private Jansen saw what he was doing and moved out adjacent to him, laying down protective fire with his M-60. The rest of his squad saw what he was doing and they, too, kept up the fight.

Mark had just released the third set of grenades when an incoming rocket propelled grenade hit the ground to his left. There had been a high whistle, then a boom, and Mark was sent flying into the brush.

Jansen hit the deck as dirt and rocks rained down around him. A burning sensation stung through his shirt, and he was certain he'd been hit. Rolling to one side, a large piece of hot shrapnel slid off his back. It had simply landed on him and burned his skin through his shirt. A split second later, Jansen felt the ground shake not once, but several times in rapid succession. The *whomp, whomp, whomp, whomp!* of exploding bombs was followed immediately by the sonic roar of the low-flying jets that had released them on the advancing enemy troops. He looked up to see two F-4 Phantoms that were nearly out of sight before the sound caught up. Passing rapidly through the valley and rising high into the clouds, they turned and prepared for another pass. A second flight of Phantoms could now be seen approaching, and the enemy broke off their attack, scrambling for cover.

Private Jansen moved quickly to where Mark was sprawled in the brush. His head was bleeding profusely, and the top of his head was peeled back as though he'd been scalped by Indians at the Little Big

Horn. Jansen screamed, "CORPSMAN! CORPSMAN!" and began applying a bandage until Doc Peters arrived and took over. While the corpsman worked to save Corporal Reilly's life, Private Jansen collapsed to the ground in exhaustion. Hands shaking uncontrollably, he fished through his pockets for an unopened pack of C-Rat cigarettes. He'd never smoked before in his life, but Vietnam was a place of many "firsts." Today was also the first time he'd ever soiled his pants from fear.

One look at the gaping head wound and the massive loss of blood, and Doc Peters knew Mark's war was over. If they couldn't get a medevac chopper in here soon…his life was, too.

On the morning of the 15th, Matt was cleaning his rifle when Gunny Shepherd approached him and dropped to one knee. He took the soft cover off his head and rubbed his palm back and forth over his graying stubble of hair. His face had that awkward look that meant bad news, and Matt could tell the gunny had something to say he'd give a week's pay to avoid. Matt had a good idea what was on his mind. He looked him in his eyes and asked, "Which one?"

With a pause and in a flat voice the gunny said, "Mark…Five days ago, near Con Thien."

"Is he dead?" Matt asked, continuing to wipe down the weapon in his lap.

"Wounded badly…His CO said he'd be surprised if he makes it," the gunny replied as he stood up. "I'll find out what I can and keep you posted."

"Thanks, Gunny."

"No sweat, Sergeant Reilly. Let me know if you need anything."

Matt waved his hand as if to say thanks, but no thanks. Nothing the gunny did would keep Mark alive…or bring him back if he was dead.

Matt had lost some friends here early on. As his tour wore on, he stopped making new ones. But he'd never lost a brother before. It was different. He felt like he'd just been told of his own impending death, and in a way, he had. Vietnam was a cancer, and it was eating him up slowly. It ate his friends…it ate his family…it ate his soul. What he did here didn't seem to matter. He was also mad as hell at God and the politicians who orchestrated this fiasco. He wished they could all have a little taste of the war. One day they'd pay, and like his namesake from the Bible, Matthew hoped he'd have the job of collecting the tax.

Jim Ashcroft approached Matt with some hesitation. The gunny had just told him about Mark, and he suspected Matt would be in a shitty mood. Feeling him out, he said, "Matt…I'm sorry to hear about your brother."

"Thanks, Ash…What's the word from the lieutenant?"

"We're going out again tomorrow," he told him. "Something's up with the gooks. They're moving more supplies than usual. The boss wants us to find another convoy and bust it up like the last one. The brass wants to make 'em nervous about their supply routes and slow them down."

"Pack your trash," Matt said as he stowed his rifle cleaning gear. "We'll move out at first light." As Ash walked away, Matt called out..."Hey, Ash? Pack some claymores."

"No sweat," he said over his shoulder, as he headed off to collect his gear.

The next day, the sniper team moved about six klicks to the west and crossed over the Laotian border. When they reached the trail, Mark and Ash scouted the area for signs made by supply convoys, and found plenty: depressions in the soft dirt made by heavy carts, and the dung from the animals pulling them, discarded cigarette butts, tracks from Ho Chi Minh sandals. This trail was a favorite, and would, no doubt, be used again.

They found a vantage point that offered good concealment and an excellent firing position, then radioed their location to the command post and began setting in for the night. The only thing they lacked was good cover. Operating in two-man teams, they couldn't afford the time or noise to dig a fighting hole. Their security depended upon never being seen, so they arranged natural foliage around them to camouflage their position.

Just before dark, Matt moved forward about twenty yards and positioned three claymore mines in a gentle semicircle facing down the hill. He camouflaged them, then ran the detonators back to their position. A claymore is different from most mines, and acts much like a large shotgun blast. The mine is the size of a child's shoebox lid, and is shaped in a slight curve. When the protective cover is removed, it reveals rows of small ball bearings imbedded in a sheet of C-4 plastic explosive. It can be detonated with a trip wire, or set for command detonation. Matt chose the latter, as he didn't want a small animal to trip the wire, and give away their position. If Charlie found them and approached from the front, the claymores would shred them like ground beef. When he returned, he cautioned Ash to keep the detonator's safety switch engaged. An accidental discharge would give away their position, too.

About an hour after dark, Matt began experiencing severe stomach cramps. Tonight's dinner had been canned tuna fish. He suspected food poisoning, as many of the rations had been stored since the Korean War. It was infrequent, but sometimes a can would lose its airtight seal, permitting the contents to spoil. Since tuna tasted briny anyway, it was hard to tell if it was bad.

He told Ash he was going into the bushes to get sick. Ash was dead set against his leaving, but Matt convinced him he was going to be sick from both ends, and didn't want to ruin their position for the night by soiling it. He took Ash's shotgun and the ammo for it and crawled off into the bushes.

Ash could hear him getting sick, and prayed that there were no gooks within earshot that could hear him, too. He stayed gone for what seemed like an eternity, and the noises from where he'd been ceased at last.

They were replaced by noises from the front of their position…where Matt had no business being.

Ash broke into a cold sweat, silently willing Matt to come back. He had no idea where he was, and their security was dependent upon each other. There was no way to call out to him, or warn him of the enemy he believed was probing their position. He nervously fingered the detonator for the claymores, and searched the darkness for signs of movement. He couldn't see anyone, but could *feel* that someone was out there.

It happened fast. Ash heard a blood-curdling scream from directly in front, then rolling and thumping in the brush. Two blasts from the shotgun rang out to his left front, and the muzzle flashes lit the darkness for an instant. He heard Matt scream, "Hit the claymores, Ash! Hit the claymoooores!"

Ash released the safety and fired the detonators. There was a blinding flash, followed instantly by an enormous *bang-whoosh* as the ball bearings mangled everything in their path. Simultaneous *thwacks* sounded through the impact area as twigs, branches, flesh, and bone shredded on contact.

Faster than a sneeze, the killing was over.

The radio handset had been keyed open during the attack. Ash had been about to call in pre-positioned mortar fire. PFC Stanley Watkins from Dallas, Texas was monitoring the radio and had heard it all. He knew where they were set in, and knew no one could go for them until morning. He cradled the handset in his lap as tears streamed down his face.

At first light, a platoon-sized recovery team was dispatched to the site of the fighting. There were only two possible outcomes awaiting them: they would find no trace of the two Marines, or discover a scene that would haunt their dreams forever. Considering that it had been a sniper team, they expected the latter. The North Vietnamese were petrified of them, and had a bounty on every American sniper in Vietnam. The amount was ten to twenty times what an average Vietnamese earned in a year.

The point man raised his hand to signal those behind him to halt, then scanned the area, looking for signs of an enemy ambush. After seeing none, he cautiously duck-walked a few meters forward then stopped again, looking for the slightest movement. He knew if an ambush was prepared, they wouldn't spring it until he'd led the others in deeper. He rose to full height and walked in closer. The bad guys weren't here. That determination made, he returned to the platoon and led them to the team's last position. There, they found what they'd prayed they wouldn't.

What was left of Matthew Reilly was propped up by a bamboo pole in a gruesome sitting position, as though he were aiming downhill at an imaginary target. The enemy had cut off his head and his hands as trophies, and as proof for the bounty. His rifle had been taken as further proof, so their commanders would have no doubt. His entire body was shredded by at least fifty ball bearings from the claymores. The only means of identifying him was the dog tag, which had been wrapped in black tape and laced into his left boot flap. James Ashcroft was nowhere to be found, but a heavy blood trail led from the scene, then abruptly disappeared.

What had happened seemed fairly clear to the patrol. Charlie had crept in and turned the claymores around to face the team's position, then made some noise to alert the team. Lance Corporal Ashcroft tried to call in supporting mortar fire, and detonated the claymores. They did themselves in, and Charley had simply put on the finishing touches. Ashcroft must have been taken prisoner, though judging from the blood trail, he probably hadn't survived the night. Every bit of the team's gear was gone.

All in all, it was as bad as it could get. Matt Reilly had been one of the best. Now he was gone. They hauled his remains in a body bag to an LZ a little more than a klick away, and a couple of helos whisked all the Marines, living and dead, from the site.

The captain would have to write a couple of condolence letters to the Marines' parents. It was a hellish task. What could he say?

"Dear Mr. and Mrs. Reilly...It is with great sadness I must tell you of your son's tragic death while fighting the enemy...He served his country valiantly and with distinction...

"Dear Mr. and Mrs. Ashcroft...It is with a heavy heart that I must tell you your son is missing and presumed dead...He was a fine Marine, and he will be sorely missed...

Captain Johnson had written the first letter many times. He'd never had to write an MIA letter before. He prayed this one would be his last.

Back at Anderson Air Base on Guam, Luke was seated alone in the non-commissioned officers club having a beer. A week ago, he was told Mark had been killed. Only yesterday he learned that had been bad scoop, that Mark had actually survived and been evacuated to Yokosuka, Japan. Luke was celebrating the mixed bag of news that his brother was alive but critical, when he felt a hand on his arm. Turning his head over his shoulder, he found himself looking into the somber face of Lieutenant Driscoll. Officers had their own club, and it was unusual for one to come into the NCO Club. The look on his face meant the news was bad.

Luke stood up. Not really wanting an answer, he asked, "Mark died after all?"

"No, Luke," Driscoll replied. "It's Matthew this time. We just got the word he was killed in an ambush two days ago...I'm dreadfully sorry."

Luke sank to his chair in complete numbness. He stared at the floor, unable to summon the words to speak. Lieutenant Driscoll turned a chair around backward and straddled it, resting his arms and chin across its back. There was nothing more to say, but he couldn't drop that news on Luke and simply walk away.

In a moment, Luke looked up and spoke. "What do I do now, Lieutenant?"

"You fly to DaNang tomorrow," he said. "You escort your brother home for his funeral. You take thirty days leave with your family, then you report to Barksdale Air Force Base in Shreveport. Vietnam is over for all of you, Luke. No one knows yet if Mark is going to make it. That makes you a 'sole surviving son.' No one in the Defense Department wants to see your mother and father bury all three of their boys. Pack your bags and go home, Luke."

So there it was. It had taken the volunteering of both of his brothers to get him to Vietnam, and it had taken the death of one, and the near death of the other, to get him his ticket home. He had let his brothers' decisions dictate his actions. Their fates now controlled his future. At that very moment, Luke made up his mind that he would never permit others to control his future again. He was the sculptor of his own destiny.

All the same, he felt an overpowering guilt. He wondered aloud if it would ever let him go.

Chapter Five

REARVIEW MIRROR

"Suddenly...
I'm not half the man I used to be...
There's a shadow hanging over me.
Oh Yesterday...came suddenly."

The Beatles

Clipped commands and responses had the room buzzing. It wasn't really conversation, but rather a form of oral shorthand. Mark wanted to see what all the commotion was about, but his eyes refused to open. He tried to ask for something to drink, yet no words came out of his mouth. Anxiety welled within him to the point of full-fledged panic, and he began to roll from side to side and thrash at his bedclothes. He nearly rolled off to the floor, and would have if not for the quick reflexes of the large black corpsman standing by the next bed who caught him with one hand.

Rolling him onto his back, Hospitalman First Class Lucias Hammond calmed him with a soothing voice from lower Alabama. "Settle down now, Corporal. You're in good hands here. I got you, and you're gonna' be jus' fine."

Mark's heart was racing, and he was confused. He couldn't see anything and feared he was blind. He could form words in his mind but he couldn't speak. He thought he must've died and gone to Hell.

Lucias sensed his fear and kept talking: "Corporal Reilly, you made it, man! No more Vietnam for you! You're in the Naval Hospital in Yokosuka, Japan. You got bandages over your eyes, but you got both of 'em, and they ain't damaged at all. You took a whole bunch o' shrapnel in the head and damn near lost it, but you're one tough *Marine* and you're going home to *The World*."

Mark's breathing slowed as his anxiety began melting into the crisp cotton sheets. He was covered up, and yet the room felt cool. He didn't realize it was air-conditioning, but he could tell it was a welcome change from the Vietnam heat.

Continuing with his reassuring chatter, Lucias said, "You'll be talking soon enough. The medication's wearing off. Give it some time, and you'll be talking up a storm. My name's Lucias Hammond, and I'm gonna take care of you 'til you're ready to go home. We're gonna get to know each other real well. You rest easy. I'm gonna get the doc and tell him you're comin' around."

The anesthesia surged through his system again, and he dropped into a deep sleep. After a while, he woke again…this time with a little clearer head, and a better idea of where he was. Once again he could hear the clipped jargon of the doctors and nurses.

"Water…" Mark whispered. "I need some water" he strained, a little louder this time.

A passing nurse stopped and poured some into a cup from a pitcher on his bedside stand. She stuck a straw in it and placed it on the table, then pressed a button that raised the head of his bed. Taking the cup from the stand, she guided the straw into his mouth. "Sip it slowly," she commanded.

Mark's throat was sore and burned with the first few sips. The intubation tube they'd put down his throat during surgery had scratched the lining and made it feel raw. The cool water helped. He knew someone had spoken to him earlier, but couldn't remember the gist of the conversation. He did remember, however, that whoever had talked to him had put him at ease. Still unsure of why his eyes wouldn't open he asked, "Why can't I see?"

"Because the bandage on your head is also covering your eyes," the nurse replied. "The doctor didn't want you looking around and turning your head in all directions. When he sees you later today, you can ask him when your eyes can be uncovered."

Mark grabbed for her hand and squeezed it tightly. "Are you sure I'm not blind?"

Placing her other hand behind his head and gently easing him back to his pillow she said, "No, dear, you're not blind. Both your eyes are fine."

Mark exhaled, "Thank God," and sank deeply into his sheets.

The nurse removed her hand from his and told him to lay back and rest. He did as instructed and let it sink in that he was no longer in Vietnam. His feelings were mixed. Even though he was in pain, he could tell how nice the clean cotton sheets felt. He was lying in a comfortable bed. The last place he'd slept had been rocky and hard. There was no doubt he was relieved to be away from the fighting, but he felt nauseous as he pondered the fate of his unit. It was coming back to him now. The fighting had been fierce. He remembered PFC Nichols dying in his arms. He remembered the dried-up rice paddies teeming with gooks. Did Mike Company win? How many survived? Were they all dead? He didn't know the answers, and the uncertainty upset him.

For the first time since he could remember, he wept. Half his tears were for his buddies...half were for himself. Tears of joy and sorrow, totally indistinguishable from one another, escaped from beneath his bandages. They were a cleansing luxury he hadn't permitted himself for many months.

Someone had told him he was going home. In spite of his pain, he felt anticipation words couldn't describe.

He'd done his duty. He'd acquitted himself well. He could go home proud.

Except for Saigon, Vietnam seemed an endless sea of Marine green. There was camo green, plain utility green, and vegetation green. What wasn't green was the reddish brown color of the Northern I-Corps dirt.

Sitting on the seat of the resupply helicopter was a twenty-year-old kid dressed in khaki trousers and a khaki shirt. Two Marines sat facing each other and were both quietly eyeballing the Air Force guy who'd hitched a ride with them. On his sleeve were three stripes pointing the wrong way. Neither the crew chief nor the door gunner knew for sure what rank he was. Air Force guys had more stripes than God, but they never seemed to outrank anybody unless they had about seven of them. Not only did he look like a fish out of water, but he also looked as nervous as a cat.

Both Marines broke their gaze when the pilot began speaking through their headphones. The crew chief stood and poked his head out of a side window and the gunner stood and let the bolt slam home on the chopper's M-60 machine gun mounted in the opposite window. The bird made a high circle over the airfield and, drawing no fire, began to descend. The crew chief slid the door open on the UH-34D and dismounted. The door gunner pulled back the bolt of his machine gun, removed the ammo belt, and cleared the weapon. Luke Reilly, wearing his crisp summer "1585's", hopped out of the chopper and bent lower than necessary to avoid the blades that were winding to a stop.

Holding his hat tight to his head with his left hand and grabbing his flight bag with the other, Luke stoop-walked the 15 feet to clear the rotors, then straightened up. He could see a sign on the hangar across the field. In letters of gold on a blood-red background, it read:

WELCOME TO DANANG

HOME OF THE 3RD MARINE DIVISION

Luke walked toward an ambulance parked about fifty yards away. A guy was sleeping in the driver's seat, his cover pulled over his eyes in an attempt to block the sunlight. Luke tapped him on the shoulder and startled him enough to make him bang his head on the roof.

Pushing his cover back onto his head, the Navy corpsman cast a condescending look toward the kid in khaki clothes and said, "What the hell do you want?"

"Could you tell me where the Graves Registration Unit is located?" Luke asked. "I'm here to escort a body back to the States."

The corpsman was about to give Luke a flippant reply when something caused him to think better of the idea. There was something in Luke's eyes that said this wasn't a routine escort assignment. "Who are you here for?" he asked.

Turning his head to look down the flight line, Luke said, "I'm here to take my brother home."

The corpsman closed his eyes and shook his head, thankful to God he hadn't been his usual smart-assed self, and then motioned Luke to get in the ambulance. "Hop in," he said. "I'll take you there."

At the far end of the air base was a large warehouse. It was marked with the same red and gold signs found on Marine bases all over the world. This one simply said:

BUILDING 10

GRU

Nothing more was needed. Everyone on the base knew what this building was, and everyone without official business kept his distance. In the States, kids considered it bad luck to hang around a graveyard. This was the morgue, the closest thing to a graveyard in DaNang, and most of the guys on the base weren't much more than kids.

Luke entered the building and was surprised to find it was air-conditioned. All he'd heard from both his brothers was that air-conditioning was something the Marine Corps didn't believe in. In a split second, he realized why it was. He had to chuckle to himself at the thought of all those Marines in the field that would give anything for a little air-conditioning. It was here for the asking; only the price wasn't *anything*...it was *everything*.

The gunnery sergeant at the front desk looked up and asked, "What d'ya' want, Airman?"

"Sir, I'm here to escort my brother's remains back home," Luke replied.

The gunny was about to launch into the standard Staff NCO tirade, "Don't call me 'Sir'"...when he heard the word *brother*. He swallowed hard and rose from his chair. "I'm sorry, son," he said, as he thought about what an awful task it would be to take a dead brother back to his parents.

"What's the KI..." He caught himself before he finished saying KIA, which stands for "killed in action," and said, "Excuse me, son," and started over. "What's your brother's name?"

"Reilly," Luke answered. "Sergeant Matthew Reilly, USMC."

"So, you're Matt Reilly's brother?" he said with admiration. "I didn't know him, but I knew of him. He was a legend around here."

"So he told me...every chance he got," Luke said with a faint smile.

The gunny laughed. It was typical Marine bullshit to brag to one's brother...especially if the brother wasn't a Marine. The gunny flipped through his clipboard, began walking, and motioned for Luke to follow him. "I thought Sergeant Reilly's brother was a Marine," the gunny said as he pushed open a swinging door.

"He is," Luke answered. "Mark is our other brother. He's a corporal in the 26th Marines."

When the gunny heard "26th Marines," he stopped in his tracks and turned around slowly. This morgue was *filled* with guys from the 26th Marines. He looked at Luke and asked, "Have you heard from him lately?"

Luke looked the gunny squarely in the eyes and said, "I got word he was wounded badly on the 10th. They said he was sent to Japan, but I've had no further word about his condition. My CO told me his chances were slim. Is there any way you can find out anything for me before I leave?"

"I'll give it my best shot, kid," he answered.

The room they had entered had floor-to-ceiling racks that held rows of aluminum caskets devoid of excess ornamentation. Some had crosses on the lids...some had the Star of David. The gunny stopped at the one that matched the name on his clipboard. Like the rest it was closed, but this casket's latches had been sealed.

Luke asked, "May I see him?"

The clipboard described the condition of the body inside. The gunny shook his head from side to side, looked at Luke and said, "Son…God has your brother now, and He's the only one that needs to see him."

Luke had only been told Matt had been killed in an ambush. He listened quietly, his head held low with tears flowing down his face, as the gunny explained the condition of the body.

"Was your dad in the service, son?" the gunny asked as he placed a hand on Luke's shoulder.

"Yes…World War II," Luke replied without looking up.

He thought a moment and said in a voice not much louder than a whisper, "He's going to want to lay his eyes on his son. It's up to you to see that he doesn't. I'm sure he's seen soldiers in similar condition, but they weren't his own boy."

Luke nodded in understanding. As he dried his eyes he said, "I've never had to do this before. What am I supposed to do?"

The gunny smiled. "You leave everything to me. When the paperwork is done and he's ready to leave tomorrow, I'll expedite your travel itinerary. You'll both take a bird to Tan Son Nhut Air Base in Saigon. You'll catch another plane there and fly to Okinawa. You'll have an overnight on The Rock, then catch a flight to Norton Air Force Base outside Los Angeles. From there you'll be flown to Andrews Air Force Base, outside DC. Your folks have requested that the funeral be held in Arlington National Cemetery with full military honors. The duty officer from Marine Barracks 8th & I will meet you at Andrews. He'll also get you hooked up with your parents at their hotel and lay out the details for the burial."

Luke thanked him for his help. The gunny nodded and said, "No sweat, son." Then, shattering the silence of the noiseless room, he barked, "Corpsman!"

The ambulance driver who'd brought Luke to the morgue burst through the swinging door. "Here, Gunny!" he said.

"Take this man to the transient barracks and get him settled in. Then I want you to take him to the NCO Club." The gunny shoved some scrip into the corpsman's hand and quietly said, "Buy him a drink." In the gunny's opinion, Luke's face matched the color of his shirt. He stuffed some more scrip in Albertson's hand and said, "Buy him a couple of drinks."

"Sure thing, Gunny," Albertson said as he herded Luke toward the door. All three walked back to the gunny's desk at the entrance.

Gunny's last instruction was somewhat terse: "Be here at 0900, Airman Reilly, and I'll have everything ready to go. If there are no delays, you should be airborne by 1200."

After Albertson and Reilly left, the gunny plopped down hard in his chair and banged his palms flat on his desk. He thought everything about this job sucked…but a brother taking another brother home to bury was too awful to contemplate. He picked up his phone and began trying to track down Corporal Mark Reilly's whereabouts in Japan. He prayed to God that *he* wasn't already in a box and on his way home, too.

✯ ✯ ✯

True to his word, the gunny had all the paperwork ready and all the skids greased for a hitch-free flight to Washington. He greeted Luke with a warm smile and said, "I've got some good news for you, Airman Reilly!"

"Really?" Luke said. "What'd you learn?"

"Your brother Mark is in the naval hospital at Yokosuka, not far from Tokyo. He's in stable condition, and all indications are he's gonna make it. He lucked out!"

"That's great news, Gunny," Luke said, breathing a deep sigh of relief. "I really appreciate your finding that out."

"Happy to do it," he said. "In this job, I'm nothing but an undertaker with stripes on his sleeve. I seldom get to give anybody good news." He handed Luke a large manila envelope with all pertinent forms to document the casket he was accompanying. "Your brother's casket has been loaded on the truck. Doc Albertson will drive you to the plane. The casket will be loaded aboard, and you can get on. Once you're on the plane, everything will pretty well handle itself until you're home. There'll be layovers at Tan Son Nhut and Okinawa. You won't need to stay with the casket. It'll be fine. My suggestion is to find the NCO Club at each place, have as many drinks as you can without getting drunk, and return to the terminal. If you're drunk, they won't let you board the plane. If you're feelin' just right, however, you can probably sleep most of the way home." He looked at Luke and asked, "Son, do you have any questions?"

62

"No, Gunny, you've been great," Luke replied. "I really appreciate all your help."

The gunny simply nodded this time. Luke shook his hand and turned to leave. As Luke opened the door, the bright sunlight from outside nearly blinded the gunny, and he shielded his eyes with the palm of his hand as Luke stepped out into the scorching heat.

The gunny called out, "Hey, Airman Reilly?"

Luke turned to face him.

"Tell your parents they raised three fine young Americans."

"I will, Gunny. Thanks again."

The hand shielding the gunny's eyes also prevented anyone from seeing the moisture welling in them. After he closed the door, the room momentarily plunged into darkness. He rubbed his eyes to adjust them while thinking about how glad he was to be rid of the Reillys. The past twelve hours had been much too personal. Shifting gears, he picked up the roster of new arrivals and added it to his clipboard. Today was a brand new day. He pushed open the swinging door to the morgue and muttered a flippant saying Marines often use when times are tough: "Every day's a holiday…every meal's a feast. Another day to love and serve the Corps!"

In the club in Saigon, Luke finished two stiff bourbons and a beer chaser and considered having one more. Then he remembered the gunny's warning not to get too drunk to board the plane, and picked up his hat and left. Returning to the terminal, he bought a magazine and found a chair to kill some time until the plane departed. He flipped through the pages swiftly and, for the moment, found nothing that grabbed his attention. Luke thought about the gunny in DaNang, and realized he never got his name. Life was funny like that. Sometimes the people who crossed your path and made a memorable impact were people whose names you never learned.

He looked around the terminal and noticed three distinct types of soldiers. The new arrivals were clean, young, and innocent. They had an apprehensive look on their faces that was powerful enough to feel across the room.

But it was the second group in the room, who were laughing and carrying on about being on their way home, that most caught his attention. Luke suspected that this group was primarily comprised of what his brothers had called REMF'S. This was a disparaging nickname for support troops in the Rear Echelon. They, too, had served a yearlong tour if they were Army or Air Force, or a thirteen-month tour if they were Marines. The only difference was that the REMF'S had spent their tours "in the rear with the gear."

Luke wasn't judging them; it was just a fact of life. For every combat soldier in Vietnam, there were four or five more in support. Their jobs were to keep the war fighters combat-ready. The support troops served well, and weren't immune from danger. On many occasions they were wounded or killed in enemy attacks. They suffered their share of loneliness and anxiety. Most, however, didn't face the imminent danger faced around the clock by those who did the fighting. These guys looked a little more mature than the newbies in the first group, yet they didn't have the worn-and-torn look that etched the faces of the third group in the terminal.

The last group sat or stood together and kept to themselves. They looked older than the others by as much as ten years, even though they weren't. Their skin was weathered and dark from living outside for months in the intense heat. Some observed every movement around them, while others slept, trusting their buddies to remain alert and watch over them. They wore clean uniforms that had fit perfectly when they arrived but now seemed a little large on their stark frames. Even with the weight loss, it was evident that every remaining pound was pure muscle. All of them wore at least two rows of ribbons. Some had as many as four. These men had seen too much. They, too, were on their way home, but the look in their eyes was more relief than joy. Any joy they'd brought with them to Vietnam had been bled and sweated away as they'd humped the hills and jungles for the past thirteen months. Fear and adrenaline had made their senses sharp. Each one reminded Luke of a coiled snake.

In the midst of these men were two empty seats. He couldn't help but picture Matt and Mark seated in them. If they had been, he knew they would've fit right in, wearing the same look as these guys.

The loudspeaker squawked an announcement to board the plane. By rank, all three groups filed out the door and onto the tarmac, the bright sun and sweltering heat as oppressive as always. One by one, they filed up the stairs and entered the plane to find their seats. Civilian stewardesses smiled and welcomed them aboard. It was a commercial airliner, chartered by the Military Airlift Command. For many of the men, these were the first women they'd seen in over a year. They were certainly the first "round eyes"—the Marine slang for American girls—any of them had seen in months. They were more than beautiful, they were *home*: living symbols of the world they'd left behind, reminding every man aboard that it was great to be alive.

Twenty-two minutes later, the Freedom Bird rolled down the runway and blasted into the late afternoon sky. As the wheels cleared the pavement some let out a huge sigh, while others cheered out loud. The outburst lasted for only a few seconds, then the passengers fell quiet as a church congregation. Vietnam was in the rearview mirror. It was an experience to put in the past. From this point forward it would merely be a memory. None of them had any idea that the memory would last forever.

Chapter Six

HURT

"Every day's an endless stream of cigarettes and magazines...uhm."

Simon and Garfunkel

U.S. Naval Hospital, Yokosuka, Japan – September 1967

When a man lies for days in a hospital bed with bandages over his eyes, he becomes keenly aware of the sounds and smells all around him. By now, Mark could tell the footsteps of Corpsman Lucias Hammond as he approached. His attendant made it a point to stop by several times a day and reassure Mark that he was going to be fine.

Hammond wasn't alone. The Chanel No. 5 perfume in the air announced the presence of the nurse who'd been checking on him over the past couple of days, a woman who had a gentle touch and a voice like an angel. She told him her name, but he hadn't heard it clearly. *Goodwin...Goodson...Good something.* He struggled to remember.

The presence of a female after so many months of nothing but men around made Mark long to go home and find the girl of his dreams. He hoped he would find her only after he'd gone through a couple of hundred that didn't quite fit the bill.

There was a third voice in the room, addressing him now, that was unfamiliar. "Corporal Reilly, I'm your doctor, Commander Vincent.

67

I'm going to remove your bandages and have a look. Just sit forward and relax for me."

"Sir, they tell me I'm not blind." With apprehension in his voice Mark asked, "Are they telling me the truth?"

"They are," the doctor said. "Your eyes are fine." He began removing the bandages from Mark's head. "You came damned close, however, to having your head cut in two. By all rights, you had little chance of surviving when you were medevaced from the field."

Upset by this remark, Mark asked, "Whadya' mean, sir?"

"I mean a good-sized piece of shrapnel entered your head just above the hairline on the right side and opened your head up the way Indians used to scalp settlers," Commander Vincent explained. "You lost a great deal of blood. The combined force of the shrapnel and the concussion cracked your skull over a large area. Imagine cracking a hard-boiled egg on a countertop. All the pieces stay in place, but the shell is severely weakened. Your head injury is much the same."

"What's that mean, Doc?" Mark asked, struggling to come to grips with what he was being told.

"For one thing, it means the war's over for you, Corporal: You're going to remain with us awhile and get strong enough to have some more surgery. We're going to put a thin metal plate in your head to replace the damaged portion of your skull. When you've recovered sufficiently, we're going to ship you home."

"Will everything heal all right?" Mark asked.

"I can't think of any reason why not," the doctor replied.

The last turn of the bandage fell away and brushed Mark on the shoulder, leaving his eyes covered by only two round gauze pads. The doctor asked the orderly to draw the blinds and dim the overhead lights, then removed the pads from Mark's eyes, saying, "Open them slowly. You'll be a bit sensitive to light for a while."

He did as he was told, and at first could only discern a fuzzy glare. A second later, he detected movement as someone's form broke the ray of light. In a matter of seconds he could distinguish shapes. Finally, he was able to focus on three people near his bed. Sitting on the edge of the bed was the doctor, busily examining the sutures on the side of his head. His voice a rapid monotone, he dictated observations in a language that made no sense to Mark.

Standing at the foot of the bed was a heavyset black man who appeared to be about nineteen or twenty. The man was nodding his head up and down while giving him a "two thumbs up" gesture. He had the biggest ear-to-ear grin Mark had ever seen. Lucias Hammond genuinely cared for his patients, and was delighted to see Mark...and be seen by him.

The third person was a Navy nurse who appeared to be in her mid-thirties. She wasn't particularly pretty, but had a figure that a twenty-year-old exotic dancer would envy. This was the first American woman Mark had seen since he'd left the States. She was a little too old for him, was an officer, and had a ring on her finger, but to him she looked like Miss America. He was so grateful to be seeing her at all that he forgot he was the one being examined and just stared longingly at her breasts. She looked down at him knowing full well

69

what was on his mind, gave him a brief smile, and continued recording the doctor's notes on the chart in her hand.

Summoning his best pick-up line, he asked, "What's your name, baby?"

"To *you,* Marine, I'm Lieutenant Commander Goodman." The kind smile on her face belied her stern tone.

Humor. Lust. Gratitude. All of these feelings ricocheted around his heart, and he was overcome with emotion, ecstatic to know that he was alive, could see, and still had all the body parts he'd brought with him to Vietnam. Life was good, and it was going to get a lot better.

*Good**man** hell,* Mark thought. *Good**body** is more like it!* The nickname would be forever etched in his mind. From now on, she was "Nurse Goodbody" to him.

The examination continued for several more minutes. Doctor Vincent asked Mark to look at items all around the room, testing his ability to focus on objects near and far, large and small. With flying colors, he passed every test. He made some notes on Mark's chart, clicked his pen closed, and placed it in his pocket. Then he looked at Mark through the half-glasses perched on the end of his nose and said, "My prescription for you is a great deal of rest. In a few days when you've gotten stronger, we'll perform the surgery to repair your skull."

As the doctor stood to leave, Mark grabbed his wrist to keep him from walking away. "Sir?" he said. "Thank you. I really appreciate what you've done for me."

"That's my job, Corporal. Knowing you're going to make it home has made my day."

"Sir?" Mark said as his eyes began to sweat. "You don't understand what I'm saying. You made more than my day, Doc…you made my life."

Doctor Vincent shook his head in gratitude and turned to leave. He didn't want Mark to see the tears in his own eyes. Too many of his patients had been unable to make such a statement. He'd been unable to save *their* lives. Those defeats made this victory all the more sweet. *Sometimes you win after all*, he thought as he left the ward.

Mark looked around and saw his surroundings for the first time. There were rows of beds on each side of the room. In some, the patients were visible; others were behind screens. His fellow patients had incurred all manner of injuries. Some were burned. A few had been shot. Many were missing limbs. The majority was suffering from shrapnel wounds, as was Mark. Tubes were everywhere. Men had them in their throats, protruding from their noses and sticking out of arms and hands. Other tubes ran from catheters into drainage bags suspended from the bed frames. The amount of pain and disfigurement in this ward defied belief. Mark closed his eyes and prayed. He thanked God for sparing his life. He thanked Him for giving him the opportunity to continue it. He said a prayer for those in this room in worse shape than he. At the last, he prayed for his buddies still in the field.

Opening his eyes, Mark found himself staring at a Navy lieutenant standing beside his bed. He hadn't heard him walk to his bedside, and it frightened him. He had survived for months because of his sharp senses, and they had failed him just now. He was in the process of silently chewing himself out when he realized that it didn't matter any more. No one here wanted to kill him. The people here were friends, not enemies. He could let his guard down now. This wasn't Vietnam.

Mark turned his focus to the lieutenant's collar. On one side was a set of silver bars that looked like railroad tracks. On the other side was a small gold cross. The man by his bed was a Navy chaplain.

"Corporal Reilly?" he asked, looking uneasy as he spoke.

Mark nodded his head and said, "Yes, sir."

"I'm Father Jack Harmon, the Catholic chaplain here at the hospital."

Mark chuckled and said, "If you're here to give me the Last Rites, Father, I won't be needing 'em."

"No, son," he said with a forced smile. "Your doctor tells me you're going to recover fully. I'm so pleased for you."

"Father, you're nowhere near as pleased as I am," Mark replied.

"I'm sure that's true, Corporal. Do you mind if I sit on the foot of your bed?"

"No sir," Mark said. "Make yourself comfortable."

"Corporal Reilly…" The chaplain paused and looked at the floor for a moment, then brought his eyes up to meet Mark's. "There's no easy way to break the news, so I'll just tell you flat out. You've lost your brother, Matt."

"Lost…as in missing?" Mark asked, incredulous.

"No, son," he said. "He was killed in action nearly two weeks ago. Just a couple of days after you yourself were wounded."

Mark's heart began beating rapidly, and his head throbbed as the blood rushed to it. He felt like he'd been kicked in the gut by a horse, and he wanted to throw up. He'd lost so many friends in Vietnam. Good guys, every one. Most were no older than boys. He'd learned to distance himself from the hurt. He'd learned to block out the pain so he could stay focused on the living. He was responsible for his men. He had a responsibility to get them and himself home in one piece. Dwelling on the dead only increased the chances of others joining them. Nonetheless, this news hit him in an entirely different way. Mark's war was over. His responsibilities were finished. This feeling, however, couldn't be flushed from his mind. This death wasn't a fellow Marine he hardly knew. It wasn't a friend he knew well. It was his brother. How was he supposed to react to the death of his own brother? He didn't know what he was supposed to do...and the confusion made his head hurt all the more.

Father Harmon continued, feeding him details Mark could barely assimilate: "Sniper mission...got caught by the enemy...ambushed...his partner missing in action."

Mark, lost in his own memories of Matt, only caught every few words.

The chaplain was still talking when Mark turned toward him and said, "Father? I don't mean to be rude, but would you mind leaving me alone for a while? I want to know what all happened...but I really can't listen right now."

Father Harmon nodded. "I'll come back tomorrow," he said as he clapped Mark on the shoulder. "We'll visit more then."

As the chaplain walked away, Luke flashed through Mark's mind, and he cried out, "Hey, Father!"

Father Harmon spun to face Mark.

"Do you know if my other brother, Luke, is okay?"

The chaplain gave Mark his first genuine smile. "Yes, Corporal Reilly, he is. He escorted Matt's body home to your folks for the funeral. This war's over for *all* the Reillys." With that, he left.

Mark sank back into his bed and stared at the ceiling. He'd been numb so long he had no idea how to grieve, so he stared at the ceiling and just hurt. He hurt all over. He thought about praying, but was too mad at God to talk. He didn't pray any more. He just lay there and wondered if he would hurt for the rest of his life.

Chapter Seven

THE HEARTFELT THANKS OF A GRATEFUL NATION

"All the leaves are brown…and the sky is gray.
I've been for a walk…on a winter's day."

The Mamas and the Papas

Alexandria, Virginia – September 1967

The late September weather in DC is unpredictable. It had rained hard all night the night before, and had slowed to a drizzle by morning. Mary Quinn Reilly came from a long line of worriers. She had worried about her three sons while they were fighting halfway around the world. This morning, she worried about the rain messing up the funeral, and about maintaining her composure at the gravesite. The worrying had done no good then, and it wouldn't change today's weather, or anything else she wanted changed.

Today she would bury her eldest son, Matthew. Mark was alone in Japan, recovering from surgery to repair his wounded body, and it saddened her that he couldn't be here. She had no idea if his face had been disfigured, and that caused her to worry again.

Luke, wearing his Air Force dress uniform, touched her arm. He was prepared to lead her to the waiting limousine. She looked in his face and saw not one son, but three. She reached up and hugged him tightly around the neck, her sobs muffled in his shoulder as her body trembled. For a brief moment she seemed fragile to the point of breaking. Then John Francis Reilly stepped to her side and gently placed his hand on her shoulder.

As if transformed by his touch, she straightened instantly and forced the tears to cease. She dried her eyes with a white linen handkerchief and did what Southern women have done since the beginning of time—she bucked up. Wrapping herself in the mantle of stoicism, she prepared to play out her part. There would be no tears at the cemetery, no public display of grief. Her emotions were her own, and not for show. She'd deal with them later, in the privacy of her own bedroom. Each of her sons had done his duty. She would do no less. In the America of the future, her behavior might be labeled "dysfunctional." In 1967, and in the world in which she had been raised, it was simply a code of honor.

Luke opened the door for his mother. His father held her hand as she sat down and swiveled her legs into the car. She slid to the middle, and John Francis sat down next to her and closed the door. Luke walked to the other side, and as he opened the door, felt acid burning in his stomach. The rest of today would be a heavy dose of bitter medicine, sugarcoated in the traditions of honor and glory to make it easier to swallow. He got in and closed the door. For the fifteen-minute drive to Arlington, no one uttered a sound.

The limousine pulled to the curb in front of the reception center at Fort Myer, located adjacent to Arlington National Cemetery. Waiting for them was a group of Marines in dress blues. The detail was comprised of the officer in charge, the pallbearers, the honor guard and the bugler. Waiting with them was the Reillys' parish priest, Monsignor Richard Flannigan, from the cathedral in Atlanta.

Luke exited the car and placed his hand on the rear door handle, prompting his father to lower the window and say they wanted to remain inside the limo until the hearse arrived. Luke said "Okay" and walked to the assembled Marines, giving the captain a crisp salute as he approached. The captain returned it, extending his hand to Luke to offer his condolences.

Luke held his hand out to Monsignor Flannigan, who ignored it and embraced him instead. He had known all three boys since the first grade, and had always considered them special...a unique miracle of God. It pained him greatly to know that one of them had been taken from the others. They were three individuals, yet God had brought them into the world together. It seemed odd to call them home one at a time.

Luke looked at the sky. The weather would hold for the funeral. His eyes turned skyward, and he heard the tires on the wet pavement before he saw the car. The brakes of the black Cadillac emitted an ear-piercing squeal as the hearse stopped directly in front of the parked limousine. It reminded Luke of fingernails on a chalkboard, and it had the same effect. Luke excused himself from the captain and approached the car again. Through the lowered window he explained the procedure as it had been explained to him. His parents got out of the car and joined the others.

Monsignor Flannigan turned to the Marine captain and asked, "Are we ready?"

"Whenever you are, sir."

"Let's proceed, then," said the priest, and waved his hand in the direction of the gravesite.

The captain gave a nod to the gunnery sergeant in charge of the honor guard, who broke the serenity of the morning by calling the unit to attention. It wasn't done in the loud bark of the parade ground, but was a muted version of the same command. Once at attention he ordered "Left Face! Right Shoulder Arms! At the slow step...Forward March!"

In unison, every left foot stepped out and hit the pavement as one. The funeral procession was in motion. The pace was intended to be reverent, and was slower than a standard march. The Marine in the casket had given his all for his country. There would be no rush to send him on his way.

Ten paces behind the honor guard, Monsignor Flannigan fell into step. The hearse followed him, another ten paces back. On each side of the hearse marched three Marine pallbearers. Ten paces behind the hearse was the family. Luke and his father walked on either side of Mary Quinn.

Even with a bit of time to absorb the change, Luke was stunned at how much his parents seemed to have aged in the past year. His mother was only forty-eight, and yet she looked ten years older today. His father, fifty-one, could easily have passed for sixty. It had never crossed Luke's mind before that the folks at home had also been suffering through the war.

The only other mourners were his Aunt Jennifer and her husband Arthur, who lived in Maryland, and his father's two brothers, William and George. The family had already held a memorial service in Atlanta for the extended family and friends. It had been the largest service ever held at Christ the King Cathedral. People who barely knew the family, and some who didn't know them at all had come to pay their respects. But Mary Quinn and John Francis wanted only the immediate family to attend the interment.

The procession came to a halt on the road near the place where Matthew was to be laid to rest. Once again the Cadillac's brakes squealed in pain, as though the inanimate car was the only one with guts enough to scream. The pallbearers formed at the rear of the hearse to retrieve the casket. As it slid on rollers to the back of the vehicle, the bright colors of the American flag radiated in contrast to the gray September sky. Executing a slow "five step turn," the pallbearers rotated the casket from a position perpendicular to the gravesite to a position in line with it, and then carried it to the framework positioned over the open grave. There, they placed it on the hoist.

Two Marines near the head of the casket folded the flag back to reveal a silver cross mounted to its top. The six stood facing one another at attention, saluted in unison, and slowly dropped their salute. Three faced left, three faced right, and they marched away from the grave to a position opposite the honor guard.

Making the sign of the cross, Monsignor Flannigan began speaking. "In the name of the Father, the Son, and the Holy Spirit…Amen." He poured holy water from a vial in his left hand into his right and proceeded to sprinkle it over the cross on the top of the casket, then continued the Burial Rites of the Church as the eyes of the mourners remained fixed upon him.

The priest paused and looked at the three family members in the front row. Then he began his sermon: "John Francis…Mary Quinn…Luke…This is not how any of us envisioned Matthew's return. We should be celebrating his homecoming in your backyard with a barbequed pig we spent all night roasting. We should be toasting his safe return after more than eighteen months of honorable service to his country. Mark should be sitting with us at this feast, instead of recuperating from wounds received in combat. Indeed, every mother's son should be home in America today instead of placing their lives in danger for the sake of others. This is how it should be. But this is not the reality of our times. Matthew cared for others more than he cared for his own safety. He served with honor and distinction, as did his brothers Mark and you, Luke…"

This is where Luke tuned him out and drifted toward a world of his own thoughts. "The reality of our times" the monsignor had said. Whose reality? What did he know about the reality of the times of young men at war? The closest thing to tragedy Monsignor Flannigan had experienced was losing his grip on a quart of Jack Daniels Black and smashing it to pieces as he was getting out of his car behind the rectory. Luke and his brothers had witnessed the scene as kids while passing by on their way to the playground behind the church and the school. The monsignor had sat there stunned, one foot in and one foot out of his Buick, with a look of disappointment all over his face. All three of them thought it was hysterical.

The monsignor droned on, "...Jesus said, 'Greater love hath no man than to lay down his life for his friend.' Matthew was this kind of hero..."

Luke tried to listen again, but found himself staring at the faces of the Marines in the honor guard. They looked strong and resolute. Several of them wore only the National Defense Medal on their chests, indicating that they hadn't yet been to Vietnam. Even so, they had the chiseled jaw of true believers in the cause. They were probably soaking up the priest's every word, trying hard to contain the urge to shout "Ahroooogah!" as Marines the world over shout to express their enthusiasm.

Luke had never engaged in violence that was up close and personal. That had always been the purview of Matt, and to a lesser extent, Mark. As he listened to Monsignor Flannigan, he could barely control his urge to stand up and knock him to the ground. Matthew was dead. He'd gone to another man's country and waged war. The other man resented his being there and killed him. End of story. All of this flag-waving might be comforting to his parents, but to him it was pure bullshit. That was what he wanted to scream.

The monsignor's voice reentered his consciousness. "...and so I say to you folks, grieve not, for Matthew is at the table of his Heavenly Father. The fatted calf has been prepared for him, and he awaits the day when we shall all join him at the feast. The living bear the pain of those who have left us. Those who have attained their reward bask in the glow of eternity, free from the travails of this world." He bowed his head, and the others did the same. "Father, we ask Your mercy on the soul of Your servant, Matthew, and upon the souls of all the faithful departed. May perpetual light shine on them, forever…and ever…Amen."

Again he made the sign of the cross, closing his prayer book as he stepped to the side to speak to the family. As he did, two Marines moved to each end of the casket, gripped the corners of the flag, and raised it to waist level, holding it taut. The sounds of rifle bolts slamming home preceded the first of three volleys of gunfire.

The gunnery sergeant in charge of the honor guard commanded, "Readyyyyy…Aim…Fire!"

Seven rifles fired simultaneously.

"Aim…Fire!"

Again the rifles cracked in unison.

"Aim…Fire!"

The last rifle report echoed throughout the cemetery.

On the hill, adjacent to the gravesite, stood a Marine raising a bugle to his lips. The haunting refrain of "Taps" wafted across the hillside and carried to the river below. As it played, the same thought occurred to Luke and his father, though neither ever shared it with the other. They each had the distinct impression that the occupants of every grave were listening to the bugler and recalling their own brief lives. This place emanated a powerful aura of sacrifice, unparalleled duty, and commitment. A massive price had been paid by thousands of young men resting in this field and others like it, for the privilege of living in this great land. As the bugle ceased, the residents of Arlington welcomed one of their own to their ranks.

The flag detail sidestepped four paces, and then halted to begin the ceremonial folding of the flag, thirteen carefully made folds, each with symbolic meaning. Fold one is the symbol of life. Fold two represents our belief in eternal life. The third fold is in honor and remembrance of the veteran departing our ranks, who gave his life in defense of our country; the fourth reminds us of our weaker nature, requiring us to trust in God and turn to Him for divine guidance in times of peace and war. The fifth is a tribute to our country; the sixth fold represents where our hearts lie, pledging our allegiance to one nation, under God, indivisible, with liberty and justice for all. Fold number seven is a tribute to the armed forces that protect our land from all enemies, within and without her borders. The eighth is for the One who entered the valley of the shadow of death, that we might see the light of day. The ninth fold is in honor of womanhood, for it has been through the faith, love, loyalty, and devotion of women that the character of the men and women who have made this country great has been molded. The tenth is a tribute to fathers, for throughout history they have given their sons for the defense of the country. The eleventh, in the eyes of the Hebrew citizen, represents the lower portion of the seal of King David and King Solomon, and glorifies in their eyes the God of Abraham, Isaac and Jacob. The twelfth fold, for the Christian citizen, represents eternity and glorifies the Father, Son, and Holy Spirit. The thirteenth fold completes the task and leaves only the blue field of white stars showing. The stars remind of us of our nation's motto of "In God We Trust."

The Marine sergeant executed a right-face and handed the flag to the captain, who saluted slowly, paused briefly and lowered his salute in the same slow motion. The captain approached the family and stood directly in front of Mary Quinn Reilly. As he handed her the flag, he said, "Please accept this with the heartfelt thanks of a grateful nation." He then saluted her in the same way the sergeant had just done.

To her credit, she kept her pledge, holding the tears in the corner of her eyes and refusing to let a single one fall. Luke watched in awe, as did every Marine within view. She was stronger than them all. The women always are.

Chapter Eight

KEEPING THE FAITH

"Through your tears you look around...and there's no peace of mind to be found.

Reach out...Reach out for me...I'll be there."

The Four Tops

Lake Burton, Georgia – April 1968

Geese flew in a wide "V" formation directly over Mark's head as he lay in a lounge chair on the dock. Their honking woke him from the light sleep he'd drifted into. He reached in the cooler next to the chair and pulled out a cold Budweiser, popping it open with the beer opener attached by string to the cooler's handle. He took a long pull on the beer, and it pleased him immensely. One thing in short supply to the grunts in Vietnam had been cold beer. On occasion a warm one could be had, but cold ones were few and far between.

The family's cabin had never had a telephone or a television, so Mark was enjoying the cool afternoon solitude when he heard the crunch of tires on gravel as a car came down the driveway. He instinctively reached his hand under the newspaper that lay folded on the table next to his beer. The sound of John Francis Reilly's hello set his mind at ease, and he casually removed his hand and retrieved his beer.

John Francis walked down the hill to the dock and pulled up a chair by his son. "You got one of those for your old man?" he asked.

Mark opened a beer for him and passed it across the table. As he did he brushed the newspaper, revealing the Colt .45 pistol it had been concealing. The sight of the weapon alarmed John Francis, and Mark could see the concern on his face.

"Relax, Dad," he said. "I'm not suicidal, and the weapon isn't even loaded. The magazine of bullets is in my front pocket."

The question had to be asked. "Why do you have it, then?"

"Insecurity," he answered. "When I'm around Marines, Dad, I feel okay. When I'm alone, I feel like I'm still in Vietnam. I know I'm not, but I *feel* like I am. Just having it near makes me feel better. I guess it's like a pacifier for a baby. It doesn't do a damned thing, but it makes him feel a whole lot better."

John Francis took him at his word, and changed the subject. "Your mother sent me to find you. She's worried about you. You haven't been home in days, and you haven't called to let us know where you were. I figured I'd drive up here and see if this is where you were hiding out."

"Sorry, Dad. I didn't mean to worry you or Mom, but I needed some time to think. This seemed like the best place to do it."

In fact, Lake Burton had always been Mark's favorite place to do anything. Nestled in the foothills of the Blue Ridge Mountains, in the upper right-hand corner of Georgia, it was a magic place. There were no bad memories here. God could live here and be content. John Francis had built the small cabin soon after his war. The Georgia

Power Company had made leases available for ninety-nine years. When the triplets were young, it was a chore to get here. From Buckhead to the cabin was two and a half hours of winding, two-lane roads that gave way to the final two miles of a single-lane dirt road. Over the years the roads had improved, and the drive time had decreased to about an hour and fifty minutes. It was worth every minute of the drive then, and now. When Mark permitted himself to dream in Vietnam, this place occupied more of his thoughts than Atlanta. Now, it was helping him to keep his thoughts off of Vietnam.

The concern evident in his voice, John Francis asked, "What's on your mind, son?"

Mark wrinkled his brow and answered, "I'm tryin' to figure out what to do, Dad." He paused a moment, then continued. "The whole time I was in Vietnam, I couldn't wait to get out of the Marines. I dreamed about it every morning over breakfast. All I wanted to do was get back to the real world. Well I'm back now, and the real world isn't here any more. I've got nothing in common with the old crowd, and a lot of them don't want anything to do with anyone, or anything, from Vietnam. The only guys I'm comfortable around are Marines."

"So what are you wrestling with?"

"I used to be wary of the lifers…the guys who'd been in the Corps forever," he said. "They had a different way of thinking. The more I think it through, the more I believe I'm a lifer already, and just haven't owned up to it yet."

John Francis mulled it over, then said, "You could choose worse careers. How long would you have to reenlist?"

"Anywhere from three to four years if I remain an enlisted Marine," Mark replied. He stopped as if unwilling to share the rest of his thought, but then continued. "The commanding general of 2nd Marine Division has recommended me to the Naval Academy."

"You'd be the first officer in the family," his dad said. "Do you want to take that route?"

"Dad…There were two kinds of officers in our unit: Great ones, and shitty ones. The great ones taught us how to survive while accomplishing the mission. The shitty ones got people killed. They either learned to become great ones, or failed to learn, and became dead. Dad…I believe I learned the skills to be a great one. I know I can be a damn good one."

John Francis sipped his beer and looked at his son. Mark had just turned twenty-one, yet he had a maturity in excess of his years. He was strong, he was true, and he had a deep sense of honor. This made his reply no easier. "Son," he said, looking him straight in the eye, "it broke our hearts when we lost Matthew. We damned near lost you in the same week. That would have been more than either your mother or I could bear." He looked out over the lake. "Personally, I wish you'd choose another career, but I believe you know your own mind. I know you kept many a mother's son alive over there, and I'm sure you can do more as an officer. I think the Marines, and the country, will be glad you stayed."

Mark was overwhelmed. His dad had always been a man of few words around his boys. This was the first time his father had ever expressed complete confidence in him. It made him proud.

"If you stay in, is there any chance you could be sent back to Vietnam?"

"It's unlikely if I can get into the Academy. Even though I've got a year of Georgia Tech under my belt, I'll be starting over as a freshman. There'll be four years of school, and at least a year of officer training. I don't think America has the stomach to be there that long. Dad..." Mark began, but stopped abruptly. He was looking for the right words, and wasn't sure there were any. "Dad, I'm sorry I wasn't able to bring Matt home with me...alive."

John Francis looked at his son, and simply shook his head. "That wasn't your job, son."

"Ever since I got the news, I've felt bad that I couldn't be at the funeral. I've been sitting here most of the day just looking at this cove. We used to play World War II all over this lake." Mark pointed at a vacant lot across the cove that had a brown sandy beach, unlike the rest of the lake's rocky shore. Jerking his head toward the fishing boat turned upside down on the other end of the dock he continued. "We used to run that little aluminum boat up on that beach, cut the motor off, and pile out like we were assaulting Normandy. We ran all through these woods fighting the Germans and the Japs. It was all just a game then. There was no blood, and when you died, you just got up again and kept on fighting." Mark thought about the death and maiming he'd witnessed and experienced the past year and let out a deep sigh. "I wish it worked that way for real."

John Francis reached into the depths of his own memory and said, "I remember you boys playing like that. One day I'd been working on the cabin and stopped to get some iced tea. You three boys weren't much older than ten, and you were conducting a ceremony down here on the dock. I stopped to watch you. It took me a moment to realize what you were doing, and then it hit me. You were conducting a burial at sea."

He pointed to the corner of the dock and continued, "Mark, you were standing behind a lounge chair just like the one you're sitting in now. Matthew was lying on the chair, wrapped head to toe in white towels. Luke, as usual, was running his mouth, sending him off in fine fashion, 'Commending his bones to the sea…until the sea should give up her dead.' Then the two of you lifted the back of the chair and slid Matthew into the water. You'd tied the towels around his arms so tight he couldn't swim, and he just about drowned. You jumped in and pulled him out, then both of you ran like hell to keep him from kicking your butts." The memory made him chuckle for a moment. "In a little while you were all lying around together on the dock, laughing. While you boys were having a ball, I was standing there reliving the scene for real from 1943. I thought I was going to puke."

Mark didn't reply, but just sat there looking out over the cove.

John Francis rose from his chair. "So don't worry about missing the funeral, son. You buried him once, right here, already. One funeral for a brother ought to be enough for any man."

Mark felt as though a large weight had been lifted from his shoulders. "You know, Dad, I saw Matt just days before we were both hit. Of all the Marines I ever knew, I'd have never believed he'd be killed. He was the toughest guy I've ever known. Pain never bothered him. He seemed to have a destiny, and I don't think it was to die in a stupid ambush. It all seems so random. It all seems such a waste."

"Yeah, Mark, it does at that. Look, why don't we head back to Atlanta? Your leave is about over, and your mother would love to spend a little time with you. We heard from Luke last night. He's getting out of the Air Force in July. He's enjoyed living in Louisiana. He says the politicians there are like nowhere else on earth. He's been accepted to Tulane University in New Orleans."

Mark smiled. "That's great, Dad. That ought to be right up his alley." He looked back at the water and asked, "Will you tell Mom about my decision to stay in the Corps and about the Naval Academy?"

John Francis howled with laughter. "Boy...you must have lost part of your brain when they tried to blow your head off! I'd rather sandpaper a tiger's ass in a phone booth than break *that* news to your mother!"

Matt grinned. "You're all heart, Dad."

Chapter Nine

THE BIG TIME

"Can't understand...it's so simple to me...
people everywhere just gotta' be free."

The Young Rascals

Washington, DC – January 1968

This pub wasn't the kind of place where most guys would take a date. Located in a less-than-genteel part of town, Matt Kane's Bit o' Ireland was the kind of bar that attracted a tough crowd. On any given Friday night, you'd find groups of young Marine lieutenants from The Basic School at Quantico, Virginia. Saturdays, the place was full of Americans of Irish descent rustling up financial aid (and other support) for the Irish Republican Army. Various soldier-of-fortune types frequented the bar at will. It was a hard place full of hard men, and those who liked to think they were...noisy, smoky, and full of guys getting a head start on the next day's hangover. Business was frequently done in the booths that lined the walls of the large room. In Matt Kane's, if it wasn't *your* business, you minded your own.

Two men occupied a booth in the back of the bar. The lighting was low, and none of the other patrons paid them a second thought. One of the men was heavyset and muscular for his age, with flame-red hair and a bushy beard trimmed and combed like a sea captain in an old Errol Flynn swashbuckler. On his bear paw-sized hands, he wore a large gold ring with a flat, black onyx stone. In bias relief inlay, the stone sported a skull and crossbones. He had been christened Michael Patrick O'Rourke in 1915, and had gone by that name as an officer in the OSS during World War II. When the war ended, he stayed on to be a part of the newly formed Central Intelligence Agency. For the next twenty-five years, he lived under a variety of names and identities. Those who knew him well indulged his fascination with the pirates of old and had nicknamed him Redbeard. To avoid the obvious cliché, they simply called him RB. Last year, at the age of fifty-three, he retired from the agency and hung out his own shingle, joining the ranks of the freelancers. If you had a problem, and an appropriate amount of cash, RB could see that your problem disappeared.

Seated across from him was a dark-skinned man in his mid forties. He had jet-black hair, combed straight back, and wore his mustache closely trimmed, giving him the look of a Spanish aristocrat. In reality, he was an American of Portuguese descent. He too, was a freelancer who frequently performed odd jobs for the FBI. The Bureau guarded its reputation closely. Tasks that might prove embarrassing if they were to go awry were often outsourced to him. RB had known him for years as Raoul.

The two men ceased their conversation when a young man in his early twenties approached their booth. He was lean and hard and had purpose in his walk. Like Raoul's, this man's hair and moustache were also closely trimmed. Wearing dark slacks, a knit turtleneck, and a well-worn leather aviator's jacket, he looked like he'd just landed a Phantom on a carrier deck. He smiled and said, "Greetings, RB...Mind if I join you?" He slid into the booth on RB's side before getting an answer. Raoul knew the type immediately. Young, dangerous, competent...and ignorant of just how much he had yet to learn.

RB introduced them. "Raoul, I'd like you to meet my young friend, Cain. Cain, meet my very old and trusted friend, Raoul." They shook hands over the table. To the surprise of neither man, the handshakes were firm, and their eyes never looked away from each other. Each man appraised the other in a matter of seconds.

"It's very nice to meet you, sir," Cain said. "RB tells me I might be of some help to you."

Politeness? This *did* come as a surprise to Raoul. He'd expected a surly and brash demeanor to accompany Cain's physical appearance. Instead, he was deferential and accommodating. Raoul's first impression was under revision. This young man had potential. With a little care and grooming, he could move in circles that would allow him proximity to the rich and powerful. Along with his technical skills, outlined earlier by RB, he had the total package to become a first-class operator.

RB absorbed the scene with relish. Cain was his discovery, and was now his protégé. If he passed muster with Raoul, RB was confident his career as an assassin was unlimited.

With complete candor Raoul asked, "Tell me Cain, is there anyone you could not kill?" Raoul searched his eyes for a reaction of concern, or discomfort with the question. Cain gave neither.

With no hint of sarcasm or disrespect, Cain said, "Please clarify your question, sir. Are you asking if there's anyone I *could not* kill, or *would not* kill?"

"Is there a difference in *your* mind?" Raoul replied.

"Yes sir, there is. If you're asking *could not*…the answer is no one. If you're asking *would not*, the answer is…it depends." Cain offered clarification without prompting. "If I have ample time to plan the mission, I don't believe there's anyone on earth I *couldn't* kill. If it's necessary that the target die, there are only two people I *wouldn't* kill."

"And who would those be?" asked Raoul.

"My mother and father."

Pressing further, Raoul asked, "Would you have any problem killing a woman?"

"No."

"Would you kill a child?"

"Not a problem."

"Perhaps the time would come when you'd be asked to kill a member of the clergy…say, a nun or a minister."

"That would depend on the importance of their being killed," Cain replied.

This final question was the most important to Raoul. "And who, my young friend, would decide whether or not their death was important?"

Cain's eyes hadn't left Raoul's through the entire questioning. They remained fixed on him as he answered in all sincerity, "The people paying the money."

Raoul looked at RB and nodded his head in approval. Cain was entirely satisfactory. The plan would proceed.

Nashville – March 1968

"And that's the way it is...Monday March 15th, 1968. For *CBS News*, I'm Walter Cronkite...Goodnight."

Raoul switched off the television and walked to the window. March 15th. Julius Caesar had been warned "Beware the Ides of March." Raoul's timetable was a couple of weeks longer than William Shakespeare's.

Holiday Inn motels looked identical wherever you went. Had it not been for the card on top of the TV that said "Welcome to Nashville," it would have been easy to forget where he was. He had been on the road constantly since the first of the year. There had been many preparations to make. If one wanted to kill an important person and not spend the rest of his life in prison, it was crucial to make sure that someone else would. His mother had always said, "The Devil is in the details." She'd been right, and he was still playing the game because he had taken her advice to heart. His travels had taken him to Atlanta, Birmingham, Memphis, DC and now Nashville. Several of these cities he'd been to more than twice. All his travels had been by car. Different ones each time, as well as different motels. All his gas, meals and lodging had been paid in cash. He wanted to leave no trail to follow.

The slamming of a car door outside alerted him that the party he was meeting had arrived. He parted the curtain to see Cain walking toward the stairwell. Taking the stairs two at a time, he reached the second floor balcony quickly. Raoul's door was at the top of the stairs, next to the corridor that contained the vending machines. Through his door he could hear Cain put a quarter in the Coke machine. The bottle dropped into the tray and Cain placed the neck in the bottle opener. As the cap popped off, the spewing noise could be clearly heard.

Cain took a sip and walked toward the balcony overlooking the lot where he'd parked his car. Had anyone been following him, he was to walk to the other end of the balcony and knock three times on the door of the last room. If anyone answered, he would excuse himself and say he had the wrong room. If no one answered, he'd look at his watch, knock again, wait, and then leave. Either way, he would return to his car and drive away from the motel. Scanning the parking lot and the street below, he was satisfied no one had followed him. He went to the door marked 201 and knocked twice. Two knocks meant everything was all right. Raoul opened the door and Cain stepped inside.

"Pleasant trip?" Raoul inquired, closing the door.

"Yes, sir," Cain said with a slight grin.

Raoul pointed to the glasses and ice bucket on the counter. "Would you like some ice for your Coke?"

"No thanks. It's plenty cold."

"Let's get down to business, then. It's been arranged for you to do a little plumbing work in Memphis the first week of April."

Cain looked puzzled but said, "Okay…Tell me all about it."

Raoul spent the next two and a half hours doing just that—one detail at a time.

Memphis – April 1968

The Ford utility truck slowed to a snail's pace to await a break in the oncoming traffic on South Main Street. When one appeared, the driver turned left into the parking lot between the fire station and Canipe's Record Store. He parked the truck perpendicular across three spaces, got out, and walked to the back. Putting on some heavy work gloves, he grabbed a webbed nylon strap and pulled hard. The strap was attached to a metal ramp designed to slide out of its cradle in the base of the truck bed. He pulled it all the way out and laid it on the ground. Lifting the top edge, he fitted two tabs into slots at the back of the truck, and the ramp became rigid and flush.

On the side of the truck's doors was a logo with the picture of a neatly dressed workman in an Eisenhower-cut jacket, bow tie and cap. The name of the company was below the logo, printed in simple red letters that read "Garmon's Plumbing & Electric Company." The workman driving the truck looked nothing like the one on the door's logo, and if one ever did look like him, he hadn't dressed like that since 1950. This one had a dark gray pair of Dickies work pants and a shirt to match. Half his shirt was tucked in, and the tail was hanging out. He was at least forty pounds overweight. Above the left breast pocket was a four by three inch white oval patch that said "Terry." His red baseball-style hat, with the company name on it, was pushed back high on his head, revealing the bushiest eyebrows this side of an ape. The hat capped off his shoulder-length ponytail, and his face had a three-day growth all over, except for the bushy Fu Manchu mustache that completely covered his upper lip.

Terry walked up the ramp and unstrapped a sturdy hand dolly from the side of the bed. Although the Ford wasn't very high off the ground, the incline of the ramp was fairly steep, only six feet long by thirty inches wide. The sides were about six inches deep and the surface of the ramp was about an inch below the upper edge of each side. This left a recess nearly five inches deep on the ramp's bottom side.

Terry slid the base of the dolly under a tall water heater bearing a General Electric label. He wrapped the strap securely around the unit and tightened it by pulling on a handle. Taking care to avoid slipping, he crouched down and slowly rolled the dolly down the ramp. At the bottom he stood the unit upright, then walked to the cab of the truck and put on his tool belt. He retrieved his clipboard, returned to the dolly, and placed the clipboard on top. Grabbing the handles, he placed his foot against the bottom and leaned the load backwards, then rolled it to the rear door of the adjacent building labeled Jim's Grill. With the side of his fist, he banged hard on the door three times.

A couple of minutes later he was greeted from the other side by a gravel-voiced man. Between a couple of hacks and coughs the guy barked, "Who is it and whad'ya' want?"

"Hey man...I'm Terry Miller from Garmon's Plumbing & Electric. I've got a work order to install a new water heater upstairs in the rooming house."

"Hold your horses," the man yelled as he slid a bolt open to unlock the door. When he opened it, he was greeted by the dumbest-looking man he'd ever seen, standing there unkempt, unshaven, and chomping on a huge wad of bubblegum.

Terry showed him the work order and the man waved him inside. "Wait right here and I'll go get you the keys to the upstairs door."

As he turned to go get the keys, Terry blew a big bubble and popped it loud, briefly startling the man. He turned and gave Terry a dirty look, then shook his head in exasperation and continued walking. When he returned, he handed Terry a pop-bead chain with two keys on it and a tiny replica of a Coca-Cola bottle hanging from the other end. Pointing at the dolly, he said, "You need to take that thing back outside and wheel it between these two buildings. You'll see a set of stairs back there that'll take you up to the rooming house. Don't you lose them keys, boy. You bring 'em back when you're through." He spoke to Terry like he was talking to a five-year-old kid.

Cain's desired reaction had been achieved. Terry Miller was the kind of man no one paid any attention to, and who looked like he didn't have enough ambition to pour out of a boot. He could work in the building for hours and no one would mess with him, because he wasn't the kind of guy anyone cared to talk to.

The owner of Jim's Grill was just happy this dumbass was installing an electric water heater. If it'd been a gas one, he would've worried that the stupid bastard would blow the whole building up. With an electric one, the worst he could do was to electrocute himself and trip the main circuit breaker. Fortunately, it was a little after four o'clock and the lunch rush was over. If he killed himself now, it wouldn't really matter.

Cain took the keys and put them into his pocket, then looked at the man and said, "Thanks for your help. I'll probably be up there for a couple of hours."

After wheeling the dolly upstairs, Cain rolled it to the common bathroom at the end of the hall. He placed a handwritten sign on the door that read, "Bathroom under repair. Please use the restroom downstairs. Thanks. Garmon's Plumbing & Electric Co."

Cain wheeled the load into the bathroom. Once inside, he locked the door and shoved a wedge-shaped doorstop under the door to make sure no one with a key walked in on him by surprise. Then he removed the water heater from the dolly.

The unit was lighter than it should have been, because the heating element and controls had been removed. Cain opened the top by turning it a quarter-turn counterclockwise, then lifted off the lid. He reached inside and extracted a long object wrapped in a dark green cloth. After laying the object on the counter, he went to the window and opened it. From this vantage point he could see over the back lot of Jim's Grill, clear across Mulberry Street to the motel. He smiled; confirming what he already knew, his view of the balcony overlooking the pool was unobstructed.

Loosening the strap that had held the water heater to the dolly, Cain turned the unit around, then unbuckled three small latches like the ones found on most toolboxes. This permitted him to remove the water heater's white aluminum outer skin. Taking a roll of masking tape and a can of blue spray paint from inside the unit, he painted the top of the already installed water heater. In less than ten minutes, the top of it looked brand new. There was nothing really wrong with the old heater. Cain had been here several days earlier, disguised as a hardware salesman from Little Rock, and had rented a room. While using the bathroom that night, he disconnected the control panel and rigged the unit to leak water at a steady rate. He complained about the lack of hot water to the rooming house manager, who called Garmon's to schedule the installation of a new water heater.

Cain replaced the washer around the valve that had made the unit leak—the same washer he'd removed the week before. With a screwdriver, he removed the faceplate to the panel, pulled it out, and reattached the wires. Then he peeled away the masking tape and tossed it inside the fake unit, along with the unused tape and the paint can. As the final step, he wrapped the old water heater in the aluminum skin of the unit he'd brought with him and latched the three clasps at the rear. In a grand total of twenty minutes, the old water heater was made to look and work as if it were brand new.

Without its shiny new skin, the water heater shell on the dolly now looked like an old unit. Cain was impressed with his miniature Trojan horse. Removing the cloth from the object in the corner and tossing it into the open water heater, he picked up what it had been protecting—a Remington 30.06 rifle with a telescopic sight. It made a big noise, and a big hole. From his pants pocket, he pulled out a pair of foam earplugs, rolled them between his forefinger and thumb, and put one in each ear. With his foot, he pulled up a stool from under the sink and took up a comfortable firing position. He loaded only one round. At this range, he knew that's all he would need. Through the scope, he could read the number on the door clearly…306.

Moments earlier, while Cain was trundling his load upstairs, a man parked his white Mustang on Mulberry Street and entered Jim's. Just as he'd been instructed, he rented the room down the hall from the second floor bathroom. He put his things in the room and went to use the toilet. Seeing the sign on the door, he did what anyone would do…he ignored it and tugged on the door handle anyway. Cain turned instantly, and with the reactions of a cat, pulled his pistol from his waistband at the same time. The lock and doorstop prevented the door from being opened, and he breathed a sigh of relief.

Cain said, "Sorry friend...I can't let ya' in right now. I got the water and the electricity off for a while. Use the one downstairs, like the sign says, okay?"

"Sure," the man said, and walked down the hall to the stairs.

Cain returned his pistol to the holster underneath his untucked shirt, and once again took up his firing position. Around five thirty, several men walked out on the balcony from the rooms on either side of room 306. They seemed to be in fine spirits as they spoke animatedly to one another. A black Olds 98 moved from the parking lot next to the pool and pulled to a stop below the motel balconies. Two men got out of the car and began speaking to the men standing on the third-floor balcony above.

At six o'clock sharp, the door to room 306 of the Lorraine Motel opened, and the man made his appearance. He spoke to his associates, then waved to his friends in the parking lot. Through the scope, Cain could tell he was a fine-looking man—right up to the moment the bullet smashed into his head. The time was exactly 6:01 p.m.

The only word to describe the scene was panic. Half the men fell prone on the balcony while others ran for cover. The target was dead before he hit the ground. The bathroom window closed immediately.

Cain shoved the rifle back into the fake water heater, and tossed in the pistol and earplugs, too. He replaced the top and turned it a quarter-turn clockwise to seal it shut, then laid the unit and dolly on its side and unlocked the door. Removing the wedge, Cain looked outside. The corridor was empty, but he could hear footsteps climbing the stairs, then pounding down the corridor towards the bathroom. When the men burst through the door he was sprawled on the floor next to his dolly, struggling to get to his feet. They asked what the loud bang had been, and Cain explained he had lost control of the dolly and dropped the old water heater on the ceramic tile floor. He got to his feet, tipped it upright, and walked out as one man held the door for him.

Cain hurried down the stairs to his truck, and wheeled the dolly onto the bed. After securing it to the sides with a strap, he climbed down and began to disconnect the loading ramp. Two policemen came running into the parking lot and approached him, their pistols drawn. Cain put his hands in the air and acted like the moron they assumed he was. They searched him quickly. Asked if he'd seen anyone leaving the area in a hurry, he shook his head no...and the cops left him and entered the grill.

Cain shoved the ramp into its slot halfway, leaving about three feet hanging out, then climbed into the cab and drove slowly to the curb of South Main. Looking both ways and seeing no one, Cain pulled the air vent lever under his dashboard. The cable connected to the vent lever released a latch under the recess of the loading ramp that secured a bundled canvas bag in place. The bundle dropped from the ramp into the gutter of South Main. In it was a rifle identical to the one just used—except this one held the fingerprints of the fall guy, as well as a few of his personal effects.

Cain turned onto South Main and accelerated the truck, then popped the brakes hard, causing the ramp to slide forward and lock in its recess. He gently pressed the accelerator and left the scene. In less than five minutes, he was miles away.

After leaving the bag in the room upstairs and trying to use the bathroom next door, the man who'd nearly interrupted Cain had gone downstairs and used the toilet in Jim's Grill. There he bought a couple of beers, and took them to his car. Cranking up his Mustang, he wheeled it into traffic and headed east toward Nashville. He was enjoying his beer, as well as his good fortune. He'd just made an easy five thousand dollars for doing next to nothing. He'd bought a pair of binoculars, some sporting goods and some clothes, and left them in the room he rented for a fella he'd met in New Orleans named Raoul.

He was halfway to Nashville when the radio program was interrupted with a special bulletin:

> *"Dr. Martin Luther King, Jr. has been gunned down in Memphis this evening, shortly after 6:00 p.m. Witnesses reported seeing a man in a white Ford Mustang leaving the scene shortly after the shooting."*

His jaw dropped open, and his beer fell to the floorboard. He swore out loud, saying, "*James Earl*, you are one *stupid* son of a bitch!"

Once he regained his senses, he decided what to do. He had friends in Atlanta that would help him leave the country. The draft dodgers seemed to think Canada was a safe place to get away. Maybe it would be a good place for him to duck the law, too.

The next morning, the owner of Jim's Grill was on the phone waiting impatiently for someone to answer. On his desk was the April 5th morning paper. Bold headlines read:

MARTIN LUTHER KING
SHOT DEAD IN MEMPHIS

A woman with a pleasant voice finally answered the phone. "Garmon's Plumbing & Electric. How can I help you?"

In a perturbed tone he snapped, "You can help me by tellin' that idiot, Terry, to bring me back my damned keys!"

"Terry?" she said, confused. "We don't have anybody named Terry working here."

Chapter Ten

CHASMS

"The battle outside that's ragin'...will soon shake your windows, and rattle your walls.
For the times...they are a changin'."

Bob Dylan

New Orleans – October 1968

Freret Street splits Tulane University's campus in two. Students lined both sides of the street waiting for the traffic to ease, or the light to turn green, so they could cross. Luke was on his way to Dr. Randall's International Policy class. In his opinion, Dr. Randall was the brightest professor he'd ever known. Now in his mid-forties, Randall had received his undergraduate degree from Princeton and his doctorate from Yale. Luke had toyed with the idea of applying to an Ivy League school but knew, deep in his heart, he would hate them all because of the cold New England climate. There was no denying the fact that he was a Southerner through and through.

Days like today confirmed he had made the right choice. New Orleans in the fall was like a holdover from summer any place else. Blue sky, devoid of a single cloud, perfectly framed the midday sun. The temperature was a pleasant eighty-one degrees, and no one was in a hurry. Nearly the whole student body was wearing shorts, which meant some beautiful legs attached to a bunch of girls of every shape and size. Life was good in Louisiana.

Luke had returned to school in Shreveport while he was finishing his enlistment at Barksdale Air Force Base. At night, he attended classes at Centenary College. This allowed him to take the coursework necessary to complete his sophomore year. He had considered returning to Emory upon his release, but concluded he no longer wanted to be near his parents. Mark had been accepted as a plebe at The U.S. Naval Academy and would be home very little. Were he to go back to Emory, Luke felt he would be the sole focus of his mother's attentions. The last thing he wanted was to be a living reminder of Matt.

Tulane fit the bill perfectly, and New Orleans was a fascinating town. Five hundred miles from Atlanta, the school was nearly as liberal as Emory. Unlike Emory, the school had a football team that played on Saturday nights, although it was a rare surprise for them to win. Completing the package was great food of every description and the absolute best laboratory in the world to study politics. There was a surface civility in politics—everywhere else but Louisiana. In political campaigns countrywide, candidates typically referred to their competitor as "my esteemed colleague," or "my worthy opponent."

Just the previous evening, Luke had seen a campaign ad for one of the candidates for governor. The man had looked straight into the camera and said, "Hell, boys...you know we're all crooks. What makes me a better choice is that I'm less crooked than either of the other two guys who want the job!" It made for great theater, and the odds of him winning were pretty high. Folks in Louisiana appreciated candor, even from a liar.

Luke had been at Tulane for exactly two months, and he felt right at home. His future was in politics, and there was no better place to learn than Louisiana. If you learned what it took to win here, it would be a cinch to win anywhere else in the country. It was an exciting time to be politically active as well. Politics was the primary focus of the whole country. Some folks appeared disinterested and tried to sit on the sidelines, but by and large, most folks had a position. You were either *for* it in a big way, or just as strongly *against* it. What constituted "it" covered a multitude of issues...the war...civil rights...ROTC on college campuses. Luke loved the electricity that filled the air in the University Center, the coffee shops and the bars near campus. His friends were using their minds and formulating belief systems that shook the establishment to its foundation. As Bob Dylan had said, the times indeed were changing.

The friends he now associated with were vehemently against the war. He listened to what they had to say, and could find no fault in their reasoning. He had seen firsthand what a waste it all was, although he'd kept silent about his own participation. There was nothing to be gained, and much to be lost, if it became widely known that he was a veteran. Better to keep his mouth shut and work to bring the war to a close. When it ended, there would be time to decide whether to admit to having been in the service.

As Dr. Randall's class ended that day, students slid from their desks and made their way toward the door. Luke was the last to reach it just as Dr. Randall called out, "May I have a word with you, Luke?"

"Sure, Professor. What can I do for you?"

"Are you planning to come to the rally tomorrow night?" he asked. There was a protest rally planned for Friday night on the UC Quad. Dr. Randall was going to speak, along with several other members of the faculty and a few students.

"Yes, I am," Luke answered.

"Good. I wondered if I might ask a favor."

"Certainly."

"Take my speech home with you this afternoon and look it over." He handed Luke a half-dozen handwritten pages, stapled together. "I'd like to have your assessment."

Luke was speechless. Fumbling for the words, he finally managed to say, "I'd be honored to look it over."

"Can you meet me tomorrow evening? Say, six o'clock at The Rat?"

"I'll see you there, Professor." He smiled at Dr. Randall and added, "I appreciate your confidence in me."

"You're a good man, Luke. I trust your judgment. See you tomorrow at six."

Luke knew Dr. Randall was impressed with him. He'd told him so before. Luke was a little older than most of the kids in his classes. He had a maturity about him, and he appeared to hold deeper feelings about the war than many who were protesting simply because it was

111

the "in" thing to do. Luke liked the attention and respect from someone he felt was a kindred spirit.

He read the speech that evening and felt as though he were privy to the words of a master. Dr. Randall's vision was so clear, so moral, so correct. Luke made some notes on a separate page to discuss with him later the next day. He didn't want to seem presumptuous by marking up the margins of the original.

Luke felt great all day Friday, but was wishing the clock would move quicker to bring about his meeting with Dr. Randall. He had some time to kill after his last afternoon class, so he drove home to take a shower. As he pulled his Camaro to the curb at the corner of Broadway and Spruce, he could see someone sitting in the shadows on the front steps of his apartment. He threw the shifter into park and opened his door as the guy on the steps rose to his feet and stepped into the light. Spinning a white hat in his hand, dressed from head to toe in Navy blue, stood his brother, Mark. They both smiled from ear to ear as they approached each other.

"Maaark," Luke shouted. They gave each other a strong hug, punctuated with some slaps to the back. "Damn, it's good to see you. Why didn't you let me know you were coming to town?"

"I didn't know until this morning," Mark replied. "A few days ago, I told my company commander I had a brother at Tulane, and he wrangled a pass for me to come to the football game on Saturday. We've got liberty until 1600 Saturday when we assemble for the game. I'm free again afterward until 0900 on Sunday. We fly back to

Baltimore at 1300." Mark gave his brother an appraising look. "What in the Sam Hell happened to your face?" he asked in a sarcastic tone.

Luke smiled. "You like the beard and longer hair?"

For the first time ever, they didn't look identical. They simply looked like brothers.

Mark wasn't impressed with the new look, but what the hell? It was Luke's life, and he'd earned the right to live it as he pleased.

"Come on in." Luke said. "To tell you the truth, I forgot Tulane was playing Navy tomorrow. Want a cold beer?" Without waiting for a reply, he reached into his refrigerator and grabbed two Budweisers.

"Slide one over," Mark said. He grabbed the can and was caught by surprise. It seemed as though the can had shrunk, or his hand had grown. He looked at the side of it and discovered he was right. Instead of twelve fluid ounces, as most beers contained, this one only held ten.

"What's with the puny beer can?" Mark asked.

Luke laughed and said "Creative competition." He pulled a Dixie beer from the fridge and slid it across the kitchen counter to Mark. "Jax Brewery and Dixie Beer have the dominant market share in New Orleans. They price their beer really cheap, and they should 'cause you'd be better off pouring it right back into the horse it came from. That being said, the locals love the stuff, and buy it by the caseload. The only way the national brands can compete is by offering less product for the same price as the local beer."

Mark took a swig and wiped his mouth with the back of his hand. "It sounds like what you told Mom about the politicians down here…style over substance."

Luke shot Mark a piercing glare, as though he felt rebuked.

"What'd I say?" Mark asked, realizing he'd struck a raw nerve but not knowing which one.

"Not all politicians are scumbags, Mark," Luke said in disgust. "One day, another guy will come along and finish what John Kennedy started. When he shows up, I'm going to help him succeed."

"More power to ya', baby brother," Mark said in a condescending tone.

There it is, Luke thought. They'd been together less than five minutes, and the pecking order had been trotted out. Matthew, the strong and powerful eldest son…Mark, the middle child who could do no wrong…and pulling up the rear was Luke, the *baby* of the family. To hear Matt and Mark tell it, you'd think they were all separated by years, not minutes. There had always been competition among them. It had primarily been between himself and Matt. Mark usually intervened to restore the peace. Every so often, however, Mark would say something like he just did, and the anger at Matt would bubble to the surface like a festering wound.

Luke knew that Mark would object to tonight's rally, and he'd planned to send him on the town with his buddies, and hook up with him later. He would have, too, but that *baby brother* remark pissed him off. It was time to put Mark in his place, and Matt— vicariously—at the same time.

Like the Judas goat that leads the lambs to the slaughterhouse, Luke turned to his brother and asked, "Do you have any *plans* for the evening, Mark?"

Luke drove to the Fountainbleu Hotel at the corner of Tulane Avenue and South Carrollton, and pulled to a stop under the portico. Mark, waiting inside the lobby, pushed open the door as soon as he saw the Camaro pull up. Even civilian clothes couldn't disguise the fact that he was a Marine. He wore a navy blue knit shirt with an alligator on the left breast, khaki pants and a pair of Bass Weejuns that were polished to a bright shine. Capping the look were the ever-present black military socks. Wally Cleaver would've loved the look. In contrast, Luke was wearing jeans that looked like they'd been dragged behind his car at high speed, topped by a tee shirt that said "Stop the War!" and a red and white bandana. On his feet was a pair of worn-out combat boots he'd obviously picked up from an army surplus store, since his had never been off an Air Force base tarmac.

Mark got in and closed his door. With the swift appraisal of a drill sergeant, he absorbed the scene in one glance. "Nice look, man," he said. "Did I miss the memo? I thought we were going out tonight."

"We are," Luke replied as he spun the wheel and turned onto Carrollton Avenue. "We're meeting some friends of mine at the school, and then we're going to a little party later tonight."

"A party sounds good." Mark said. "I hope there'll be some girls there. Lately I've felt like I'm in the priesthood rather than the Academy."

"There'll be girls, but they might not be your type," Luke muttered, looking straight ahead.

Mark could tell Luke was in a crummy mood. It never ceased to amaze him that a guy who had so much going for him in the brain department could have so little grace. Too often, Luke could be the proverbial turd in the punchbowl.

Mark was right about his brother's frame of mind. Luke was quietly seething under the surface. For years he had taken crap from his siblings. Matthew was dead and gone, but this afternoon Mark had brought it all back with one innocuous remark. Matthew had always felt himself superior, and had always imposed his dominance on the other two boys. Mark had always been strong enough to fight back, and Matt respected him for it, so he let up on him. Though he'd never said it to his face, Luke knew that Matthew considered him weak. Matt had always hated weakness, and he bullied those he thought couldn't cut it.

Mark was strong. He'd survived months of hardship in Vietnam. He'd fought intense battles and had spent months recovering from painful wounds. Seeing him on his front steps today, wearing three rows of campaign ribbons, including the Purple Heart and the Navy Cross for extraordinary heroism, made Luke feel inferior.

The war had defined both of his brothers. It had shaped him as well, but he was not going to let it be the foundation of his manhood.

Principle was what he intended to have shape his future. Tonight was about principle. Luke stomped on the gas pedal and beat the changing traffic light as the yellow turned to red.

Mark reached down to find his seat belt and buckled it up. The action wasn't lost on, Luke and a smile formed at the corner of his lip. *That's right, big brother,* he thought. *Buckle up tight! You're going on the ride of your life tonight.*

It was still daylight outside as they pulled up to the University Center, and some people were putting the final touches on a platform at the other end of the Quad. The UC was the nerve center of student life on the campus. It housed a dining facility, a bowling alley, the campus radio station, *WTUL,* and the campus newspaper, *The Hullabaloo.* In the basement was a pub called The Rathskeller, known affectionately by the student body as "The Rat." This was the first stop on Luke's itinerary.

In contrast to the outside daylight, the room behind the large wooden door was dark. There were large, heavy tables around the room. At the far end was a cafeteria-style counter holding pizza, hamburgers and sandwiches. Behind the counter, beer taps mounted on the front of fake barrels were attached to the wall to give the appearance of recessed kegs. The place achieved the desired effect. It looked like a German beer hall, safely tucked into the basement of the school.

Against the far wall were long upholstered benches with six-foot-long tables in front of them. On the other side of the tables were wooden ladder-back chairs. Seated in the middle of the vinyl bench sat a middle-aged man with bushy, long hair and a beard to match. On either side of him sat several students, dressed in attire similar to Luke's. By all appearances, the man was holding court. At first blush the scene looked like a hippie rendition of DaVinci's painting, "The Last Supper."

Luke approached the table without waiting for Mark. The man in the middle saw him enter the pub and waved him over. "Luke" he said, "I'm so glad you could join us." He took note of Mark and asked, "Who's your friend?"

Luke paused and said, "Dr. Randall, I'd like you to meet my brother, Mark. He's in town for tomorrow's football game between our own Green Wave and the Midshipmen from the Naval Academy."

Mark wasn't sure what was happening here, but he had no difficulty detecting Luke's snotty tone. He had a burr under his saddle about something, and Mark was pretty sure *he* was about to pay for Luke's foul mood. The table fell silent, and he could feel the suspicious reactions of the students sitting there. He had experienced similar looks in the Los Angeles Airport as he waited to catch a flight home to Atlanta last November. He was wearing his uniform then, adorned with a chest full of ribbons. It was the first time he'd worn them, and he'd been proud to be a Marine combat veteran. He had no idea why so many people seemed aloof, but after a few months back in the real world he'd come to accept it as a fact. A lot of people in

America were against the war. He could understand that. Hell, he'd been in it and hadn't liked it much himself! What he couldn't understand was why the people who were against the war were also against the soldiers. They hadn't started the damned thing. Luke's hero, JFK, had been the one who thought Vietnam was a good idea.

"Ah, Mark, welcome to New Orleans," the professor said, waving his hand like a king, inviting him to take a seat at his feet. "So you're a cadet at the Naval Academy?"

"*Midshipman*, sir," Mark answered, looking him straight in the eyes.

Astonished, he said, "Excuse me?" as though he were incapable of making an error.

"I'm a *midshipman*, sir. *Cadets* go to West Point. I attend The Naval Academy."

"Yes, yes…whatever," he said, as if all military pawns were indistinguishable.

"Luke," Mark said, "I'm gonna go get us a couple of beers."

Luke said "Fine," and became engrossed in the table's conversation as Mark got up and walked over to the service counter.

Mark paid for a pitcher of beer and asked for two glasses. While the young girl behind the counter pulled the tap and poured off the initial foam, he looked around the room. In one corner was a group of fraternity boys. Many had jerseys with the letters ΣAE in gold letters on the front. They didn't impress him much, but sitting with them were three of the prettiest girls he'd ever seen. He felt like joining them instead of his brother's group.

He thought better of the idea as he remembered his last visit to a fraternity house at Georgia Tech, last spring. While on leave in Atlanta he'd gone over to Tech to visit his old friends at the **KA** house. They were all seniors now, and had the college experience down pat: "Drink until you puke…keep your grades high enough to maintain your draft deferment…and thank your lucky stars you're not eating lunch in a rice paddy." In comparison to what he'd been doing the past couple of years, it seemed pretty juvenile.

He'd been sitting in a rocker on the front porch for just a few minutes when a couple of guys started talking about "the niggers." Mark interrupted them and told them to watch their mouths. He explained that two of the best Marines in his squad were black. Many of the Navy corpsman in 'Nam were black, and his good friend Lucias Hammond, who'd nursed him back to health in Japan, was, too. They were as fine a group of men as he'd ever known.

That's when the other guy said, "Well, Mark, I guess you must've turned into a real nigger lover since you've been gone."

Mark had sprung from the chair like a cobra and, in one swift motion, smashed the heel of his palm into the boy's chin. The kid's jaw shifted backward and popped from its joints. Blood spewed from his lips and his head split wide open as it smacked hard against the brick siding of the house. It happened so fast the other guys on the porch couldn't have stopped it if they'd tried. Four guys had to intervene to keep Mark from hurting him even more.

At that moment Mark knew he no longer wanted to be a frat boy. Instantly, his former fraternity brothers at **KA** reached the same conclusion about him.

Mark returned his attention to where his brother was sitting, and the same sick feeling returned that he'd had while visiting the **KA** house. This was his brother's turf. He had no desire to embarrass Luke in front of his friends. He hoped Luke felt the same way. Nonetheless, he would try to be pleasant and get along for the night. Taking the pitcher and the glasses, he walked back to the table.

As he pulled up a chair, the professor turned his way and said, "So Mark, your brother tells us that *you* actually served in Vietnam."

The emphasis on the word "you" made him wonder what Luke had, and hadn't, told them. Once again he fixed his gaze directly on the professor and said, "Yes sir, I did."

"Didn't it bother you to be a participant in the killing of innocent women and children?"

The trap was sprung, and he was the lamb at the table with the pack of wolves. Pizza wasn't on the menu tonight...*he* was.

Mark took his time formulating his answer, then calmly replied, "I never saw any."

"You never saw any *what*?" chimed a loud-mouthed girl wearing small round eyeglasses and a loose-fitting peasant blouse.

"Any *innocent* civilians," Mark said, without raising his voice to match hers.

"You don't think little children should be spared the horrors of war?" asked the boy sitting to the professor's left.

"I think everyone should be spared the horrors of war," Mark replied. "But you should never confuse age with innocence."

"What do you mean by that?" asked the overweight, out-of-shape grad student straddling a chair turned backward.

Mark poured his beer and took a sip. "Let me tell you a little story," he said. "One morning I was getting ready to open my daily can of peaches. Y'all ought to try canned peaches for breakfast every morning for a few months—*they really grow on you.* Anyway, this little Vietnamese kid about ten years old was standing there eyeballin' that can, so I gave it to him. He just took it and ran away. No 'thanks. No "screw you, GI.' He just took it.

"A couple of hours later, my platoon left the village and moved out down the trail. About two hundred meters out we heard a grenade explode, followed by a lot of screaming. The point man moved up to check it out and saw a kid lying in the middle of the trail with his leg and his arm blown off. One of our corpsman rendered medical attention and saved his life. I took one look at the kid and recognized him as the one I'd given the peaches to earlier."

"So you prove our point," said the professor. "The innocent are maimed because of us."

"No, Professor. You didn't let me finish. You see…about six feet from this kid, wired to the base of a tree, was the empty peach can I'd given him. He'd pulled the pin on a grenade and shoved it into the can. He'd already attached a long piece of wire to it and was trying to tie the other end to a tree across the trail. The idea was for one of us Marines to trip it and blow a few of us to Hell. He'd gotten tangled up in his own booby trap and accidentally pulled it out of the can. The dumb little shit blew *himself* up. You see folks, he should have tied the wire off first, *and then* pushed the grenade into the can. He wasn't but about ten, but I can assure you of one thing—he was a *combatant*, not an *innocent*."

The kids at the table sat speechless as Mark added one more parting shot: "I'll say one thing for him though: He put his life on the line for what he believed. He had more balls than any bunch of pampered college kids and ivory-tower professors I've ever met."

Luke was about to challenge Mark, but Mark's cold stare caused him to hold his tongue. Dr. Randall appraised his outspoken adversary and found him strong and quick-witted. Mark Reilly was indeed a dangerous man, and his tongue-lashing strengthened the professor's resolve. Dr. Randall felt men like Mark were barbarians who'd outlived their usefulness.

Mark refused to break his lock on the professor's eyes. He said, "Professor, I have a question for you."

"What would you like to know?"

"Has Luke told you much about our family?"

"Not very much," replied the professor. "Just that you're his twin, and you were a Marine in Vietnam."

"*His twin?*" Mark thought to himself, working to shield his shock. That said it all. Luke had never mentioned Matthew, or his death. He apparently hadn't mentioned his own service, dropping bombs from B-52's, either. His brother the politician was a revisionist historian. He planned to start over and forget his past ever happened.

Mark looked at Luke with disgust. He'd made a choice, and it was these academic pukes over his family. He started to lay it all out for them…then he saw the look in Luke's eyes, pleading with him not to blow his cover. Luke needed these people, and wanted desperately to fit in. His omissions of the truth were designed to win their approval. Mark thought it was fitting he should have it—and *them*.

"Folks," Mark said as he stood up, "I'm gonna' say goodbye now." Glaring at his brother, he said, "Luke, I'll get home on my own. Have fun at your party." Then he turned and walked away without looking back.

The rally appeared to be a huge success. Mark had been really pissed when he left The Rat, and walked around the campus for a while to cool off. He returned after the rally had already begun, and leaned against a bike rack outside the UC. He was on the outskirts of the crowd, as were a lot of people who wanted to see what was going on but didn't want to be a part of the demonstration. Dr. Randall was whipping the crowd into outrage with chants against America's warmongering, and chants in support of Ho Chi Minh. Luke was sitting on the stage in rapt attention, as though seated in the presence of Christ, so caught in the moment he hadn't noticed Mark had returned and was watching from the wings.

Mark stared at him for several minutes. He must have felt the piercing gaze, for he finally turned his head in Mark's direction and their eyes met. Neither spoke. Then Luke simply turned his head away. Mark felt a familiar pain. A year ago, he'd lost a brother to an ambush in Vietnam. Tonight he'd lost another to an ambush in New Orleans. Battle lines had been drawn. From this moment on, there was a huge chasm between them.

There was nothing more to say tonight, or for many years to come. He turned around and left the grounds.

Chapter Eleven

HONOR – COURAGE - COMMITMENT

"Feelin' alright...Not feelin' too good myself."

Traffic

Annapolis, Maryland – May 1972

Life on the "Yard," as the Naval Academy campus is called, is stressful whether you're a plebe or an upperclassman. Midshipmen live in close quarters. They work and study together around the clock. Private time is a rare commodity.

Early in his third class year, Mark discovered a spot to get away— the roof of Bancroft Hall. Now a First Classman, his time at the Academy was nearly over. Graduation was tomorrow. As a senior, he had rank, status and privileges he hadn't rated in his first three years. Even so, he treasured his time alone above anything else. At least once a week, he'd venture to this private refuge for the luxury of clearing his head and harnessing his thoughts. Tonight was his last night on the roof.

Mark had always required less sleep than most people, and used it to his advantage. While the rest of the brigade lay sleeping in their rooms, he'd use the service ladder to access the roof. From up here he could see farther than from anyplace else on the Yard. He liked looking at the lights on both sides of the Severn River. Sometimes, late at night, boats would pass one another and signal with a blast from their air horns. The smell of the river filled his senses and made him thankful he was alive. So many guys his age no longer were. He'd never heard the term "survivor's guilt," since psychologists wouldn't coin the phrase for a few more years. Nonetheless, he had a strong case of it, and it troubled him from time to time. The roof was his place to deal with it.

Mark heard a noise behind him and turned to see a figure illuminated in the open doorway. He could clearly see that he was a Marine officer, so he immediately snapped to attention. Captain John Hall, the Officer of the Day, had seen the doorway to the ladder-well ajar, and climbed the stairs to investigate. He stepped through the door and approached Mark.

"Good evening, sir," Mark said as he saluted the captain.

Captain Hall returned his salute and said, "Midshipman Reilly. What the hell brings you up here at 0115?"

"Just looking for a quiet place to think, sir," he replied.

"Tomorrow's your big day. You're gonna' be draggin' ass if you stay up all night."

"True for mere mortals, sir, but this midshipman needs little sleep. It must be a holdover from Vietnam."

Captain Hall was a tactical officer on the Academy staff. He taught small unit tactics, and commanded the respect of everyone, including his superiors. He was a brilliant field commander, and was a recipient of the Medal of Honor for gallantry above and beyond the call of duty. He also wore two Silver Star medals and three Purple

Hearts. To put it bluntly, the captain was a living legend of the Corps. He motioned to where Mark had been sitting and said, "At ease, Mr. Reilly. Take your seat."

Mark did as ordered, and the captain sat down on a vent hood across from him. He crossed his left ankle over his other thigh and retrieved a pack of Marlboros that were tucked in his sock. He lit one, replaced the matches in the cellophane wrapper, and tossed the pack to Mark.

Mark tossed them back and said, "Thanks, sir, but I'm not a smoker."

Mark noticed that Captain Hall cupped his hand over the glowing end of the cigarette to hide it in the darkness. The precaution took him right back to Vietnam. He nodded his head toward the captain's hand and said, "Old habits die hard, don't they, sir?"

Captain Hall realized what Mark was looking at, and smiled in understanding. "I guess they do, Mr. Reilly."

"Sir?" Mark asked. "I've been wrestling with something for a long while. May I ask your opinion?"

"What's on your mind?"

In a pensive tone, he asked, "Do you ever feel we're out of step with the rest of the world?"

"What do you mean?"

Mark said, "I mean…I sometimes wonder if the rest of the world gives a damn about us. We protect them. We fight for them. Many of us die for them, and they act like we're Neanderthals. For my money, I feel like they're the strange ones."

"Are you here for *them*...or for something bigger?" the captain inquired.

"I'm not sure I understand the question, sir."

"Are you here to serve the *American people,* or are you here to serve *America*?"

"If there's a difference, sir, I'd love to hear what it is. I thought I *was* serving the American people until I got home from Vietnam. I couldn't believe the cold shoulder, and downright hostility I received from people I thought were my *friends*, let alone from total strangers. I knew I couldn't live with those people anymore, so I decided to come to the Academy. Now I'm about to become a Marine Corps officer, and my job will be to defend the same people who tossed us on the garbage pile when we came home."

"Grow up, Mr. Reilly. The average American citizen of today isn't fit to shine your shoes. He's either self-centered, thinks the country owes him something, or is so into trying to improve his miserable lot in life that he doesn't give the military a passing thought. If you're looking for gratitude, look in Webster's Dictionary. That's the only place you'll find it. The military is a lot like an insurance policy that's been bought and filed away in a drawer. It's of value only when it's needed, and of no use whatever when it's not.

He took a long glance at the river before continuing. "America? Now she's a different matter altogether. She's worthy of your loyal service, and perhaps one day, even your life. She's superior to the citizenry that comprise her. America is a noble idea that offers hope to a world that simultaneously admires and envies her greatness. Our heritage as military men is what's preserved her for nearly two hundred years from threats from outside her borders—and within." He fixed Mark with a look that was more stern than Mark had ever seen from him, and said, "You need never worry about whether the American people appreciate you. Few ever will. However, you serve a greater entity—America herself."

Mark soaked in every word.

The captain asked, "Mr. Reilly, have you read much of Rudyard Kipling?"

"No, sir…not really."

"Get a copy of his poem "Tommy," and teach it to your Marines before they go to war. It might spare them the confusion you're suffering now."

"How's it go, sir?"

"Kipling bemoans the treatment of the English soldier upon his return from war. In the slang of his day, soldiers were called 'Tommies,' and he wrestled with the same problem as you:

It's Tommy this, and Tommy that, an' 'Tommy go away';
But it's 'Thank you, Mr. Atkins,' when the band begins to play.
It's Tommy this, and Tommy that, an' chuck him out, the brute!'
But it's 'Savior of 'is country' when the guns begin to shoot.
Then it's Tommy this an' Tommy that, an' Tommy 'ow's yer soul?'
But it's 'Thin red line of 'eroes' when the drums begin to roll.

"Mr. Reilly," the captain continued, "there's no difference between the England of the 1880's and America today. The military is loved when it's needed, and shunned through peace and prosperity. If you want to be popular, run for Congress and give away other people's money. If you want to serve America and belong to The Brotherhood of Arms, you're in the right place."

"You served America bravely in Vietnam. If her citizens don't love you, that's their problem. You've excelled here at the Academy, and you've got a bright future in the Corps. Duty. Country. Corps. These things matter. You belong to something much bigger than you'll ever be. Most Americans, on the other hand, will live their lives never spending their best efforts on anything meaningful. Thoreau said, 'The mass of men lead lives of quiet desperation.' Don't agonize over the meaning of your life, son. History will decide whether or not you mattered."

It took Mark a minute to respond, then he said, "Thanks, Captain Hall."

"You're welcome, Mr. Reilly."

The captain stubbed out his cigarette on the vent hood. Peeling the remaining paper from the butt, he placed it and the filter in his pocket, then crumbled and dropped the remaining pinch of tobacco on the roof. Realizing he'd just performed a field ritual he'd learned long ago in boot camp, he laughed and said, "You're right, Mr. Reilly. Old habits die hard, indeed."

Mark couldn't have been more honored if he'd been Moses receiving the Ten Commandments from God Almighty. In one brief conversation, Captain John Hall, Marine Corps Legend, put in perspective all that had been eating at him for the past five years. He remembered an old saying: "For civilians, no words can express the special bond Marines have with one another. For Marines, no words are necessary." Another old expression said, "A man joins the Army…he joins the Navy…but he *becomes* a Marine."

When he returned from Vietnam, Mark had reservations about becoming a lifer. It was made clear tonight that he already was. He now knew he'd be a Marine forever.

Captain Hall's voice broke into his reverie. "Hit the rack, Mr. Reilly! You may not require much sleep, but I do."

The next afternoon crowned four years of sweat, perseverance and honor with the ultimate prize of graduation and commissioning. On his hand, Mark Reilly already wore the first gold symbol of his tenacity—his class ring. In a few hours he'd wear the second—the gold bars of a Marine lieutenant. There were times when Mark thought he'd never see this day; now it seemed to have arrived in the blink of an eye. He stood with his class, resplendent in his midshipman dress whites, knowing it was the last time he'd ever wear the uniform of the Navy. Graduation concluded with the commissioning ceremony and the oath of office:

"I, Mark Reilly, having been appointed an officer in the United States Marine Corps, do solemnly swear that I will support and defend the Constitution of the United States against all enemies foreign and domestic; that I will bear true faith and allegiance to the same; and that I will obey the orders of those officers placed over me. I take this oath freely, and without any mental reservation or purpose of evasion; and I will faithfully discharge the duties of the office on which I am about to enter, so help me God."

Immediately upon the commandant of midshipman pronouncing them "Officers and Gentlemen" in the naval service of The United States, each officer threw his hat as high into the air as four years of bottled-up frustration would allow. It was a magnificent sight, and brought tears to the eyes of parents and combat veterans in the audience.

Mark left, briefly, to exchange his white Navy blouse for the slightly different white blouse of the Marine Corps. Unlike the Navy whites, with shoulder boards bearing an ensign's single gold stripe and star, the Marine version had epaulets to hold his gold second lieutenant's bars, and the front of its rigid collar sported an "Eagle, Globe, and Anchor" emblem on each side. When he returned, Mark smiled as his mother and father pinned a gold bar on each of his shoulders. May 23rd, 1972, Second Lieutenant Mark Reilly, USMC was born.

His brother, Luke, did not attend. Mark hadn't invited him.

Georgetown, DC – May 1972

Only an hour's drive from Annapolis, Luke Reilly was finishing the last exam of his first year at Georgetown University School of Law. When he was done, he reviewed his Blue Book and judged it satisfactory. He had no doubt he would receive an "A" in constitutional law. Luke turned in his exam, bought a Coke from the machine in the hallway, and took a seat on the steps of the law school building.

His mother had told him today was Mark's graduation and commissioning, and she'd pleaded with him to come. He begged off, citing the need to take his final. Had he not been taking the exam, he still wouldn't have gone. He and Mark hadn't spoken a word to each other since the night of the anti-war demonstration two years earlier in New Orleans. It had been a childish performance on his part, and he'd regretted it many times since. He was a proud man, though, as was Mark. They both had access to a telephone, and neither of them had a broken arm. Since neither had called or written a note, Luke assumed their estrangement was simply a sad fact of life. Their mother was aware of the rift between them, but had no idea about its cause. Ever the peacemaker, she tried valiantly to bring the brothers back together. Luke's thoughts flashed back to another time when, as teenagers, she'd tried to smooth their ruffled feathers.

At fifteen, Luke had fallen hard for Mary Beth Jensen. She had blond hair and aquamarine eyes, her skin was the complexion of cream, and every time Luke saw her, his heart beat faster. Life was never simple back then, with three brothers the same age attending the same school. Mark, it seemed, had developed a crush on her, too. They argued for days over who was going to ask her to the homecoming dance. The arguments actually came to blows one afternoon, and the two wouldn't speak to each other for several days.

Their mother stepped in to make peace. Mary Quinn told them they should never let anyone outside the family come between them. Girlfriends would come and go, she said, but they'd be brothers forever.

The situation resolved itself when Matt walked through the door the following Monday after school and announced that *he* was taking Mary Beth to the dance. It was the typical move one could expect from Matthew. He had no interest in her at all. He just knew that Luke and Mark did, and that snaking their girlfriend would piss them both off.

He was right. As Luke thought about it, even now, he was still angry with him. Matt had been in his grave for five years, and he still had the power to make Luke mad. Of course, Mark got over the homecoming incident in a few days. He and Matt could never hold a grudge as long as Luke. He thought hard about this fact and concluded that, for Mark to remain angry for four years, he must have really been hurt by the shabby treatment he'd received at his hands. Luke had repeated the same mistake his mother had warned him about at fifteen—he'd let someone outside the family drive a wedge between himself and Mark. To win the friendship and approval of Professor Randall, he alienated his brother. For the first time, Luke realized Mark must've viewed his behavior in New Orleans as a serious betrayal of trust. He felt a little like Judas must have felt after betraying Jesus. The sweetness of the Coke in his hand couldn't remove the sour taste from his mouth.

He tried to weigh in his mind what he'd traded for the respect and love of his brother. *Access to power* was the only thing that he could call to mind. Through his friendship with Dr. Randall while at Tulane, he'd made a number of friends in the Louisiana Democratic Party. He was working part-time now for Senator Russell Long in his Washington office.

The atmosphere on "The Hill" was electrifying, and Luke was determined to spend the rest of his life there, in one capacity or another. Capitol Hill was the epicenter of the world's power. If it mattered, it was happening here. Access to power was how he could change the world for the better.

Luke's value on the Hill was his talent with the major polling services. He believed, and others agreed, that he had a real gift for extracting the essence of what the reports contained. Luke could put his finger on the pulse of a poll, and get it right every time. It wasn't enough, however, to have the data—but Luke knew whether to heed or ignore it as well. He read incessantly. He'd read *The Washington*

Post and *The New York Times, Newsweek, Time,* and any number of periodicals with a more conservative point of view. He'd learned one thing in the Air Force, and the lesson was reinforced during his political activism in college: As important as it is to know what you believe, it is vital to know how, and what, your enemy thinks.

Luke tossed the empty can in the trash and walked to where he'd parked his Camaro. Leaning against the fender was a stunning young woman named Samantha Abernathy. She, too, was a first-year law student who shared several classes with him. She also shared his bed.

Samantha was from Boston, and was the daughter of well-connected Democrats. She did some part-time work on the Hill for Senator Teddy Kennedy. She was three years younger than Luke, and was a product of the "free love" Sixties. Standing there in a short denim skirt and calf-high leather boots, Luke thought she had the best set of legs he'd ever seen...and oh, how he had a weakness for great legs.

"So how did you do on your Con Law final?" she asked.

"I aced it. Did you expect anything less?"

She smiled and said, "I suppose not." She stood on her tiptoes, wrapped her arms around Luke's neck, and kissed him hard on the lips. Staring seductively into his eyes, she said, "Unlock the car, smart guy, and let me in."

Luke put the key in the passenger door and held it open for her. The three years' difference in age showed, as did the thousand miles between Boston and Atlanta. For all his arrogance, Luke was still a southern gentleman: raised to have good manners and to abide by a chauvinistic code of conduct. Samantha found it amusing that, in the enlightened Seventies, he still felt compelled to hold doors open for her. She thought it an anachronistic practice, but down deep, she also thought it was an attractive quality.

She looked at Luke and said, "I'm hungry. Let's get something to eat."

"I'm game," he replied. "Where do you want to go?"

"Anything but pizza or Chinese," she said. "Let's eat at a *real* restaurant and celebrate completing our first year of law school."

"Your wish is my command," Luke said as he cranked the car and put it in gear. He looked in his sideview mirror and pulled away from the curb.

They drove to Baltimore, where they found a tiny restaurant that served nothing but steamed blue crabs. They ordered a dozen and a half and a couple of beers. It was a messy dinner to eat, but they both thought it was a feast. Luke had become fond of seafood while at Tulane. Being raised Catholic in Atlanta in the fifties and sixties meant eating a lot of fish on Fridays. The problem was, in those days, you couldn't get fresh fish in Atlanta. His mother could do wonders with canned salmon, tuna, or crabmeat. She'd make up some concoction, and the rest of the family would wonder what it was. Until he lived in New Orleans, he didn't know shrimp had heads or legs; he thought they swam around the ocean with heavy breading on them, like the Mrs. Paul's Frozen Shrimp his mother served. There was no doubt these crabs were the real thing. He'd come to like Maryland-style steamed crabs even better than the spicy boiled ones from New Orleans. Boiling crabs sometimes made them gummy. Steamed crabmeat was always firm and delicate. Luke thought crabs and beer were better than caviar and champagne. Looking across the table at Samantha, he also thought he had the prettiest girlfriend in DC.

They met while working on a bill cosponsored by their respective bosses. The attraction was immediate and mutual. Although they were both handsome people, they were also drawn to each other by the fact that both were exceedingly bright. Samantha had dated her share of football heroes, and found them all lacking. After high school, she made the mistake of thinking college athletes would be different. By the end of her freshman year she'd sworn off jocks completely, finding herself attracted to intellectual men with inquisitive minds. To her, it mattered little whether they were fellow students or professors. It mattered even less if they happened to be married. In fact, she liked it better if they were. Married men were certainly eager to please her, and they were much easier to dump when they became tiresome. A single guy won't always go away when he's told. A married man with a career goes quietly into the night when he's threatened with exposure.

Luke was the first single guy she'd been involved with in more than two years. Perhaps it was the fact that he was slightly older than her. She also felt his military service had matured him beyond his years. Luke wasn't inclined to talk much about having been in the Air Force, but one evening while in bed together, a nightmare made him bolt upright in a cold sweat. She'd asked what was wrong, and he'd recounted the tale of escorting his dead brother home from Vietnam. The memory of the morgue, with its metal coffins stacked from floor to ceiling, had frequently haunted him ever since. Occasionally he'd dream that *he* was in one of those coffins by mistake, and that he was still alive. It made him sick to think a mistake like that could've been made with Matt.

Luke knew he was dead, but it had always bothered him that he hadn't been allowed to see Matt's body. He'd been told that he'd been grotesquely dismembered. Still, without the closure of seeing his body, he'd always clung to an irrational fantasy that Matt hadn't really died.

Samantha smashed a large crab claw with a wooden mallet, sending juices and pieces of shell across the table at Luke. She giggled in amusement and squirmed in her chair, tickled at his reaction. With debris on his face, Luke raised his glass, smiled at her and said, "Thank you, Miss Grace."

The diversion was welcome, but not quite enough to distract him from his thoughts. He was sitting in the safety of a Baltimore restaurant, having dinner with the girl of his dreams, and yet he was daydreaming about a time in his life he desperately wanted to forget. He'd been home from the war for five years. He wondered how long it would take to let the past go, and enjoy the present. Tonight was a good time to start.

He paid the bill and took Samantha back to his apartment.

Chapter Twelve

LIEUTENADATES

"I beg your pardon...I never promised you a rose garden."

Joe South / Billy Joe Royal

Quantico, Virginia – The Basic School – Summer 1972

Post graduation leave was over, and Mark had driven all day yesterday, from Atlanta to just south of Richmond. He spent the night in a motel and, that morning, dressed in uniform so he'd be ready to report on station.

With the top down, and little traffic to interfere, he passed quickly through the city on Interstate 95. Behind the wheel of his new car, he felt like a million bucks. He thought every young man should experience the joy of owning and driving a Corvette. Twenty miles out of town, he downshifted and pressed down hard on the accelerator. The Vette hunkered down over the rear tires and began eating pavement like a ravenous tiger. Out of the corner of his eye, the road's white lines flew by rapidly.

According to his map, the Marine Corps Base-Quantico exit was about forty minutes north. From there it was four miles of winding, two-lane road to Camp Barrett, home of The Basic School. This is where the Marine Corps put its young lieutenants through an intensive six-month training course.

He was enjoying the way the car handled, and the throaty noise that accompanied the speed. It had been a graduation present of sorts from his folks. Upon returning from Vietnam, he'd purchased a two-year-old GTO. It had been a great car and he would've kept it, but he wasn't permitted to own one as an underclassman at the Academy. During his plebe year, he asked his father to sell it and put the money in the bank for later. He'd been frugal at the Academy and had saved most of his pay. His plan had been to purchase a new Pontiac Firebird a few months before graduation. In the first week of April, he placed the order through a General Motors franchise in Baltimore.

His dad was visiting him that weekend, and accompanied him to order the car. As they walked into the dealership, Mark's head was turned by the brand-new Corvette on the showroom floor. It was a dark metallic color called Steel Cities Grey, with red leather seats and a black convertible top. With its raised white-letter tires, he thought it had to be the sexiest thing on four wheels, but after one look at the sticker he shook his head in disappointment and proceeded to order the Firebird. The dealer completed the forms, thanked Mark, and assured him his parents could pick it up in mid-May when they flew into town for his graduation.

Two blocks from the dealership, John Francis told Mark he'd left his glasses on the salesman's desk and needed to go back for them. He urged him to go on to the hotel and get ready for dinner, saying he'd catch up with him soon. Without Mark's knowledge, his dad wrote a check for the difference needed to purchase the Corvette. When his parents arrived for graduation in May, they rolled up in the shiny roadster, with the top down. Mark's eyes nearly popped from his skull. It was the best surprise he'd received since he was six years old and still believed in Santa Claus.

His reverie was shattered by the sound of the state patrolman's siren, and the flashing lights in his mirror. Mark took one look at his speedometer needle and knew he was fried. He slowed the car down and pulled to the highway's shoulder.

Mark was wearing the Marine's brand new summer service "Class A" uniform that consisted of a long-sleeved khaki shirt and tie, a pair of dark green trousers and a matching coat that Marines called a blouse. On the seat next to him was his green garrison cover, with the black Marine Corps emblem on one side and a single gold bar on the other. In keeping with Corps tradition, the uniform itself was nondescript. What made this one special were the eleven campaign ribbons and personal decorations pinned above the left breast pocket. There were four Vietnamese ribbons representing medals including the Vietnamese Cross of Gallantry. From his own country he wore the National Defense Medal, a Presidential Unit Citation, a Marine Expeditionary medal, and a Marine Good Conduct medal. The upper rows were especially impressive. He wore the Combat Action Ribbon and the Purple Heart medal with a small bronze star in lieu of a second award. Topping the three rows was his highest decoration: the Navy Cross, a dark navy blue ribbon with a vertical white stripe in the middle. This is the second highest honor the United States bestows for valor in combat. Only the Medal of Honor is more prized. Few of either medal is awarded. Even fewer are ever worn, as most are awarded posthumously.

The state trooper stepped from his car and put on his hat. Expending little effort, he sauntered to the driver's side of Mark's car, prepared to light up the lead-footed college boy driving a car that would easily cost a cop a year's salary. Mark already had his license out and held it between his fingers, tapping it on the sideview mirror. The trooper pulled a pen from his breast pocket and opened his ticket book. He hadn't said a word yet, and neither had Mark. He was about to ask him if he knew how fast he'd been traveling when he looked at him closely, for the first time. Clean cut, squared away, and sharp as a razor, Lieutenant Reilly made quite an impression.

The trooper absorbed the scene quickly, including the decorations, and his attitude changed right away. "Lieutenant," he said, "you look like a thoroughly capable man who made it through Nam without getting himself killed. Why the hell do you want to die out here on *my highway*?"

Mark knew by the way he said *my highway* that the trooper had once been a Marine. From boot camp on, Marines laid claim, as if it were their very own, to everything that wasn't nailed down. My hooch…My barracks…My mess hall…My parade deck. One also learned in boot camp that excuses are like assholes—everybody has one. In the Corps, the only acceptable reply to a reprimand is "No excuse, sir."

Mark thought this would be a good time to invoke the same response. "Officer," he said, "I have no excuse for speeding. I just allowed myself to daydream."

The trooper laughed and asked, "When were you in Nam?"

"Sixty-six to sixty-seven," he answered. "How 'bout you?"

"I hit Chu Lai two weeks before the Tet Offensive in '68," he said. "I got home in '69, and got out in '70. Been in the state police since then." He shifted the pen to his other hand and extended his right hand to Mark. "John Tanner's the name, sir. What's yours?"

"Mark Reilly," he replied. Still shaking the trooper's hand, Mark added, "I'm sorry to be meeting you here, John, but I'm glad we're both on the right side of the grass."

"Me too, Lieutenant." Even though Tanner was no longer on active duty, the former Marine couldn't bring himself to call an officer by his first name.

"That's the shiniest set of butter bars I've ever seen, Lieutenant. They don't have a scratch on 'em yet. You gotta be on your way to The Basic School."

"That's right," Mark said. "I finished the Naval Academy in May. I report for training today." Mark knew better than to ask for a warning, but he summoned the nerve to ask the trooper for a smaller favor. "John, I know I deserve a ticket, and you have to give me one, but I'd sure appreciate it if you could cut me some slack on the speed. As fast as I was driving, a judge might just take my license."

"No ticket for you today, Lieutenant," the trooper said with a toothy grin. "Consider it my good deed of the day, and my gift to the Corps' newest second lewie."

The smile vanished from his face in an instant, and his next words were stern. "I shit you not, Lieutenant. This little chariot's gonna get you killed if you don't slow it down. It won't bother you none, cause you'll be dead—but I don't want to be the one who has to scrape you off my road and talk to your family."

Trooper Tanner's tongue-lashing took Mark back to the morning in Vietnam when he'd chewed out Privates Nichols and Jansen for screwing up on guard duty the night before. His tone and his words were just about identical. Mark shook his head affirmatively and said, "Message understood, Trooper Tanner. I'll try to comply."

"Don't try...do!" John Tanner shook Mark's hand, and then did something totally unexpected—he stood at attention and executed a crisp salute.

Mark was more than stunned; he was honored. He sat as erect as he could in the low slung Vette and returned the salute. As Mark watched in his sideview mirror, he noticed the change in John Tanner's walk. The arrogant saunter displayed earlier had been replaced with a brisk marching cadence. *You can take the man outa' the Marines,* Mark thought, *but you can't take the Marine outa' the man.* Then, under his breath he added, "Semper Fi, Marine." He pulled onto the highway and waved. For the next forty miles, the speedometer needle didn't crack sixty-five.

★ ★ ★

Just as he'd done at the Naval Academy, Mark excelled at The Basic School. His age, maturity, and combat experience earned the respect of the school's instructors, and his peers.

Most of the subjects taught at TBS were deadly serious. Good Marines might die someday if a lieutenant failed to master the subject matter at hand. Calling in artillery fire, land navigation in daylight or darkness, and small unit tactics were important lessons to learn. It was a bit of an inside joke that every instructor believed his class was so important that each one began with the same introduction: "Class…Today's lesson may very well…**save…your…life!**"

This wasn't true of every class. Some were so mundane that even the instructors rolled their eyes when they opened this way. Regardless of the lesson's gravity, the gallows humor never failed to make the lieutenants come to order and pay attention.

By this time in October, Mark had four months of TBS under his belt. Most of the subjects pertaining to individual skills had already been taught. The company was now embarking on squad, platoon and company level tactics. The weather was cooling off, and Mark, who felt at ease in the woods and confined in the classroom, was looking forward to spending fewer days inside and more time in the field. He was eager to lead, and was anticipating his first opportunity to command a Fleet Marine Force platoon.

Today's lesson was a refresher on individual cover and concealment, and was to be conducted under actual field conditions.

Most TBS instructors were captains, and a few first lieutenants who had already served in the fleet. Some subjects were taught by veteran enlisted men with specialized combat experience.

Upon arriving at the outdoor classroom, the lieutenants took seats on folding campstools. From the woods to their rear came the booming voice of a very large Marine: "GENTLEMEN! There's no doubt about whether or not today's lesson will save your life. Five years ago it damn well saved mine every day."

The officers turned and searched for the man speaking to them, but saw no one.

After several moments of silence, the Marine stood from his position of cover and concealment and strode to the front of the class wearing camouflage from head to toe. His chest and arms were so big he looked like the tree he was trying to imitate.

"My name is Staff Sergeant Jansen," he said. "I was a screwed-up eighteen-year-old PFC who learned cover and concealment the hard way—at the hands of my squad leader. In a foxhole in Quang Tri Province, he showed me just how easy it would be for my enemy to sneak up on my noisy ass and slit my throat. A few days later, that same corporal led his men in close combat, repelling an enemy assault.

"His actions saved countless lives that day—mine among them. For his leadership and bravery, our country awarded him the Navy Cross. We recommended him for the Medal of Honor, and he deserved it. Someone at a desk in Washington, who didn't see what we saw on the battlefield, decided the Navy Cross was enough. My squad leader taught me well, gentlemen, and today I intend to pass along what I learned. Listen well, and you'll be able to teach your men how to survive, like that squad leader, *your classmate*, taught me."

There was only one classmate in the company wearing the Navy Cross. Every head in the class turned in Lieutenant Reilly's direction. He was both embarrassed by the attention, and flattered by the respect Staff Sergeant Jansen was bestowing upon him.

The big staff sergeant continued, "The day he earned that medal is the last time I saw him, and I never had the chance to say thanks. Lieutenant Reilly...would you permit this grateful Marine to shake your hand?"

Mark stood slowly and stepped around the randomly positioned stools as he made his way to Sergeant Jansen. Both men were fighting back years of stifled emotions. They shook hands, then embraced with the familiar bear hug of comrades in arms. As they did, the class raised closed fists in the air, and shouted "Aahhrooogha!"

Mark said, "We've got some catching up to do, Staff Sergeant."

"That we do, sir," Sergeant Jansen replied.

Mark returned to his seat with a look of shock pasted on his face. It was a good thing he was already skilled in the art of cover and concealment, because his mind wandered back to the timeframe Sergeant Jansen had just described, and he heard nothing more for an hour.

✯ ✯ ✯

Staff Sergeant Don Jansen invited Lieutenant Reilly to his home for steaks on the grill the following Saturday night. They drank beer and had a great meal. Jansen was married to a pretty young woman named Maureen, from Oceanside, California. The still of the evening was broken by the fussing of their year-old baby son. Maureen warmed a bottle and fed him while rocking in a patio glider. Don beamed when he looked at his family, and Mark could tell he loved both of them more than life itself. As if he had heard Mark's thoughts, Don hoisted his beer bottle in Mark's direction and said, "If it weren't for you, Lieutenant, neither of them would be sitting here tonight. I would never have made it home."

"Mrs. Jansen," Mark said, "he either has a very poor memory, or else he must've banged his head harder than I did after I got hit. The story I was told in the hospital was that your husband and a Doc Peters saved *my* life, not the other way around."

"As I understand it, Lieutenant, your recollection is correct," Maureen said. "But I can't count the times I've heard him say *you* taught him what he needed to know to stay alive. He's never forgotten that you took the time to teach him…and he's made it his mission in life to see that no Marine he instructs dies because he wasn't taught well." She rose from her seat and brought the sleeping boy over to his father so he could kiss him goodnight. "Enjoy the rest of the evening. I'm going to put Reilly to bed and leave you two guys to your sea stories."

The baby's name took Mark by surprise, and he asked, "His name is *Reilly?*"

Both of them smiled. "Yes sir," Maureen said. "He's named after you."

Mark was speechless. Holding the baby, Maureen offered him her free hand and said, "Lieutenant, thanks for being there for Don. I didn't know him then, but I'm so glad you did. I know we'll be seeing you again. Goodnight."

The two Marines didn't spend the rest of the evening reminiscing. There were no old times to talk about; five years earlier, in Vietnam, they'd hardly known each other. Instead, they spent the rest of the evening remedying that situation, drinking beer and filling in the gaps. The Marine Corps is unique in one regard. At fewer than 190,000 members, Marines are a tightly knit fraternity. The longer one stays in, the more people a Marine is likely to serve with again. Over the next two decades, these two men would cross paths often. They were both destined for the top.

The following month, Mark and some friends made the forty-five minute drive to Washington for a night on the town. Since most of his Basic School friends were new to the Corps, and hadn't served in Vietnam, the National Defense Medal was the only one they rated. The red and gold-striped ribbon is awarded to all service members on active duty during an armed conflict. The students at TBS sometimes called it the "Highway Medal." Since they had yet to do anything to earn any awards, and yet it was the only one they wore, they needed a heroic story about it to tell women. The reasoning went, if you could make it back to Camp Barrett in one piece after a long night of drinking in DC, you *deserved* a medal.

Even so, there were no medals in sight tonight. They were all dressed in civilian clothes, and their destination was Matt Kane's Bar. After a big meal of Italian food, they arrived at the bar around nine. Mark was shooting pool with Dave McKee and Tommy Clarke. McKee's dad was a Marine colonel and had been a regimental commander in Korea. Clarke was a graduate of Ole Miss and was one of the funniest people Mark had ever known. He could insult a man twice his size, avoid the beating he ought to get, and have the guy buying him drinks for the rest of the night. The fourth Marine with them, Benji Barton, was a nice looking guy that girls initially liked—until they talked to him for a while. He was the pushy sort who thought every girl should sleep with him on the first date. Consequently, he had a lot of first dates, and very few second ones. His real name was Phil, but Tommy Clarke had nicknamed him Benji for Ben Franklin of hundred-dollar bill fame. The closely guarded joke was that even if he had hundred-dollar bills hanging out of his pockets, Barton couldn't get laid by a prostitute. Barton never had a clue what the nickname meant.

Mark threw his empty Budweiser bottle in the trash and made his way to the head. When he finished, he returned to the bar and ordered another one. As he turned to leave, he bumped into a large man with a flame-red beard. The collision caused the man to spill his drink, and Mark apologized right away. "I'm terribly sorry, sir," he said in a voice loud enough to be heard over the blaring music. He grabbed some napkins from the bar and handed them to the man, saying "Please let me buy you another one."

"No need, my friend," the man said, startled by the face looking back at him. "It was nearly empty anyway." As he wiped liquid from his shirt he shouted, "When did you get back from Belfast?"

Mark was puzzled by the question and said, "I've never been to Belfast, sir." He thought he might have mistaken him for Luke, so he said, "You may have me confused with my brother over at Georgetown Law, or Capitol Hill where he works part-time."

"Ah, yes. That might explain it," he said. "I have some associates on the Hill. I think I've met him before. Does your brother's name begin with an L? Lewis...Leonard?"

"Luke, sir. Luke Reilly. I'm Lieutenant Mark Reilly, United States Marine Corps."

"Nice to meet you, son." He extended his hand. "My friends call me RB. I've had a number of good friends over the years who were Marines."

Mark shook his hand and said, "Good to meet you too, sir. Are you sure I can't buy you another drink?"

"If it makes you feel better, I'll have a double scotch on the rocks."

Mark paid for the drink, toasted him by clinking his beer bottle against the highball glass and said, "If you'll excuse me now, sir. This is our last weekend on the town before we graduate from The Basic School. I need to get back to my friends."

"Thanks for the drink, Mark."

"No sweat, sir," he replied.

RB downed the scotch and left the bar. He stood on the curb long enough to light a cigarette, then turned up the collar of his coat. He walked away pondering the uncanny resemblance.

Three weeks later, Mark donned his dress blues and graduated from The Basic School as the Honor Man of his Company. For six months, two thousand second lieutenants jokingly referred to themselves as "lieutenadates," a sarcastic term for a hybrid being slightly lower than a fleet lieutenant, but higher than an officer candidate. There was no doubt they were officers, but since they commanded no troops, and were herded from class to class just as they'd been when candidates, the term seemed appropriate.

Mark had one more course to attend before reporting to the Fleet Marine Force at Camp Hansen, Okinawa. After a couple of weeks of leave in Atlanta, he would report to the eight-week long U.S. Army Ranger School. The Ranger program was considered one of the toughest endurance tests in any branch of the military. It would be long weeks of hell, but he was one of very few Marine lieutenants chosen to attend, and it would prepare him to be one of the best platoon leaders in the Corps. As he drove away in his Corvette, he looked forward to some time with his folks. But before he allowed himself to settle into daydreams about his mother's cooking, he had one image he wanted to burn into his memory.

In one respect, Vietnam and The Basic School shared something in common: the most beautiful view of both places was the one in your rearview mirror. As he drove away, the last building to fade from view was O'Bannon Hall. He downshifted to second and stomped on the gas, thinking, *Bring on the Fleet.*

Chapter Thirteen
STOCK IN TRADE

"When ya comin' home son?
I don't know when...but we'll get together then...
Ya' know we'll have a good time then."

Harry Chapin

Bailey's Crossroads, Virginia – April 1975

Cain remained in his car, observing the restaurant from the parking lot. Families entered and left, as well as the occasional out of town business traveler. The Peking Gourmet Inn was his favorite Chinese restaurant in the Washington area. At five minutes till seven, a white Oldsmobile Cutlass drove into the parking lot and pulled into an open space.

There was enough daylight to see without headlights, but Michael O'Rourke was a cautious man, and he turned the lights off and locked the car door before heading for the restaurant. He scanned the parking lot without turning his head very far in either direction, and made sure not to pause when he noticed the man sitting in the black Porsche looking at a street map. O'Rourke entered the first of two glass doors, and as the tinted glass closed behind him, he turned to get a better look at the man in the Porsche. The general appearance was similar, but he wasn't completely sure; Cain made a practice of seldom appearing the same way twice. O'Rourke opened the second door and entered the restaurant's foyer.

A middle-aged Chinese woman greeted him with a short bow and a big smile. In Chinese-laced English, she asked, "How many in yo' pahty?"

"Two. Please," he replied. "A friend will join me in a few minutes."

She grabbed two menus from a holder at the front desk and proceeded to show him to his table. He sat in the back of the restaurant, facing the entrance. The waiter appeared and took his order for a double scotch on the rocks. As he walked away, O'Rourke placed his napkin on the table and went to the restroom at the rear of the large dining room. From behind the small window in the swinging door, he saw a man who looked middle-aged but muscular walking toward the table, following the same woman who had shown him to his seat. He ordered a beer and sat down. Although he'd never seen Cain in this disguise, he was satisfied it was him.

RB returned to the table, shook Cain's hand and said, "Welcome home, my friend. It's been much too long."

"Nice to be back, RB," Cain said as he shook hands with his mentor.

"You must've become a distrusting soul in the past few years," RB said—more a statement than a question. "Were you expecting someone else to show this evening?"

"Just force of habit now. You spotted me when you arrived?"

RB stirred his drink and said, "The Porsche was a nice touch, although not particularly discreet. I thought I trained you better than that. You know ego will get you killed."

"You're slipping, RB," Cain said with concern. "You bought my decoy. The guy in the Porsche is a bookie. I told him we'd meet to pay off a bet. The open map was for identification. I was in a..."

"Dark blue Buick LeSabre," RB interrupted. With a curt wave of dismisal, he added, "License number NQL-326."

The reprimand stung. Cain was good, but RB had been at the game a lot longer.

"My young friend," RB said, "I've been snoopin' and poopin' in dangerous places longer than you've been alive. You've learned a lot since we first met...but don't you *dare* presume that you're ready to become my teacher."

Even though nearly sixty, his mentor's sharp powers of observation missed nothing: not even Cain's slight reaction to being upstaged. "My apologies, sir," he said sincerely. "Living in Europe and the Middle East *has* made me more cautious, but it would never occur to me to try to instruct you."

RB studied the man sitting across from him. He had matured. Many of the rough edges were now polished. There was no doubt he had become one of the most lethal men in the world. He was proud of his protégé. Softening his tone, and the mood, he said, "Let's order dinner, and you can tell me about your travels."

The corner table permitted quiet conversation, yet the restaurant was noisy enough to speak without concern of being overheard. They were far from the family tables and the business diners. Everyone was too busy enjoying their meals to pay them any attention. For the next hour, Cain brought him up to speed on his new skills.

With the help of RB and Raoul, Cain had fled the country in '68 after the job in Memphis, first driving from Tennessee to Niagara Falls. From there he crossed the border to Toronto. Travel documents were waiting there, identifying him as an Irish businessman. He left Canada for Ireland, and spent the next two years with RB's old friend, Andrew Flynn. "Drew" led a small cadre of radicals in the Irish Republican Army, providing good training for the young man who knew how to kill with a rifle, but who needed a postgraduate course on additional techniques. Belfast and Derry proved to be ideal training grounds.

From there he spent some time in London, repaying the IRA for his education. As an unknown American, he wasn't on anyone's watch list in England. This allowed him to gather information and, on occasion, place a small explosive charge in a public place to embarrass and demoralize the English government.

While in London, RB had arranged some additional training with an old friend from the SAS, England's counterpart to the America's wartime Office of Strategic Services. Nigel Pennyman and RB had worked together several times during the war. Under Nigel's tutelage,

Cain perfected to an art form two subtle methods of assassination: murder made to appear as suicide, or accidental death.

Over the years, these would become his stock in trade. There was no denying that a high-powered rifle at the right distance was effective, but it had three main drawbacks. At the time of the kill, the assassin needed to be attached to the other end of the rifle. Add to that the logistics problem of getting the rifle to and from the ambush site, and the risk of discovery increased. The third limitation was that sniping is a young man's game. As a man ages, many of the skills required to be a long distance shooter diminish. Eyesight begins to falter, and hands become less steady. Although this wasn't one of Cain's present concerns, he was smart enough to realize that one day it would certainly become an issue.

Cain conducted field trials of his newfound skills in various countries around Europe. To his credit were four assassinations that had all been ruled suicides by the authorities. A member of the British Parliament was found in the apartment of his mistress. It appeared to all that, after shooting her, he'd placed a revolver in his mouth and blew off the top of his head. The facts were never made public that the mistress was a Soviet agent through whom the official had been funneling classified intelligence information to the Russians for several years.

In Belgium, the chairman of an international banking conglomerate leapt to his death from his twentieth floor office after the bank became aware that large sums of money had been embezzled. The subsequent investigation uncovered a paper trail of bad investments, and an addiction to high stakes gambling. None of the two million francs was ever found. Just moments before he was helped over the balcony railing, however, Cain became the proud new owner of the banker's numbered Swiss bank account.

RB congratulated Cain on his professional achievements, and then changed the subject: "Now that Nixon's out, the Agency is under a lot of scrutiny. A lot of their work will need to be outsourced to avoid the prying eyes of congressional oversight committees. I thought this might offer you a chance to find some work here in the States."

"Sounds fine to me," he replied.

The discussion turned to news of what was happening in Vietnam. The ARVN forces in the south weren't going to be able to hold off the North Vietnamese Army much longer. Both men knew the end was near, but neither had a clue when the house of cards would collapse.

RB opened his fortune cookie and said, "Nixon wasn't Watergate's biggest casualty. *Vietnam* was." He read the Chinese proverb, smirked a little, and tossed it on the table. "When he left office, the NVA grew a new set of balls. Gerald Ford is the country's only person ever appointed, rather than elected, to both the vice presidency and the presidency. General Giap knows the American people won't support putting ground troops back in Nam, and Ford doesn't have the political capital to lift a finger to stop him. A lot of people who worked with us are in for a real bad time."

Cain shrugged his shoulders and said, "Screw 'em."

His callous comment irritated RB. For all Cain's feigned politeness and charm, his underlying personality trait was ruthlessness. He had no tolerance for weakness, and no compassion for people who caved to the will of the strong. Fight or die was his creed. RB reminded him, "There were some folks over there that saved your ass a time or two."

"Well I'm not there *now*, RB, and neither is anyone I give a rat's ass about."

Disgusted, RB pushed the slip of paper with the fortune on it toward Cain, who picked it up and read it silently to himself: "A loyal friend is a treasure for the ages."

Cain tossed the paper on the table, along with the cash to cover the bill. Without another word, the men stood and left.

★ ★ ★

Across the Potomac, the lights were burning brightly on Capitol Hill. Richard Nixon's August '74 resignation had emboldened more than the North Vietnamese; it had opened the floodgates for new legislation from congressional Democrats.

Luke Reilly had a long night ahead of him. He'd just finished a couple of pieces of pizza and was settling into his analysis of the latest Gallup polls. He'd promised Senator Long a summary, along with Luke's observations, on his desk by morning. He figured he wouldn't see his bed before three a.m. He'd pay for the lack of sleep, but he knew from past experience that adrenaline was a powerful stimulant. He got a rush every time he walked into the Senate office buildings.

In the background a television was on, but the sound was muted. Chaotic scenes from Saigon were flashing across the screen. The population was becoming painfully aware of what the rest of the world wouldn't learn for several more days. The Communists were coming—and no one in South Vietnam had the power to stop them.

Chapter Fourteen
SPRINGTIME CHRISTMAS

"I'm dreaming of a white Christmas.
Just like the ones I used to know."

Bing Crosby

U.S. Embassy, Saigon, Republic of South Vietnam – April 1975

As hot as Okinawa had been, Vietnam was hotter still. Mark thought he had flushed the oppressive heat from his mind, yet from the instant his feet touched the tarmac at Tan Son Nhut, it was as though the ensuing seven and a-half years had never happened. He'd been in his new job for less than two weeks. He was assigned as the executive officer of the Marine Security Guard Detachment that protected several U.S. embassies throughout Southeast Asia. Ordinarily there are few officers assigned to embassy duty, but it was obvious that America would soon be leaving Vietnam for good. He'd been sent from Okinawa to Saigon to assist the officer in charge, Major Jim Kean, with organizing and conducting an orderly withdrawal of the Saigon embassy when the time came.

Mark assumed his time in Saigon would be short, so he decided not to tell his family, letting them assume he'd extended his tour in Okinawa and would be home in a few more months. Assumptions sometimes let folks sleep better than they would if they knew the truth. He did nothing to set them straight.

The embassy was jammed with reporters from all over the world, and they were becoming an irritant to the Marines. On the afternoon of April 28th, all hell had broken loose.

At first no one knew the details, but a turncoat South Vietnamese Air Force captain and four of his men had commandeered a flight of five U.S. made aircraft and launched an attack on Saigon. The population of the city went nuts, and all hope of affecting an orderly withdrawal went up in smoke. Early the next morning, NVA gunners began firing mortars at the Vietnamese military at the Tan Son Nhut airfield. One of the runways was severely damaged, and two Marine security guards were killed. Around noon, Ambassador Graham Martin let Washington know that the situation was untenable, and that he required helicopters to evacuate the embassy. Armed Forces Radio began playing Bing Crosby's "White Christmas," the coded signal for all U.S. personnel to make their way to the compound for evacuation.

Preceding this, nearly 45,000 people, including 5,000 Americans, had fled the city. There were still a huge number of Vietnamese nationals who also wanted to leave, and the American ambassador had opened a Pandora's box two days earlier when he announced that any Vietnamese who wanted to come to America was welcome. It was a promise that couldn't be kept, and made a bad situation worse in no time flat. With thousands massing around the embassy, jockeying for a way out, Mark thought the scene must be similar to what Noah saw as the floodwaters lifted the Ark from its cradle.

Many of the Americans entering the embassy compound brought Vietnamese friends they wanted to help flee the approaching Communists.

The ambassador asked the major if the American flag should be lowered. Major Kean recommended it be left in place to avoid panic on the part of the crowd. The decision had already been made to clear the large tamarind tree in the embassy courtyard to make room for helos to land. Lowering the flag would cause everyone in sight to lose hope and start panicking.

Mark and the major had each served combat tours earlier in the war. Some of the enlisted men had too, but several had no combat experience. Although most of the crowd was unarmed, and were supposedly "friendlies," it was unnerving to see and feel them press in waves against the compound gates. None of the Marines had ever faced such a large and angry crowd before. Unarmed or not, if they panicked and stormed the walls, a lot of people were going to die. Though the choice was unpleasant, the Marines would ensure the Vietnamese would do the dying, and not the Americans they were here to protect. There was concern that North Vietnamese saboteurs were among the local crowds. Machine guns had been placed at strategic locations, along with sodium nitrate burn barrels that could provide a wall of fire between the crowd and the Marines.

Inside the embassy, Mark passed by a couple of State Department employees who were busy destroying several million dollars worth of new U.S. currency. It was a surreal scene he would've never believed if anyone else had told him they'd seen such a sight.

The sun began to set, and in the distance the whipping roar of large rotor blades could be heard. The first of the CH-53 Sea Stallions touched down in the courtyard just after five o'clock. The Marines directed the loading, trying to make sure that families weren't separated while making sure that the evacuees traveled light. As soon as a bird was loaded, it would lift off and another would take its place. Along with the 53's were CH-46 Sea Knight helicopters. This is also a big helo, with two large horizontal rotors, one up front and one in the back. Periodically, a small Air America UH-1 Huey would land on the embassy's rooftop. Whatever arrived was loaded and sent on its way to the ships standing offshore.

Back in the real world, the heavyweights on Capitol Hill watched, in stunned fascination, the footage taken by news crews that hadn't yet departed. The chaotic scene was unfolding with little commentary from the screen, or the audience. For once, even those who'd vehemently opposed the war kept their mouths shut as the lid of the coffin closed on U.S. involvement in Vietnam.

Luke was sitting on the edge of the long table in Senator Long's conference room. Sitting by his side was Samantha, and leaning forward in his chair, arms resting across his knees, was Michael Anderson, the Senator's legislative assistant.

There was a twelve-hour time difference between Saigon and Washington, and the footage they were watching had been shot earlier in the day. Samantha shifted her gaze periodically from the television set to Luke. He hadn't said a word, but the muscle in his jaw was visibly twitching.

Onscreen, a Marine officer approached two other Marines and gave them instructions. They ran in different directions in response to his orders. As he turned to walk away, his face filled the screen and the camera zoomed in as he shouted orders to a Marine in the guard tower atop the wall. Samantha gasped in shock and turned to Luke in time to see the color drain from his face. The Marine's face also surprised Mike Anderson, who said what Samantha was thinking: "My God, Luke, that soldier looks just like you!"

"Marine," Luke said, just above a whisper. "He's not a soldier. He's a Marine. He looks just like me because he's my brother."

Stunned by Luke's statement, Samantha asked, "I thought your brother was killed in the war."

"Matthew was killed. The guy on the TV is Mark. We're triplets."

Speechless before, now Samantha really didn't know what to say. Luke seldom talked about the war, and he'd told her little about his family. She was aware that Matthew had been killed, but she had no idea there was another brother, and certainly not a triplet. She didn't know whether to be angry or hurt. She was living with a man she thought she knew, but this revelation made her painfully aware she hardly knew him at all.

Unaware of, and certainly unconcerned with the emotions Samantha was experiencing, Luke reached for the telephone and dialed Atlanta. His mother answered the phone on the third ring.

When he said hello, she beat him to the punch and asked, "Have you been watching the news?"

"Yes ma'am, I have."

"We thought your brother was in Okinawa," Mary Quinn said. "Your dad about had a heart attack when he saw him at the Saigon embassy!"

"I didn't know he was there either, Mom. Mark and I haven't talked in quite a while."

"I know," she said, "and I've been pushing the rosary beads every day for seven years praying that you two would get right with each other."

Luke could feel the frustration in her voice as she continued chastising him, just as she had when he was little, but he said nothing.

"I'm through asking God to make it happen, Luke," she said. "When Mark gets home, you go see him and bury the hatchet. It's time to get over whatever is between you two."

He turned from the television and answered in the same way he always had when she scolded him as a child. "Yes, Mother." Then he hung up the phone and returned his attention to the chaos unfolding before the world. Moments later, he caught another glimpse of his brother directing the movement of his Marines. His mother's order to make amends echoed through his mind. He hoped he'd have the chance to bury the hatchet, rather than his brother. One Marine funeral had been more than enough.

The helicopter pilots had flown non-stop for hours. It became increasingly difficult to handle the birds, but none would stop flying until ordered to. The ambassador had cajoled the president into ordering more flights than had originally been planned. The deadline for having the ambassador out, along with all U.S. nationals, had been 2200 hours. The birds were still flying nearly six hours later.

President Ford finally called a stop to further airlifts, and ordered the ambassador to leave. At 0330 in the morning, the CH-46 approaching the embassy received the code words "Tiger! Tiger! Tiger!" This was the signal indicating the ambassador was to board the next inbound bird and depart. Major Kean spoke by radio to the general aboard the *USS Blue Ridge*, who was in charge of the evacuation. His orders were clear: no more foreign nationals were to be evacuated, only U.S. civilians and Marines. As Ambassador Martin took his seat in the chopper, Major Kean handed him the embassy colors, which had been lowered, without ceremony, after dark.

The ambassador's departure enabled the Marines to pull back from the walls and gates. After making their way to the rooftop, they locked the controls to the elevators. The remaining crowd below knew they'd been abandoned, and things deteriorated in a hurry. Several more birds arrived and took out fifty more Marines. Eleven Marines waited for the last chopper to arrive and whisk them to safety. They had no idea they would be waiting for quite a while.

★ ★ ★

RB sat in a thick leather chair in the study of his Alexandria home. It was a little early for a double scotch, but as the saying went, it was after five o'clock somewhere in the world. The bottle of Dewar's remained open and handy on the table next to his chair while he watched the television with a mixture of morbid fascination and deep sadness. He'd fought in three wars. The scorecard wasn't much to brag about. World War II went in the "win" column. Korea had been a draw. The collapse of Vietnam, unfolding on the television, put ten years of blood and pain squarely in the *lost* column. The politicians and the American people had finally done what no American fighting man had done on the battlefield—they gave up and abandoned their friends.

RB had never lost before, and he didn't like the feeling. Although no one else was in his house, he knew he wasn't really alone. There were many men like him, all over America, slamming fists on tables, throwing things against the wall, or choking back the rising bile in their throats that kept them from shouting at God. RB downed his scotch, then swore under his breath at all the weak-kneed politicians that knew how to start a war, but had no resolve to finish one.

The phone on his table was unlisted. It rang twice, and he picked it up without saying hello. The caller on the other end didn't identify himself, but the voice was unmistakably Cain's.

"Are you looking at the news?"

"Yes."

"I apologize for my remarks at dinner the other night. You invested more in that country than I did. I was out of line." As if they had but one mind, Cain said what RB had been thinking: "I've come to the conclusion that killing politicians is a noble profession."

With that, the phone clicked, and the call abruptly ended.

The eleven remaining Marines had been hard at work for more than seventy hours. Half remained on alert while the other half grabbed a little sleep. Below them they could hear the rampage taking place inside the embassy as the crowd that missed their ride was now busily looting the place. It was hard to fathom why, but some may have thought they could use the items to buy mercy, or barter with the conquering North Vietnamese. The other answer was that they were just thoroughly pissed off, and were taking out their anger on the abandoned remnant of what had been the United States' presence in Southeast Asia.

Several hours before, a significant error had taken place of which the Marines, as of yet, had no clue. When the ambassador's helicopter departed, Henry Kissinger announced on television that the evacuation was over. No one knew troops remained at the embassy, so no one had dispatched another chopper to bring them out. It was hours before anyone in the States, or the ships offshore, realized they'd been left behind.

All the Marines on the roof knew was that there were no birds on the horizon, and no sound of rotors in the distance. They prayed that they hadn't been forgotten or left for dead. A young corporal looked at Mark and said, "Lieutenant...are you afraid to die?"

Mark thought it a perfectly valid question, and recognized it as one he'd been asked before, during his first tour. He answered the young Marine the same way he'd answered then. "I'm not afraid to die, Corporal. Heaven is better than this hellhole, so dying isn't that scary." He paused, then continued, "I *am* afraid of getting myself seriously screwed up and having to go on living. I don't want to be a blind man, I don't want to live in a wheelchair...and I want to keep my balls where they belong so I can have a family. I think living can sometimes be a lot harder than dying."

The corporal thought about his answer and said, "I got no argument with that, sir."

The morning sun washed away the darkness, but not the previous evening's bad dream. Reality remained as ugly as before. Looters roamed the streets below, weaving in and out of stunned refugees who waited in the parking lot, some still sitting on their luggage. In the distance, the popping sound of rotor blades broke the stillness of the morning air. Sunlight reflected off a lone CH-46 as it banked at a sharp angle and dropped quickly to the rooftop helipad. The Marines hustled to the lowered tail ramp and boarded.

After they were all aboard, the senior enlisted man, Master Sergeant Valdez, stepped off the bird and snapped a final picture. He hopped back on, and the last Marines in Vietnam left the ground.

More than 100,000 people had been evacuated from Saigon in the previous three days. It was a lot, but not enough. Those left would be subjected to the merciless wrath of the conquering Communists. For the Marines, it was a bitter pill to swallow.

The bird rose swiftly and banked toward the sea. Like everyone else who'd paid dearly to serve, Mark felt the pain of seeing their sacrifice abandoned in the ruins. He had an odd feeling of finality as he watched the Vietnamese scenery pass beneath him for the last time. He had always felt that leaving the country unconscious, when he'd been wounded in '67, left things open-ended. One minute he was fighting for his life and the lives of his friends, then the earth shook and he was out like a light. He had no memory of his helo ride from the battlefield to the hospital ship off the coastline. On *this* trip he was awake, and as the land gave way to the sea below, he felt like he was leaving Vietnam for the first, and last, time.

Even with the realization that America hadn't accomplished what it set out to do, he had no recriminations for the efforts of his fellow fighting men. They had served with honor, and had done their duty. It gave him a small sense of personal peace.

It came at a hell of a price.

Chapter Fifteen
HUMBLE PIE

"Hello stranger...seems so good to have you back again.
...how long has it been?
Ooooh...it seems like a mighty long time..."

Barbara Lewis

Georgetown, DC – April 1978

The cherry blossoms were starting to bloom, and Washington was awash in pink and white. It was the sort of day that brought pretty women out in droves, and Luke was glad he was a single man in Georgetown.

Samantha was a distant memory. After the fall of Saigon in 1975, she decided she'd had her fill of Luke Reilly. He couldn't say he blamed her. He'd been absorbed with his work and had never really been open with her. There had been a lot of personal information he held close to the vest, and he was learning how much women detested that in a man. He was also coming to the conclusion that he could care less what women wanted. He was comfortable with the fact that he was totally self-centered, and he liked himself fine that way.

Samantha, true to form, didn't stay unattached for long. Within a month of deciding he wasn't the man for her, she found a new lover. Mike Anderson was more than happy to take over the side of the bed

Luke had been sleeping on. The only one unhappy with the new arrangement was Mike's wife. Three months later she filed for divorce, and two months after that, Mike and Samantha married. To nobody's surprise, their union lasted less than a year.

Luke thought about her from time to time, but came to the conclusion that she'd done him a huge favor by leaving. She seemed to sow misery in the hearts of every man who got involved with her. For years, she'd left piles of debris in her wake. He felt he'd been lucky. Samantha was a hundred pounds of bad news wrapped in a pretty package and tied up with a bow.

For the past six months, Luke had been seeing a young woman who was an assistant to President Carter's press secretary. Angela Latimer was her name, and she lived up to it, a true angel in every sense of the word. She was good, beautiful, and trusting. Goodness and beauty made her an ideal girlfriend for Luke, because she showered him with care and great sex. Her trust was an added benefit. To please him, she'd do anything—including sharing confidential information from the White House press office.

Earlier in his life, Luke would've felt guilty about using someone so blatantly. Not now. He'd just turned thirty-one, and had been in Washington long enough to know the Hill was made up of takers and givers. The givers were in short supply. He felt no guilt about expanding his network of assets, human or otherwise. It was a fact of life in Washington politics: you were only as good as your information.

Angela had one more thing going for her. The young woman who shared her apartment worked on the Hill for Hiram Smith, a Republican senator from Wyoming. Angela's roommate was particularly close to the senator, and knew his positions intimately. She wasn't romantically involved with him, though she loved him dearly. Becky Smith was the senator's only daughter.

Hiram Smith was invariably on the opposite side of any legislation put forth by the Democrats. Luke took to heart Marlon Brando's advice in *The Godfather*: "Keep your friends close, but your enemies closer." Becky wasn't inclined to volunteer information, but if Luke got her wound up, he could frequently count on her to unwittingly tip the senator's hand.

Tonight she was going to be helpful to Luke in another way. She had agreed to be Mark's date for the evening. Luke had spent nearly a week trying to convince her to go, and only secured her agreement yesterday after blurting out, "He's nothing at all like me!"

When Becky heard that, she responded, "Well you should have said *that* days ago."

Luke figured Mark and Becky would hit it off fine. She was a strikingly beautiful brunette...petite, with a terrific figure. On top of that, she was intelligent and sweet as they come. Mark, however, had always had a penchant for blondes, so Luke knew Becky would make a great date for the evening, but not the long run, keeping Mark from become a recurring visitor. Luke had no idea how the night would go, but he promised his mother he'd set things right with his brother. In typical fashion, he took his own sweet time getting around to it, but he thought, *better late than never*.

Mark was stationed for the second time at Quantico, about forty-five miles south of DC. He was a captain now, as well as a student at Amphibious Warfare School. Earlier in the week, Luke finally worked up the nerve to call him on the phone and apologize, then extended an invitation to come to Washington for a more personal apology. His plan was a face-to-face talk, followed by a peace offering of dinner with a couple of beautiful young ladies. Hopefully this would end the years of bitterness, and they could bury the hatchet as their mother had ordered. He hoped Mark wouldn't try to bury it in his skull.

Luke's phone call had come as a real surprise to Mark. A lot of water had passed under the bridge since that painful night in New Orleans when he'd written him off. In the past decade, Luke had matured enough to realize that harboring bad feelings hurt the grudge-holder worse than the offending party. He was tired of the hurt, and ready to cut it loose.

Luke had crossed Mark's mind many times, and he'd come close to picking up the phone to initiate a reconciliation. Things he couldn't explain—perhaps reasons, or just lame excuses—conspired to prevent him from dialing the numbers. Or maybe it had been easier to simply let go of his anger, yet maintain his distance. Luke's call forced his hand; he would either have to continue holding his grudge, or let it go. He chose to forgive, though he didn't say so over the phone. Their conversation had been brief, but it was a good start. Luke had finally said the only thing that Mark wanted to hear: he'd been an ass, and he was sorry. Much to Luke's dismay, Mark agreed that Luke *had* been an ass, then added that his own actions hadn't been much better.

At the call's conclusion, Mark felt relieved to shed the load he'd carried for nine years. Like acid, anger eats at the soul.

Mark was further thrilled by Luke's offer to sweeten the pot with the best dinner in town, in the company of a pretty girl. With the exception of San Diego, the Marines aren't known for having a wealth of duty stations in big cities full of single women. The kind of women he wanted to date were scarce near a base, and when found were usually competed for by dozens of Marines in heat. He was more than ready for a date with a nice girl who hadn't been burned by dating Marines.

He arrived at Luke's apartment around six o'clock, put the top up on his Corvette, and locked it. As he stepped away from the car, he paused to admire its lines. It looked as good as the day he first saw it on the showroom floor, six years before. It had low mileage too—a by-product of his having spent a lot of time out of the country.

He rang Luke's doorbell, expecting a bushy haired hippie to answer the door. He was pleasantly surprised to, once again, see his own mirror image. The only difference in their appearance was Mark's high and tight Marine haircut, close-cropped and flat on the top and absolutely skinned on the side. Luke now wore his hair reasonably short, but long enough to require a comb.

Neither one spoke at first, and there was an awkward moment where they didn't know whether to shake hands or hug each other. They settled on simply saying "Hey," and Mark stepped inside as Luke walked toward the kitchen and opened the fridge. He tossed Mark a beer and popped one for himself, then hopped up on a barstool at the kitchen counter. Mark planted both palms flat on the counter next to the stove and pushed up, sliding himself into a sitting position, then propped his feet up on the bar counter where Luke was sitting.

The silence in the room spoke volumes. Though they both wanted to end their feud, neither one seemed to know where to begin. Luke took the first stab: "I'm truly sorry Mark, and if you hate me…I understand. I hope you'll forgive me for the way I treated you the last time we were together. I've had a lot of time to think about why I shit on you the way I did that night. It wasn't any single statement you made…but rather my frustration at the way you and Matthew always made me feel inferior…like I wasn't as good as the two of you. You said something…I can't even remember the words…but it was in that condescending tone that Matthew always used toward me. I think I was madder at him than you, but you were there and he wasn't. I made you take the heat."

Mark listened without interrupting, because it was apparent from Luke's face that he wasn't yet through.

"You two always thought I couldn't cut it. That I wasn't as tough as you were. I may not have slept in the mud and the rain like a

Marine, but I paid my dues in that damned airplane. You fired bullets, and a few guys hit the ground. I looked down and saw the blast of those bombs cut a swath fifty yards wide and hundreds of yards long. I'm responsible for more death and destruction than you and Matt combined. If I hadn't been just as strong as you two, I'd be in a mental ward somewhere. But I'm not...I survived."

Mark sipped his beer and chose his words more carefully than he ever had with his brother. "Luke, I can't speak for Matthew, but it was never my intention to make you feel inferior. You're my brother, and I've always loved you. I haven't always *liked* you—and it's been pretty apparent you haven't always liked me. We've hurt each other plenty. But hate and love are just two sides of the same coin. There's no way to separate them. People *dislike* folks they don't know, but *hatred* is an emotion that requires a person to burn energy. People usually reserve that for folks they know *too* well.

"I've never hated you, and I'd bet my last dollar that Matthew never hated you either. We're about as different as they come, and for the rest of our lives we're going to piss each other off more times than we can count. I'll make you this promise though: from this moment forward, like you or not, I'll *never* hate you. You also have my word that nothing you say or do will ever cause me to turn my back on you. I'll accept your apology if you'll accept mine...and take me at my word about the promise I just made."

Luke thought it over and agreed. Wiping his eyes and extending his hand, he said, "You bet." With that, the peace was made. Strangers might find it hard to believe it could happen this easily, yet for triplets it made perfect sense. Remaining estranged was like cutting out one's own heart.

Neither brother was certain if they'd ever be close again, but they were no longer at war. It was enough. They talked for an hour and filled each other in on the missing pieces of their lives. Like it usually is with a close friend one hasn't seen in years, the conversation came easily. They stayed away from politics, and steered clear of further discussion of Vietnam, except for a single comment from Luke just before they left to pick up the girls.

"When I saw you on the TV, in the embassy courtyard in Saigon…" He paused for a second and choked a little on his words. "I felt sad, and sick at the same time." Staring at the ceiling to avoid losing his composure, he said, "It should've turned out differently. You and Matt bled too much for it to have ended as it did. Mark…I'm just sorry *any of us* ever had to be there."

Mark looked at Luke and said, "Ya' know, Luke, sometimes I think you bled worse than Matt, or *me*. You didn't shed a drop…but the war tore you up on the inside." He said nothing more; he simply walked to his brother's side and embraced him.

Both men's eyeballs began to sweat. When they let each other go, they both felt like brothers once again.

For the first time ever, Luke felt as though someone finally understood. Better still, the one who understood was his brother. The respect he'd always craved had finally been offered. It was the finest birthday present Mark could have given him. Tonight was going to be worthy of the celebration he'd planned.

✯ ✯ ✯

Angela answered the door and greeted Luke with a big hug and kiss, then surprised Mark by letting Luke go and repeating the procedure with him. She was a good kisser, and a knockout to boot—but he didn't know what to make of her actions, and he didn't want to start another long feud with Luke. He looked at his brother, and could tell he was a little ticked, when all of a sudden she laughed and said, "I win!"

Luke asked, "You win what?"

She flashed a big grin. "Becky and I made a bet about whether twins kissed exactly the same. She bet you did...it's *obvious* you don't...so I win!"

Mark held his curiosity in check and didn't ask who *obviously* kissed better. He broke Luke's awkward silence by introducing himself to Angela, who grabbed them each by the hand and led them into the apartment.

The stereo was playing an old Barbara Lewis song, "Hello Stranger." Mark loved the tune; it took him back to pleasant times in high school. He walked to the stereo and became lost in his thoughts as he looked at the album cover. Luke and Angela went into the kitchen to open a bottle of wine. He heard the bedroom door open behind him and turned to catch a vision that took his breath away. Becky Smith stood in the doorway, illuminated from the lamp on her bedside table. The effect made him feel he was in the presence of royalty. Regaining his composure, he hoped his mouth wasn't hanging open. He approached her and said, "You must be Becky. I'm Luke's brother, Mark."

"Nice to meet you, Mark," she said with a warm smile and a voice as soft as silk.

The term for what he was feeling was "thunderstruck," and just as a booming artillery piece makes a violent thump in one's chest, Mark felt the same sensation now. It happened in an instant, but there was no flash and no noise.

Becky felt it too. She'd known Luke for months, and had never been attracted to him. There was no denying he was handsome, but his arrogance overshadowed his looks. Mark was another story altogether. He shared the same features, but there was gentleness in his eyes that Luke would never have. She had a feeling Mark was special.

Angela and Luke returned from the kitchen with some wine and cheese. Luke watched Becky and Mark stare at each other in silence, and he knew immediately his brother had fallen. *Hard.* He'd seen the look before, when they were fourteen and both of them had a crush on Mary Beth Jensen. *Put a fork in this guy,* he thought. *He's done.*

The two couples had a wonderful dinner at a place called Dominique's. The menu was exotic, and the atmosphere was conducive to good conversation. Luke paid the bill and suggested they go back to his apartment for a nightcap. Mark agreed, though he was wishing the evening wouldn't end. As they drove across town, Luke could see in the rearview mirror that Mark was holding Becky's hand. No one noticed him shake his head in amazement. All he'd wanted to do was patch things up with Mark and get on with his life. He figured they'd make peace, then go on ignoring each other. Now he had a sneaking suspicion he was going to be seeing his brother on a regular basis. *So much for the brunette theory.* They walked into his apartment with the satisfaction that comes from having had a perfect evening.

As Luke opened the door, he found an envelope shoved under it. It was from Ben Harvey, one of the interns in Senator Long's office. He read out loud, "Luke, your father had a heart attack this afternoon. He's in Piedmont Hospital. Call your mom at home. I hope everything turns out alright."

The men looked at each other, and the girls fell silent. Luke dialed Atlanta. The phone was answered by their parents' next-door neighbor, Pat Walker.

"Who's this?" Luke asked.

"Mr. Walker, Luke. We've been hoping you'd call soon."

"Mr. Walker, please put Mom on the phone."

"The doctor gave her a sedative, Luke. Martha's in there with her now. I doubt she'll wake up 'till morning."

"How's Dad?" he asked.

There was a long pause, and Luke closed his eyes, knowing what the next words would be.

"Your dad's gone, son. About three hours ago."

He shook his head from side to side, and Mark stood in silence, taking the blow. Becky squeezed his arm.

"Luke? Your mother wanted me to ask if maybe now, you'd find your brother and settle things with him. She wants you both to come home for the funeral."

Luke cleared his throat, but it did little to bring his voice above a hoarse whisper. "Mark's standing next to me, right now, sir. Ah…Mr. Walker, when Mom wakes up, let her know we're flying in tomorrow, together. She'll understand."

Chapter Sixteen

CHANGING OF THE GUARD

"I'll be seeing you...in all the old familiar places."

Tommy Dorsey

Atlanta, Georgia - April 1978

The "Early Bird" to Atlanta was scheduled to depart National Airport at 6:15 a.m. It was after midnight when they received the news about their father, so they decided they'd catch a catnap on the hour and a half flight, and remained awake. Luke took the two women home while Mark called the base for permission to leave the area. It was nearly two in the morning before he got it. He'd contacted the American Red Cross in Atlanta and asked them to send official verification of his dad's death to the commanding officer of AWS. The officer of the day arranged his emergency leave, then told him to check in from Atlanta on Monday. There was no need for him to return to Quantico before flying home; he'd come with clothes for the weekend, and Luke loaned him a dark suit and a couple of ties. They each packed a bag, and were ready long before it was time to leave for the airport.

There were few people in the concourse on Saturday morning. Washington is a "suitcase town." Many members of Congress commute from their home districts on a weekly basis. On Sundays and Thursdays, the airport is a zoo. Most of the business travelers are gone by Friday evening. On Saturday mornings one could fire a shotgun down the longest concourse and never hit a soul.

Luke spoke to the gate agent and arranged for each of them to have an entire row so they could stretch out. As soon as they boarded the plane, they kicked off their shoes, shoved a pillow under their heads and fell fast asleep. Between the time they boarded and deplaned, they each got a little more than two hours' sleep.

They had reserved a rental car from Hertz, and were on their way to the counter when they saw Mr. Walker coming toward them. He waved and shouted their names as he picked up his pace. The man was nearly eighty, and at a trot he could be timed with a calendar. The boys headed his way to shorten his trek. Luke was clearly annoyed, since the usual thirty-minute ride to his folk's house would now take at least an hour. Mark, sensing his irritation, quietly suggested he lighten up.

Luke had lived so long in the fast pace of politics, that he hated people that moved slowly. Mark saw things from a different perspective. The Walkers had lived next door to his parents' home for thirty-five years. They'd been like surrogate grandparents to them. Mr. Walker was doing what Southern men always did in times of trouble: honoring the code of chivalry that said when you can't do what you'd like to do…you do what you can. He couldn't bring their father back to life, but he *could* pick the boys up from the airport.

Mark hugged the old man and thanked him for getting up early to meet them. As he said it, he laughed to himself. Mr. Walker hadn't slept past 5:30 in the morning in his whole life. Through a scowl on his face, Luke thanked him too, then picked up both bags and headed for the exit. As they walked, Mark asked Mr. Walker if he'd like to ride instead of drive. He agreed right away, saying his eyesight was getting poor and he'd love for Mark to drive. Luke's disposition improved immediately.

Twenty-five minutes from leaving the airport they drove into Mr. Walker's driveway. They thanked him again for the ride, retrieved their bags, and crossed his lawn to the front door of their childhood home. Luke made straight for the door, but Mark lingered for a moment in the driveway. It had been a long time since he'd been home in April. Standing on each side of the white Colonial house were large magnolias. In addition to the trees, the azaleas lining the opposite side of the yard were in full bloom. The scent of the blossoms filled his senses, and he had to fight the urge to sit down on the brick steps and dredge up fond memories.

Regaining his focus, he walked through the front door and embraced his mother. Ever the Spartan, she held back her tears and greeted her boys with a smile.

After breakfast with Mary Quinn, Luke drove downtown to Spring Street to make the funeral arrangements at H. M. Patterson & Sons Funeral Home, located in an old estate house known as Spring Hill. North Atlanta folks subscribe to a simple creed: "The best is always good enough." Patterson's had always been the best. In his present state, of course his dad didn't care where he was prepped for burial. If he were alive though, he'd have made his preference known, and Spring Hill it would be. There would be no substandard ride to the cemetery for John Francis Reilly. Mary Quinn was running this show, and he'd have the best.

Mark stayed behind to keep his mother company. She cleared the dishes from the kitchen table and turned to face him. "I'm still mad at you for going back to Vietnam without telling us," she said, waving a bar of dark brown Octagon soap that no one in America except Mary Quinn Reilly used anymore. "I ought to wash your mouth out with this soap for lying to me."

"I didn't lie to you," he said defensively. "I just didn't volunteer information."

"Don't split hairs with me, young man. If you couldn't bring yourself to let us know where you were, *you knew you were lying.*"

The Grey Nuns of The Sacred Heart had been his grammar school teachers. Between them and his mother, he'd had guilt laid on him by the very best. Instead of calling it Christ the King School, he and his friends had jokingly referred to the place as "Our Lady of Perpetual Guilt."

Mark stared at the tiny woman standing there, threatening him with a bar of soap. He remembered vividly how bad the stuff tasted. At age six, she'd painfully taught him that lesson after he entered the house wearing cowboy boots and six-shooters and proceeded to spit on the kitchen floor. She'd looked at him in horror and demanded to know where he'd learned such a thing. Mark told her he'd been watching Gabby Hayes on television over at Mr. Walker's house, and that *Gabby* spit on the floor every time he walked into a saloon.

His mother informed him, in no uncertain terms, that *her home* was no saloon. Upon learning he couldn't spit in the house like the crusty old cowboy, he expressed his disappointment by muttering, "Well...crap!" The brown soap was in his mouth before the words echoed off the wall. Twenty-five years later, he could still taste it. His mother wanted to know where he'd heard that kind of language, so he quickly fessed up, "From Daddy."

Mary Quinn had to bite her lip to avoid smiling. Mark had never asked, but often wondered, if his dad had received the same punishment.

Now, he laughed at his mother and said, "So...you and whose army is gonna' wash my mouth out with soap?"

Mary Quinn smiled, then laughed, but it disappeared as fast as it came and was replaced by tears. She choked them back and dried her eyes with a dishtowel. In the midst of handling the loss of her husband, Mark had dredged up memories of Matthew.

When the boys were fifteen, Mary Quinn had threatened to wash Matt's mouth with soap for being disrespectful. He replied, "Oh yeah? You and whose army?" Just as quickly as she'd yanked them over her knee when they were small, she grabbed Matt around the neck and wrestled him to the ground like a rodeo calf. She ground the soap into his teeth, and he laughed so hard he nearly threw up. Mary Quinn had laughed too, and when she figured he'd had enough, she let him go. Luke and Mark had sat there astonished. Matthew ruled the streets, but their mother ruled the kitchen.

The remainder of Saturday and Sunday was the traditional parade of friends and extended family coming by to drop off food. Two days prior to any Atlanta funeral, there was enough food brought to the family to feed a third world country. In the kitchen that weekend were no fewer than three hams, two pot roasts and five chicken casseroles. Enough six-packs of Cokes had been dropped off to rival the soft drink aisle at Mathew's Grocery Store.

Along with the food came condolences and support. It was painful, yet in an odd way it was comforting. People weren't born alone, and the support of the community prevented people from having to deal with death by themselves. Mark felt the friends filling up the house epitomized John Donne's frequently quoted poem:

"No man is an island, entire of itself,
every man is a piece of the continent,
a part of the main;
if a clod be washed away by the sea,
Europe is the less, as well as if a promontory were,
as well as if a manor of thy friends or thine own were;
any man's death diminishes me,
because I am involved in mankind;
and therefore never send to know for whom the bell tolls; it tolls for thee. "

Mark *was* diminished by the death of his father, as was every person who knew him. He was a fine man. He'd done the best he knew how to raise his sons and to love his wife. Mark had no doubt his father was free of concerns for those left behind. He was standing in front of God, hearing the words, "Well done, good and faithful servant."

John Francis Reilly was laid to rest on Tuesday afternoon. Atlanta had never seemed prettier to Mark. Luke appeared introspective and had little to say all day. Mark suspected he was wrestling with his own mortality, and when they returned to DC later the next evening his suspicions were confirmed. They'd driven in separate cars to Washington's National Airport, so they said their goodbyes standing next to Mark's Corvette. That was where Luke broke his silence by saying, "Dad's death doesn't seem to have *you* very upset."

Mark shrugged his shoulders and said, "I'm going to miss him a lot, Luke, but he's better off than either of us. If I cried, they'd just be selfish tears."

"Death doesn't frighten you?"

"That's the third time in my life I've been asked that," Mark said. "Death isn't frightening, Luke. *Living* is what's scary."

"I wish I had your faith," Luke replied.

"My faith is no stronger than yours," Mark answered. "I've just had more people die around me than you. I've seen guys that grabbed life by the throat and lived it to the hilt. They may have died young, but they lived every moment. Dad was like that. I've also seen guys who are so afraid of dying, they were too afraid to really live. There's nothing sadder than that."

Luke had nothing to say. He just stood there, jingling his car keys.

"Thanks for coming back into my life, Luke. I'll call you soon." Mark closed his door, fired up his engine and headed south to Quantico.

Chapter Seventeen
CALL OF THE WILD

"When a man loves a woman, can't keep his mind on nothing else."

Percy Sledge

Alexandria, Virginia – May 1978

Seven weeks had passed since the night Mark met Becky Smith. His low-mileage '72 Corvette had come much closer to being a car of average-miles. At every opportunity, he burned up the interstate between Quantico and Alexandria. Their visits weren't confined to the weekends; Mark would drive to her apartment at least two nights a week for dinner, and she would make the trip to Quantico if he had a heavy night of homework, or an early morning field exercise. They'd packed a lot of dating into the past couple of months, and to say they were serious was an understatement.

Mark had two more weeks of Amphibious Warfare School, and he'd already received orders to report to Camp Lejeune, North Carolina by July sixth. He planned to spend his leave with Becky and her parents in Jackson Hole, Wyoming. They'd seen Mark only twice, but had received quite an earful from their daughter. From what they could tell he was a fine young man, and they liked him. This was cause for celebration, because she had dated her share of obnoxious guys from Capitol Hill. They weren't counting their chickens before they hatched, but her parents were fairly certain they were soon to have a son-in-law.

Tonight was a special occasion. He'd been invited to a real live Washington bigwigs' bash. This was an A-list ticket, and he was the guest of Senator and Mrs. Smith. He was reasonably sure that he was to undergo formal inspection by Becky's mother and a few of her close friends, so he washed his ears well.

Mark rang Becky's doorbell at seven o'clock sharp. She opened the door and, as always, looked stunning. He was unprepared for her reaction when she looked at him. Her mouth fell open, then, formed an O as she let out a low whistle. Mark was wearing his Marine dress white uniform, with full medals in the place of ribbons.

"Dashing!" Becky purred. "Come on in, sailor. You look so good we may not go to the party."

"I'll thank you not to call me a sailor," Mark said in mock indignation. "I'd rather have a sister in a bordello than a brother in the Navy."

Becky laughed at his slam on the Navy. She loved the rivalry Marines had with their military siblings.

Mark said, "We Marines have our *own* white uniform, and the sailors envy us 'cause ours looks so much better than theirs."

Becky was wearing a short black dress, adorned with just a single strand of white pearls around her neck. With her long dark hair worn down around her shoulders, she was the epitome of unaffected elegance. He offered her his arm, and she laid her hand in its crook.

She called out to Angela to say goodnight, and Mark heard her yell out from the kitchen to have a good time.

Holding the door to the open convertible, he told Becky he'd be happy to raise the top. She asked him not to and simply pulled her hair into a ponytail for the thirty-minute ride to Chevy Chase, Maryland. That simple gesture confirmed why he loved her so much. Although she was gorgeous, she wasn't hung up on her looks, and a spring ride in her boyfriend's convertible was more important than her hairdo. He knew that upon arrival, with two strokes of a brush, she'd be the prettiest woman at the party.

"So…Dad called and told you to break out the ice cream suit, huh?" she said.

"Yeah," Mark replied. "He said there'd be some heavy brass in uniform and a lot of political big shots at the party tonight. In his words, 'Tonight is a full tilt, wear your medals shindig.'"

"He didn't lie," she said. "I know who's coming, and tonight should be quite a show." She laid her head on the headrest and Mark drove in silence. He'd never known such satisfaction. He loved being a captain of Marines, he was driving a car he'd always dreamed of owning, and sitting next to him was the woman he planned to marry. The thick sweet taste of canned peaches filled his senses, and he thought back to his frequent breakfast daydream in Vietnam. Back then, he didn't know the name of the girl in his dreams, but he knew one day she'd come along. It was a bittersweet irony that Becky entered his life the same day his father passed away. John Francis would have liked her a lot. He turned to steal a glance, and his heart raced like the thundering motor under the hood.

They arrived at her parent's house to the sight of a long line of expensive black sedans. Two young valets in their early twenties were parking them. One opened the door for Becky while the other slipped into Mark's driver's seat. Mark took Becky's hand and looked over his shoulder at the parking attendant. With a sly grin, he issued a warning, saying, "I know what the odometer reads, so don't think you can take her for a joyride without my knowing about it!"

The attendant grinned. "Don't worry. I'll park her right up front. All these old guys in Cadillacs will wish it were theirs."

Mark gave him a thumbs-up as he and Becky walked through the front door.

The house was magnificent. Inside the foyer was a sweeping staircase that curved from left to right and commanded all eyes to look upward. Black and white marble tile covered the floor, and the area seemed large enough to serve as a life-sized chessboard. He suspected the chandelier alone cost more than everything he owned.

The Smiths' wealth was impressive, even more so in light of their unpretentiousness. In his limited experience with very wealthy people, Mark had already learned there were distinct types. Those who inherited wealth were, more often than not, overly impressed with themselves and snobby. Those who'd made their own money fell into two types. The first was inclined to be ostentatious, and their taste leaned toward the garish. The second type didn't let their wealth affect the way they treated others. The Smiths fell into the latter category.

Mark had a surprise tucked in his sock, and wanted Becky to have it before they reached the garden party out back. He'd intended to give it to her the previous weekend, but she'd been nursing a headache at dinner, and the mood hadn't been right. Tonight was different. He couldn't get over how beautiful she looked. He was in fine form too, and figured he might as well get full value for the dress whites he so seldom wore. Grabbing her by the elbow, he guided her into the library and closed the sliding doors.

She gave him a look like a chicken caught by a fox and said, "Don't get any bright ideas. You may be handsome and charming, but my parents are hosting a party, right now…*in this very house*."

"Miss Smith," he said, "I assure you my intentions are honorable." He guided her toward a large leather sofa and held both of her hands as she took a seat. Then he reached into his left sock and pulled out a small velvet box. Before she could even speculate about its contents he flipped it open and dropped to one knee. "Becky…I don't know if this is the right way or not," he said, "but I can't wait another minute to tell you how much I love you. Will you marry me?"

She was momentarily stunned, but her surprise turned instantly to joy. Through a huge smile she said, "You'd better believe it, *sailor*!"

He snapped the box closed and quickly stood up. "There you go with that sailor stuff again. I think I'd better find myself another girl."

She snatched the box from his hand and said, "OK, jarhead…OK. No more sailor jokes. If I'm going to help you become a general, I'd better become all Marine, too."

He slipped the ring on her finger, and she held her hand in front of her face to admire it. It was beautiful, and he was so proud he thought his brass buttons might pop. They held each other tightly for a few moments, then stood and opened the sliding doors. Standing on the other side was Senator Smith, who had been wondering who was in his private library with the doors closed.

Mark extended his hand, and the senator shifted the wine glass from his right hand to his left, eyeing him suspiciously as they shook hands. Mark looked as though he'd been caught with his hand in the cookie jar, and Becky stood behind him looking like the cat that swallowed the canary.

"What are you two up to in my study?" he asked, suspecting he already knew the answer.

"Senator, may I have a word with you, sir?"

"What's on your mind, son?"

"I've just asked your daughter to marry me, and she said yes. We'd like to ask for your blessing."

Hiram paused before answering. The engagement was no great surprise, but he wondered what to make of this heroic young warrior standing before him, assuming his blessing was a given. "In my day," he said, "a young man asked a girl's father for permission *before* asking the girl. You didn't feel the need to do that?"

Mark looked him straight in the eye. "No, sir, I didn't. I'm thirty-one, and Becky's twenty-six. We don't need your permission...but it'll make things very awkward if you refuse us your blessing."

"And what will you do, should I withhold it?" the senator asked.

"I'll marry her anyway, sir, but with less joy than I'm feeling right now. I love your daughter, Senator. I'll provide for her the best I can, though probably not as luxuriously as you have. She may want for material things, sir, but never for my love."

Hiram eyed Mark again, this time with grudging respect and admiration. "Son, I'd never want to get between you and whatever you've set your mind on having. I suspect there are some corpses around the world who once tried to deny you your objective. I have no plans to join them. You have my blessing...*and my permission*."

Becky let out a shriek that could be heard all the way down the hall. Mark let out the breath he'd been holding since he spoke his last words. Hiram hugged his daughter and put his arm around his soon-to-be son-in-law. "I believe the purpose of this party has just been changed," he said. "Let's go find your mother."

Allison Smith stood by the pool, talking with Senator Andrew Taylor and his wife Mary. She saw Mary break into a smile, and turned to see what she was looking at. Descending the back stairs from the upper patio were her daughter, Becky and her handsome Marine captain. Walking beside them was Hiram, smiling from ear to ear and waving for Allison to come and join them quickly. She excused herself from her friends and hurried to her husband. The Taylors watched from a distance as the senator announced the news to his wife. Allison's hands flew into the air. and she embraced her daughter. She turned and gave Mark a kiss on the cheek and put her arms around them both.

Though the guests couldn't hear a word, they had a pretty good idea of what had just transpired. The Smith family made their way toward the bandstand, and Hiram grabbed a microphone. "Ladies and gentleman," he said, "I have an announcement to make."

Everyone turned their attention toward the bandstand to hear what he had to say.

"You all know why you're here," he began. "You're to eat too much, drink too much, and before you leave, write very large checks on behalf of our guest of honor."

Everyone laughed the nervous little titter that meant they knew exactly how large a check he expected from each of them.

Hiram smiled at his friend who was making a bid for the White House and said, "Governor Reagan, I beg your indulgence, and *ask your permission* to steal the spotlight for just a minute." The subtle dig wasn't lost on Mark as the senator placed emphasis on the request for permission.

Ever the gentleman, Ronald Reagan smiled and yielded the floor.

"Many of you know my beautiful daughter, Becky. Standing beside her is Captain Mark Reilly. These two have just informed Allison and me they plan to be married."

Cheers, whoops, and a large round of applause filled the air. Hiram raised his glass high in the air and proposed a toast. "Becky...Mark...may you have long lives and a wonderful marriage. If you're blessed with only half the happiness Allison and I have had, you'll be among the luckiest people on earth. To young love!"

The crowd joined the toast, responding, "Young love!"

Chapter Eighteen
THE CHANGING FACE OF WAR

"You can check out anytime you want…but you can never leave."

The Eagles

Camp Lejeune, North Carolina – March 1983

Mark rose before the sun came up and took a quick run by himself. Becky and their baby son, John Matthew, were still sleeping, and the base was relatively deserted this early on a Saturday.

There was seldom rhyme or reason to assignment of base housing. Even though he was an infantry officer, he was housed at the Marine Air Station at New River. It actually worked out well because it was closer to battalion headquarters at Camp Geiger than was main-side Lejeune housing. While running, the only people he saw was a lone military police patrol.

When he'd finished his three-mile course, he settled into a cool-down walk. After a few minutes, he checked his watch and pulse, then rested his hands on his knees to take some deep breaths. He could still complete the three-mile run in less than eighteen minutes. One month away from turning thirty-six, he was in better shape now than some of his men who were only half his age.

As soon as he finished stretching, he walked into the battalion office to finish some paperwork before heading home for breakfast.

Corporal Anthony, the battalion duty clerk, snapped to attention and saluted him as he entered the building. "Good morning Major Reilly," he said in a cheery voice that belied his having spent most of the night awake.

"Good morning, Corporal," he replied. "Anything interesting happen last night?"

"Not much, sir," he said. "A couple of guys from Bravo Company got picked up in town for drunk and disorderly." He peppered his brief report with a few details, then concluded by saying, "For a payday Friday, it was pretty calm."

Mark walked toward his office, instructing Corporal Anthony to resume his post with the command, "As you were."

His latest job was executive officer of 1st Battalion, 8th Marines. This was the battalion's second in command, and the position primarily consisted of administrative duties. He wasn't fond of the job because it required him to be inside more than he liked. He much preferred his previous role as a company commander, but, as in all walks of life, to climb the ladder of success one has to pay dues.

His father-in-law was urging him to take an assignment back in Washington. The senator had several opportunities in mind, among them a post in Ronald Reagan's White House. He questioned whether that would be a good idea or not. Senator Smith assured him that President Reagan asked about him whenever they saw one another. Mark wasn't sure if that was because he remembered him fondly, or remembered him as the guy in snazzy dress whites who upstaged him at his fundraiser by announcing his engagement to the senator's daughter. It didn't really matter. He needed time in the Fleet Marine Force to be eligible for promotion to lieutenant colonel. At any rate, he'd remained in the Marines to lead troops...not to wear dress uniforms at White House functions.

The senator kept trying to explain that the *right* staff positions were stepping-stones to rapid advancement *and* command. Mark wasn't convinced. With the exception of Senator Smith and President Reagan, he wasn't a big fan of politicians. He preferred the company of his Marines. With Marines, there was no subterfuge or game playing. What you saw was what you got.

It mattered little at the moment, anyway. In the next month he was going on an extended deployment to Beirut, Lebanon. He'd be gone for at least six months, quite possibly longer. Lengthy deployments always offered plenty of time for thinking. He planned to give the senator's suggestions a great deal of thought while he was away from home.

Right now he was trying to find the words to tell Becky the battalion had received deployment orders. They'd come down on Thursday, and he hadn't told her yet. As far as he knew, the word wasn't out, but the jungle drums work quickly on a Marine base, and scuttlebutt about a deployment gets around pretty quickly. Mark wanted her to hear it from him, and not from someone else's wife. They'd been married for just over four years, and this was his second unaccompanied tour. Life had been a lot simpler when he was single. It had also been a lot lonelier.

Once again, they were experiencing what many of their married friends had been dealing with for years. Separation from family was one of the major downsides of being a Marine. The term was *sacrifice*. As a single Marine, he had thought of sacrifice as the act of putting himself in harm's way for the good of his country. As a married man, he more fully understood the nature of sacrifice that was made by Marines with families of their own. In a twenty-year career, he could count on at least five of those years being away from his family. If he stayed thirty, the number would climb to at least eight or nine, not to mention that any of these unaccompanied tours could get him killed.

Sacrifice was the nature of the business.

One thing he could say about Marine Corps life under Reagan's administration—the Vietnam hangover had ended. It had been difficult to be a member of the armed forces in the seventies. President Nixon was trying to find a way to exit Vietnam without losing face. President Ford was serving his unexpired term and had no mandate to lead, since he'd been appointed rather than elected. Other than the Camp David Accords, President Carter had come out on the short end of every negotiation he made with a foreign power.

After Nixon, neither Ford nor Carter had effectively used the military, because the mere mention of employing armed troops to project American policy brought up the specter of Vietnam. The Iranians had thumbed their nose at President Carter by holding hostages from the captured American embassy for more than a year. An ill-fated mission to free them had been aborted, and wasn't tried again. Ronald Reagan changed the whole climate. He was committed to a strong America, well enough prepared to deter any aggression. Iran's leaders understood there was a new sheriff in town, and on the day of his inauguration, they released the American hostages they'd held for 444 days.

Nixon and Reagan had one thing in common. The nation's enemies thought they were both a little crazy, and for that reason they were both feared. They were like the television commercials for the E. F. Hutton stock brokerage firm: When they spoke, everyone listened. Under Reagan, there was a renewed sense of pride in being a member of the military. If there was a president worth serving, Mark thought Reagan came closest to fitting the bill.

Mark spent about an hour and a half cleaning up some work on his desk. Before leaving, he took a quick tour of the battalion area and stopped by the duty desk. Corporal Anthony was in the process of being relieved by Sergeant Rodriguez. Both Marines wished him a pleasant weekend, and he returned the sentiment. They envied the major because he had the weekend off, while they had the duty. *He* envied the two enlisted men, because they were single and didn't have to go home and break the news to their wives about a six month, or longer, separation.

He pushed open the door and broke into a run before the air pump eased it closed. Twenty minutes later he walked through his kitchen door to the smell of sausage and eggs on the stove. Becky turned and smiled as John Matthew let out a shriek of joy at the sight of his daddy. Mark kissed Becky on the forehead while simultaneously patting her butt. He deftly spun away from her as she tried to swat him with the dishtowel she yanked from her shoulder. Then he reached in the high chair and grabbed his boy under his upraised arms.

John Matthew was nineteen months old, and was solid as a brick. He'd been an early talker, and a late walker. By the end of most days that combination made for a load on both the ears and the back. "Up me, Daddy," he said as Mark picked him up and swung him high over his head.

They sat together at the head of the table as Becky finished making their breakfast. As she served the plates, Mark placed John Matthew back in his highchair, and they ate together, watching in amazement as their little boy polished off a huge plate of food. At birth, his baby footprint had extended past the border of the footprint card. Becky remarked at the time that if baby feet and puppy feet had anything in common, John Matthew was going to be a big boy.

"So, what's happening at the office so early on a Saturday morning?" she asked. It wasn't her words but her tone that made him look up from his plate. He knew the look on her face. She had already heard.

"I'd planned to tell you this morning, but it sounds like I waited too long."

"Captain Dunbar's wife, Cynthia, called and told me last night," she said.

"Why didn't you say something when you heard?"

"I figured you'd tell me in your own good time," she said. "I just thought I'd give you the opportunity on a full stomach."

He shrugged his shoulders with a look of resignation. They'd always known that deployment orders would come again sooner than they wanted. Still, they had both hoped that if they kept their heads in the sand a little longer, the orders might not come.

"Who's fighting who over there right now?" Becky asked.

"At the moment it's the Christians and the Muslims," Mark answered, "but it seems like all the factions over there hate each other. Things change in the Middle East on a weekly basis." He shook his head, a little frustrated. "We're like a cop walking a beat…we're just out there for a presence."

She only sighed. His "presence" explanation was meant to minimize the danger, but he could tell she was anxious. Then she smiled and said, "You aren't the only one that's been sitting on some news, Marine. You're leaving John Matthew and me…but if you take too long getting home, you're going to find three of us when you return."

Mark dropped his fork, stood from his chair, and moved to Becky's side. Kneeling on one knee, he put his head in her lap, then looked up and said, "When did you learn about *this*?"

"About the same time Thursday that you were getting orders to leave." She stroked his head. "See if you can make it back before the due date, *Dad*."

★ ★ ★

Beirut, Lebanon – October 1983

It was obvious that Beirut had once been a thriving place. Yet in the past eight years of civil unrest between Christian and Muslim factions, the once-proud city looked every inch the war zone it had become.

War was nothing new to Beirut. Mark had done some reading about Lebanon before coming here. In Vietnam, he—like so many other young Americans—had known little or nothing about the country where he might die. Determined to never let that happen again, he became a student of history, making it his practice to learn as much as possible about any country where he was about to lead armed troops. He then made sure to educate his Marines about what he'd learned.

This prize port on the Mediterranean Sea had changed hands many times over the centuries. In the third century B.C., Beirut belonged to the Romans. In 635 A.D., the Arabs captured the city. Baldwin the First led his Crusaders on the city in the early 1100s. By the 1500s, it was part of the Ottoman Empire. Next came the Egyptians, and then the French. In 1921, Beirut became the capitol of Lebanon. In the first third of the twentieth century, the French built up the city in rapid fashion despite heavy tensions between Christians and Muslims.

That began to change soon after the creation of Israel at the end of World War II, when a flood of Palestinian refugees descended on the city and made it their home. Violence became a regular occurrence through the fifties and sixties, and erupted into full-scale civil war by 1976.

Mark had a working knowledge of the country's past, but neither he, nor the Marine Amphibious Unit commander, knew nearly enough about the mindset of Lebanon's Muslims. If anyone in the intelligence community knew, the information hadn't made its way to the troops on the ground. This lack of understanding would prove costly beyond measure.

As a young infantryman in Vietnam, Mark had no idea what transpired at command level. Nearly twenty years later, he was in the position to have a better idea. It troubled him greatly to know that sometimes he still didn't know squat. Once again, the hands of the ground forces were tied by people halfway around the world. The term was called "rules of engagement," and they never seemed to be set by anyone who was onsite and would have to live, or die, by them. The current rules ranged between the ridiculous and the insane. When the Marine Amphibious Unit first arrived in Beirut they were invited guests, not combatants. By October the situation had changed dramatically. They'd been invited by the ruling government to restore stability to the country torn by civil war.

The mission itself was the primary problem. Their assigned mission was "...to provide a presence in Beirut, that would in turn help establish the stability necessary for the Lebanese government to regain control of their capitol." Nowhere in his training had he heard of "presence" as a mission. It hadn't been taught at the Basic School, or at Amphibious Warfare School. In talking with his superiors who'd attended the Naval War College, they'd never heard of it either.

Mark was a quick study, and the past few months had taught him a valuable lesson: No armed military unit can occupy a war zone and claim to be neutral. The opposing sides will eventually come to the conclusion you're either friend or foe. This was the position the Marines now occupied. The Shiite Muslims had determined the Marines were an enemy, and therefore a viable target. The folks calling the shots from America were slow to grasp the change, and consequently slow to change the rules of engagement. The original rules were those in place for peacetime units, such as few weapons being carried loaded to prevent an accidental discharge that might injure civilians or Marines.

When it became apparent that stability wasn't going to occur simply because of a multinational peacekeeping presence, the Muslim factions began firing artillery, mortars and small arms at Marine Corps positions. The Marines were authorized to respond with measured and appropriate means. Unfortunately, "measured" and "appropriate" were terms that meant entirely different things to a guy having a thirty-dollar lunch in Washington and a Marine who had incoming rounds landing around his position. One of Mark's early combat lessons had been "peace through fire superiority," which means a greater volume of outgoing fire suppresses all incoming fire. Measured response prolongs a firefight; massive response ends it quickly, with the added benefit of making the aggressor think twice about attacking again.

The second problem with the rules was their inconsistency. The MAU had been on the ground for close to six months, and different units within it operated under different rules. In April, a suicide bomber drove a truck full of explosives into the American embassy, partially destroying the building. Forty people were killed, including the entire CIA contingent in the region. A platoon of MAU-based Marines was sent to provide additional security at the embassy. *Their* weapons were locked and loaded at all times, yet at the Marine barracks at the Beirut Airport, this wasn't permitted. Only the perimeter guards and Marines at remote outposts carried loaded weapons.

The final thing that made Mark uneasy was the fact that the troops were concentrated in one location. In his opinion, this wasn't smart, but they were the guests of the Lebanese government and they lived where they were told. He hated it, but it wasn't his call. He wasn't in command.

Whenever Mark was troubled, he would rise early and run. Late yesterday, he had received a letter from Becky's mother. Becky had gone into early labor the week before, and had been admitted to the hospital at Camp Lejeune. The doctors had given her drugs to stop the labor, and at present, her mother said they appeared to be working. She was on the scene with her daughter, and there was nothing Mark could do from Lebanon except pray and run. Neither activity made him feel much better. He did them both anyway. It was Sunday morning at 0600, and the day promised to be quiet. It was a good time to clear his head, and the run would be a welcome distraction from his worries.

As he ran the perimeter of the airport, he made a point to observe each security post and let the guys on duty know the battalion exec was around. He was completing the first lap when he saw a yellow Mercedes stake bed truck winding its way toward the next guard post, about half a mile away.

As the truck approached the security checkpoint, a Marine stepped from behind a wall of sandbags and raised his hand for the truck to halt. Instead of slowing, the engine roared and accelerated past the checkpoint, hurdling the razor wire and concertina obstacles. The vehicle blasted through two more checkpoints without being fired upon, weaved around two sewer pipe barriers, and flattened the sandbagged booth housing the sergeant of the guard. The truck penetrated the lobby of the Battalion Landing Team's headquarters, and detonated upon impact.

The building lifted from its foundation, imploded upon itself, and collapsed under its own weight. Hundreds of Marines, sailors and soldiers were inside asleep. Two hundred forty-one lost their lives without ever knowing they'd been attacked. More than a hundred were severely wounded, among them those standing within a three hundred foot radius of the building. Mark had been lifted off the ground and blown nearly thirty feet back. The time on his smashed wristwatch was 0622.

Several days later, FBI forensic experts investigating the attack determined the charge had been traditional explosives, enhanced by compressed gas. The resulting explosion was equivalent to a 12,000-pound bomb, and they stated in their report that it was the largest non-nuclear blast they'd ever examined.

The guided missile had been in the world's arsenals for years. Missiles guided by terrorists willing to sacrifice their own lives to deliver their payload hadn't been used against military installations since the Japanese employed kamikaze pilots in World War II. Kamikaze means "divine wind" in Japanese. The Arab word "Jihad" means "holy struggle." A new face of war was emerging. After the morning of October 23rd, the world was left wondering how to defend itself against fanatics who believed they had a one-way ticket to paradise for killing the infidels.

The question would find no satisfactory answer for many years to come.

Chapter Nineteen

STARMAKER

"You can do magic…you can have anything that you desire."

America

Chevy Chase, Maryland – December 1983

As Luke drove toward his townhouse in Georgetown, a light drift of grainy snow blew across the pavement, making the road appear to move from side to side. He'd just enjoyed a pleasant evening at the home of Hiram and Allison Smith.

He thought them kind to invite him for Christmas Eve dinner, as he and the senator had crossed swords on more than a few occasions. As the old saying went, politics made for strange bedfellows. Although their views were at polar extremes, there'd been a few occasions when they had the chance to be helpful to one another. An anomaly of politics was that it was frequently difficult to personally dislike the very people you couldn't stand professionally.

The Smiths' invitation was testimony to this very fact. Hiram Smith was a first-class gentleman. Although he disliked Luke's politics, he respected his connection to the family. Mark and Becky were home for Christmas, and his mother, Mary Quinn, had flown to town to see the new baby. She'd also come to lay her eyes on Mark, and see for herself the extent of his injuries.

To say the least, Mark had been very lucky. Instinctively he'd turned away as he saw the blast and had been, literally, blown away. He landed hard on the ground, knocking the wind from his lungs and sustaining a concussion along with a lot of minor lacerations. He remembered little, except trying to stand to run to the aid of his fellow Marines.

The effort made in planting his left foot made him crumple to the ground in pain, and the foot had felt as though it was no longer there. With the little cognitive thought he could muster, he surmised that his foot must've been blown off. When he regained his senses in the hospital, he learned that some shrapnel had severed his Achilles tendon, rendering his left foot useless until it was repaired. His leg was in a rigid brace and, for now, he walked with a cane. It would take between four and six months to heal, but the prognosis was full recovery.

Many years ago, in New Orleans, Luke had betrayed his trust and had seen the depth of his hurt and anger. The same look was back in his eyes, though thankfully no longer directed at him. Mark was grateful for the presence of their mother, and for the healthy baby boy that had been nestled in his lap all evening. Bennett Michael Reilly had been born one month early, in November. He was six weeks old now and was doing great.

Luke watched in admiration as Mark gazed lovingly at his second son. Work had kept him too busy for a family of his own, and he had no prospects for starting one in the near future. It was evident for all to see that his brother was a good father. Mark's anger seemed to disappear when he held his children, but Luke knew he had actually just stuffed it away for the benefit of Mary Quinn, Becky, and her parents. Try as he might to hide it, it percolated just below the surface, waiting to explode.

As Luke continued driving, the snow began falling heavier and the rhythm of his windshield wipers almost lulled him to sleep. He forced himself to stay awake, which became easier to do as he allowed his own anger to fester. Luke was angry at Ronald Reagan for what he perceived as his directionless employment of American troops. The news of the Beirut bombing hadn't run a full day's news cycle when it had been preempted by news of U.S. forces invading Grenada. Luke had no idea what the man's objectives were, but he seemed intent on involving America in another war, somewhere. He thought Mark's luck might be starting to run low; he had just received his third award of the Purple Heart. Arlington Cemetery was filled with men who had but one.

Unlike the past, Luke was now in a position to do something about a president with whom he disagreed. His current occupation was to groom candidates to become viable contenders. Around the time Mark and Becky married, Luke had been offered a chance to join the Washington public relations firm of Wood & Kemper. He'd performed well over the last four years, and had been made a partner. It was a wonderful job, as it incorporated everything Luke loved about Washington. It kept him involved on Capitol Hill, it utilized his skills with words and ideas, and it offered him the chance to earn a small fortune. The job had one more intangible…power. Luke liked

219

this aspect as much, or more, than the rest. He didn't wield political power in the purest sense. Better than that, he was a "starmaker," one who had the ability to lift someone from political obscurity and thrust him, or her, into the national spotlight.

He was working now on the Walter Mondale/Geraldine Ferraro campaign. He wasn't overly enamored with either candidate, but he'd fought for Ferraro's selection as a running mate, feeling the time was right for a woman to occupy a spot on a presidential ticket. Margaret Thatcher had proven in England that a woman could run a country; Luke's instincts with polls told him that the next revolution in this country would be feminine in nature, and his antenna was up for women who could hold their own on the political battlefield.

One reason for his projection was the current political landscape. Luke believed the public should've been outraged at October's military news. Indeed there had been outrage over the Beirut bombing, but instead of being directed at the president, it appeared the country wanted revenge. In Luke's mind, the invasion of Grenada had been irresponsible, yet the public applauded it, and Reagan's approval ratings soared. America's bad memories of Vietnam were fading. The public's respect for the military was returning. Luke mulled these facts over in his mind and came to the conclusion that the utilization of America's military, when popular, was a factor he'd been overlooking for too long. He would have to control his personal prejudices in the future.

He parked the car and sidestepped patches of ice as he negotiated the front stairs of his home. As he placed his key in the lock he decided that every aspect of the federal government was a potential arrow in the campaign quiver…even the military.

Hilton Head Island, South Carolina – New Years Weekend, 1984

Luke entered the restaurant in Harbor Town and stood on his toes to peer above the crowd waiting for tables. He spied his dinner partner at the bar, and jockeyed his way between people as he made his way toward him. The place was packed with beautiful women, but most appeared to be only college age. He liked *them*, but he knew they thought he resembled their fathers, so he just smiled and admired the view. He chuckled softly when he realized the song playing on the sound system was Steely Dan's "Hey Nineteen." A funky beat accompanied Donald Fagen's poignant lyrics: "Hey Nineteen…we got nothin' in common…we can't talk at all." The song wounded his pride. It was simply too true.

Upon reaching his friend, he clasped a hand on the man's shoulder. Dr. Pierce Randall turned and smiled at his former student. Now in his early sixties, and with hair turned completely white, his appearance took Luke by surprise. They'd kept in touch by telephone through the years, but hadn't seen each other face-to-face since Luke graduated from Tulane. Ordering a glass of Chablis, he pulled up the stool the professor had saved for him by draping his coat across it. They were still catching up on old times when a cute blonde in her late teens approached them and said their table was ready. Luke paid for the drinks and they followed the hostess to the table.

Luke was here at the professor's invitation, and was anxious to learn more about the upcoming weekend. As the elite had been called during John Kennedy's term, today's best and brightest were assembled at Hilton Head for a New Years weekend of camaraderie and idea exchange. Leaders in the fields of law, finance, politics and academics had made the pilgrimage to the island for what promised to be the networking event of the year. The majority of them were decidedly liberal, although a few conservatives had been invited for the purpose of sparking controversy to their faces, and for comic relief behind their backs.

Dr. Randall waited until the waiter had taken their order, then, began speaking to Luke. "I'm so glad you could join me here, Luke. You're going to meet some wonderful people this weekend."

Luke hoisted his glass of wine and offered a toast, "To new friendships...but more importantly, to the old ones!"

Dr. Randall was very fond of Luke, and appreciated his sentiment. He raised his glass and nodded in silent agreement. "Luke," he said, "there's someone here this weekend I really want you to meet. He's one of the country's youngest governors, and with the proper grooming, has the tools to go all the way." The professor lowered his voice to a whisper and exclaimed, "Better than that...he has the mettle for it, and the drive to get there."

"Are you referring to Will Norton, Professor?"

"Indeed I am. Have you met him yet?"

"No, but his name keeps popping up as someone to keep an eye on," Luke replied.

The professor seemed excited to be playing matchmaker, and acted as though he were involving Luke in a conspiracy rather than merely making an introduction. "I've arranged for him to join us for dinner in my cottage tomorrow," he said softly, smearing butter on his bread. Then he glanced at Luke. "How old are you now, Luke?"

"I'll be thirty-seven in April."

"Well, Luke…if you hitch your horse to this guy's wagon, by the time you're forty-five, I believe you'll be making government policy from the White House."

Luke actually felt a tingle run up his spine at the suggestion. From the time he'd heard JFK's inaugural address, he knew the White House was where he wanted to be.

The waiter arrived with their dinners and laid the hot plates in front of them. The seafood smelled wonderful, yet Luke anxiously wished the next twenty-four hours would pass quickly, bringing him closer to tomorrow's dinner with Will Norton.

A waitress passed by with a tray of cold beers. Luke noticed that two of them were Old Milwaukees, and he chuckled under his breath as the company's slogan flashed into mind: "It just doesn't get any better than this!"

He took a big bite of stuffed crabmeat and agreed wholeheartedly.

Chapter Twenty

BAD GUYS DON'T ALWAYS SPEAK RUSSIAN

"Wide eyed pistol wavers…with blood in their eyes."

Don Henley

Headquarters Marine Corps, Arlington, Virginia – 1985

Having spent the morning reading, Mark needed a stretch break. His leg injury was completely healed, but the Achilles tendon had the tendency to tighten up if he sat too long. He leaned against his desk and thrust his left leg as far to the rear as it would go. Bending his right leg toward the desk and keeping his left foot flat on the floor, he rocked back and forth to stretch the tendon. In a matter of minutes, he felt fine.

He refreshed his cup of coffee and returned to his desk, still brooding about the argument he'd had with his father-in-law the previous evening. Hiram Smith had pulled some strings to secure a position for him on the National Security Council staff at the White House. It was a terrific opportunity that had the potential to secure him an early promotion to colonel. Mark had several problems with the offer, and the resulting discussion heated up rather quickly.

The senator was already responsible for arranging his current assignment soon after the bombing in Beirut. Mark had told him he wanted to learn about terrorists—firsthand. Hiram spoke to his close friend, the assistant commandant of the Corps, and three weeks later he received orders to Marine Corps Headquarters, known as HQMC. He'd learned much in the last sixteen months, and was grateful for Hiram's help. Presently assigned to the Anti-Terrorism Division of the Operations Department at HQMC, his name was on the most recently published promotion list for lieutenant colonel, and he was slated to pin on his silver oak leaves sometime in the next thirty days. Those who had the power to assign command were meeting now, in the same building, and he hoped they would select him for a battalion of his own. Two staff jobs in a row were not to his liking, nor did he believe it was a good career move to refuse command if offered one. Hiram disagreed, pointing to the high profile of Lieutenant Colonel Oliver North, presently on staff at the NSC and considered by many to be a true "water walker" with general's stars in his future.

Mark had never served with North, but knew a little about him. In the spring of '72, he'd witnessed, then Captain, Oliver North put on a show like none he'd seen before or since. At the invitation of Captain Chuck Krulak, one of the Naval Academy company officers, North had come to help persuade the midshipmen that selecting the Marine Corps as their choice of service was the smart thing to do. The classes of '67, '68 and '69 had, for the first time in the Academy's history, failed to meet their quotas for Marine officers. Headquarters Marine Corps had made it known at the Academy that this trend was to be reversed. It was a daunting task, as the faces of too many young Marine officers were forever frozen in time on the Academy's Wall of

Honor. Youthful faces, shining bright with promise, had slogged their way into battle as Marine lieutenants…and never came home.

After the dinner, Captain North appeared on stage to the strains of music from the movie *Patton*. Decked out in his dress blues and medals, and sporting a rarely worn dress cape of navy blue with scarlet lining, he embodied everything noble about being a Marine. For forty-five minutes, without referring to notes, he paced the stage recanting tales of heroic deeds performed by Marines since the formation of the Corps. He whipped the crowd of midshipmen into heat by putting on the performance of a lifetime.

The following month, at service selection night, the Marines not only made their quota—they had a waiting list for the first time in years.

Ollie North was, no doubt, a contender. In Mark's mind, this was further reason to decline the NSC post. Why in the world would he want to be a brand new lieutenant colonel on the NSC staff junior to a Marine like Ollie North? Better, he thought, to command a battalion in the Fleet Marine Force.

The final reason to decline Hiram's assistance was the fact that he'd already influenced his present posting. Mark thanked him profusely for his interest in his career, but felt back-to-back assignments requested by a U.S. senator, who also happened to be his father-in-law, was as good as the kiss of death. Nobody likes a brownnose, and Mark had never had to kiss anyone's ass for a promotion. He had no interest in starting now. To avoid hard feelings, he told Hiram he'd give it some more thought. He was thinking about it now, and it was giving him a headache. He made Hiram swear to make no further calls on his behalf until the next command assignments were published. He prayed the slate would include his name so he wouldn't be coerced into accepting the White House position.

It was time to get back to work. Retrieving the report he'd been reading earlier, he became intrigued with the section detailing the available information on an assassin and advisor to numerous terrorist organizations in Europe and the Middle East. The assassin operated under ever-changing aliases and descriptions, thanks to his training in the art of disguise by a member of the Royal Academy of Performing Arts. According to a captured IRA operative, the instructor wound up floating in the river Thames in the summer of 1971. According to the report, which had been gleaned from debriefings of several terrorists captured by the English SAS and the Israeli Mossad, no description of the assassin was ever the same, and his undoctored appearance was a mystery. The code name under which he operated was "Cain."

Mark was mystified by the fact that men could grow from innocent boys to pursue careers of good, or evil. He wondered what events in this man's life could've made him choose to become one of the world's premier assassins. *Cain...the world's first murderer.* He thought to himself, *what an appropriate moniker for a hired killer.*

Washington, DC – 1986

Wood & Kemper's office was located at 701 Pennsylvania Avenue. Luke kicked back in his chair and peered from his window to the street below. Since the '84 New Years weekend in Hilton Head, his friend and mentor's words frequently crept into his thoughts. "If you hitch your horse to this guy's wagon," Dr. Randall had said, "by the time you're forty-five, you'll be making government policy from the White House." Only nine blocks away, the White House was just down this very street. For Luke it represented the Holy Grail of politics, as it did for most people in Washington. He wanted to make policy...not merely influence it. He'd made up his mind. Dr. Randall had picked a winner. He was ready to hitch up his horse and join Will Norton's team.

At their first meeting, Luke had been impressed with Governor Norton. He was quick minded, charming, and had the true gift of making whoever he was speaking to believe he was the only other person in the room. It didn't matter whether that person was a head of state, or was cleaning the head. In a word, he exuded sincerity. He had the ability to make his eyes well with tears on demand, and persuade the hardest of hearts that he not only understood their troubles, but also empathized on a deep personal level. As soon as he was out of that person's presence, he could turn off the empathy and shift gears without depressing the clutch.

When Luke first joined Wood & Kemper, he spent as much time as he could with Arthur Shields, one of the senior partners who was a legend in the world of political consulting. Shields had told him, "Luke, sincerity is the key to success. Once you can fake that, you have it made." Will Norton could fake it as well or better than anyone Luke had ever seen.

This was an art, but that wasn't what excited Luke about Norton's future. Will Norton had a priceless asset that few politicians possessed: an equal partner in the form of his wife. Sure, many politicians had the support of an ambitious spouse, who would campaign vigorously and do all the right things. Mallory Norton was different. She was, quite possibly, smarter than her husband, and he was plenty smart. She also had a clear vision for acquiring and wielding power. He had the charisma, and she was no-nonsense. Together, the two made the most formidable candidate he'd ever come across.

Luke's challenge was to move them from the minor leagues of a small southern governor's mansion to the premier residence in the world. He had no interest in playing starmaker for Will Norton as an independent consultant; Norton would require more time and attention than that. Luke was prepared to do whatever it took...as long as he got to go with them. He would insist that the Nortons adhere to the same philosophy: "Whatever It Takes." He had coined it as the insider's motto for the campaign long before he knew it had been their creed for years. In the next ten years, there would be ample opportunities for the people in and around the president to be forced to keep their WIT's. If they wanted to win, they would all do whatever it took...*every time it was required of them.*

Years ago, in New Orleans, Luke told Mark that when he found the guy that could relight the torch of Kennedy's Camelot, he would help him succeed. Will Norton was that man. It was time to grab for the brass ring. He picked up the phone and called the governor's office. In less than a minute, his call was put through. "Governor…this is Luke Reilly…Count me in."

Wood & Kemper would have his resignation in the morning.

Chapter Twenty-One
PICK OF THE LITTER

"It's gonna' take time…a whole lot a precious time.
It's gonna' take patience and time."

George Harrison

Newport, Rhode Island – 1990

Of all the places they'd been stationed, Becky thought Newport had to be the most beautiful. She had enjoyed living in California, but had spent the better part of her life in the East, and was glad to be back. New England offered four distinct changes of seasons and scenery.

Still a lieutenant colonel, Mark had just relinquished command of an infantry battalion on the West Coast, at Camp Pendleton. After the fine job he'd done, he received a set of well-deserved orders to the Naval War College in Rhode Island. Each year a select number of promising officers of Mark's grade and experience, are tapped to attend the senior most professional schools in the Defense Department. These schools are called War Colleges, and each branch of the military has such a school. To provide a broadened education to its senior officers, a cross-section from each service is sent to the various schools. Mark's superb record in the Marine Corps gave him exactly the background the Marines wanted to build upon. A tour with

231

fellow Marine, Army, and Air Force officers, along with a larger number of Navy officers, was the next right career move for preparing him for higher command.

This would be a shorter assignment than most. For the next year Mark would focus on the strategic and geopolitical nuances of national policy making, and the role of the U.S. military in carrying out these policies. He was privileged to be here, and had told Becky he planned to make the most of the opportunity by finishing at the top of his class.

This came as no surprise to her, as he'd done so at each school he had attended since the Academy. There were never any guarantees in the service, but finishing in one of the top three spots of professional schools always looked good to the promotion boards. Schools like the War College allowed for a brief respite from the family separations and demands of being a line officer in the Fleet Marine Force. That benefit aside, no assignments he'd had could surpass his three commands. Mark was born to lead troops, and had enjoyed these tours the most. As a second lieutenant, his first chance to command had been as a platoon commander. He'd enjoyed every minute of being a company commander, and he felt that no rank in the Corps was better than captain of Marines. It was a tremendous responsibility for a young man. His third command had been a battalion, and as a lieutenant colonel it had been every bit as challenging as he'd hoped. He hated having to give it up, but no command lasted forever. In the Marines it was either up or out, and Mark was in one of the up-phases of his career. After the year in school, here, he would most likely serve a stint on someone else's staff. With luck and the right sponsors at Headquarters Marine Corps, he might skip the staff job and be assigned command of a regiment or a Marine Expeditionary Unit.

The past five years had flown by in a hurry, and a lot had transpired. The most significant event, the sudden death of Mark's mother, had occurred while they'd been on the West Coast. On her way home from a Christmas party, Mary Quinn had been killed in a head-on collision with a drunk driver. The tragedy had deeply wounded the whole family, including Hiram and Allison Smith, who'd grown very fond of her. Just a month after her death, Mark and Becky's third child, Callie Quinn, had been born. They had planned on naming her Mary Kate, but changed her name in Mary Quinn's honor.

Becky was ecstatic about the Newport assignment. Mark's hours were regular. He wasn't on a ship, or overseas...and for the time being, no one was shooting at him. Life was good.

She busied herself with picking up Callie Quinn's toys while her daughter napped. It never ceased to amaze her that a four-year-old could single-handedly trash a room like the Tasmanian devil in a *Looney Tunes* cartoon. Though at times she was a handful, she was a beautiful little girl, and the apple of Mark's eye. The Lord had blessed them with wonderful children. Thankfully John Matthew and Ben were at school, which gave Becky the chance to catch her breath...at least until Callie Q's naptime ended.

She'd been cleaning the house in preparation for this evening's visitor. Luke was coming to town, and the plan was to have a drink at the house and a quick visit with his niece and nephews. Around 7:30 they were to head to dinner, leaving the children in the capable hands of their favorite babysitter, Emily. She was the next-door neighbors' daughter, and the children loved her more than any other sitter they'd ever had. Emily was a natural with children and had the charisma of a pied piper. Becky wished she could take her with them to their next duty station. Knowing her parents wouldn't give her up, she placated herself with the knowledge that Emily was now fourteen, was a knockout, and in another year would be so busy dating she'd be retired from babysitting for good. Becky smiled to herself at the realization she'd caught Emily at the prime of her babysitting career.

Lying down on the couch, she propped her feet up and tried to take a quick nap, hoping to take her mind off the fact that her stomach was churning in anticipation of this evening. No one could ever predict how a visit between her husband and his brother was likely to unfold. She'd never known two men who cared for each other more, yet could make each other furious at the drop of a hat. It was an emotional minefield she'd learned to deal with by running interference when she could…and running for cover when necessary.

The one thing you could say about Luke was that he had great passion for his work. Winning the Democratic Party's presidential nomination for Will Norton was his sole objective, and had been for the past three and a-half years. No one outside the South had any idea who the governor was just a few years ago. All that changed when Luke secured the party's invitation for him to speak at the 1988 Democratic Convention. He'd done a superb job, though most people thought he talked too long. It turned out to be the longest speech ever at either party's convention. Becky thought he projected a vibrant image, and certainly looked presidential in his own right. The other thing that impressed her was the fact that she agreed with almost everything he said. This was no small trick for a Democrat to score points so convincingly with a lifelong conservative, who happened to be the daughter of a Republican senator. She'd asked her father his thoughts, and he said Will Norton could quite possibly win the nomination, but the Democrats had no candidate that could give George Bush much trouble at election time.

Not long after she dropped off to sleep, she was awakened by the smell of secondhand cheddar cheese. Opening her eyes, she found Callie Quinn's face no more than four inches from her own. She was busy chewing a large mouthful of Goldfish crackers while holding the bag in one hand and feverishly digging in the bottom for more.

Becky glanced at her watch. The boys would be coming through the front door in a half hour, and would be hungry. She took Callie Quinn by the hand and said, "Why don't you come help Mom make the boys an after school snack?" The two walked hand in hand to the kitchen.

Sometimes she still missed the action of Capitol Hill, but she was happier raising her children than concerning herself with polls and elections. While she prepared a couple of peanut butter and jelly sandwiches, she prayed silently that tonight would go smoothly, and Luke would *go soon*.

★ ★ ★

By the grin on his face, it was apparent that Luke enjoyed seeing his niece and nephews. Though he could be a real pain in the ass to adults, he had a way with kids and dogs. The children were always happy to see him, for whenever he showed up it was a miniature version of Christmas. Like Santa Claus, Uncle Luke could always be counted on to deliver the toys.

Emily took Callie Quinn from Luke's lap and steered the boys to the kitchen to eat dinner. It was like herding cats, but she made it look easy. Becky wondered if Emily would take to being a mother with the same ease with which she handled other people's kids. Anyway you looked at it, she was going to be a prize catch for some lucky young man.

Luke smiled at Becky and said, "You've done a great job with those children, Becky."

"Thanks, Luke," she said. "Now I'd better see if I can work the same magic on my hair. I don't know about you guys, but I'm starving."

They watched her leave, then Mark asked, "Do you want another drink?"

"No, thanks," replied Luke. "I'll have a glass of wine with dinner." Both boys had significantly reduced their consumption of alcohol after the death of their mother at the hands of a drunk.

Mark pushed a tray of crackers and cheese across the coffee table toward Luke and asked, "So how long have you been in New Hampshire?"

Luke spread some bleu cheese on a cracker and answered, "A little less than a week. I've been testing the waters with the locals, and we got a pretty favorable response."

"You're sure of this guy?"

Luke made a gesture of exasperation. "Dammit, Mark, get a grip! Will Norton is a Democrat…and you're not. You won't like him no matter what I say." His voice began to rise as he continued to defend his candidate. "He cares more about social problems in America than he does about rattling sabers all over the world. He's young, he's smart, and he's going to shake up the fat cats of the world who've gotten rich during the Reagan and Bush years."

"Gee, Luke," Mark said with a hint of sarcasm. "Have you been reading Karl Marx again?"

Luke was about to fire back when Becky entered the room and said, "Okay, gentlemen, I'm ready for dinner." She was wearing a simple white dress with a matching sweater. She looked stunning, and her entry made both men forget what they'd been arguing about. Holding her purse clamped under her arm as she secured the back of her earring, she called out, "Emily?" She didn't answer, but instead, entered the living room with Callie Quinn on her hip and the boys following behind.

Luke gave them all big hugs and kissed Callie Q on the forehead. Then he looked at Mark and said, "Her eyes remind me of Mom's."

Mark nodded in silent agreement, and Becky breathed a low sigh of relief. Once again she'd diffused a ticking time bomb that looked as though it was about to go off. She had indigestion already, and she hadn't taken her first bite. Kissing the children goodnight, she said, "We'll be at The White Horse Tavern, Emily. I've left the phone number on the fridge, and we should be home by 10:30."

Emily said, "Have a good time." Ever the polite young lady, she looked at Luke and added, "Nice to meet *you*, Mr. Reilly."

They left through the garage. Becky's station wagon was closest to the kitchen door, and parked next to it, under a car cover, was Mark's '72 Corvette. Luke chuckled at the sight of it. "You planning to keep that thing forever?"

Mark said, "Why not? It's a classic now." He raised the garage door and they got in Mark's Jeep Wagoneer for the short ride to the restaurant. According to the owners of The White Horse Tavern, it is the oldest continuously operated tavern in the country. Of course you can travel all over New England and find a dozen places that make the same claim. At any rate, it was a wonderful place to eat, and Mark had been looking forward to it all day. Becky was less enthusiastic. She was looking far past dinner to Luke's departure in the morning.

At the dinner table, Becky took a gamble and asked Luke questions she'd never before asked about growing up in Atlanta with Mark and Matt. The strategy worked; it changed the subject from politics to family, and the rest of the evening was spent recounting adventures, great and small, undertaken by the Reilly boys.

This evening she learned a lot. Matthew had generally been a touchy subject to bring up, yet with the triplet's parents now dead he seemed a less sensitive topic than before. Luke would tell a story about him, and Mark would chime in with contradiction or amplification. It was obvious to her that both brothers had made observations of the same man through very different eyes. The resulting picture was of a brother quite different than the two sitting with her tonight. Matthew had been an enigma to her for all the years she and Mark had been married. Between the tales she'd been told by her husband and Luke's take on the same events, she was forming a picture in her own mind. She came to the conclusion that Matthew was a loner, forced to share the spotlight with siblings who looked just like him, but who consistently outperformed him. Capable in the classroom, but frequently too bored to put forth the necessary effort, he earned marginal grades. Aloof, and disinterested in making friends other than Mark, he liked to fight, and had no concern for the damage that might result from his anger. Unlike the rest of the family, his moral compass appeared to have no true north.

As the brothers spoke about Matthew, Becky's mind wandered to a book she recently read that panned the "self-esteem" movement of the past twenty years. As the psychologist-author had stated in his book, "You can compliment Johnny all day long about how hard he's trying to read, and how proud you are of his efforts, but at the end of the day...Johnny knows he still can't read." In his estimation, the friction between these two realities had the potential to spark deep-rooted violence in the underachiever with an inflated self-esteem. He concluded, "Gangs in America are led by, and prisons are full of, men with high self-esteem and no real accomplishments."

To her, the subject he was describing sounded much like Matthew Reilly as a young boy. As much as she disliked being around Luke, she thought she might have found herself even more uncomfortable around Matthew. The Lord worked in mysterious ways. Perhaps it had been a blessing that he'd been killed before she met Mark. Had she met him *and* Luke prior to meeting her husband, she'd have probably never given him a chance. She'd never known the boys' father, but had known Mary Quinn well. She found it discomforting to think that such a wonderful woman could have raised three sons in the same household and have them turn out so differently. It made her wonder if her own children would grow up to cause her grief, but believing that God had a plan for everyone, and no amount of worry on her part would change its outcome, she dismissed the thought.

When she returned her attention to the conversation, Mark was talking about his attendance at the Vietnam Memorial dedication in 1982; seeing, for the first time, Matt's name etched in the black granite wall. "It was rough," he told Luke, "like reliving the death of every guy there all over again. But oddly though, when I got to Matthew's name, it was different somehow. I can't say why, but it just seemed wrong that his name was there."

Luke made no reply, and didn't mention that he'd experienced a similar sensation in the past. To everyone's relief, the subject changed as their waiter arrived with the dessert cart. The rest of the evening was uneventful, and Luke begged off the invitation to stay overnight, saying he had an early flight from Providence in the morning. They dropped him at his hotel and said their goodbyes.

On the ride home, Becky said, "I hope I didn't upset you by bringing up Matthew this evening."

"Not at all, sweetheart. It felt good to bring him to life for a while. I've always thought the three of us were happy together as kids, but to hear Luke tell it, I guess he must've felt differently."

Becky looked at Mark in silent admiration as he drove her home. She had no illusions about the man she'd married. The Reilly boys had been identical strangers...as different as puppies in the pound. Becky had no doubt she'd gotten the pick of the litter.

Chapter Twenty-Two
A LINE IN THE SAND

"I gotta' find...my place in this world...my place in this world!"

Michael W. Smith

U.S. Central Command,
MacDill Air Force Base, Florida – November 1992

In the disembodied state every driver has experienced, Mark was in control of his car, but lost in his thoughts. With the top down on his Vette, he was wheeling his way in the Florida sunshine toward his office at U.S. Central Command. Two years can pass in a flash, and in that time the collective consciousness of the world can change.

In 1941, after the Japanese navy broke off their engagement at Pearl Harbor, Admiral Yamamoto was congratulated by his subordinates on his successful surprise attack. Somewhat less exuberant, his response was, "I fear we have awakened a sleeping giant."

America had been attacked because she was perceived as isolationist and weak. It is said that people who are ignorant of history are doomed to repeat it. Even after their victory in World War II, America in the 70s and 80s was still perceived by many of the world's despots to have no stomach for prolonged military action, even if justified. Vietnam, they believed, had taken the fighting spirit out of her people. In that way, America resembled the big guy in high school who looks imposing, and is afforded deference and respect based solely upon his size. Invariably this kid is confronted by a smaller, meaner one who appears on the scene and takes him down. To the shock of everyone who once feared the big kid, they realize he didn't even know how to fight because he'd never had to. Everyone had always left him alone.

On August 2nd, 1990, Iraq's President Saddam Hussein came to the same conclusion. He wanted his neighbors' oil fields, and thought he could take them like a schoolyard bully takes a weaker kid's lunch money. He was counting on the big kid to stand on the sidelines with his hands in his pockets and his eyes on the ground. It was a mistake. History indeed repeated itself, and as Yamamoto had learned a half-century before, the giant was awakened once more. Desert Shield was launched immediately to prevent Iraqi forces from grabbing the oil fields of Saudi Arabia. For the next five and a-half months, the Coalition forces assembled under the leadership of President George Bush engaged in the most massive buildup of combat troops since the Vietnam War. It had taken six years to reach a half million troops in Vietnam. It was done in less than nine months in the Persian Gulf.

On the 16th of January, at 7:00 p.m., the White House announced that "the liberation of Kuwait has begun under the name Operation Desert Storm."

Mark's wife, Becky, had written him that she was cleaning up the dinner dishes when the boys' TV program was interrupted with that announcement. The news caused her to drop a handful of plates on the floor. Prior to the commencement of ground hostilities on the 24th of February, the talking heads on television news programs had been predicting heavy casualties. There were even reports that the Pentagon had shipped in excess of a hundred thousand body bags to the Gulf.

Becky had no idea where Mark was, but upon graduating from the Naval War College, he'd been promoted to colonel and given command of one of the Marine regiments that was committed to the operation. All she'd known was that, once again, the bullets had begun to fly…and the one man in the world that mattered to her most was once again in harm's way for someone else's country.

Mark had known that she would be nervous and upset. All military spouses know they'll be separated from their loved ones many times, and their spouse will be in danger. Whenever the call to arms goes up, regardless of the Marine's rank, every spouse silently questions why their Marine has to go.

For the first time ever, Becky found herself in agreement with her brother-in-law, Luke. They both thought Mark might be pressing his luck as a combat Marine. He'd been wounded twice in his first Vietnam tour, and had flirted with death when he was left behind during the evacuation of Saigon in 1975. The bombing of the Marine barracks in Beirut resulted in another wounding, which could have left him permanently crippled. Now at the ripe old age of forty-two he was back in combat, leading a regiment comprised primarily of Marines half his age or younger. Cats were thought to have nine lives, but there was no such luck for Marines. One death was all each one had been issued.

Mark had assured them both that this war would be different and, as it turned out, he was right. For the first time in his military career, the generals had stood their ground with the politicians. They clarified the ground rules before the troops were committed, and they got the president's approval to conduct the war from the battlefield, rather than the White House. Generals Colin Powell and Norman Schwarzkopf had been young captains and majors in Vietnam. They understood what made sense and what didn't, and they got concessions their predecessors didn't have in Southeast Asia. The Gulf War wasn't reported by the media in the same way as Vietnam; reporters were kept at a distance and fed information, *after* the fact, in daily briefings. Video footage the brass wanted played was delivered *after* the engagement was concluded. The Defense Department was determined not to permit the media to demoralize the country, or the troops, before the mission could be completed. These generals also had something else they'd been denied in their youth—before the hostilities began, they had their country's permission to win.

The Gulf War was prosecuted more along the lines of traditional theater warfare. The objective was to win ground and hold it, rather than seize terrain and relinquish it in a matter of hours or days. There was a four-phase plan to waging this war: Phase I was a strategic air campaign, designed to knock out specific Iraqi resources, especially those that enabled the Iraqi commanders to communicate with their subordinates; Phase II was to be a short but very intense air campaign to establish complete air superiority in the region; Phase III would consist of attacks on specific Iraqi Army units and Hussein's Republican Guard troops; the final phase, Phase IV, would be a full-scale ground offensive supported by air and naval forces.

The Coalition countries had assembled so much air power in the region that the first three phases of the air war were conducted simultaneously. For a little more than five weeks, the Iraqi forces were subjected to an unparalleled number of air sorties.

When the ground conflict began, Mark found himself in a position he'd never before known. His mission was clear, his enemy identifiable, and there were few constraints imposed by higher authority. The Coalition forces, and in particular his Marines, were there to kill the enemy, free a sovereign country, and right a terrible wrong.

As it became apparent that Iraq's forces were being routed, Saddam Hussein resorted to acts of ecological terrorism. Oil pipelines were breached, permitting the free flow of crude oil into the waters of the Gulf. Refineries and oil fields were set ablaze, blanketing the Arabian sky with clouds of dense, black smoke. The amount of damage to the earth was devastating.

Mark had looked forward to kicking Hussein's army all the way to his palace steps, and being present as one of his men put a bullet through his heart. Short of this outcome, the man deserved to be captured and tried for high crimes against humanity. He was a megalomaniac that had acted like a spoiled child, throwing a temper tantrum when denied his way. Mark's Marines had performed splendidly, and his leadership had been exemplary. His poise on the battlefield did not go unnoticed by his superiors. Colonel Mark Reilly was a bona fide water walker with a general's star in his immediate future.

Exactly one hundred hours after the ground assault began, Kuwait was freed and a cease-fire declared at 0800 on the 27th. The only problem was that the Marines weren't standing on the palace steps, and Saddam Hussein wasn't in handcuffs or being zipped into a body bag. It left a bittersweet taste in Mark's mouth. In his mind, and the minds of most of the Marines, it was an incomplete victory, which fell far short of what everyone wanted.

As he drove along the Florida turnpike some twenty months later, he had concluded that the war's outcome was as it should be. Men should come away from war with something less than joy in their hearts. It shouldn't be something satisfying. During the War Between the States, upon seeing a federal charge repulsed at Fredericksburg, Robert E. Lee had said, "It is well that war is so terrible, or we should grow too fond of it." Saddam Hussein had drawn a line in the sand, and the rest of the world kicked his ass back across it. It didn't seem enough…but it would have to do.

Two years had passed in a flash, and much had changed. Who would've believed that George Bush, emerging victorious from the Gulf War with the highest job approval rating of his presidency, would lose the White House and Will Norton would be moving in this coming January? Bush had been poised to cruise to reelection…until the fateful day he uttered the phrase, "Read my lips…No new taxes!"

In the next budget negotiation, he'd been maneuvered into breaking his pledge. He had figuratively put a gun to his head, and Will Norton and Luke Reilly had been more than willing to pull the trigger. Mark had to hand it to Luke. When presented an opening, he'd gone for the throat. The entire tone of the presidential debate had changed from a question of character to a sole focus on the economy.

On the military front, much had changed, too. General Schwarzkopf had retired a national hero, and had become an unlikely celebrity. General Colin Powell was retiring, and most folks figured that in a few years he had a legitimate shot at the White House, or any political post he desired. Marine Corps General Joseph P. Hoar had taken over as commander-in-chief of the U.S. Central Command. He'd long been a champion of Mark Reilly, and had assisted his rise through the ranks. Once again, at the war's end, the general weighed in on his behalf.

As Mark approached the entrance gate to the base, the armed sentry snapped to attention and rendered a crisp salute. "Good morning, General Reilly," he said. "That Corvette sure is a looker, sir. Any chance you'd sell it to me when you're tired of it?"

"Not a chance in Hell, Sergeant," Mark replied with a smile. "I bought this car when you were still in diapers." He rubbed the chrome strip on the top of the door with affection and said, "I have only four things that money can't buy: my wife, my kids, my dog, and this car."

The sergeant smiled, waved the new brigadier general through, and admired the car until it was out of view. Mark swung it into a spot in front of the headquarters building that bore his name, then sat behind the wheel for a moment and concluded his ruminations about the war. The mission had been to liberate Kuwait, not to crush Saddam Hussein, yet he would never be happy that Hussein remained in power after all he'd done. He hoped that the decision to leave him alone wouldn't one day come back to haunt the world. Mark believed strongly in the phrase, "People ignorant of history are doomed to repeat it."

He left the top down, grabbed his briefcase from the passenger seat, and bounded up the stairs to the building. As he opened the front door he couldn't resist taking one last look over his shoulder at his car.

Washington, DC – December 1992

Luke hadn't anticipated a Christmas like this one since he'd been a kid. The present he'd visualized for years would be his in less than a month. William H. Norton was to be sworn in as president after the New Year. Luke was going to get the office in the White House he'd always dreamed of having.

As he looked back on the campaign, he realized how close the candidacy had come to being derailed. One accusation after another had been leveled against his man. Luke had performed like an explosive ordinance disposer, diffusing landmines on a daily basis. There had been accusations of marital infidelity, financial improprieties, and campaign irregularities. The fact that many were true only made Luke's job more difficult.

He'd learned a huge lesson in 1987, at the expense of presidential candidate Gary Hart of Colorado. Thankfully, Senator Hart hadn't been Luke's client when he made a colossal error that no one who aspires to be president can afford: Hart underestimated the press, and had the audacity to let them know he thought they were rubes.

There had been rumors that the senator was a player, and inclined to enjoy the company of women other than his wife. This was no novelty on Capitol Hill, and would've probably gone away had he not succumbed to arrogance and dared the press to follow him around. They did, and caught him with a stunning young blonde named Donna Rice...and the rest, as they say, is history. The picture of a smiling politician with a bikini-clad woman half his age sitting on his lap might have been forgivable had the name on the boat's transom not been visible in the photograph. "Monkey Business" was painted in large letters right below the smiling couple. It served as too poignant a caption for the press to look the other way.

Watergate was still a vivid memory, and the country wasn't interested in any more "monkey business" in the White House. Luke was of the opinion that the picture offended the sensibilities of a lot of female voters, and pissed off a lot of men who envied Hart the good time he was apparently having. He may have gotten the girl...but the public didn't have to condone it by awarding him the White House, too.

As the story gained momentum, Senator Hart was forced to play defense, and he didn't know how. It was the shortest presidential campaign ever, and the scandal eventually sent him packing to write his memoirs in Colorado. The joke all over Washington was that his book should be called, "Six Inches from the White House."

The priceless lesson from Gary Hart's misfortune proved invaluable to Luke in salvaging Will Norton's candidacy four years later. He would never allow his candidate to become defensive. He executed a three-pronged strategy that had worked like a charm: Phase I was to deny the charges and label the accuser a liar. Phase II was to stonewall on releasing information, whether requested or subpoenaed. Phase III was to attack the accuser and assassinate his or her reputation.

Luke knew his brother understood military strategy, but he wondered if Mark had any idea what a master strategist he had become in the political arena.

There were roadblocks, surely. In the sixties, the press had turned a blind eye to philandering politicians. In the seventies and eighties, the women's movement demanded that boorish behavior be severely punished. Even now, in the nineties, had Will Norton's problems belonged to a Republican candidate, he would've been tarred and feathered, then run out of New Hampshire on a rail. But the press had evolved in the past decade and a-half. It had been twelve years since a Democrat had occupied the White House. Norton was their best hope. His positions on everything from the economy, to abortion, to the military were in line with those of the Washington elites. Neither the press nor the feminists could afford to trash his chances.

Luke could barely contain his enthusiasm. Will Norton was going to be a great president. His wife, Mallory, was going to turn government policy on its head. He was going to help them both accomplish their dreams, and at the same time realize his own.

It wasn't John Kennedy's Camelot…but it was damned close.

Chapter Twenty-Three
THOSE ARE OUR PLANES

"Don't stop thinking about tomorrow…
…yesterday's gone…yesterday's gone."

Fleetwood Mac

Washington, DC – January 1993

Hiram Smith would've been there in person, but he had just come home from a lengthy battery of tests at Bethesda Naval Hospital, where he'd been put through the wringer. As he sat in the study of his Chevy Chase home, watching the inauguration of William Hamilton Norton, he was reminded that the only certainty in politics is its very uncertainty. He felt that he, along with the entire Republican Party, was guilty of underestimating the American electorate's capability of doing the unthinkable. George Bush had the highest job approval rating of his presidency at the end of the Gulf War, and with more than forty years of service to his country, was being sent back to Texas in favor of a self-absorbed, slick-talking Southern governor.

It was beyond comprehension. The man was a well-documented womanizer, and yet he had the support of the same liberal women's organizations that had earlier called for the heads of Bob Packwood and Clarence Thomas. He'd dodged the draft during the Vietnam War, and yet this endeared him to the country's youth. It defied logic.

The Republicans had run on the customary rhetoric central to presidential elections since George Washington's day: George Bush was a man of character…and Will Norton was not. The voters didn't buy it. Hiram was reminded of the old joke about the dog food company president who wanted to know why sales were so poor when his dog food had every essential vitamin and mineral a dog needed. The sales consultant put it in perspective for him when he said, "Yes, sir, it has all those things…*but the dogs won't eat it.*"

Luke Reilly had determined what the voters would, and wouldn't eat. With his genius for conducting and evaluating polls, he was delighted to let the Republicans hammer away at the character theme. He understood clearly what they didn't. In the 1990s, Americans from the heartland were eating up the character message. The American voter was another matter altogether. Those who were going to vote for character had two choices—George Bush, or the independent candidate, Ross Perot. The rest of the voters in 1992 could care less about character. They were voting their pocketbooks.

Hiram wondered if one day Will Norton would sit in that big chair in the Oval Office and become frightened that he was surrounded by hundreds of millions of people that didn't think character mattered. Somehow, he doubted he ever would.

Luke had kept the campaign focused on one theme throughout: the economy. He'd been absolutely right. The Democrats voted for Norton…and the Republicans fragmented. Some voted for Bush, some voted against him by casting a vote for Perot, and some just stayed home. The end result was a win for Will Norton without ever having obtained a majority of the vote.

Hiram poured another scotch as he listened to the chief justice of the Supreme Court administer the oath of office. He had to admit that Will Norton had a true gift, one that politicians the world over would kill to possess. The television camera loved him, and he skillfully used the inanimate cyclops to make the people love him too. Norton was a man of seductive charm, the consummate actor…not so much a deep believer in the things he said, but a deep believer in the image he wished to portray. For a man with so few personal character traits, once into character he could move the masses.

Thankfully, his inaugural address was briefer than most of his speeches. He touched on the myriad attributes of the greatest nation on earth. This of course was the same nation that—according to his earlier campaign speeches—had been on the verge of financial collapse. He addressed the working families who work ever harder for less, and those unfortunates who were unable to work at all. He touched on the devastating cost of health care, and the millions of poor children in our land.

As Hiram Smith listened, he was hearing the opening salvos from weapons that would be aimed his way throughout this administration. There were millions of poor people everywhere…panhandlers who Democrats and Republicans alike crossed the streets to avoid, or simply passed without notice. The plight of the poor was more emotionally compelling when the anonymous face of a poor adult became the pitiful face of a child. Becky had warned her father years earlier that this guy could inspire people. She'd found herself agreeing with much he said in his speeches, all the while knowing that his proposed solutions were as impractical as Solomon cutting the baby in two to please two mothers. Norton quoted Thomas Jefferson, and his belief that the preservation of the nation required "dramatic change" from time to time. Hiram Smith was a man who was suspicious of politicians with agendas full of dramatic change.

Hiram thought about what his son-in-law must be thinking. Mark despised Will Norton to the soles of his shoes. Two years earlier, when his brother Luke had first begun grooming Norton for president, Mark had known nothing about him. During the campaign, as the stories and accusations began to cause cracks in the dike, Mark strongly suggested that Luke distance himself from the man, warning that if only half the allegations were true, Will Norton was a walking time bomb that would destroy himself and everyone around him. Luke would have none of it, and in typical fashion had become vitriolic in his defense. He accused Mark of being jealous of the fact that, although he was a Marine general, he would technically outrank him, since he would have daily access to the ear of the nation's Commander-in-Chief.

Luke had never learned how to fight without going for the throat. Once again, he'd tried to swat a fly with a sledgehammer. As usual, it worked…but was hard on the furniture. Mark was pissed that his brother had reduced his genuine concern for his welfare to something as base as petty jealousy. Luke had always needed the approval of the powerful, and always seemed willing to pay whatever it cost. This time, Hiram thought, it had paid off mightily for Luke.

Hiram returned his attention to the television screen. The new president was shaking hands with the members of Congress from both sides of the aisle. Mallory Norton was standing next to Luke, and they were all looking and pointing into the clear Washington sky. The network switched to another camera, which zoomed in on the tight formation of the approaching Navy Blue Angels fighter jets. The camera panned back to the reviewing stand, where the Nortons were greeting their supporters. Hiram couldn't tell what Luke was saying to the new first lady, but the close-up camera made it easy to lip-read her response. Later, from a colleague who'd been standing next to them, he learned what the entire exchange had been. It seems that Luke had commented that "he'd prefer, never again, to see American warplanes in the sky."

The first lady had responded, "You're missing the point, Luke. Those are our planes now."

It was going to take more scotch than Hiram Smith had on hand to make him feel better about the next four years.

Chapter Twenty-Four
ANYTHING BUT CHINESE

"But it's all coming back to me now."

Celine Dion

The White House – 1996

Children are miserable creatures when they don't get what they're promised. Just ask any father who has ever told his children he'd take them to the zoo, and later reneged. A lot of grown-ups don't take disappointment any better, especially when it's a lifelong dream that's been shattered. Kids believe in fairytale endings, while adults put their faith in ideals. Luke's ideals had taken a pounding over the past four years, and he was feeling more than disillusioned...at the moment, he was lower than whale crap. He'd come to the realization he'd hitched his wagon to an illusion. Will Norton, the young visionary with the ability to dream big and the passion to act even bigger, was turning out to be a bad magic show made up of smoke and mirrors.

In 1987, during one of the vice presidential debates, Lloyd Bentson scored a knockout blow against his opponent, Dan Quayle, when Quayle compared his age and experience to that of President John Kennedy at the time he was elected. Senator Bentson looked across the stage and said, "Senator, I knew Jack Kennedy, I worked with him...and you sir, are no Jack Kennedy."

When Luke first met Will Norton, he believed he had the potential to bring back Camelot. It had all been an act. Will Norton was no Jack Kennedy, either. Luke had signed on with the Nortons to formulate and influence government policy. Instead, his political skills were being used to extricate the president and his wife from minefields, more often than not of their own creation. No sooner than he'd diffuse a potential landmine, one or both of them would make a promise to someone who'd leave several more strewn all over the White House grounds. In recent years, it seemed an increasing number of these people weren't even from the United States, but rather the other side of the Pacific Ocean.

Along with the potential problems they left for him to handle, they left behind substantial amounts of money. Questionable campaign contributions had been coming in to the Norton campaign and the Democratic National Committee since well before the first term. For this administration, there were only two givens about fundraising...it was to continue without end, and there were few, if any, prohibitions about where, or from whom, the money came. Everybody's money was the same color green.

Of late, Luke's job was to keep the media focused elsewhere. This wasn't all that difficult, for it was sympathetic to both the Democrats and the Nortons, and wasn't particularly fond of Republicans. Since 1994's change of congressional majority, there was no shortage of folks with an "R" after their name to demonize. The press was only too happy to focus their energies on the likes of Newt Gingrich and company. The questionable land deals and futures trading of a Democratic president and first lady didn't outrage the liberal media, but it was scandalous that a Republican speaker of the house should receive an advance of four and a-half million bucks for a book deal.

The fact was that many politicians from both parties had used their office for personal gain. Right now, however, there was a lot going on in the White House that couldn't pass the smell test. To Luke's relief, the public was absolutely ambivalent. The "Me Generation" of the sixties had come of age. As long as their 401-K's were growing and their economic futures were on the rise, the activities of their public officials were of little concern.

Luke was no prude. He understood as well as anyone that political machines run on dollars, not gasoline. He could hold his nose and look the other way while the Lincoln bedroom was sold to big donors from Hollywood, but he was troubled by the ease with which big-time contributors now opened doors to the Commerce Department and the intelligence community.

International bankers and overseas corporations, whose partners included the People's Republic of China, were receiving briefings and classified reports they had no business seeing. No one else in the administration seemed overly concerned that a man born in China, who once worked for a multibillion-dollar Indonesian conglomerate, was now an assistant secretary of commerce. This same Indonesian concern was a huge backer of both the Democratic Party, and Will Norton. To those investing hundreds of millions of dollars in countries like China and Vietnam, a heads-up on U.S. political positions was worth billions.

Much of what they were seeing had more than just commercial value. Missile guidance technology and manufacturing processes with military applications were among the files shared with the Chinese government through their front companies. If anyone seriously probed the situation, it could be construed as more than just bad judgment—it bore the earmarking of treason.

If treason seemed too harsh a word, it was clearly influence peddling in the form of selling sensitive information to a longtime adversary. Either way, it was a slippery slope on which the Nortons could easily lose their footing.

Indonesian investment bankers, Chinese Communists, huge domestic corporate donors, and sexual escapades with young women were a far cry from restoring confidence in public education, moving welfare recipients to the ranks of the employed, and providing affordable health care to every American. Greatness had all been within his grasp, yet Will Norton was squandering his chance to make a difference. Luke thought the past four years had yielded little meaningful change and, thus far, the second term resembled a house of cards waiting on a strong breeze.

In the middle of the first campaign, his brother, Mark, had tried to persuade him to dump Norton. The general avoided playing politics as much as a high-ranking officer could, but when he had to play, he was good at it. Luke had been so focused on his ambition to work in the White House that he'd become what folks in the South had always called a "Yellow dog Democrat." This phrase came from the South's old days, when there was no such thing as a two-party system. If you wanted to get elected, you were either a liberal Democrat or a conservative Democrat. No one in the South voted for a Republican. It was said the Democrats could run an old yellow dog against any Republican and the dog would win the seat.

Right now, Luke felt as though he was on the other end of Ole' Yeller's leash.

Mark thumbed through a copy of *The Washington Post* while he waited for Luke in the lobby of the Mayflower Hotel. Now wearing a pair of stars as a major general, he was serving at the Pentagon in a support role to the Joint Chiefs of Staff. His duties required him to give an occasional briefing before the president and the National Security Council. He longed for another command of his own, and the chance to put some distance between himself and the politicians…both military, and civilian. He'd spent the morning at a series of meetings at Headquarters Marine Corps, and the plan was for Becky to meet them, here, for dinner at eight.

Luke walked through the revolving door and fished through his overcoat pocket as he trotted down the stairs to the lobby. Finding what he'd been rummaging for, he peeled the wrapper from a roll of Maalox tablets and popped two in his mouth. He walked to the center of the lobby and flopped on the sofa opposite Mark.

"Tough day at the office?" Mark asked, folding his paper and laying it aside.

Luke just shook his head, implying that Mark wouldn't believe it if he told him. No words were uttered, but Luke's silence spoke volumes.

"You want to get a drink?" Mark asked.

"No," he said. "I want to get several drinks."

Mark said, "Fine with me. I'll buy your first one—then you can buy the rest. As of this morning, I'm unemployed."

Luke stopped chewing his Maalox and said, "Say that again…"

"I resigned this morning. There'll be a small ceremony in eight weeks, and I'll retire."

As they walked into the bar, Luke asked, "What prompted this decision? Were you passed over for promotion?"

"No," Mark replied. "I've actually been offered another star and command of the Third Marine Division, which has been my dream for years, but personal reasons make it impossible to take the assignment."

Luke didn't pry, figuring Mark would elaborate on those reasons when he was good and ready.

They ordered some beers and found a quiet table in the corner, away from everyone else. As they sat down, Mark asked, "Why don't you resign too? Maybe we could start a defense consulting practice here in town."

Luke smiled. The thought of being set free from his own rat race was appealing. "No," he said a moment later. "I think I'd better stay right where I am."

"You haven't had enough yet?" Mark asked. "You're just chomping Maalox by the roll for grins?"

"I won't deny that every day's a challenge," he said. "But I'm needed now more than ever." Luke grew impatient waiting for Mark to open up, so he said, "I've never known you to quit anything. What's going on?"

Leaning across the table so he could talk without being heard, Mark said, "I'm tired, Luke. I'm tired of my men being deployed too much, and I'm tired of asking my men to serve a president I can't stand. He's everything I detest in a man. He's self-serving, and he uses the military like a pissant South American dictator. If the heat's on him for anything, he whips up a little military op. Luke...he's increased the military's commitments every year he's been in office, while cutting military funding more and more each year. I've got Marines who've been deployed all but a few months of his entire presidency. The Navy has it even worse. Those poor bastards are at sea all the time. The number of ships and crews has been drastically reduced, yet we have carrier groups committed to operations all over the globe. God help the Navy line officer."

Luke was listening, but said nothing.

"Look at where we've been since he took office," Mark said, in the same quiet voice. "We've been in Haiti, Somalia, and now the Balkans...and there's no end in sight. We've never really left Saudi

Arabia and Kuwait. We've become the world's police force, and no one in the military knows how to be a cop except the MP's. I enlisted as a private, and I've been fortunate enough to wear two stars. Major general is enough."

"That's not enough for me," Luke said, all the more convinced something else had motivated his brother to resign.

"*What's* not enough for you?" Mark asked.

"That explanation you just gave isn't enough to make you throw in the towel," Luke said. "There has to be more to it than that."

There was no fooling Luke. Mark took a long pull on his beer bottle, then looked away. He was silent for what seemed like minutes. Then, very softly he said, "Becky's got cancer."

For a moment, Luke couldn't say anything, then he found the will to say, "Mark...I'm so sorry."

"I know," Mark said. "We're all sorry."

"How bad?"

"The doctors have given her six months to a year," Mark answered. He spun an ashtray on the table and kept his eyes riveted on it. Without looking up, he added, "There's no way I can take a new command and leave her to battle this on her own."

Luke asked, "Is there anything I can do for you two?"

"Not for us, but you can watch your own ass. I want you to stay alert whenever you're in public with the president. I'm not the only one in this country that can't stand the guy. If someone should ever try to take him out, make sure you aren't standing too close. They might miss and get you."

Luke laughed at the scenario…until he looked at Mark's face and realized he wasn't laughing with him. The topic unsettled him.

Thankfully, Becky stepped into the bar and made her way to the corner table, bringing the uneasy conversation to an end. Luke saw her first, and stood to take her coat. He embraced her warmly, and she knew from the hug that Mark had spilled the news. In all the years she'd known him, Luke had never hugged her like that. She looked in his eyes and saw something there she'd never seen before: sincere compassion. Perhaps there was hope for him yet.

Becky looked at Mark and could tell he was unhappy. She held his hand and could feel his aggravation melting away. He ordered her a drink, and they all sat and talked for a while.

Luke had paid the bill and was putting his American Express card back in his wallet when Becky said, "I'm in the mood for some Peking duck. What do you guys think?"

Luke was the first to answer. "I'll buy dinner if you let me pick the place."

Mark said, "That sounds like a deal. What do you have in mind?"

After the past few weeks of dismantling landmines from the Pacific Rim, Luke said, "Anything but Chinese."

Chapter Twenty-Five
UNSUNG HEROES

"These are the sweetest days of all."

Vanessa Williams

Stafford, Virginia – 1996

Mark called out Becky's name as he walked into the kitchen from his morning run. The house was still, and she didn't answer. Calling out again, he took the stairs two at a time. The bed was empty; she wasn't in the bathroom. His heart began to race and he ran back down the stairs. He checked the garage and found that her car was still there. Becky had been undergoing chemotherapy for her cancer, and it had a tendency to make her sick. He feared she'd had a bad episode while he was out running, and had called a neighbor for help.

He was on his way to the phone to call her cell phone when, out of the corner of his eye, he saw movement in the backyard. From the bay window, he saw Becky sitting outside, swinging in their porch swing. Taking a deep breath, he waited for his heartbeat to slow down and watched her from the kitchen window. She was still beautiful, even though she'd lost a lot of weight and her skin was sallow. She was holding their orange cat, Sailor. She'd thought it was great name, and laughed out loud when she told Mark she was going to call him that.

"Now when you're gone on deployments," she'd said, "I'll always have a sailor around."

At this moment, watching her doing something so profoundly normal, he loved her as much as the day they were married. She was dying, and it was killing him and the children to watch it happen.

He'd seen a lot of death during his career. Most had been violent. All had been swift. His father had passed without warning, and his mother had been snatched in the blink of an eye by a man who couldn't keep his car keys in his pocket after too many drinks. He'd never had to watch someone die slowly, and it hurt more than he could describe. Even so, Becky was handling her illness with courage and dignity.

He poured two cups of coffee and walked out on the back deck. Holding one high in the air he said, "Interested in some coffee?"

She smiled and said, "Sure...come join me in the swing."

He walked toward her, sidestepping their black Lab, Otis, lying prone in the morning sun. He handed Becky her coffee and sat down beside her. They swung for several minutes without speaking, then she said, "I've been admiring the flowers. When you stop worrying about the children's carpools and the rest of the chaos of family life, you can really see how beautiful each one is. I suppose it's the same with people. We spend so much time caught up in our own problems that we don't take time to see how beautiful each person is."

He shook his head in amazement. If it had been him sitting here battling cancer, he'd have been thinking how much he was going to miss being around. He would've selfishly focused on his own problems. Becky was of another stripe entirely. She was always thinking about others.

She was too good for him...and he didn't want to face the prospect of raising three children without her. He wasn't sure he could bear the loneliness. His hand began shaking involuntarily, and he spilled his coffee in his lap. Becky leaned closer and wrapped her arms around him. They embraced for a long time, and Mark buried his head in her shoulder. *What's up with this?* he thought. He'd seen things that would give Jack the Ripper nightmares...and here was his dying wife comforting him. Typical Becky.

She whispered in his ear, "Mark, I want to go somewhere before I'm too tired to enjoy it, and I want you to go, too."

"You name it, we'll go," he said. "Europe...Alaska...or would you like to go on a cruise?"

She said, "I want to go on a Walk to Emmaus." He had no idea where or what that was, so she explained it to him: "It's a three-day spiritual retreat that you'll attend with a group of men over a long weekend. The next week, I'll attend with the wives of the men from your retreat. There's one coming up in three weeks. Terri and Allan Connor have offered to sponsor us."

Prior to getting sick, if she'd asked him to go on a spiritual retreat, he'd have probably refused. Mark had been a practicing Catholic all his life, and he had exactly the kind of relationship with God that he wanted. God took care of the big stuff and the major problems...and he took care of the rest. He felt he had a strong faith that had gotten him through some very difficult times. He didn't need this...*but it was apparent that Becky did.*

He agreed without hesitation.

Allan Connor drove Mark to the camp where the Emmaus retreat was being held. They arrived around seven o'clock on Thursday evening, and had a light dinner in the kitchen. It was a chance for the men who were attending to get acquainted.

Mark looked around the room and immediately had second thoughts about having agreed to come. Most of the men were in their forties and fifties. There were a couple of guys in their sixties, and about half a dozen still in their thirties. He was trying to size them up, just as he'd done throughout his military career. At boot camp, the Naval Academy, and every advanced school he'd ever attended, he had sized up his competition before training began. Now, he was measuring himself against everyone here, and he had no doubts that if the weekend required any kind of competitive effort, he'd come out on top.

After dinner, it became apparent that about half the men at the camp were working as servers, and the other half were attending. The group met in a large conference room. Each man was asked to introduce himself to someone else and tell that man something interesting about himself. After a few minutes devoted to this task, they were asked to stand. Instead of introducing themselves, as Mark expected, they were asked to introduce the man they'd been talking to. It was a nice icebreaker, and smoothed the sharp edge of having been left for the weekend with a bunch of guys he didn't know. After hearing background stories of the other men, Mark felt somewhat better, as the men he'd been measuring earlier didn't seem to be the losers he first thought they were. Mark's interesting fact was that he was a triplet. This worked every time, because no matter where he went—unless Luke was in the room—he was bound to be the only triplet there.

They were assigned to tables of eight men for the rest of the weekend. The leader of the Walk gave them an idea of how the next three days would unfold, and asked that they suspend their expectations and just open their ears and hearts to what would take place. Later in the evening, they were asked to observe silence until the following morning's breakfast. It was a pleasant way to end an otherwise uneasy orientation.

There were about thirty men sleeping in his section of the open dormitory. In short order, the snorers began sawing logs. It bothered some, but for Mark it was reminiscent of barracks and tents he'd occupied for thirty years. He promptly fell asleep and slept like the dead.

The next two days were filled with talks, by lay people and clergy, on a variety of subjects. What was impressive was how much each speaker's words seemed to come from the heart. Talks on priorities, grace, study, and Christian action were subjects about which he'd never given much thought. He thought it amazing, however, that as each man spoke, it was as though he was speaking only to him.

The talk on grace seemed to move him the most. The concept was nothing new to him. He'd been the recipient of it many times. Becky was a gift of God's grace, as were his three children. The fact that he hadn't been killed in Vietnam and Beirut were gifts of grace, yet something about how the speaker framed his remarks grabbed him by the throat and wouldn't let him go. For the first time ever, he realized that he hadn't earned any of the grace God had sent his way. By the time the weekend was over, he'd clearly seen grace manifested in the unselfish servanthood of the Emmaus team members. Mark had never known so many masculine men who were, clearly, God's men as well.

Throughout the weekend, the lay leader recited the same prayer each day: "Lord, be with those who need this weekend the most, and with those who think they need it the least." Mark came not because he needed to, but solely because Becky had asked him to. By Sunday evening, he realized he had needed this more than he'd ever imagined. He'd always been a headstrong Christian, meaning that his concept of God was mostly intellectual. He knew who God was, and he believed in Him, yet during the seventy-two hour retreat, for the first time he had actually seen His face. He'd seen the Church in the actions of these fine men. He had unfairly judged them when he first saw them on Thursday evening…and he had overestimated himself. He had believed them to be weak, and that he was stronger and more squared away than any of them.

He'd been prepared for a competition, but had instead been humbled.

After hearing stories of struggle, challenge, despair, and ultimate triumph, he realized he was among as strong a group of men as he had ever known. The Marines awarded him medals for valor and faithful service throughout his distinguished career. Not one of these guys wore medals on his chest, yet each one had proven his valor in the face of life's challenges. They were unsung heroes, and he felt blessed to have been here. Once again, Becky had known him better than he knew himself.

Mark had been angry for many years, yet he could never put his finger on the reason. During this weekend, it was revealed to him. War had cheated him of his youth, and made him grow old much sooner than he should have. He'd been mad at God for thirty years, though unlike Luke, he'd never seen fit to take Him on hand to hand.

Knowing it was a battle he'd lose made him even angrier. He had questioned God's mercy every time he recalled holding PFC Nichols in his arms as his life poured into the Vietnamese dirt. After the massacre in Beirut, he was really at a loss for what God had in mind. Every soldier knows that one day he might die in battle for a worthy cause...but where was God's compassion when a suicide bomber slaughtered Marines as they lay sleeping?

And now there was Becky, the most precious gift he'd ever had. He had been furious with God for permitting her to die slowly, allowing cancer to ravage such a wonderful woman. This weekend made it clear she wasn't leaving him; she was going home to join God, where she ultimately belonged. Through His Holy Spirit, wiser men than he had helped him realize that everyone we love is only on loan…not a permanent gift. We hold their love and well-being in stewardship until God wants them back. For the first time since learning of Becky's illness, he realized that God had reserved a place for both of them in His magnificent home. They were simply due to arrive on different dates.

The weekend had been nothing short of a miracle. Through grace, God prepared him to let her go. He had made peace with Mark.

Becky had loved Mark from the moment she first laid eyes on him, standing in her apartment, holding a record album and humming along with the stereo. He'd become a wonderful husband and father. He had always been a man of faith…but not a man of God. It was a serious flaw in someone who, in every other respect, was a rock. She'd always wanted him to come to know Christ in his heart, not just in his head. When Allan's car pulled into the driveway, she could tell by the look on Mark's face that his faith had made the eighteen inch journey from his head to his heart. It appeared her prayers of the past seventeen years had been answered.

When her turn arrived the following Thursday, Mark kissed her goodbye and packed her off with Allan's wife, Terri. As she drove away, all he could think about was the simple little prayer he had heard so often the weekend before: "Lord, be with those who need this weekend the most, and those who think they need it the least."

He had no doubt she'd have a wonderful experience...but nowhere near as life-changing as his. Prior to last week, God had been like a famous celebrity, known only from a distance. God had always been in his life, yet had been no more than a casual acquaintance, rather than an intimate friend. Things were different now. The famous stranger had become the best friend he would ever know.

Becky's circumstances were different. She was going on a retreat with the God who'd been her best friend for years. She had been walking hand-in-hand with Him all her life.

She was one of the ones who needed it the least.

Chapter Twenty-Six
HONOR AMONG THIEVES

"Smiling faces...sometimes...pretend to be your friend."

The Undisputed Truth

Alexandria, Virginia 1996

Chimes rang as the elevator doors opened on the ground floor of the Inova Cancer Center. The man stepped out and slowly strolled the hospital corridor, reading the numbers on the doors until he found the room marked "121." He knocked lightly, then poked his head inside the partially opened door. Lying motionless was the gaunt figure of his once-robust friend.

He walked to the side of the bed and laid his hand on top of RB's. Startling from his sleep, the sick man opened his eyes to see who was in the room. Recognizing Raoul, he smiled and tried to sit up. "What brings you around an awful place like this?" he said.

Raoul helped him into a more comfortable position and propped some pillows under his head and back. "I heard an old warrior friend of mine was here," he said. "I thought I'd come see if the rumor was true."

"Much to my chagrin, it is. It's good to see you, Raoul. Thanks for coming."

"I'm sorry to see you like this, old friend. What are the doctors saying?"

"They're saying I should've died years ago," he answered. "Can you believe this? Three wars, and more tight scrapes than I can count, and I'm going down to cancer. To tell you the truth…I'd much rather have taken a bullet."

Raoul nodded in understanding, all the while wondering why RB hadn't elected that option. He knew that if *he* were facing a prolonged and painful death, he would strongly consider eating his pistol. There was no way he would endure what RB was going through.

As if he could read his thoughts, RB said, "You're wondering why I haven't blown my own head off, aren't you?"

Raoul nodded again. "That's exactly what I was thinking."

"Nuns," he replied.

With a raised eyebrow, Raoul indicated he didn't follow.

"Years and years of Catholic schooling by the nuns," he answered. "Suicide's a mortal sin. According to the nuns, it's an express ticket to eternal damnation."

Raoul laughed out loud. "I would think killing yourself would be just so much icing on the cake, as far as your sins are concerned. After eighty years of living like you have, I'd bet you've had a standing reservation in Hell for quite some time."

"Probably true, my friend. But, that's the beauty of a lingering illness. It gives a man the chance to confront his mortality and decide if he wants to repent."

"And do you?" Raoul asked.

"I'm giving it serious consideration. The Catholic chaplain has visited me every day. He says it's not too late for me. The problem is, absolution requires repentance, and repentance requires remorse. I'm damn well sorry for a lot of things I've done in my life, but there's a whole lot of people I've killed that needed killing. If I had it to do over…I'd kill most of 'em again."

Raoul listened with amusement, and smiled to himself. He figured he wouldn't be alone when *he* showed up in Hell. No matter how much time RB spent with the hospital's chaplain, he'd be there holding the door open for him.

"Close that door for a minute," RB said, bringing him out of his thoughts. "I want to tell you a story."

Raoul did as he was asked, pausing to watch an orderly wheel a gurney into the room next door. The woman on it had obviously been ill for some time, and looked like she wasn't long for this world. He could hear her family welcoming her back from surgery, even though she was still under anesthesia and was only semiconscious. *Hospitals are terribly depressing places*, he thought. Then he closed the door and took a seat in the chair by RB's bed.

"Before I check out," RB began, "there are some things about our friend Cain that I want you to know."

Raoul sat back and crossed his arms and legs. "I'm all ears."

RB squirmed in the bed to get more comfortable, and the movement seemed to cause him a great deal of pain. Raoul asked if he needed any help, but he just waved him off. When he regained his breath he continued his story:

"I've never told you how Cain and I first hooked up. We met in Thailand during the war. He was a sniper in the Marines, and I was still working for the CIA. While he was on R & R, we struck up a conversation in a bar. I tried to recruit him then and there, but he was skeptical." RB chuckled, although the effort cost him. "He told me to take a hike. He had two brothers who were serving there at the same time. One in the Marines, and one in the Air Force…"

RB proceeded to lay out the whole story, including who those two brothers were and the positions they held today. He was aware of one of them, and had often thought he bore a striking resemblance to Cain…although Cain varied his appearance so often, Raoul had never been certain exactly what the *real* Cain looked like.

"Something happened to him just a few weeks after we first met," RB continued, his mind clearly focused on that time. "His brother had been severely wounded, and Cain was told he wouldn't make it. The loss was too close to home, I guess. He snapped, big time. He'd been responsible for a lot of death, but, up to that point, he'd handled it all right. Hearing that his brother was dying sent him over the edge, as though he, too, was dying. From that day forward, I don't think he wanted to ever again be close to another living soul.

"That incident caused him to cut off ties with the world, and he became the loner we both know. To make a long story short, he contacted me through some guys at Phu Bai, and we arranged to pick him up. Before his last patrol, we planned to rendezvous at an LZ just inside Laos. He wasn't sure when he'd be able to get there, so we agreed to land a chopper there each night, at 2100, for three successive nights. He showed up the first night."

Raoul found the story intriguing, but couldn't figure out why a man on his deathbed would expend so much effort to recount it, at this late date. Again, RB must have read his thoughts: "Hang in here with me for a minute," he said. "Believe me...this story affects *you,* directly."

Raoul signaled he was still listening, and RB said, "He's planning to kill you."

Now the story was personal, and Raoul was, indeed, all ears. "What for?" he asked.

"Because he's preparing to retire. He's begun eliminating anyone who knows him well enough to identify him. I'm sure it didn't escape your notice that our old friend, the former director of the CIA, turned up drowned last week near his vacation home on the Wicomico River. The news said no foul play was suspected." Another faint smile crossed his face. Then he said, "My old Irish dad used to say, 'I don't mind them pissin' on my shoes...but it insults m' intelligence when they try to tell me it's only rainin'.' No foul play, my aching ass!"

Raoul chuckled. Even on his deathbed, RB was a colorful old pirate.

He droned on about the former spymaster's death. "Tell me how it is that a man who operated behind enemy lines in Nazi-occupied France, and who ran the whole shootin' match in Saigon, was stupid enough to go canoeing on a river being swept by storm winds." He glanced at Raoul, who nodded in understanding, then continued. "By the way, he didn't just go canoeing in a storm. He got up from his dinner table to go canoeing in a storm. An Agency friend of mine told me the food on the table was barely touched…sorta' like he got up from dinner to answer the door. I'll bet what little life I've got left that our friend Cain paid him a short visit."

"So what does Mr. Colby's death have to do with me?" Raoul asked.

"Colby knew him in Vietnam. I've been running Cain for years, and I've got just days, maybe weeks to live. You've been helping plan his jobs for the better part of the last two decades. I know the guy, and so do you. If he's planning on retiring, and I'm sure he is, he won't leave any loose ends. He'll wait until he completes a mission he feels is worthy of his talents, then he'll pull the plug and disappear for good."

"That mission may be on the horizon," Raoul said, nodding pensively. "I've been contacted by some powerful people in Indonesia. They sound interested in trimming some loose ends of their own."

"Hand me my shaving kit. I've got something I want you to have."

Raoul retrieved the kit from the bathroom and handed it to RB. He looked through it until he found a set of keys, clustered together on a small, unmarked metal ring. He handed the ring to Raoul and said, "Take the safe deposit box key from that ring. It opens a box at the Duke and Washington branch of First Virginia Bank. You're already authorized access to the box. There's a large manila envelope inside with your name on it. It contains information that might help you leverage Cain into leaving you alone. I'd planned to use it myself, but I won't need it now."

Raoul could only say, "Thanks, RB."

Again, as if reading his thoughts, RB just nodded.

Raoul thought about his upcoming meeting in Jakaarta. With the information RB had just shared, it troubled him to know that Cain was the only man for the job. He looked at RB and said, "We've all been friends for a long time. Cain has never given me any indication that he'd ever turn on his friends. I hate to rely upon honor among thieves, but I have a hard time imagining him turning on me. Why do you believe he would?"

"Because that's how he disappeared from Vietnam. He faked an ambush of his position and killed his partner. He carried the kid's severed head and hands all the way to the LZ in a haversack."

The line on the vital signs monitor went flat. At the same instant, an alarm buzzer sounded at the nurse's station, causing several nurses and a doctor to come running in a hurry. They passed the room where RB and Raoul were concluding their visit and burst through the door of room 123, directly next door.

Unlike the man in the next room, this woman's suffering was over. She'd fought the good fight, but had finally run out of strength.

Mark Reilly sat at her side, stroking Becky's head and holding her lifeless hand.

Chapter Twenty-Seven
GREETINGS FROM UNCLE SAM

"Come together...right now...over me."

The Beatles

Washington, DC – November 1996

Six months had passed since Becky's death, and Mark and the children had begun settling into new routines. They'd bought a home over the summer, just around the corner from Becky's parents. Allison was looking after the children, which made her feel needed and helped her deal with her own grief. To Mark, she'd been a Godsend, for he was overwhelmed by the needs of his three children. He wondered, often, how a man capable of leading thousands of Marines could be so over his head with two teenage sons and a ten-year-old daughter. Becky had always made it look simple, and he realized now that he'd never understood how tough her job had been.

The kids had been great, and had really pulled together in the last few months of their mother's life. They were continuing to get along, and were helping out around the house, which made a painful situation more bearable. Yet, like him, they still missed their mother every day.

Mark had joined his father-in-law's senate staff as advisor on military affairs. Since Hiram Smith was an influential member of the

Senate Armed Services Committee, it gave him a sense of doing something positive to obtain the funding the military so desperately needed. Even so, he missed the Corps. Retiring from the Marines hadn't been what he really wanted, but it had been the right decision. He'd never regret the last few months he had with Becky.

Mary Townsend stuck her head into Mark's office and said, "General...your brother Luke is on line three."

"Thanks, Mary." Lifting the receiver he said, "Hey Luke...what's up?"

"I need to see you. Soon. Are you free for lunch today, or dinner this evening?"

"I'm having dinner with the children tonight, but I could meet you for lunch in about an hour and a-half. Where do you want to go?"

"Can you meet me here at the White House?"

"Well let me see. I can eat at any old restaurant in Washington, or I can come to the White House for lunch. Uhm...I think I'll join you at the White House."

"Great!" Luke said, laughing. "I'll put your name on the pass list. They'll be expecting you at the gate at 12:45."

Mark hung up the phone and wondered what Luke had up his sleeve. He usually preferred to eat "outside the gates" so he could check out the pretty girls. Lunch at the White House meant he wanted some serious privacy. This should be interesting.

The White House security guard held up his hand, and Mark brought the Wagoneer to a stop. He rolled down his window and handed the guard his driver's license.

"Good afternoon, General. Do you need directions, or do you know where you're going?"

"I do need directions," Mark answered. "I've never been here before in my own car, and I don't know where to park."

The guard showed him where he could leave his car, and directed him to the right entrance. "By the time you enter the door, General, there will be someone there to escort you to your brother."

Mark thanked him, retrieved his driver's license and parked the car where he'd been told.

As he approached the side entrance to the White House, a Marine in dress blues executed a sharp salute. Mark was about to return it when he remembered that not only was he not in uniform, he was now a civilian. As he entered the building, he smiled at the sergeant and said, "Semper Fi, Marine."

A pretty young woman named Leticia Williams was coming down the hall at a brisk pace. "Excuse me, General, for not being here when you arrived. I got stuck on a call I couldn't gracefully bring to a close." She shook his hand, and stared just a little longer than was polite.

Mark couldn't help but notice, and she finally realized what she was doing. "Forgive me for staring, sir...It's just unusual to find grownup twins who still look so much alike."

Mark didn't correct the misconception that he and Luke were twins. After nearly thirty years, it was still awkward to explain that he was one of two living triplets. People always wanted to know what happened to the third one…until he told them that Matthew had been killed in Vietnam. After all this time, most people still wanted to change the subject at the mere mention of the place.

"If you'll follow me, General, I'll escort you to your brother."

"Lead on, young lady," he replied.

She led Mark to a small conference room just down the hall. Upon entering, he noticed the table was set for two, and Luke was reviewing some notes. Seeing his brother, Luke stood and gave him a quick embrace and a couple of pats on the back. He motioned for Mark to take a seat, and slid a fancy 5x7 inch card across the table. Printed on it were four entrees, three salads, and a choice of two soups. "Tell me what you want and I'll order it for you," he said.

Mark perused the menu for a moment, then, said, "I'll have the Caesar salad, the filet of sole, and the crab corn chowder."

"Good choices…I'll have the same." He picked up the phone, placed the order, and then poured Mark a glass of iced tea from a nearby pitcher. "If you want something stronger, I'll get it for you."

"No, thanks," Mark said. "I don't drink during the day. It makes me sleepy."

The pleasantries over with, Luke looked at his notes and said, "Mark…I need your help."

"Ask, and it's yours," he said. "What do you need?"

"I appreciate your willingness, but you need to hear my request before you agree so readily."

"Quit beating around the bush, Luke. Something's on your mind. Let's hear it."

Luke proceeded to tell him about the frequency of staff turnover that had taken place since the first term. This was one criticism of the administration that the press wasn't reluctant to make. In their view, there were too many people employed by the White House who were very young, and had too little experience. In short, there were too few *adults* in sensitive positions.

Luke was of the opinion that the media complained so much about this because their traditional friends and peers were no longer inside the gates. It required a whole new Rolodex to gain access to the White House, and many of the established media folks didn't want to expend the effort to cultivate "the kids" now inside.

Mark listened attentively, but still wondered where Luke was heading.

The food arrived, and Luke stopped talking until the dining room steward finished serving them and left the room. He had taken a mouthful of his salad and was glancing at his legal pad when Mark said, "Do you mind if I say a short blessing?"

Luke stopped in mid-bite and said, "Not at all…"

Mark asked a brief blessing on both the meal and the subject of their meeting. When he finished, he spooned his chowder to let it cool.

"Nice touch," Luke said. "Grace before meals isn't done around here much."

Mark just shrugged his shoulders as though that was no surprise.

Picking up where he'd been interrupted, Luke laid out the rest of the story. When he was finished, he looked at Mark and said, "The president would like for you to become his national security advisor."

Mark nearly choked on his soup. As soon as he recovered, he stared across the table and smiled. Finally finding the words, he said, "You've got to be kidding me."

"I'm serious as a heart attack."

"Why me, Luke? You know I can't stand the guy. I'm a Republican...*Hell*, I work for a Republican who's always been a thorn in Norton's side! There has to be any number of folks who'd do a fine job and be thrilled to work for him."

"There most certainly are," Luke said. "That's why he wants *you*. He knows you're no fan of his, but he respects you as a military man, and knows you'll shoot straight with him. There are far too many people inside the gates that tell him only what he wants to hear. That's been a big problem for a long while."

"If he *respects* me so highly, and *wants* me on the team...why isn't he here?"

"Because he knew if he asked, you'd say no. If I asked...he figured you might say yes."

Mark mulled over Luke's offer. It was certainly a position he'd never aspired to hold. He'd have to serve a man he fundamentally disagreed with on nearly everything. He wouldn't, by any means, be the first person to serve on a presidential staff of the opposition party. As national security advisor he would know, for the first time in his life, what was going through the minds of the president and the Joint Chiefs of Staff regarding the use of the nation's military. As he weighed the pros and cons, he knew, deep down, it was an offer he would regret taking...but it was also one he knew he would regret turning down.

It would be a terrific opportunity—if he just didn't despise the man so much. "I'd like to think this one over, Luke. Do I have your permission to discuss it with Hiram?"

"Of course," Luke said. "But please let him know it's of the highest confidentiality, at the moment."

"Understood."

They finished their lunch without any further discussion of the offer. Luke gave Mark a brief tour and showed him where he'd be working if he accepted the position. They walked to the doorway where he'd entered the building and said their goodbyes. Mark asked, "Luke...how do *you* feel about my coming to work here?"

"Not only does the president need you, Mark...*I* need you. As I'm sure you already know, politics has its fair share of people you can't completely trust. You and I won't agree on many things politically...but I know I can trust *you*. Right now, that means a lot to me."

"Thanks for lunch," Mark said. "I'll call you with my answer by tomorrow evening."

As Mark approached the door, it was opened by one Marine as the other one saluted. General Reilly smiled at them both. When Vietnam was going on, guys his age, including the current president of the United States, dreaded receiving notification from their draft board saying, "Greetings from Uncle Sam." Mark hadn't been drafted...he volunteered. Two hours ago, he'd have bet everything he owned that he'd never be drafted into serving on Will Norton's staff.

Yet now, as he looked at these two fine young Marines, guarding the very man who'd called in favors to avoid the draft, stating in writing that he *loathed* the military, he knew in his heart that he couldn't refuse. They deserved someone who would look after them, and ensure their security. As far as he was concerned, these men represented the best of the nation.

National Security Advisor. Mark owed Hiram the courtesy of discussing his decision...but he knew in his heart it had already been made.

Chapter Twenty-Eight
FOX IN THE HENHOUSE

"We're lost in a masquerade."

Leon Russell

Chevy Chase, Maryland – November 1996

Mark cleaned up the stove while Callie Quinn and Ben loaded the dishwasher. He had made spaghetti for dinner, and the kitchen looked like someone had offered a human sacrifice in it: Sauce was all over the tile backsplash, and there were noodles stuck in the colander and in the pot. It was a mess, but everyone had enjoyed the meal.

Spaghetti night had always been more than just a weekly dinner…it had been Mark's way of giving Becky a night off. The kids joined in the act as they grew older, and their role was to keep their mom out of the kitchen from start to finish. Tonight was the first spaghetti night they'd had since Becky died. Cooking the meal and cleaning up afterwards brought back pleasant memories. The fact that they could smile about it meant they were all on the mend.

John Matthew was standing at the kitchen counter, pulling his history book from his book-bag and preparing to do his homework. The other two kids were heading for the stairs when Mark called for them to come back. Sighs of exasperation could be heard from the stairwell; Callie Quinn and Ben figured their dad had a few more chores for them.

Mark said, "I need to talk with all three of you for a minute."

John Matthew swiveled in his chair and leaned on the counter. Ben pulled up a stool next to his brother, and Callie Quinn took a seat at the kitchen table. Ben said, "What's up, Dad?"

"I had lunch with your Uncle Luke today. He's under a lot of pressure at the White House, and he asked me if I'd give him a hand. Upon his recommendation, the president has asked me to become his national security advisor."

John Matthew's eyes grew wide. "What's up with that?"

Ben said, "Dad, I've always heard you say you didn't like the president. How can you work for a guy you can't stand?"

"Good question, son. The answer is…I don't really know. I don't like the man who is the president, but right now, he's the guy in the Oval Office. It's like…" He paused a moment, looking for the right words "…the office of the presidency is something that'll always be bigger than the man—or one day, the woman who holds it. I have to decide if I can set aside my disdain for the *man*, and loyally serve the *president*."

Callie Quinn didn't understand anything her dad was talking about, but she knew it was important, and she was glad he included her in the discussion. When their mother had gotten sick, both her mom and dad had told her brothers, and her, what was going to happen. Big decisions in their family weren't made in secret, and then dumped on the kids. She was only ten, but she knew her dad was asking their permission to take the job. "Daddy," she said, "who needs you more…the president, or Granddaddy?"

"Well, sweetheart, I'd rather work with your grandfather…but I believe I'm needed more by the president."

"Then that's who you should work for," she said.

Both boys looked at Callie Quinn in a mild state of shock. Wisdom sometimes springs unexpectedly from the mouths of babes. In one sentence, she'd boiled an important decision down to its essence.

Their dad was rendered speechless. He finally smiled and walked over to give her a hug. The boys nodded in agreement, and the family part of the decision was made.

"I need to go over to Granddaddy's house and visit with him for awhile. You guys finish your homework. Callie Q…brush your teeth and be in the bed by 8:30."

She said, "Okay, Dad."

Mark grabbed his coat and his keys and headed to the garage. After he cranked the Wagoneer, he turned off the radio, *Then that's who you should work for* still echoing in his head. Ten years old, and she had the instincts of her mother. Becky would've been proud of her tonight.

Hiram swirled the ice in his glass of scotch, and took a moment to collect his thoughts before replying to Mark's news. He looked in his eyes and saw the same resolve he'd seen, in this very room, the night Mark told him he was going to marry Becky…with or without his blessing.

"You have to know this is a bad move, don't you?" he began. "The political dumpster, not to mention several prisons, is strewn with former friends and associates of Will Norton. He uses people up, then discards them when their usefulness is over. A few years ago, you tried to warn Luke of the very same thing. Dammit Mark, you're a respected former major general with a future so bright you need sunglasses! You're a bona fide war hero as well. If you play your cards right, my senate seat is yours for the asking when I step down. Why in Hell would a man with your integrity willingly walk into that viper's nest?"

"Because I'm needed there, Hiram," Mark replied. He told him what Callie Q had said just an hour before.

Hiram smiled, then a scowl quickly crossed his face. He was proud of his granddaughter's sense of civic duty, but he was concerned the successor he'd been grooming for his senate seat might wind up as the captain the administration might order to go down with the sinking ship. He cautioned him further: "Once upon a time, you know, Ollie North was needed there, too. Promise me one thing, son."

"What's that?"

"Confine yourself to national security matters only. Stay out of the stuff that's pure politics. Leave that crap to Luke. Maintain a wide berth from the Democratic Party advisors, the White House staff, and the money raisers. *Keep very far away from the money raisers.*"

"I will."

"And Mark...keep your brother at a distance, too. He's been the lead pit bull for the Nortons for a long time. If he's ever viewed as a liability rather than an asset, they'll put him down just like the mean dog he's been."

"I'll watch my ass, Hiram."

"You'd better. Where you're going, I can't watch it for you."

One week later, Mark passed through the White House gates. This time he knew exactly where he was to go. He pulled into the parking space marked with his name and title: "Mark Reilly, National Security Advisor."

When he walked into his office, he was greeted by a sharp-looking Marine major named Tim McGuire. He brought the general a cup of coffee, prepared exactly the way he liked it. Along with it he presented him with an overview of matters of importance to the National Security Council, as well as hot spots the staff was keeping their eyes on. It was just what he would've expected, and he was impressed with his new assistant.

Mark thanked him for the information and asked him to return in two hours to answer questions he felt certain he'd have. He posed his first to the major as he was leaving his office: "Major McGuire," he said.

The major turned and said, "Sir?"

"How did you know how I take my coffee?"

The major smiled. "General, I'd be a pretty poor aide to the national security advisor if I waited for him to tell me something as easy to find out as that. I called a mutual friend of ours—Sergeant Major Jansen—and asked a few heads-up questions."

"And what else did the good sergeant major tell you about me?" Mark asked, allowing a slight grin to cross his face.

"He told me to make sure I kept my mouth shut and didn't smoke in a foxhole if you were anywhere in the area, sir. He said the only time it was okay to smoke around the general was if I happened to be on fire."

Mark shook his head and said, "Dismissed, Major." Tim McGuire was smart, quick...and had a good sense of humor. He would do just fine.

The National Security Council, or NSC, was established shortly after the end of World War II to advise the president on national security and foreign policy issues. After reorganization in 1949, it was placed under control of the executive office of the president, who chairs the council. The NSC is comprised of the vice president, secretary of state, the secretaries of defense and the treasury, and the national security advisor. The chairman of the Joint Chiefs of Staff is the statutory military advisor, and the CIA director advises the president on intelligence matters. To say a meeting of the National

Security Council is filled with hard-charging personalities is a massive understatement. It takes an enormous room to contain all the egos, and the members guard their respective turf like Dobermans in a junkyard.

The president introduced Mark to the other members, many of whom he already knew. With a few perfunctory presidential remarks from Will Norton, Mark's first NSC meeting was underway. He listened a lot, and had little to say. The Marine Corps had taught him that it was better to be quiet for the first several days at a new command. There would be ample time to formulate positions and decide which battles were worth fighting and which ones to avoid.

As he sat quietly, observing the others at the table, he found himself making swift judgments about the members of the council. There were two in the room, in addition to the president, about whom he felt he should be wary. They were the kind of men who held personal agendas close to the vest, and they talked for the sheer joy of hearing their own voices. He thought of Ben Franklin's comment, "It's better to remain silent and be thought a fool, than to open one's mouth and remove all doubt."

One hour and fifteen minutes after the meeting began, Mark knew no more about the nation's security than he'd known when he entered the room. He had learned a lot, however, about the people with whom he'd be working. The president adjourned the meeting and the members began milling about the room, some speaking loudly, others in hushed tones. The president put his hand on Mark's shoulder and asked him if he'd accompany him to the Oval Office.

Will Norton, in person, was a surprise. He was engaging and warm, with a terrific sense of humor. There seemed to be more substance to the man than he originally thought. Over the years, Mark had known many politicians, and learned that even those with whom he disagreed vehemently had one common trait...they were all charming people. If they weren't, the voters would never have elected them.

The president was a *thoroughly* charming man. As they walked the corridors of the White House, Mark experienced a queasy feeling. At first he couldn't put his finger on it, and then the word he was reaching for entered his mind...majesty.

Walking with the president, within the walls of the White House, was a heady experience. It had nothing to do with the man, and everything to do with the majesty of the presidency. Mark couldn't figure out why such an aura would cause uneasiness in his stomach, yet it did, and alarm bells began clanging in his head. The warning bells receded as another word came to mind...seduction. Majesty, power, fame, and prestige were all seductive emotions. They could make a man feel more special than he had any right to feel.

Therein was the *Big Lie*...the belief that because of one's position the rules that applied to ordinary men were indefinitely suspended. There was an expectation in many of the people he'd met in this White House that the rules existed for everybody but them: that the privileged were above the law.

In the best of times, this was an easy place to get into trouble. With the allegations and rumors surrounding this president, it was a more dangerous place than ever. Add to that the fact that those who worked here didn't want anything to bring it to an end, and it was easy to see why being a counselor to the president was a tough position. Life in the White House was temporary, but the seduction made one believe it would last forever. No wonder no one in ancient Rome had had the guts to tell Nero he wasn't wearing any clothes.

Chapter Twenty-Nine

BAD DOG

"You ain't never caught a rabbit and you ain't no friend of mine."

Elvis Presley

The White House – 1997

Will Norton broke fresh ground in 1993 when he arranged for his wife, Mallory, to have an office and staff of her own in the West Wing of the White House. No first lady before had occupied such a high profile in her husband's administration. Her first assignment was the complete overhaul of the country's healthcare system.

The Nortons had come to Washington with the impression that the White House and the U.S. Congress were just larger versions of the governor's mansion and state house they'd known inside and out. Things worked differently here, and they learned in a hurry that revamping something as large as the healthcare system wasn't going to happen by holding some closed-door meetings, railroading a bill through Congress, and informing the public after the fact.

The healthcare industry represented nearly seventeen percent of the country's gross national product. That was a lot of sacred cows grazing in pastures throughout the country. Rather than be led placidly to the slaughterhouse, the herd had stampeded. The result was an overturned chuck wagon and a lot of bloody cowboys. In her role as trail boss, the first lady had been severely trampled.

There were a lot of things about Washington that the Nortons and their staff didn't know. Like everyone else who'd ever tried to take on this town, they learned. Some lessons were learned painfully, and some were learned with relative ease. The key was to learn quickly.

An administration only had two years to learn the ropes. At that point, a great deal of focus would shift toward getting reelected. Failure to do that meant having too little time to leave a lasting legacy. It was in the second term that policy strides could be made. Policy was the focus of every second term, since presidents were limited to only two, making further campaigning unnecessary.

Even so, there'd never been a presidency quite like the Nortons. The country had only elected Will, but Mallory was every bit his partner. *He* couldn't run again…but *she* sure as hell could. Much of the first four years had been devoted to grooming her to be a viable candidate to succeed her husband. The plan was eight years for him, and eight years for her. Franklin Roosevelt's twelve-year presidency had left its mark all over the past fifty years. If they successfully executed a Norton tag team presidency, they could count on more than a legacy—with sixteen years, they could change the world.

Once again, the concept had been borrowed from the Kennedy family. Joseph Kennedy had planned to run for president himself. A number of things transpired to make that impossible, so he mapped out a plan for his sons. Joe Junior was the oldest, and the original plan earmarked the White House for him. His death in World War II put an end to that dream. John was next in line, and old Joe poured his considerable wealth and influence into making him first a U.S. senator, and then the president.

The overall plan was to have sons John, Bobby, and Teddy serve two terms each, with the other two out-of-office brothers serving key positions in each administration. Had it not been for the assassinations of John and Bobby, and the poor driving skills of Teddy, it was a viable scenario. The Kennedy Dynasty...twenty-four years at the helm of America's political ship. It would've been the closest thing to a royal family this country had seen since the days of King George.

Mallory Norton was determined to accomplish what Joe Kennedy had been unable to do. That was the subject of today's meeting. In attendance were two of her husband's key political advisors, two of her own, and of course Luke Reilly, who'd been with them since the beginning.

The discussion revolved around recent focus group polling, conducted to determine if the country was ready to elect a woman president, and more to the point, *this woman* in particular. As expected, the data indicated she could carry the states along the West Coast, New York, a lot of New England, and the heavily unionized states in the upper Midwest. The rest of the country would most likely tell her, and her husband, to take a jump off a high pier. The good news was the population of the U.S. is heavy in the states she could carry. The bad news was that the Electoral College, not the people at large, actually elects the president.

The founding fathers, in all their divine inspiration, had seen fit to assure that the states that made up the federal government had an equal voice in selecting the leader of the republic. Were it not for the Electoral College, the tiny state of Rhode Island would forever be outvoted by the likes of California or Texas. If the system permitted only the popular vote to elect the president, the ten most populated states in the country could consistently render voiceless the population of the other forty states. The conservatives in the heartland weren't anxious to have Mallory Norton succeed her husband. The discussion was heated as strategies were debated for securing enough electoral votes to win.

Luke had a friend at the Gallup Organization who was conducting an independent poll about a number of female politicians, and their chances to win higher office. It was certain that, although not an elected official, Mallory's name would be on the list. Luke leaned over to her and suggested, quietly, that he give his friend a call while the others continued their discussion. She nodded in agreement and whispered for Luke to use the phone in her private office, then asked if he would retrieve a folder she needed from her desk and bring it to her when he returned.

"Certainly, Mallory," Luke quietly responded. "Where is it?"

"It's on the center of my desk, directly in front of the computer monitor. It's in a red folder labeled 'Personal and Confidential.'" She touched his arm and added, "Thanks, Luke."

He rose from his chair and walked through the door to Mallory's office, closing it quietly behind him. The door to her secretary's office was already closed. He took a seat behind Mallory's desk and dialed his friend at Gallup. The phone was answered on the second ring. With little enthusiasm in her voice, the receptionist said, "Good morning...Gallup Poll News Service."

"This is Luke Reilly at the White House...Phil Sims, please."

Changing her mood on a dime, she said, "Thank you sir, I'll ring his office."

Those three simple words, "the White House," had a way of making people hop who were otherwise just plodding through their day.

After three rings, a recording of Phil's voice asked the caller to leave a message. Luke complied, stated the time, and asked him to call him back in about two hours. As he picked up the file Mallory had asked for, he brushed the computer mouse on the top of her desk, causing the blank screen to burst into life. It wasn't his intention to nose around the first lady's computer files, but one's own name in a document stands out like an elephant in the parlor. This is especially true when the subject line of the document has that name in bold type.

The memo was one Mallory was preparing for discussion with the president. Luke could quickly tell his performance was the subject, and that she was questioning his continued value to the administration. To say the least, he was stunned. He'd borne the brunt of both her anger and the president's on more than a couple of occasions, but in the end, he believed all had been smoothed over. The tone of this report indicated she was plenty pissed off, and had been stewing about it for a while. He knew better than to sit here reading her computer screen, so he clicked the mouse and printed a hard copy, then tucked it in his portfolio and stood to leave the room.

He took two steps toward the door before remembering to grab the red folder she'd asked him to get. He wasn't sure why, but he was already in the doghouse with the first lady. It wouldn't improve matters to return to the meeting without the file she'd requested.

As he walked to the door, he thought about Hannibal, the old German shepherd dog that had lived down the street when he was a kid. Old man Sanderson would beat that dog unmercifully with a newspaper, then turn around and try to pet him on the head. From the look in Hannibal's eyes, Luke had always thought he was waiting for the old man to get so infirmed that he could take him. What the dog didn't know was that he was aging seven times faster than the old man. By the time Sanderson was too old to hit, Hannibal was much too old to bite.

After he handed her the file, she offered a sincere smile and said, "Thanks, Luke." He could feel the sting of the rolled-up newspaper as he returned to his chair.

Just a few yards down the hall, Mark scanned through his personal address book and found the number he needed. He dialed the phone and waited for an answer. A woman with a pleasant voice said, "Hello."

"Hey, Maureen, this is Mark Reilly. Is the sergeant major around?"

"Yes he is, General. He's in the garage. Let me get him for you."

Mark could hear her walk to the door to call Don's name. He heard her footsteps as she returned and picked up the phone. There was an awkward silence as she paused to collect her thoughts. He knew she wanted to say she was sorry about Becky. She wanted to ask how he and the children were doing. She wanted to let him know she cared. Mark spoke up and let her off the hook. "Maureen?"

His voice snapped her back to the here and now. "Yes, General. I'm still here."

Putting her mind at ease, he said, "We're all doing fine."

She breathed a sigh of relief. "I'm so glad to hear it, General. I just didn't know how to ask you that."

"I know," he said. "It's the love and support of people like you and Don that help us all hang in there. It's been hard, but we're adjusting. I hope to see you soon."

"Me, too," she responded. "Here's Don."

With a heavy dose of sarcasm, the sergeant major said, "Good afternoon, General. How're things in the *Big House*?"

"It's the White House, Sergeant Major, not the Big House," Mark retorted.

"Yes, sir. That's what I meant to say. Of course, when I read the newspapers, I sometimes confuse the two."

"Same ole sarcastic bastard, aren't you?"

"Humor keeps me young, sir." Then he asked, "Things treating you okay?"

"Life's getting better," he answered. "How's retirement treating you?"

"I'm bored shitless, sir," he replied. "Retirement is for old farts."

Mark was happy to hear that his old friend might be interested in having a little less time for golf and fishing. Don Jansen was the kind of man one could always rely on when the chips were down. Flyers called this kind of ally a "wingman." Infantry grunts like the general and the sergeant major didn't have a wingman. The guy they relied on was another set of eyes to cover your back. Mark said, "If you could use some excitement...I could really use your help."

"When and where, General?"

"Can you meet me at my home at...say, 2100 tonight?"

"I'll be there, sir. And, sir? Thanks for the call."

The line went dead.

Mark hit the end-button on his cellular phone and slipped it into the holder attached to his belt. He hadn't lied to Maureen. By no means were he and the children over the loss of Becky, but they were adjusting to her absence. He'd always thought the term "getting over" a loved one was a stupid choice of words. People are too important to "get over." You can get over losing a home, a car, or even losing a job, but people are an entirely different matter. A person's body has a limited life, but the same person's soul lives through eternity. There was no reason to get over Becky. She was with him always.

Mark had an able assistant in Tim McGuire, but he was young, and he was an active duty Marine major. There were things he might want to delve into that he would not ask the young major to do. He thought about Ollie North, following the orders of Mark's predecessors, issued from this very room. In the 80s, they'd placed him in some indefensible positions. He had no intention of doing that to Major McGuire.

Tonight he planned to ask Don Jansen to come to work for him. They had worked together many times over the years, and they had a sixth sense between them that, without requiring words, frequently allowed each to know what the other was thinking.

In this White House, that could be a real asset.

As soon as the strategy meeting ended, Luke hurried to his office and asked his assistant to see that he wasn't disturbed for thirty minutes. He closed his door and plopped into his chair to read Mallory's report.

It was a summary of everything he'd ever done to make her angry. All the infractions listed had been things for which he'd thought he'd been forgiven. The report told another story. Mallory, it seemed, was capable of *forgiving*…but, apparently, was incapable of *forgetting*.

He remembered every incident, and believed most were trivial— unless one wanted to use their cumulative weight to bury the transgressor. There were a couple of altercations where he'd crossed an invisible line, and the first lady had shoved his positions right down his throat. He sat there reliving the one that had been most awkward and painful:

It had been early in '94, and a number of staff members had been sitting around discussing the latest Norton scandal, and its likely consequences. There were allegations that they had been up to their ears in the failure of one of their state savings and loans during Will's term as governor, and that they'd personally profited from it, along with their investment in a failed real estate development.

It was apparent at the time that not just Republicans but also influential Democrats were calling for an investigation by a special council. As usual, the Nortons had denied any wrongdoing, labeled the allegations partisan attacks, and stonewalled on providing information. The tactic had worked successfully with the press for years, but, as healthcare reform should've taught them all, Capitol Hill was a different ballpark.

When the likes of well-respected Democrats like Daniel Patrick Moynihan and Bob Kerrey began calling for an investigation, it was a sure bet there was going to be one. Luke had been making the point to the others in the room that the White House should go ahead and ask for an independent counsel to look into the matter. Even now, he could still feel grinding in the pit of his stomach as he recalled everyone that had been agreeing with him, saying, "Yeah, yeah…that's what we should do…" becoming silent as a tomb. It was the same sick feeling he'd had when he was twelve, and his mother had walked in as he and his brothers were talking about sex.

That day, he could tell by the looks on his brothers' faces that his mother was standing right behind him. In the White House, thirty-five years later, the looks on the faces of the staff told him that it wasn't his mother, but Mallory Norton who was standing behind him in the doorway.

Since he'd been the last one talking, he thought it only fair to tell her about their discussion, and what he had recommended. "I think we should go ahead and ask for the special counsel ourselves, instead of looking defensive and waiting to have it forced upon us by Congress," he had said.

The volcanic eruption of Mount St. Helen's had been only slightly more violent than hers. She jumped down his throat with a vitriolic personal attack, unlike anything to which he'd ever been exposed, accusing him of disloyalty...of jumping ship...of cowardice.

He was able to let those remarks roll off his back, but she added one accusation that he'd felt was more than unfair...it was untrue, as well. She looked him right in the eyes and said in front of everyone, "You've never believed in us! You've been riding the bandwagon for years for your own benefit, not ours."

Luke sat there silent, humiliated, and deeply wounded on a personal level. No one had ever believed in them more than he.

Had she not been blocking the only door, the rest of the staff would've bolted for the exit like kids running home after breaking the neighbor's window with a baseball.

When it was over, he had shrugged it off and put it behind him as a tantrum of a strong woman under a great deal of pressure. She'd obviously been unwilling to put it behind her. What was of more immediate concern was her opinions about his views on fundraising.

Electing a woman as president would require a tremendous amount of advertising. It was a concept that needed to be sold to the American people. Madison Avenue ad agencies had been convincing the public for years that they couldn't live without fancy cars and vacations they couldn't afford. To them, the public was a mindless herd that required someone else to tell it what it really needed. It was time for a woman to be president. The country didn't know it yet, but Mallory did. By the time her campaign ads blanketed the popular media…the public would want it as badly as she did…but that would require a huge advertising budget.

Her memo detailed Luke's reluctance to "get on board" with the ambitious fundraising program. She outlined the amounts of money that still needed to be raised for her campaign by both the DNC, and themselves. If Luke wasn't in, she reasoned…he needed to be out. Her memo was intended to get Will's support for firing him. She was making the argument that although she knew he was, by far, the best poll analyst in Washington, her campaign needs might be better served by someone else.

Mallory Norton was calling for his head on a platter. As Luke saw it, he had two choices. From today forward, he could demonstrate his value to Mallory at every turn…or he could dust off his résumé.

He wasn't ready to leave the White House just yet. To do so now would give credence to her accusation that he was a deserter, unwilling to fight for a ship in distress. He was determined to stay to the end. Even though he was tired of the daily balancing act between the legal troubles of the first family and the political battles, he had too much of himself invested in these people to leave in disgrace.

The Nortons had a way of draining the energy from the people around them. Luke felt he had little fuel left in his tank. It seemed he'd aged seven years for each year he'd known Will and Mallory. At that moment, he felt even more like old Hannibal the dog than he had just an hour ago.

Chapter Thirty
PULLING THE PLUG

"A change would do you good...
uhm uhm...a change would do you good."

Sheryl Crow

Hong Kong – December 1997

Landing a commercial airplane in Hong Kong is a true test of skill for most pilots. The head winds usually blow from the harbor, which means the plane must approach from over the mountains. The bottom seems to fall from the plane as throttles pull back and air speed slows, causing it to drop hundreds of feet in a hurry. Adding to that difficulty is the fact that space is at a premium in Hong Kong, and apartment buildings line each side of the approach to the runway. As the plane lines up for landing, the wingtips seem ready to strip the laundry hanging from balconies that seem close enough to touch. It's an eerie feeling to be able to identify the eye color of children sitting on those same balconies.

Raoul wasn't a nervous flier, but landing in Hong Kong always caused him to grip the arms of his seat a little tighter than anywhere else in the world. He breathed easier today: visibility was good, and there was no fog to make the approach even more nerve-wracking.

After clearing customs as Anton Ricardi, an Italian clothier on a buying trip, he was met by a chauffeured Rolls Royce belonging to the Peninsula Hotel. Less than thirty minutes later, he was registered and settled in his suite. His dinner meeting was scheduled for eight o'clock, so he had plenty of time to enjoy the spa.

Western people tend to mistake expensive toys and high-tech gadgets for luxury. The Orientals understand that luxury is a state of mind, induced by indulging the body. The average American of means considers the heated seats in a Mercedes Benz to be luxurious, but until one has experienced a bath in the Far East, the concept of luxury is alien. Westerners bathe to clean the body—Orientals bathe to cleanse the soul.

Raoul entered the spa and was taken to the shower, the first step in stripping away the grime of civilization. From here he entered the bath, which in reality was a small swimming pool. The water was very hot, and the four foot deep tub was lined with seats, allowing him to rest in water over his shoulders. After fifteen minutes, his muscles relaxed and the tension that had built on the long flight from Vancouver began to dissipate. He returned to the showers and rinsed once again. After drying off, he was escorted to a massage table. He lay down on it with his towel covering his buttocks. A young Chinese girl, dressed in white, approached and introduced herself as Ling Tao. It was a beautiful name, and he knew enough Chinese to translate it as "delicate peach," which indeed she was.

Raoul remained on his stomach with his head facing to the right, resting on his arms. Ling Tao sprinkled his back and the backs of his

315

legs with powder and rubbed it in thoroughly. She began working the hamstrings with her strong hands. It felt as though she was kneading bread. She worked her way down his legs to the Achilles' tendons and then on to the bottoms of his feet, one leg at a time. Placing one hand behind his knee, the other under his foot, she raised and lowered each leg. Each time she raised it, she would bring it further toward his buttocks. By the time she finished, she could just about touch his calf to the back of his thigh.

Ling Tao moved to the small of his back, working with her strong hands up the right side first, then returning to the small of his back and working her way up the left side. The shoulders and neck came next and, when finished with them, she instructed him to turn over. She massaged his feet with her thumbs and the heels of her hands. The sensation was just this side of pain, but felt wonderful as soon as she was through. She gave the front side of his body the same treatment he'd just received on the back. Unlike portrayals in the movies, he remained covered at all times. Hong Kong had its share of prostitutes, but Ling Tao wasn't one of them. Raoul was in the spa of the Peninsula...not a Hong Kong whorehouse.

When the massage was completed, she bowed and thanked him. He returned her thanks, put on a heavy terrycloth robe, and went out on the patio, where he took a seat in a comfortable chair overlooking the harbor and ordered a cup of hot tea. He allowed himself to bask in the glow of pure ecstasy, feeling like a rubber band that had been stretched to the point of breaking, and then allowed to return to rest.

Victoria Harbor was breathtaking. The average temperature in December is 62 degrees. Today was slightly warmer at a comfortable 68. There was a pleasant breeze coming off the water, and Raoul believed this was the best time of year to visit Hong Kong. The massage, tea and the lounge chair combined with a fourteen-hour flight to make him fall asleep. In a few moments he awakened and decided he should move around for a while. Jet lag has a less wearing effect if one stays up as long as possible before sleeping. He would have a long rest after the conclusion of his dinner meeting.

Raoul returned to his room to find his bags had been unpacked, and his clothes put away. His suits were pressed and his shoes had been shined. Nothing but pampering at the Peninsula. Pure luxury. He looked at the nightstand clock and decided he'd take a walk to kill some time until dinner. Dressed in casual clothes, he decided to stroll around the Kowloon business district.

Although the British had returned Hong Kong to the Chinese just this year, there was little difference to the casual observer. The one notable exception had been the Chinese soldiers carrying automatic rifles at the airport. It was a little unsettling to see, and gave him the sensation of being back in Vietnam. He chalked it up to the propensity of communist regimes to delight in displaying their ever-present ability to apply force if it became necessary. In their eyes, the garish display reduced the need to use it.

Driving the communists from his thoughts, he continued his interaction with the merchants in the shops. Unlike the bored and disinterested teenaged clerks in American shopping malls, the people in these stores genuinely wanted to sell you something, and made you feel special when you walked through their door. They all spoke English, but warmed up even more when he attempted to use his rusty Chinese. Few people in the world care if you master their native tongue, but the effort expended in trying is usually returned tenfold in kindness. Courtesy is a disappearing art, and making the effort to employ a little earned him a warm response from the jewelry store owner: he purchased a gold Rolex watch for twenty-five percent less than he'd been quoted just moments before he began speaking Chinese.

Returning to his room, he dressed for dinner, selecting a handsome dark suit with a deep blue and gold tie. The highly polished leather shoes and the shiny new Rolex completed the look of the successful clothier his travel documents said he was. At eight o'clock sharp, he presented himself to the maître d' at Gaddi's Restaurant. He was shown immediately to a private room where his host, Mr. Umar Farida of Indonesia, greeted him. Extending his hand, the heavyset man said, "Welcome to Hong Kong, Señor Ricardi."

Raoul gripped his hand and replied, "Thank your for your kind invitation, Mr. Farida."

Seated next to Farida was a rather stern-looking Chinese man who was introduced as Yong Hu. The name meant "courageous tiger," which was fitting even though it wasn't his real name. A high-ranking official in the communist government of China, as well as head of Chinese military intelligence, the man's real name was General Po Sin Sheng. Raoul joined them at the table.

Farida waved his hand, and a waiter appeared to take their drink orders. There was no mistaking the black military shoes, the bulge under his jacket, or the ruthless look in his eyes. For this evening only, he would play the role of their waiter. If the need presented itself, he'd quickly revert to his primary job of being General Sheng's bodyguard.

There was no need to order dinner. It had been arranged in advance. Gaddi's is one of the finest gourmet restaurants in Hong Kong. Mr. Farida was a frequent patron, and the food would be the best the city had to offer. The serving staff would serve the meal and withdraw. General Sheng's man would retreat to an unobtrusive observation post, and they would be free to conduct their business in private. Dinner conversation was confined to small talk until the serving staff was through.

Mr. Farida was the first to get down to the formal agenda. He leaned across the table, and in a low whisper said, "They tell me you have people who can eliminate relationship problems, no matter where...no matter whom. Is this true?"

"It is," Raoul answered without a trace of false modesty.

Nodding toward the general, Farida said, "My esteemed friend from the Chinese mainland, and some close friends from home, are becoming nervous about events unfolding in America. Certain members of the U.S. Congress are taking an unwanted interest in our affairs. If a few key business transactions should ever be thoroughly investigated, they could prove both embarrassing, and costly."

"And how may I assist you with your concerns, Mr. Farida?"

Farida slid a picture across the table. Raoul looked at it without picking it up. Mr. Farida continued, "Should your congress get serious about its probe into the sources of various large contributions…it is crucial that certain parties are unable to verify their origin. What, to this point, has been a mutually profitable business deal, has become of questionable value. Our partners consider it time to cut our losses."

Raoul looked at the Chinese general, who had yet to say anything. Then, returning his gaze to Farida, he said, "It will take some time…and a great deal of money."

"We have a great deal of money, señor. Time, on the other hand, is a precious commodity."

"You've chosen a very well-protected party," Raoul said. "The planning will take several months."

Farida looked displeased, but not surprised. He stirred cream into his coffee and said, "Another scandal is about to be dropped at the doorstep of your president. Within a few weeks, allegations will be made that he has engaged in a series of sexual improprieties."

Raoul simply smiled as if to say *you're wasting your time*. "Sex scandals bounce off this guy like rubber balls, my friend."

"Not this one," Farida replied. "This allegation involves a young woman, not much older than his daughter, who works in the White House as an intern. It is not just an affair. As an American friend of mine so delicately put it, he's been dipping his pen in the company inkwell."

Raoul took a moment to absorb the news. The press had recently been alleging that Chinese money and policy concessions had been exchanged for American technology…that that there had been influence peddling for contributions from Indonesian billionaires. Now there were going to be allegations of sex with an employee. Though of greater importance, the first two wouldn't spark the interest of the talk shows like the third one would. It had all the trappings of a political nightmare and a media sensation. The feminists would have a field day over it.

Raoul said, "Mr. Farida, if what you say becomes public, it will take months to sort it out. The wheels of justice turn slowly in the United States. The president's problems with this young lady should grab the television spotlight and push your issues into the shadows for months. We'll have sufficient time to plan."

"That was our thinking as well," Farida said, his relief evident. "We will have the story leaked to our contacts in the American press. When are you leaving Hong Kong?"

"The day after tomorrow."

"Before you leave, I will expect you to let me know your requirements. You may name your price. Do we have a deal?"

Raoul nodded affirmatively.

Without a word, the enigmatic general bowed and left the room.

Chapter Thirty-One
CHASING MERCURY

"Across my dreams…with nets of wonder…
I chase the bright elusive butterfly of love."

Bob Lind

Washington, DC - March 1998

The American political landscape had suffered a mudslide in January. All of Will Norton's previous troubles were swept aside, leaving the latest one center stage. As much as the president's dilemma pleased the Republicans, they troubled Hiram Smith—as a man, and an American citizen. The detonation of this latest landmine brought into question the president's fitness for office.

The public might be too self-absorbed to concern themselves with foreign campaign contributions, or the administration's routine abuse of the law, but their antenna always tuned in to charges of sexual misconduct. The past five years had sorely challenged Hiram's regard for the public. Whatever the abhorrent behavior, the widely held conception that "everybody does it" had made few sins unforgivable in America.

For twenty years, feminist groups had vilified any man who abused his position of authority to have sex with a woman who worked for him. The implication was that, even if the sex was consensual, by definition it had been coerced because the man held authority over her. Now, these same women's advocates were defending the president and excusing behavior that they had universally condemned before. Because of Will Norton's positions on women's issues, gun control, and minority programs, he was too valuable to crucify. The opportunity to make an example would wait for other politicians who held politically incorrect views. For the moment, the president would have to be excused. Television news covered little else, and it was the principal topic on The Hill, but his recent news from Bethesda was of more importance to Hiram. The drive from the Naval Hospital to Chevy Chase felt as though it was taking years, and in a sense it was, for the journey had actually begun five years earlier. Hiram had been lucky back then, but luck was a finite commodity.

In 1993, during his annual physical, colon polyps had been detected. God had smiled upon him then; after extensive testing, they had been determined to be benign. A few weeks ago, he'd had another physical. New polyps were found. Another battery of tests was ordered. This time, his doctor wore no smile when he entered the room. From that clue, Hiram concluded God must've stopped smiling too. The news was bad. This time it was cancer. The prognosis was no better: perhaps a year, possibly longer.

Allison, seated next to him in the car, was taking the news poorly, since it caused her to relive the terrible hurt of watching her daughter wither away. The thought of going through it again with her husband of forty-seven years was too dreadful to consider. They were both sixty-eight years old, and had married right out of college in 1951. Becky had been born the following year. They had dated for two years before marrying. She could hardly remember the first nineteen years that Hiram wasn't in her life, and she didn't want to imagine how many years might lay ahead without him.

Sixty-eight used to sound ancient, but people seemed to live forever nowadays. She stared out the passenger window and watched the raindrops roll over the glass, pushed along by the wind. The drops seemed an appropriate metaphor for life itself—they came from above, and rolled across the surface until blown away by a force they could no longer fight. Allison wanted to hold her husband tight and never let him go, but knew it was no more possible than for the raindrops on the window to cheat the wind.

Hiram shared her sadness, but was lost in his own thoughts. He was contemplating the one remaining goal he wouldn't live to pursue. He had accomplished much in his life. He'd built a successful business, and made a fortune. He had an enviable record in politics. The crowning achievement of his life had been his happy marriage to Allison, and his wonderful daughter, son-in-law, and grandchildren. He had no reason to complain; yet he was human, and he felt cheated in one regard—he had spent the last few months assembling a team to help him run for the presidency in two years.

His chances received a boost when the news broke of Will Norton's inappropriate relationship with one of his female interns. Hiram was disgusted that the media could minimize what had happened by using the word "inappropriate." *Wearing white bucks before Easter or after Labor Day is inappropriate,* he thought to himself. *Sex with an intern in the Oval Office is just plain wrong.* Even so, Will Norton didn't know the meaning of the word "wrong." He had no reverence for the office. He only revered the power, not the presidency. Hiram believed he'd be good for the country, and that he could return dignity to the office. He wasn't the first to have his bubble burst. In spite of that, it hurt to think he'd never have the chance.

He reached across the front seat and held Allison's hand. She turned from the window and gave him the bravest smile she could muster. Patting her hand, he said, "It's going to be all right, dear." The cell phone rang, and he pulled it from his pocket. Mark was returning his call. Hiram asked him to meet him at the house at six o'clock. "We've got some talking to do," he said. "Bring Callie Q with you, and the boys if they're going to be around tonight. They can keep their grandmother company while we visit."

Mark was stunned at the news, and sorry was the only word he could muster.

"I'm sorry too, son...I really am." Hiram poured himself another scotch, and poured one for Mark. He knew Mark didn't really want it, but he needed another one, and didn't want to drink alone. "Mark, I've always said my senate seat was yours for the asking whenever I decided to step down. That decision has been made for me. You and

Becky long ago established your official residency in Wyoming. How do you feel about launching your own senatorial campaign?"

"Hiram, you know I'm no politician."

"Don't give me that self-effacing bullshit. You didn't become a major general in the Marines without being a natural politician. You've handled your post as national security advisor with competency and skill. In the best interests of the country you love, you work for a man you despise. That's the very definition of a politician. It's in your blood, son, or you wouldn't be working at the White House right now."

Mark looked out the window, but could feel that Hiram's gaze hadn't left him. When he turned back toward him, Hiram's look of determination was clear to see. He said, "The thought of your senate seat has crossed my mind on a few occasions, Hiram, but I'm just not sure I'm cut out for elected office."

"Mark…please don't patronize me. It's unbecoming. You've always been a straight shooter, and you know your own mind. Who the hell do you think *is* cut out for politics? It certainly isn't the majority of people who are in it now. Damn, son…the only things most people need to be a politician are a pulse, a smile, and someone else's money."

Mark chuckled as Hiram took a sip of his scotch and got ready to put on the hard sell.

"Now, being a leader…that's another matter entirely. You, sir, are a leader. You've been one since you were nineteen years old, and since that time you've never shirked the chance to lead. You work in

Norton's White House—not because you want to, but because your leadership is needed. It has to feel like a rudderless ship over there, doesn't it?"

Mark nodded affirmatively, indicating the White House was even less fun since January than it had been when he first arrived.

"It's time to chart your own destiny. When my health problems become known, there'll be half a dozen folks in Wyoming who'll want my seat. Whoever I endorse will win. No brag...just fact. If I tap you, no one else will run."

Hiram could tell Mark wasn't completely sold. His reluctance to run was what was going to make him a terrific senator. He didn't need the post for his ego. "Plato said it best, Mark: 'The penalty good men pay for indifference to public affairs is to be ruled by evil men.'"

Mark certainly agreed with the quote, but still made no reply. Hiram slapped his palm flat on the table and said, "Nothing's changed in politics since Plato said that in the fifth century B.C." He walked to his desk and retrieved a piece of paper from it. "Son, I want you to read a letter I got from one of my constituents a few days ago. His name is Bill Henry. I've never met the man, but his letter made me think of you."

Mark put on his reading glasses and took the letter from his father-in-law. It read:

Dear Senator Smith:

Can he still lead?

This is the fundamental question that faces Congress and the American people.

Sex is not the issue. Neither is it relevant whether this matter is private or public. For better or worse it is public, and the public trustworthiness of Will Norton is now the central issue. He is a master of words, and is highly skilled in choosing them. He is not, and has never been a man of his word. He has been less of a leader, and more a proponent of whatever the polls indicated the country wanted at any particular time. If he was ever capable of leading, from this point forward it is no longer possible.

As a captain in the Marines, it was my honor to serve my country. My brother served as a Marine, and died in combat in Vietnam. Regardless of anyone's opinion of that war, he served his country with honor, and died for it. Marines hold duty, honor, and country above all else. A man with no honor is not fit to send America's best to fight and die for their country.

Please note that I said a man without <u>honor</u>, not a man without <u>sin</u>. We're all sinners. All of us have made mistakes. All of us have deeds in our past that we would refrain from doing if given another chance. The president has had many honors bestowed upon him by others, but true honor comes from within.

America deserves an honorable leader. A sinner can still maintain his honor. A man doesn't lose it by making an immoral choice, but restores it by making the moral choice more often than not. It comes from the wisdom derived from having made poor choices. It comes from the maturity of regularly choosing the more difficult right, rather than the easier wrong. It comes from self-denial, and self-discipline. Will Norton has never lived this way. He is not an honorable man.

As a man and a sinner, he is deserving of another chance, but God is the only one who should grant it. As a nation, we would be foolish to look the other way and excuse our president and Commander-in-Chief. The chance to seek forgiveness, atonement, and redemption may indeed be private. However, the privilege to lead our nation and the moral authority to send our young people into combat is a public trust.

Many of President Norton's policies have been wrapped in the mantle of what is best for our children. My brother was twenty-one when he died. The bulk of our armed forces are twenty-one or younger. He was, and they are, barely more than children. Is President Norton the best example of leadership for them?

My teenage sons are just a few years away from being old enough to serve. I have no trust that Will Norton values the sacrifice he might order them to make. I have no trust that he wouldn't use them as pawns for his own political gain.

There are several presidents with whom I've differed politically. I disagreed with their vision for our country, but I served under their leadership without reservation. They were all men of honor. I would not choose to serve, nor would I want my sons to serve Will Norton.

Fitness reports evaluate soldiers on a variety of leadership traits. Judgment, loyalty, courage, integrity, and presence of mind, are a few. A below-average evaluation in any of these areas will usually end a service career. If I were writing a fitness report on Will Norton he would be marked poorly on each of these traits. Why? Because he is a man who serves his own interests first.

There is talk of impeaching him. For political reasons, Congress probably wishes this problem would just go away. Doing what's best for the country will require the same character traits mentioned above. The press and the polls say impeaching the president will cause our country pain. It may, but we've survived pain many times before.

To carry out its duty, Congress will need the leadership traits I've mentioned.

Vince Lombardi said, "Pain makes cowards of us all." It was self-indulgence that caused the president to do what he did. It was the selfish desire to avoid embarrassment and potential loss of face that caused him to lie. It is the dread of a painful public discourse that makes the public want to do as he asks and "put this behind us." I pray that the fear of pain doesn't make cowards of Congress. If it does, then our nation will face much greater pain when world events require a leader with honor, and Will Norton remains our president.

Respectfully,
Bill Henry

Hiram was the first to break the silence. He said, "Leadership abhors a vacuum, Mark. When there's a leadership void, someone always rises to the occasion. The country needs leadership...the country needs you, son."

Mark's two sons were just a year or two away from draft age, and Bill Henry's letter echoed his own feelings about the Commander-in-Chief. It had never been easy to serve him, and it was becoming more difficult every day. Mark handed the letter back to Hiram. Mark's boys were out on the town tonight with their friends...not much

331

different than he, Luke, and Matt had done on a high school Friday night. For them, the world held endless promise—as long as honorable people took their duty seriously. He said, "Let me sleep on it, Hiram. I still a lot have on my plate at the NSC."

Hiram nodded his understanding. "We have a few months before any decisions need to be made. You'll make the right one…You always do." He offered Mark another scotch, which he declined. Pouring one more for himself, they left the study to join Allison and Callie Q in the kitchen.

Mark lifted Callie Q onto the counter and asked, "What did you girls make for dinner?"

In unison, she and her grandmother said, "Reservations!"

Across town, at the White House, Mallory Norton was dealing with a similar realization. Her husband's appetites had made her bid to succeed him more than doubtful. She was as shattered as her dreams. She had stood by him throughout his political career, no matter what allegations had been leveled, or by whom. Infidelity was nothing new, and she could deal with it as long as it wasn't flaunted in her face, or the public eye. Theirs was a working partnership, but this time he'd let his partner down in a very humiliating way.

Whether Will served out his term or not, some time would have to pass before America was ready for another Norton in the White House. Mallory would not pass go, collect two hundred dollars, and proceed to the Oval Office. She suspected her best bet would be to spend a little time in the Senate.

On Monday, she would convene a meeting of her advisors and discuss her options. This kind of environment was where Luke Reilly had always been invaluable. She was glad Will had talked her out of letting him go, but she still planned to cut him loose as soon as he helped her secure a seat.

Mallory Norton and Hiram Smith had but one thing in common on this rainy Friday night. Neither of them would be running for president in the year 2000. In 1966, Bob Lind's song "Elusive Butterfly" lamented the frustrations of pursuing one's dream of love. The presidency was even more elusive. One could spend a lifetime preparing and still need the luck of a lottery winner to get close enough to even have a shot. Like trying to round up mercury from a broken thermometer, the presidency fled from their reach and eluded their grasp.

Chapter Thirty-Two
LUCK OF THE DRAW

"Every breath you take…every move you make…I'll be watching
you."

The Police

Georgetown, DC – July 1998

Luke's heart pounded and he flew from his bed at the wailing siren of the burglar alarm. He flipped on lights in his bedroom and hallway and tried to determine, over the noise, if anyone had actually entered his home. Satisfied that it was a false alarm, he turned it off and phoned the security company.

This was the third time this week that his alarm had been triggered, and each time there had been no actual disturbance. The repairman was already scheduled to come later this morning. Luke's schedule was too full to miss work, so he told them his next-door neighbor, Mrs. Jackson, would open the house for the technician and stay until he finished his repairs.

He retrieved a bottle of Perrier water from the refrigerator and opened it. Sitting at his kitchen table, he sipped it slowly, waiting for his heartbeat to return to normal. He didn't know why he even had the damned alarm. The stupid thing always scared his socks off when it started blasting, and he doubted seriously that it would ever deter a professional burglar. An alarm system just seemed to be one of those necessities in expensive neighborhoods. It was no guarantee against being burglarized, but not having one was tantamount to issuing a personal invitation to Washington's thieves. He chalked the aggravation up to one more aspect of living life in the fast lane.

The clock on the stove read 3:30 a.m. He had a series of important meetings in a few hours, and he really needed his sleep. If the alarm company couldn't fix the problem, he was going to have them remove the system. Luke had little patience for incompetence. Turning off the lights, he went back to bed.

A little before seven thirty in the morning, two panel vans left the lot at Guardian Security Company on Duke Street in Alexandria. Arturo Rodriguez and Harold Martin drove two blocks to the McDonalds and pulled in for a quick breakfast before beginning their separate rounds.

Neither man paid any attention to the maroon Buick following them into the parking lot.

The man in the car dialed the number on the side of the truck and asked for the dispatcher. The woman he was speaking to said her name was Judy, and that she would be delighted to help him. Identifying himself as Luke Reilly, he informed her he was expecting one of their repairman this morning. Judy said the repairman was on his way, and that his house was the first stop of the day. The man in the Buick asked what the repairman's name was, and Judy told him it was Arturo Rodriguez.

"Judy," he said. "I need to postpone today's service call. Would you tell him it won't work out for him to come today? I'll be at the White House all day, and I just learned my neighbor will be traveling this week and won't be able to let him in. I'll call you to reschedule at a better time."

"No problem Mr. Reilly," Judy said. "We'll wait to hear from you."

Cain put the phone in his pocket and walked into the restaurant. He stood directly behind the two repairmen, who were waiting for their food. The walkie-talkie on the shorter man's belt hissed and scratched, and was followed by a woman's voice saying, "Artie, come in...this is Judy."

He removed the unit from his belt and said, "Yeah, Judy...this is Artie, go."

"Artie...be advised your first call has been scratched. Cancel Reilly and go straight to the Harrisons'...Over."

"I copy that," he said. "Reilly's scratched...go to Harrisons'...Out." He replaced the radio in his belt and picked up his tray of food.

Both men had ordered the same thing: hash browns, an Egg McMuffin, and a large black coffee. It wasn't what Cain would've wanted for *his* last meal—but then again, Harold Martin didn't know it was the last breakfast he'd ever eat.

★ ★ ★

Cain read the newspaper and sipped his coffee until the men were almost finished with breakfast. While they piled trash on their trays and wiped the table with a napkin, he left his booth and walked to his car.

Arturo and Harold dumped the trash in the wastebasket, strolled leisurely toward their trucks, and then each one climbed behind the wheel. When they reached the street, Arturo turned left and Harold went to the right. Cain slipped the Buick into traffic behind Harold's truck and followed him for about three miles. The traffic light turned yellow, then red. Harold stopped the van and immediately felt a violent jolt as the Buick behind him failed to stop in time.

He put the truck into park and got out to inspect the damage. The Buick hadn't been traveling fast, and the damage was moderate. A nice looking man with a full head of wavy blond hair, with just a hint of gray at the temples, got out of the car and approached Harold. "Gee mister," the man chattered, "I'm awfully sorry. Are you okay? Gosh, I feel terrible. I just looked down to change stations, and all of a sudden...*bang*!"

"Don't worry about it, buddy," Harold said. "You didn't do any real damage to the truck, and I'm okay."

"Well, I sure hope so! Boy, I feel like an idiot," Cain said. "I'm Paul Peterson. Listen...Why don't we pull into the shopping center parking lot and I'll give you my insurance information? I feel bad enough about hitting you, and I hate to make things worse by tying up traffic."

Harold said, "Sure thing."

Both men got into their vehicles and turned into the strip mall entrance. Cain motioned for Harold to come join him in the Buick. He held his left hand under the newspaper he'd been reading earlier.

As soon as Harold sat down in the passenger seat, Cain fired two shots from the silenced automatic he held under the paper. The bullets entered Harold's chest, striking the lungs and heart. He died instantly. Cain looked over his shoulder and saw no one around, so he pushed the man's lifeless body to the floorboard, pulled his wallet and car keys from his pockets, and removed the Guardian Security hat from his head. Pulling a heavy bedspread from the back seat, he covered up the body. To give the appearance of a load for the laundry, he threw a pile of shirts and trousers from the rear seat on top of the spread.

That done, Cain retrieved a box from his trunk, locked the car, and got into Harold's van. He was heading east less than five minutes from the time he'd bumped the truck. The body in the car wouldn't be found until the next day. With luck, perhaps a little later. It was, however, the middle of summer, and even with the windows tightly rolled up, the decaying corpse would announce its presence soon. Cain peeled off the surgical gloves he'd been wearing and shoved them in his pockets.

The Alexandria police would have no trouble solving this crime. The car had been stolen in Maryland. It was hurriedly wiped of prints, but if any remained, none belonged to Cain. On the Buick's damaged front end was paint the color of the alarm company's truck. They would conclude that someone had rear-ended Harold Martin, lured him to the car, and killed him for his wallet and his truck. By nightfall, when Cain was through with the van, it would disappear in the Upper Potomac River. This morning, Cain had a house call to make, and for the next few hours he needed it more than Harold did.

Cain parked the van in front of Luke Reilly's townhouse. He stripped off the lightweight black windbreaker he'd been wearing all morning, revealing a khaki shirt with the name Paul stenciled on it. He put on Harold's hat, and then trotted up the stairs to the townhouse next to Luke Reilly's and rang the doorbell. A spunky little woman in her mid-seventies looked through the leaded glass door and saw what she expected to see: a technician from Guardian, and his truck parked in front. She picked up her book and her reading glasses from the foyer table and opened the door.

"Good morning, ma'am," Cain said. "I'm Paul Peterson from Guardian Security. Mr. Reilly said you'd let me in next door."

"Good morning, Paul," she said. "I'm Mrs. Jackson. Mr. Reilly wants me to stay there while you work. I won't get in your way. I'm just going to read my book, okay?"

"Yes ma'am," he said. "That'll be fine."

While Cain got his tools and supplies from the truck, she locked her front door and opened Luke's.

True to her word, Mrs. Jackson read quietly in the den while Cain busied himself bugging every floor of the house. In addition to the phones, he placed miniature cameras in each television set to observe Reilly as he watched TV. There were additional cameras in the bedroom, the bathroom and the kitchen. Cameras and microphones were also strategically placed to observe his favorite spots to read and work.

As he passed through the den, he saw Mrs. Jackson fast asleep, her glasses askew and her book open on her lap.

Setting up today had been a snap. Last week he'd paid a visit to the offices of Guardian Security, posing as a phone company repairman. Under the guise of servicing data transmission lines, he bugged the receptionist's phone and the phone on the service desk. Two days later, he began tripping Luke Reilly's alarm in the early morning hours. By the third night's disrupted sleep, Luke had called for help. Cain knew exactly when the repairman was scheduled to visit the townhouse.

He gathered his tools and pulled a note from his pocket that he'd written in advance. It read:

Mr. Reilly:
Your system is fixed now. We're sorry for the inconvenience.
There's no charge.
Paul

Leaving the note on the table, he woke Mrs. Jackson and told her he was finished, and offered to escort her home.

She seemed embarrassed about having fallen asleep on guard duty. "You won't tell Mr. Reilly that I fell asleep, will you, Paul?" she said.

"Mrs. Jackson," he said, "if you don't mention my visit, I won't either."

She smiled. "You're a nice young man. Come see me again sometime."

"Yes ma'am," he said. "I'll do that."

On the other side of town, Cain pulled the van into a mini storage facility, unlocked the padlock on the unit's sliding door, and backed it into the stall. He got out of the van, closed the sliding door, and opened the rear doors wide. Placing a metal ramp to the back of the van, he walked a lightweight Suzuki trail bike up the ramp. He closed and secured everything, got back into the van, and slept until dark. When he woke up, he took a long drive out of town to the upper end of the Potomac.

There were lights on the ramp from a pick-up truck belonging to the last fisherman to leave the river. Cain waited, out of sight on a dirt road overlooking the launch ramp, until the truck and trailer drove out of the park. He drove the van straight down the parking lot, aiming it at the launch ramp, and left it running with the parking brake engaged. Opening the panel doors he climbed in the van, started the Suzuki, and jumped it out the back of the truck. He spun the bike to the side and put down the kickstand.

He released the parking brake of the van and let it roll down the boat ramp into the river. It bobbed up and down and proceeded to sink, nose first. The current swept the vehicle into the middle of the river, and in the dim moonlight, Cain saw it disappear under the water. Straddling the lightweight dirt bike, he flipped up the kickstand with his heel, and sped away from the boat launch.

As Cain rode back to his apartment, he marveled at the power he wielded over life and death. Arturo Rodriguez was absolutely clueless that he'd come close to being murdered today. Had Harold Martin been assigned the Reilly service call instead of him, Rodriquez would be the one with two bullets in him, and Harold Martin would be watching TV with *his* family tonight.

It would've been a serious mistake to kill the service technician that was scheduled to repair Luke Reilly's system today. If Rodriguez had turned up dead, the police would take an interest in every call he was to have made on the day he went missing. The fact that Luke Reilly worked for the president would have been reason to alert the Secret Service, and perhaps the FBI. As it stood now, the cancelled Reilly call would never come under scrutiny. Instead, the police would concentrate on the calls Harold Martin was to have made.

Luke Reilly would come home to a system that had been repaired. He would never receive a bill, so he would have no reason to talk further with anyone at Guardian Security. Mrs. Jackson would never admit to falling asleep on duty, and would tell Reilly that the service man had been quite professional. He'd toss the note in the trash, and would never suspect his every move was being observed on *Candid Camera*.

Cain felt no remorse about killing Harold Martin. There was no malice in it. Today was simply his appointed date with death. It was just like choosing a target from a column of patrolling enemy troops when he'd been a sniper in Vietnam. Why pick one guy over another? No reason, really. Bad luck…wrong place at the wrong time…*fate*. It was no more than the luck of the draw that Arturo Rodriquez was alive tonight, and Harold Martin was dead. It was as random as death on the battlefield. Cain would lose no sleep over it. Everybody had to die, sooner or later.

Chapter Thirty-Three
HEARD IT THROUGH THE GRAPEVINE

"Believe half of what you see...son...and none of what you hear."

Marvin Gaye

Office of the National Security Advisor
The White House – Late October 1998

Mark's two-year anniversary at the White House was approaching soon. Though he would never have dreamed it, he considered his time here well spent. He'd learned more than he imagined he would, and now held a much different perspective than he'd brought with him to the job.

When asked to join the team, his initial impression of the role was to advise the president regarding threats of a military or terrorist nature. He'd been surprised to learn that there were many threats to national security, running the gamut from economics to education to environmental concerns. The job had broadened his knowledge of the government's influence over the lives of its citizens.

Mark, following Hiram's advice, had carefully trod the delicate line between advising the president and attempting to formulate policy. His role required him to organize and mobilize the information reaching the president from the divergent perspectives of the Security

Council members. Absent his efforts, much of the raw data available to him would be of little use in making good decisions.

He performed his role differently than some of his predecessors, and kept a very low profile. His style was to avoid making statements to the media, referring them instead to the chairman of the Joint Chiefs, or the appropriate Cabinet secretary.

The president valued his performance, for he provided not only sound advice, but advice that was clear and, for the most part, free from personal bias. Perhaps Hiram knew him better than he knew himself. Deep down, he was a gifted politician...and he'd made a difference at the National Security Council.

He had been giving serious consideration to running for the senate seat of his ailing father-in-law. At fifty-one, he felt he still had a lot of service left to offer his country. He couldn't stay in the Marines, or the White House, forever...but if the people of Wyoming sent him to the Senate, and sent him back a time or two, he might be able to make a lasting impact. He never thought he'd sound like Luke, but he did.

Raoul entered the Metro station through the L'Enfant Plaza Hotel and office complex. He took the escalator to the lower level and bought a subway ticket. The pass card disappeared in the slot, and he passed through the turnstile like the thousands of other bureaucrats who commuted by train each day. For first-time visitors, the station's high ceiling naturally draws the eye. The regular commuters look neither up nor down. They just look ahead, paying little attention to anyone else.

He arrived just as a train was pulling away from the platform. A man in a khaki-colored raincoat stepped away from the departing train and walked toward a bench near the wall. He laid his copy of *USA Today* on the bench, and put his right foot up to tie his shoe. Raoul took a seat next to him and laid his newspaper over the other copy. When finished tying his laces, the man picked up the top newspaper and began walking toward the hotel entrance. Unlike most amateurs, he'd done exactly as he had been told.

Another train slowed to a stop, and Raoul took the first newspaper and boarded. When the train picked up speed, he looked in the fold of the paper to discover a white envelope with a return address that read:

The White House
Washington, DC

----- -----

$200 fine for personal use

He'd spoken too soon. This was more than an amateurish mistake...this one had the potential to be fatal. There'd be more to pay than a $200 fine if the contents of this envelope were ever seen by the FBI or Secret Service. His next communication would reemphasize the need for using *unmarked* envelopes, handled only while wearing gloves.

When he was safe in his living room, Raoul studied the envelope's contents: the proposed presidential itinerary for the next sixty days. It was subject to change, but would give them some options to consider. Also in the packet were security procedures for passengers traveling aboard Air Force One and Marine One aircraft.

Three months ago, his planning with Cain got an unexpected lift. An old colleague from the FBI, who was offering his services as a consultant to this mission, had told Raoul there was a party in the White House who could be blackmailed into providing them with up-to-date information. He was willing to cooperate to avoid exposure and prison.

To date, the quality of his information had been incredible. The man who'd just made the exchange was not the source, but one of his aides, who thought he was leaking information to the media that would embarrass the independent counsel who was investigating the president and his wife. It was a good blind. Raoul had never met the real source, and the source would never meet him. If the mule carrying the envelopes was ever caught, he'd have a lot of explaining to do, but he would know nothing about what he'd been transporting.

Major McGuire placed the daily "threat report" on General Reilly's desk and busied himself reviewing information recently received from the FBI. One would think that the combined resources of the Bureau, the Secret Service, the CIA, and the National Security

Agency would paint a clear picture for the national security advisor. Unfortunately, the dots on the various agencies' reports frequently went unconnected. Once a week, Major McGuire made an effort to read between the lines and coordinate the reports.

The Secret Service and FBI each have a watch list of people who've either made threats against the president, or have ties to groups who have. At any given time there are as many as five to fifty threats against his life. Most are nothing more than hotheads venting their frustration with the man or his policies, and who are dumb enough to do it in writing. Though most threats have no teeth, all were taken seriously by the folks who protected the president and his family.

Among today's reports was a recently completed CIA investigation of last month's U.S. embassy bombings in Tanzania and Kenya. The two attacks killed 224 people, and wounded 5,000 more. Among those killed were twelve Americans. The major highlighted sections that laid responsibility for the attacks on Osama Bin Laden, a disenfranchised Arab terrorist who headed a group of anti-American Islamic fundamentalists called Al Qaida. His threats included very direct reference to the White House, the U.S. capitol, CIA headquarters, and other major American landmarks.

The National Security Agency, who handles the nation's communications intelligence, referenced at least two dozen intercepted conversations that had made reference to plots aimed at the president. These had been passed to the FBI and Secret Service for follow-up investigation. The FBI made passing reference to the last reported movements of an assassin known only as Cain. At present, he was believed to be back in the United States.

Tim McGuire took a late lunch and then drove to Headquarters Marine Corps to meet his friend, Major Harrington, for PT. They ran three miles from the main building, around Arlington Cemetery and past the Marine Corps Memorial. After continuing their run along the Potomac to the halfway point, they doubled back and retraced their steps.

When they reached the parking lot, they finished their PT with some pull-ups and sit-ups. Tim showered and put his uniform back on. He worked a lot of weekends, but planned to return to the White House and work late tonight, and every night this week, so he could keep his promise to take his family to the Smithsonian on Saturday. It was a good weekend to be with the family, anyway, for it had all the makings of a slow one at work. The president and his family were going to Camp David on Friday afternoon.

Fairfax, Virginia

School had been out for about an hour, and the residential street was filled with children on bikes and two-wheeled Razor scooters. It

349

was a Monday, and the kids were picking up where they'd left off yesterday evening, burning excess energy from being cooped up in class all day.

In this family neighborhood, 250 Sunnybrook Lane seemed out of place. There was no indication that anyone lived here at all. There were no bicycles, toys, or even a basketball goal in the turnaround. There was a tall cedar fence around the yard to afford privacy to the backyard pool…and 250 was the only house on the entire street with its garage door closed.

Cain turned into the driveway and had to hit his brakes, hard, as a redheaded kid on a scooter shot in front of his car on the sidewalk. The boy gave him a snotty look that had the same connotation as flipping him the finger.

He wondered how some of today's kids were going to make it to tomorrow. The sheltered and overindulged children of well-off parents were going to have a rude awakening when they hit the real world. Cain could envision the kid on the scooter turning twenty-one and walking into the wrong bar. He'd make a snotty remark to the wrong man, accompanied by that *screw you* look, and he'd be dead before he hit the floor.

Cain thought the old West must've been a much more civil place to live than today's world. Everybody carried a gun…and since they did, everybody watched their mouths. Impatience, insults, and sarcasm at someone else's expense must've been rare occurrences. When they occurred, the smart-mouth didn't live to become a repeat offender.

After making a mental note to run over the kid if he got the chance, he put the little brat out of his mind. Throwing the gearshift into park, he got out, walked to the front door, and rang the bell. While waiting, he looked up at the ceiling and saw a camera lens no larger than the eye of a Barbie doll. In a couple of minutes Raoul opened the door and let him in, tersely asking, "Why have you come to my home?"

Raoul was annoyed with Cain for coming to his house instead of meeting in a public place, and was indignant that he arrived unannounced. Breaking established protocols was an excellent way to destroy a clandestine network that had taken him decades to build.

To Raoul's question, Cain replied, "We need to talk, and I'm on a tight schedule."

"What do you mean? I plan your schedule...and you have plenty of time."

"Some things have changed," he said as he walked to the rear patio and took a seat at the table next to the swimming pool.

Raoul followed him there, and took a seat beside him. "What's happened...have we been compromised?"

"Not exactly," he answered. "This is the first time we've ever met that you haven't offered me a drink. I'd expect better hospitality in your own home than in a hotel room or restaurant."

Raoul stood to go to the kitchen and asked him what he wanted.

"A cold beer will be great, thanks."

Raoul walked through the sliding glass door and rummaged through his fridge for a Budweiser, finally locating a couple in the crisper drawer. He twisted off the top of one of them and returned to the patio table.

With his thumb, Cain was tapping the portable phone Raoul had been holding when he let him inside. While Raoul had gone to the kitchen, Cain pressed the redial button, and hung up before it began to ring. The last phone number called was displayed in the call window. The number was unfamiliar.

Raoul handed Cain the beer and sat back in his chair. He began sipping the scotch he'd been drinking when Cain arrived. "Tell me why you're here," he said.

Cain replied, "I've decided to accelerate our timetable."

Incredulous, Raoul slammed his fist on the table. "You accelerate nothing unless I say so! You're very good at what you do my friend, but one of the reasons you've lived this long is because I leave nothing to chance. That's my gift. My planning and my networking keep *all* of my operatives healthy and productive...*not just you.*" Continuing in the coldest tone Cain had ever heard from him, he added, "Don't you ever think about changing one of my plans."

"Raoul, you're a fine partner, as was RB before he died...but it's about time for me to hang up my cleats."

"You're not hanging up anything until you complete this assignment."

"I fully intend to carry out my mission," Cain replied. "I just don't plan to do it when, and where, you planned."

"So you think you don't need me anymore?"

"That's right," Cain said. "I don't need you anymore. You see, old friend, this is our last mission. There'll never be one bigger. It's retirement time...for all of us."

It was time for Raoul to utilize the insurance policy he'd been given by RB before he died.

"You don't even want to think about harming me, Cain," Raoul said. "If you do...you'll have nothing to retire on. The millions you have in the bank won't be accessible to you anymore."

Cain was confused...and didn't like the sound of Raoul's threat. His confusion turned to anger. His face flushed red, and his initial impulse was to choke the life out of Raoul. Realizing that if he had accessed his bank accounts that course of action would be futile, he took control of his emotions and decided to probe a little. "Raoul," he said, "please tell me you haven't been foolish enough to tamper with my bank accounts."

"All your account numbers in Geneva and the Caymans have been changed. New passwords are in place. I live...or you live with no money. That's the deal."

"And when will I regain control of my accounts?"

"When the mission's over," he replied. "Then, we'll both retire...to different parts of the world...where we won't see each other again. And we'll both die of old age."

Cain's mind was racing as Raoul concluded his case. Who in Raoul's network was capable of hijacking his accounts? Several candidates came to mind, but were immediately rejected. It would take a genius. Then it hit him…Leon Chandler. He'd bet his life the phone number on Raoul's phone belonged to Leon.

Raoul continued. "There's something else you need to know. If anything happens to me—accidental or foul play—there's a package waiting to be mailed to officials at the White House who would be very interested to learn all about you. If one of my colleagues doesn't hear from me the prearranged times, the package will be mailed."

Cain thought quickly. The file on him would throw a wrench into the works only if he followed Raoul's plan, which was to shoot the president as he spoke at the Eternal Flame in front of John F. Kennedy's grave in Arlington. November 22nd was the thirty-fifth anniversary of his assassination. Raoul had felt it fitting to take out President Norton at JFK's gravesite. The man who had so admired Kennedy would share more with his boyhood idol than just the presidency and a penchant for beautiful women: He would share the same fate.

"Cain…Cain, are you listening?" Raoul's question brought Cain back from his thoughts. "…I said…do we have an understanding?" .

Cain looked at him with resignation on his face and said, "I suppose I have no other choice."

Raoul thought it odd that his forehead began to sweat, since it was a cool October afternoon. His first impression was that his anger at Cain was making him hot, but the tingling in his arms told him it was something more. His heart began to beat rapidly, and he made an effort to reach for the gun from the holster hidden underneath the table.

When he realized he was paralyzed, it was his turn for resignation. His head pounded, his mouth got dry, and he was unable to move from the neck down. He'd been drugged, and like a fly in a spider's web, he was completely at Cain's mercy. This offered no comfort, for the man who controlled his fate was a merciless one.

Cain rose from his chair and checked his watch. The nerve agent he'd placed in Raoul's drink was too slow in taking effect. For artistic reasons, he preferred a victim that was aware of what was taking place, but on his final mission that would be a luxury he couldn't afford. Time wouldn't permit it. For the mission, he would use a faster-acting narcotic to more quickly render his prey unconscious.

He sat next to Raoul and gently held the back of his head. There was an odd mixture of fear, anger, and recrimination in his eyes. Though Raoul had expected Cain to make a move on him, he thought he'd been smart enough to prevent what was about to happen. The master planner had miscalculated...and had played his hole card too late.

"You've been a great partner, Raoul," Cain said. "Like a skilled assistant gunner on a sniper team, you've always seen the broader picture that the shooter can't see through his scope. I'll miss both you and RB."

Raoul's throat had begun to swell, and he couldn't speak.

With one swift motion, Cain smashed Raoul's head into the metal edge of the patio table. Blood ran from the deep gash in his forehead. Then he tilted him backward and allowed both the body and the wrought-iron chair to tumble into the swimming pool. Standing, he stood and rotated the table so the bloodstain paralleled the edge of the pool. Strategically arranging some of the pool cleaning tools, he set the stage to look as though Raoul had been cleaning his pool while drinking heavily. An investigator would assume he tripped over the vacuum hose and hit his head, causing him to fall across the chair and into the pool.

Cain used a towel to pick up Raoul's scotch glass and dropped it on the concrete. He took the beer bottle and cap and put them in his coat pocket. The body wouldn't be found for several days. Cain knew Raoul's cleaning lady came on Thursdays. Today was Monday. If the coroner elected to conduct an autopsy, it wouldn't happen until well into next week. He planned to be sailing the Caribbean by then.

He pressed redial again and allowed the phone to ring. After four rings, an answering machine picked up. "This is Leon, man. You know what to do at the beep."

Leon Chandler was one of the brightest computer hackers in the country. He'd been a seventeen-year-old prodigy at MIT until he was thrown out for cheating. It hadn't really bothered him because he knew, without question, he was smarter than his professors, and classes were a waste of his time. They never proved he'd changed his grades through the university's computer system, but his professors knew what his real grades were.

Four years later, the FBI agent who caught him hacking into the Pentagon's computer system was operating a little freelance business on the side. Instead of turning him in, he turned Leon into his personal asset. For substantial fees, Leon's services had been made available to, among others, RB and Raoul. It had been a profitable arrangement for everyone.

Leon's talents were confined to computers and electronics, but Raoul had stepped *waaay* over the line with his latest request. Raoul had called him about an hour ago and told him that, if he didn't hear from him again within three hours, to mail the package he'd left in his care. Those instructions made him really nervous. To make matters worse, his phone rang just a few minutes later, and no one said anything.

Leon had been strong-armed into some serious cloak and dagger shit he had no interest in playing. Raoul had some spooky associates, and Leon wanted nothing to do with any of them. The phone had rung a second time, and this call damn near made him soil his pants. He didn't answer, preferring to see if the caller would speak into the answering machine. When the line disconnected, and no message was left, he began sweating profusely. He could tell something bad was going down, and began shaking uncontrollably.

Deciding not to wait for Raoul's call, he took the package and ran down the street to the corner PostNet Mailing Center. The owner's name was Linda, and Leon gave her the package with instructions to mail it right away. She told him the last pickup by the post office had already been made, and the earliest it was going anywhere was tomorrow. Leon's eyes darted back and forth, his agitation clearly obvious. "Will that be all right?" she said, "or would you like to send it FedEx?"

Leon returned from his thoughts and said, "What?"

"The mail's gone for the day, Leon. Do you want to express mail your package tonight, or is tomorrow soon enough?"

Thinking quickly, Leon said, "No. Uhm…no…tomorrow will be fine. In fact, I'd appreciate it if you wouldn't mail it until the end of the day. I may need to put something else with it. But if you don't hear from me by noon, please go ahead and send it along."

"I'll be happy to," she said with a smile. "That'll be a dollar seventy-five."

Leon tossed two bills on the counter and said thanks as he hit the door, then hurried back to his apartment.

The longer he sat around waiting for Raoul's call, the more agitated he became. Finally, he decided to forward his calls to his cell phone, pack some clothes, and check into a hotel for a couple of days. If Raoul called, he'd go to PostNet in the morning and retrieve the package. If he didn't call, the White House would deal with whatever was in it quickly. Raoul had told him all hell would break loose if the contents of the package were ever sent. The White House was having enough troubles as it was. All hell breaking loose was something he wanted to avoid at all costs.

He grabbed his shaving kit from under the bathroom counter and tossed it onto the bed. Pulling open two drawers, he threw some underwear and socks onto the bed. He ran to his closet and got a couple of sweaters and shirts, and another pair of pants. After stepping out of the closet just long enough to throw the clothes on the bed, he reached up on the upper shelf and pulled down an overnight bag. Returning to the bed, he crammed everything into the bag and zipped it closed.

Holding the overnight bag in his left hand, Leon picked up his cell phone and car keys and looked around the room. There was nothing else he needed for a short trip. He flipped off the light and opened his door. That's when his head felt like he'd just run into a brick wall at full speed.

More to the case, a brick wall had just run into *him*. Cain's right uppercut caught him just under the chin, shattering several of Leon's teeth. The blow lifted him from his feet and he landed hard on the coffee table in front of his couch. Cain closed the door and was on top of him before he could move or cry out.

Leon had only seen the man standing over him once, from a distance. From his violent greeting, he knew he was in for a very bad time. His only hope of survival was to rely on his mind, not his body. He knew he was no match for a man like this. The best he could hope for was to convince him that he couldn't help him...that he'd come too late. He shouted, "It's already gone, mister...It's already gone!"

Cain struck him again across the bridge of his nose and ordered him to be quiet. "What's gone, little man?" he snarled in a menacing tone.

"The package I was told to mail," he whimpered.

359

"According to my watch, you weren't supposed to have mailed it, yet," Cain said.

"I got scared and mailed it already," he cried.

"And what made you scared enough to jump the gun like that, you little shit?"

Wiping his bleeding nose and mouth on his sleeve, he said, "The two phone calls a while ago with no one on the other end."

Cain said, "I don't need the package, Leon. I've got you." He stood Leon on his feet and helped him to his computer. He'd hurt him just enough to let him know that he'd be hurt even worse if he didn't do as he was told. "I want my money back, Leon."

"What money?" he asked, holding his throbbing nose. "I don't have your money."

"You're a genius, Leon. Don't act like an imbecile. You changed my accounts and passwords." Cain pulled his right arm behind his back, just short of breaking it. Leon cried for mercy, and Cain released a little pressure. "Leon," he said, "you know I can break your arm in so many places you'll never be able to use it again?" He applied more pressure and leaned closer to Leon's ear. "You don't want to make me do that...do you?"

Tears streamed down Leon's face as he shook his head no.

"Restore my accounts and codes...or I will. Then you'll have to restore them with your other arm. If you refuse after that...you'll never feed yourself again, much less make a living as a computer hacker. I suspect it would be difficult to be a good one if you had to use your toes to type. Am I right?"

Leon sobbed openly and he could taste the blood running down his throat from his mouth and the back of his nose. "Don't hurt me any more," he pleaded. "I'll restore your access...please don't hurt me any more."

Cain released his arm. Leon took a few moments to recover from the pain, and to get the circulation back in his fingers. He switched on his computer and waited for it to warm up. He'd never been tortured before, and he sensed it could get a lot worse at the hands of such a ruthless man.

He opened the file labeled, "Abracadabra. doc." The history of what he'd done opened up, and he began to restore the original account numbers and pass codes. When he was done he said, "Everything's as it was, sir."

"How do I know you haven't lied to me, *genius*?"

Leon answered, "You don't strike me as someone I ought to lie to, mister. Access your accounts. Transfer money between accounts. It'll work, I promise you."

Cain was satisfied. This little puke wouldn't dare screw around after the pain he'd just endured. "Delete your file," Cain ordered.

Leon highlighted the folders and hit the delete key, knowing it was the last keyboard stroke he'd ever make. The only consolation he'd take to his grave was that he had just spirited away his tormentor's entire fortune.

When he'd originally hacked into and changed the accounts, he'd programmed them to accept a change to the original accounts and codes only one more time. They could be accessed only twice after that. On the third attempt, the accounts would revert to the new numbers he established when he first stole them. *Abracadabra. Now you see 'em…now you don't.*

His face hurt too bad to smile, so he smiled in his mind. These instructions were included in the package he'd just left at PostNet.

Cain spun Leon's chair around and looked deeply into his eyes. There was no longer any fear. He knew what was coming. "Leon…this isn't personal." Cain placed a hand on each side of the young man's face. With one quick twist, Leon's neck snapped in his powerful hands.

He searched the apartment to be sure the package wasn't still there. Satisfied he'd been told the truth, he prepared to leave. He pulled a good-sized package of marijuana from the nightstand next to Leon's bed. It never ceased to amaze him how brilliant people could succumb to the lure of drugs. It must have something to do with turning off the thoughts that never seem to allow their brains to rest.

Cain moved the body to the floor by the coffee table and tore open the package, sprinkling a small amount on the floor next to Leon. He flushed the rest and the bag down the toilet. He took Leon's bag back to his bedroom, unpacked it, and put the clothes where they belonged. He threw the overnight bag onto the closet shelf.

It was a shame he hadn't arrived soon enough to intercept the package, but it was of little concern. It warned of an attempt on November 22nd—nearly a month away. This coming weekend was Halloween. The president wouldn't be eating candy come Monday.

He came back to the living room and looked over the scene. Another DC drug deal gone bad. The bad guys tossed the apartment looking for cash, or more drugs, and beat poor Leon to death. There was just too much crime in this city.

Chapter Thirty-Four
TRICK OR TREAT

"Every chain...has got a weak link."

Aretha Franklin

Office of the National Security Advisor
The White House – Late October 1998

Tim McGuire was looking forward to calling it a night and heading home. It had been a long week of late hours, and he was ready for some time off with his wife and kids. Stretching his arms over his head, he rubbed his eyes and sat back in his chair. He looked at his in-box and saw that someone had put more mail in it while he was at lunch. A thick brown envelope caught his attention, so he reached for it with one hand and for his letter opener with the other. One more report from an intelligence agency was all he needed to cap off his week. He pulled the material from the envelope and began reading.

"November 22nd...Arlington Cemetery...assassination..."

The major sprang from his seat and ran to the general's office. "General Reilly, sir," he shouted, "You gotta see this!"

The general wasn't at his desk. Major McGuire came running out and slapped his hand on Sheila Oliver's desk. She jumped at the sound and said, "Major, please..."

Tim cut her off mid-sentence. "Sheila, where's the general?"

"He's gone for the weekend, Major, and he didn't say where he'd be."

"Where's the sergeant major?"

"Major, I have no idea. What's the matter with you?" she asked.

He went back to his desk and tried calling the general on his cell phone. It was unlike him to turn it off, and even more unlike him to steal away for the weekend without letting him or Sheila know where he was going. Murphy's Law had many corollaries. This was one of them: "When the boss wants you...you're always available. When you really want the boss...he's nowhere to be found."

Chapter Thirty-Five

RESURRECTION

"I can see clearly now the rain is gone. I can see all obstacles in my way."

Johnny Nash

Georgetown, DC – October 1998

No one in Washington pays any attention to a gray Ford Taurus. For that matter, no one *anywhere* does. DC is full of lost tourists, and the residents of trendy neighborhoods don't give a passing glance to a man studying a map spread across his steering wheel.

In his rearview mirror, the door of the elegant townhouse was reflected clearly off the rain-drenched street. A black government sedan pulled slowly to the curb and stopped. Luke Reilly grabbed his briefcase from the back seat and stepped out. He jogged spryly up the front stairs, and fumbled with his keys for the right one as the car pulled away. With a twist of the key, he opened the door and stepped inside. Lights came on in the front foyer, and a few seconds later, the bedroom lamp shone through upstairs curtains that were slightly ajar.

Folding the map and laying it on the passenger seat, Cain opened his door and stepped out of the car, then swung a small canvas bag over his shoulder. There was no one on the street, so he crossed quickly, hopped the standing water in the gutter and bounded up the stairs two at a time. He pressed the front door bell a couple of times. As he glanced over his shoulder to confirm that the street held no passers-by, he could hear Luke coming down the stairs. The door opened and Cain turned to face him.

Surprised to see his visitor, Luke said, "What in the world brings you here?"

Stepping inside and closing the door with his left hand, Cain pulled his right hand from his pocket and shoved the instrument he held against Luke's chest. Luke recoiled with a jolt, collapsing to the floor with a thud and trembling uncontrollably as though having a seizure. Cain locked the door and turned out the downstairs lights. He lifted Luke from the floor and carried him upstairs to his bedroom. The stun gun had run enough voltage through him to immobilize him for several minutes. Before it could wear off completely, Cain bound Luke hand and foot to the four posts of the brass bed.

Luke shook his head, trying to regain his focus and make sense of what just happened. It was as though he'd suffered a heart attack. One moment he was answering the door. The next, he was in excruciating pain. He was further frightened by the fact that he couldn't move. Looking up his arms to his wrists, he realized they were securely tied to the bed, as were his feet. He watched in confusion as his brother, Mark, stood on the opposite side of the room, rifling his briefcase and picking up items from the top of his dresser.

Mark then entered the closet and emerged with Luke's Barbour jacket, a plaid shirt, a pair of khakis, and his Rockport moccasins. Every item was the finest outdoor clothing money could buy. Typical

367

of Luke, none of it had ever been in the woods, but it provided just the right look for a weekend with the first couple at Camp David.

Struggling to speak, he moaned, "Maaark?"

Cain turned to face him, and smiled. *He looks different*, Luke thought. Something he couldn't put his finger on.

And then he spoke. The voice sounded like Mark's, or his own, but had a menacing tone all too familiar from his youth. "Greetings, little brother," Cain said with a wink and a smile.

Luke's mouth dropped to his chest and his heart pounded so loud he could hear it. His eyes grew wide, and tears welled in them as the recognition swept over him. In the process, he regained his composure and his voice returned. "Matthew? My God...it can't be you...you're dead!"

"Not hardly, pal," Matthew said as he began exchanging his clothing for Luke's.

Luke was awash in a sea of emotions. Shock...anger...confusion.

Matt bent over Luke and removed the ID badge from his lapel that identified him as a member of the White House staff. Rolling him from side to side, he removed his wallet, then emptied Luke's front pockets of change, a small Swiss Army knife, and a roll of Maalox tablets. From his coat pocket, Matt took Luke's reading glasses and tried them on, amused to discover that their prescriptions were almost identical. Matt could still shoot the eyes from a man's head at several hundred yards, but he had trouble reading a phone book in a brightly lit room.

Matt pulled a small overnight bag from the closet and packed enough clothes for a two-day trip. He tossed in a book, and Luke's shaving kit, and set the bag beside Luke's briefcase by the bedroom door. Finally, Matt pulled two small pouches and some other items from the canvas bag he'd brought with him and placed them in the side pocket of Luke's oilcloth jacket.

Events were moving too fast for Luke to comprehend. He lay on his bed, trussed like a Thanksgiving turkey, while his brother who'd been dead for thirty-two years moved around his home as though it were his own. *How did he know where everything was?* he wondered. Then he asked, "What are you doing? Why am I tied up...and what did you hit me with?"

Matt moved his face close to Luke and said, "You've been invited to a weekend getaway that I need to attend. We can't both show up, so you're going to stay home."

Luke became angry at that. "I don't understand...what are you up to?"

His tone callous, Matt replied, "I've been hired to kill your boss and his wife."

Luke's eyes widened in horror, and he tugged at his bonds. He opened his mouth to shout, "No! You can't!"

But the words never came out. Matt pointed a large pistol at Luke's chest and pulled the trigger. There was a muted spit, and Luke felt something penetrate above his left breast. His eyes rolled back, and his world went black.

Matthew Reilly, known throughout the shadow world as Cain the assassin, picked up the overnight bag and briefcase, turned out the lights, and descended the stairs as though he'd merely swatted a fly. This shot had been more than just business…*it was personal*.

The government car had returned, and was waiting for him at the curb. He laid the bag and briefcase on the backseat, got in, and the car headed toward the White House. As they pulled away from the curb, he waved to an elderly man out walking his golden retriever.

Puzzled, the old man shook his head in disbelief, and watched the reflection of red taillights on wet pavement until the car braked hard and turned the corner. He knew who Luke was. He'd passed him while walking Amos at least fifty times over the last five years. This was the first time the pompous ass had ever acknowledged him.

He reached down to pet his dog's head and said, "Amos, that's the first smile I've ever seen on that man's face. The president's job approval numbers must be on the rebound."

The limo slowed to a stop at the White House security gate, and Cain lowered the rear window. The guard rested one hand on the open sill and peered into the car. Checking the clipboard in his other hand, he flashed a warm smile and said, "Good afternoon Mr. Reilly. Are you still joining the Nortons for the weekend at Camp David?"

"I am," Cain replied in Luke's typical condescending manner. The guard waved him through with a wish for a pleasant weekend.

Charlie Thompson was a career civil servant, and had manned the employee entrance to the White House for sixteen years. It never ceased to amaze him that the closer a person was to the president, the more distant he became from everyone else. Charlie had never gotten more than a couple of words from Luke Reilly. He found that funny, since every time he'd seen him on television, he appeared to have diarrhea of the mouth. Charlie had met his kind before. Luke Reilly was one of those people who believed that if you couldn't help him get what he wanted, you didn't matter. Charlie Thompson knew he was no Tim Russert from *Meet the Press* or Tom Brokaw from *NBC Nightly News*. He was simply one of the little people…which, to Luke Reilly, meant he didn't exist.

When the car stopped, Cain got out and pulled his luggage from the backseat. He gave his overnight bag and briefcase to a young Secret Service agent to stage with the other luggage to be searched and loaded onto Marine One, the president's helicopter. Then, *as Luke*, he walked to the South Lawn entrance of the White House, where he was scheduled to meet the first family before boarding. Cain had studied Luke closely for months, and knew his habits intimately. The audio- and videotapes from the bugs he'd planted allowed him to imitate his every mannerism and nuance. Many were easy, for they were much like his own.

Luke was known to be distant in his personal relationships, but he was equally known for his weakness for animals, especially dogs. From the ground floor corridor, a young agent named Pete Wilson emerged sporting two springer spaniels on chain leashes and choke collars. One was black and white; the other was brown and white. Their coats were thick and shiny, and they looked splendid in their matching tartan plaid sweaters. Oscar and Felix were their names, and like many things this administration offered for public view, they were purely for show. They made their appearance anytime the president and first lady were on the White House grounds. The dogs made them look like the average American family, no different than yours or mine.

The facts were quite different. Neither Will nor Mallory could stand animals of any kind. They shed hair, had bad breath, and were inclined to pass gas whenever they were allowed in the couple's quarters, which was for photo ops only. They had been named by the Secret Service after the principal characters from the movie *The Odd Couple.* Will and Mallory were clueless to the inside joke the names represented. Their guardians, the Secret Service, considered the first couple to be odder than the movie characters the dogs were named after.

Felix and Oscar required a potty break before parading across the White House lawn. It wouldn't look good to have them stop to do their business while the president was on the other end of the leashes. The dogs had no bond with anyone but their caretakers, so they gladly accepted attention from anyone else who'd show them some. When Cain approached them, extending his hand, they began wagging their nubby tails excitedly.

Cain bent down to let them sniff his face while he scratched their ears. He told Agent Wilson he'd give them a walk while waiting for the president. Pete was happy to accommodate him, for he knew Mr. Reilly loved the dogs and they were in safe hands. Pete remained at the door looking alert. Like any branch of government service, the Secret Service has its shit details, but being the dog guard really was one, and Agent Wilson hated the fact the job was *his*.

Taking hold of the leashes, Cain led the dogs around the corner, out of view of the waiting press corps, and let them relieve themselves in the tall bushes next to the White House. When the dogs were through, Cain knelt down to give them each a Milk Bone biscuit he'd brought in his pocket. He casually looked over his right shoulder to make sure no one was paying him any attention, then removed a flat black pouch from his jacket pocket. He slipped it inside the stomach of Felix's sweater, and then quickly placed a similar pouch inside Oscar's. Each one was three-quarters of an inch thick, but was unnoticeable because of their thick coats and the plaid pattern of the sweaters. If by chance they passed close to a metal detector, the assumption would be that the chain leashes were the cause of an alarm.

Returning the dogs to Agent Wilson, Cain entered the corridor to await the arrival of the first family. Without acknowledging the Marine guard at the metal detector, he passed through without making a sound.

In the White House residence quarters, the president was completing his last phone call of the week. Through the cracked door of Mallory's bedroom, she and her daughter Kelli could clearly be heard having an argument. Kelli was being chastised for the umpteenth time for some perceived transgression regarding her choice of clothing. Mallory Norton was keen on the *proper image*, whether there was substance behind it or not. No matter what, Kelli would look perfect…just as her mother always did. A combination of anger and frustration on her face, Kelli stormed from the bedroom and went to her room to change clothes as she'd been ordered.

Life under the public's microscope was no way for a teenager to live. Kelli was looking forward to a weekend at Camp David about as much as she looked forward to a trip to the dentist. No one else her age would be there, and she was missing the Halloween dance at her prep school. Her mother impressed upon her that the polls would change favorably if they appeared before the cameras as a loving and unified family, pulling closer together in a time of crisis. Kelli could care less what the polls said. Her dad was a philanderer, and she thought her mother was a domineering witch. She was the only person in the family with a decent moral compass, and she was only seventeen. *God help the country,* she thought to herself.

Accompanied by three Secret Service agents, Will, Mallory and Kelli stepped out of the residence elevator on the ground floor. The entire group looked like they were on their way to a funeral instead of heading to the premier retreat of the presidency. The family walked in silence down the corridor that led to the South Lawn while one of the agents talked quietly into his microphone. As soon as Mallory saw Luke inside the entrance foyer, the scowl left her face, replaced instantly with a smile. One had to admit, both she and the president always worked the crowd, whether it was thousands of people or just one.

"Luke," she said warmly, extending her hand, "I'm so glad you're joining us this weekend. Will and I want to go over the latest polling data with you after dinner. I promise that will be all the business we'll do while we're there. All of us need a little break from the media sharks. The weather is supposed to be perfect. The rainy front passed through this morning, and it's supposed to be cool for the next couple of days. With the leaves at peak color, it'll be beautiful at Camp David."

"Mallory," Cain said, taking her hand, "I'm so happy to be included. You're taking me to one of my favorite places." Cracking a little joke to which only he was privy, he added, "If you died at Camp David, there'd be no need to go to heaven. You'd already be there."

The heavily armed Secret Service agents passed through the metal detector, causing it to ring like a Vegas slot machine. The rest of the entourage passed through without so much as a ding. Outside the door, the president took the leashes from Pete Wilson. He made no friendly gesture toward either dog until he saw the first reporter with a camera. As if he'd been cued, he reached down and rubbed the ears of both animals while they pranced in place with excitement. The waiting photographers dutifully recorded the mutual admiration of the president and his canine pals. Oscar and Felix led the way to Marine One as the rest of the party quick stepped to keep pace.

The Marine sergeant at the foot of the steps saluted the president as he and the dogs boarded. When the remaining passengers and agents were aboard, the guard climbed in and pulled up the steps. The brightly polished olive drab-and-white helicopter lifted slowly and banked away from the White House grounds.

Will Norton held Felix in his lap until he was sure they'd climbed beyond the reach of a long camera lens. When he was sure he couldn't be seen, he pushed the dog away and began brushing the hair from his clothes. "Damned dogs!" he muttered to no one in particular. Mallory rolled her eyes, then continued reading reports while the president closed his eyes to escape through a few minutes' sleep. Kelli put on headphones and turned up the volume so she could hear over the rotor blades. Cain sat behind the first family, and in front of the Secret Service agents in the rear of the aircraft. He shook his head in amazement at the sight before his eyes. *One big happy family!* he thought with irony.

Oscar and Felix curled up in the seat beside him and fell fast asleep. He gently stroked their heads. As in Memphis in '68, his tools of death were once again hidden inside a Trojan horse.

Upon touching down at Camp David, Mallory looked with disdain at the dogs sleeping with their heads in Luke's lap. In her mind it defied logic that a smart man like him would give the hairy mutts the time of day. As if reading her thoughts, he said, "Mallory…I've loved dogs all my life. We had a couple of retrievers when I was a kid, and I hate that the 24-7 White House schedule keeps me from having one of my own. Would you mind if I kept Felix and Oscar with me for the weekend?"

She laughed and shook her head as though he were nuts. "Knock yourself out," she answered. "I'll tell Agent Wilson they're all yours. He'll be thrilled!"

The senior agent on site, Hank Atherton, greeted the man he believed to be Luke Reilly and respectfully asked if he would follow him to the security office. Other than the Secret Service agents, he'd been the only non-family member aboard the chopper. Although he was a trusted advisor of the president and held the country's highest security clearances, he was still subject to undergoing a final search.

Atherton requested permission to look through his briefcase and bag. Though asked politely, Cain knew it wasn't really a request, so he offered no objections. While the search took place, another agent swept him with a metal-detecting wand. There was nothing out of the ordinary, as Agent Atherton knew would be the case. He returned the briefcase and thanked him for his cooperation.

Cain couldn't resist poking a little barb at the man responsible for protecting the first family. "You know," he said with a wink, "you'd think, after all these years, you'd consider me trustworthy enough that this wouldn't be necessary."

Atherton responded just as Cain predicted he would. "Sir, you know better than that. The Secret Service extends courtesy and respect to *all* who serve the president…but we never trust *anyone*."

Cain gently slapped Atherton's shoulder and said, "I knew that's what you'd say! No one will ever hurt the president while you're on the job."

Agent Atherton didn't crack a smile, but Cain knew he was beaming with pride on the inside. Flattery is one of the quickest ways to disarm an enemy, and though the Secret Service didn't realize it, they'd just lost this bout's first round.

As Cain walked to his guest cabin, he saw Pete Wilson standing outside his door minding the dogs. Cain knew that Luke had a reputation for being curt with subordinates and a brownnose with superiors. Secret Service agents didn't report to him, but Luke would never consider treating Agent Wilson like a peer. In his whole life, Luke had never believed he had any peers, and as a senior presidential advisor, at best he had very few. Knowing this, Cain summoned the agent with his best impression of his arrogant brother. "Agent Wilson?" he called. "I'll have a word with you, please."

"Sir?" he replied.

"Did the first lady inform you Felix and Oscar wouldn't be spending the weekend in the kennel?"

Wilson nodded affirmatively. "Yes, sir. I'm glad they're going to get some attention. You know the president and Mrs. Norton don't acknowledge they're alive."

Cain nodded in understanding and said, "I'll take them with me now, if you don't mind."

"Have a fine time with the guys, sir," he said, smiling as he handed over the leashes. Ecstatic to be relieved of pet patrol for the weekend, he headed for the security office. Perhaps he'd get the chance to act like a *real* Secret Service agent for a couple of days instead of a thirty-year-old pooch valet.

Cain stepped inside his cabin with the dogs in tow. Closing the door, he led the dogs toward the bedroom and said, "Come on boys...we have some unpacking to do."

The property now called Camp David was appropriated during WWII to provide Franklin Roosevelt with a safe retreat from the heat and humidity of Washington. Once the war began, spending time aboard the presidential yacht *Potomac* presented too tempting a target. German U-boats were plying the waters off the Atlantic coast, and the Secret Service wanted a self-contained retreat that could be properly secured.

Located in the gentle mountains of western Maryland about sixty-five miles from DC, Camp David's temperatures run roughly ten degrees cooler than the city all the time. The property was formerly owned by the government for the recreational use of federal employees, and was then called "Camp Hi-Catoctin." It fit the bill perfectly, and was renamed "Shangri-La" by the president in tribute to the utopia of the same name in James Hilton's novel *Lost Mountain*. The retreat for *many* federal employees became the private retreat of one. Years later, Dwight Eisenhower renamed the camp in honor of his grandson.

Most Americans imagine Camp David as a massive, rustic lodge. Instead, it's a collection of modest but well-appointed cabins and service buildings arranged in a compound nestled in the center of the property. If it were ever necessary, the president could go belowground to a large bunker complex built to withstand a nuclear attack. This portion of the camp is off-limits to everyone, including the first family. They have no need to see it unless the world loses its mind.

The security office where Cain had been searched was located in the cabin named Hickory. In addition to the security office, this building houses the White House Communications Agency, commonly known as "the comm center." The comm center contains every imaginable piece of office and communications equipment that the president, or any guest, might require. The grounds contain a complete fitness center called Wye Oak, which holds a gymnasium, sauna, racquetball court and locker rooms. There's also a swimming pool, a three-hole golf course, and a chapel on the property.

The camp is further protected by a forty-man unit from Marine Barracks 8th & I, located in Washington. This is the same organization that conducts the Friday evening parades during the summer months. Though in dress blues they put on a splendid show, the unit isn't comprised of toy soldiers. These men are a hundred percent Marine.

They patrol the perimeter of the property and control ground access at the gates. At night, a number of them remain hidden in the woods. The Marines are always armed, equipped with night vision aids, and well concealed. Guests are free to remain outdoors, but are instructed to stay in the lighted areas of the compound. Anyone in the woods past 2200 is considered fair game.

The first family had already settled into the president's quarters, a sprawling single-story cabin named Aspen. Cain was assigned a private suite in Walnut, a cabin just a few buildings away, connected by a meandering stone path.

Aspen looks just as you would expect a mountain retreat to look…rustic, but comfortable. In the lounge, there's a large stacked stone fireplace at one end, offset by a heavily beamed ceiling of stained tongue-and-groove pine boards. The walls of the lodge are random width pine with a warm stain that has darkened over the years. The dining room is located adjacent to the lounge, and is similar in many details. It too, has a large stone fireplace and matching beams in the ceiling. After a few cocktails in the lounge, and a short meeting, dinner would be served there.

The dining steward setting the table had always felt the formal dining room furniture seemed out of place with the rest of the rustic surroundings. The long table had been shortened by two leaves and was set for four, instead of five. The fourth place-setting was for a guest President Norton had said would be arriving by helicopter, later in the evening. In an effort to avoid her mother, Kelli was having dinner in her room. Under his breath, the steward said a short prayer for the lonely child, and then proceeded to light a fire in the fireplace.

The Nortons had excused themselves for a couple of hours. Mallory wanted a sauna and a massage; Will had grabbed his small carry bag of golf clubs and set off for the golf course, alone. He knew Luke didn't play, which was just fine because he didn't really want to spend any more time with him than he had to. By himself, he would be able to play all three holes before it got too dark to see. Kelli was in her room, talking on the phone to one of her friends back in town. Cocktails were scheduled for eight thirty.

In Cain's bedroom in Walnut, he reached in Luke's briefcase and pulled out a CD called "Frank Sinatra: The Voice...The Music," and put it in his jacket pocket. He thought the song titles said so much about the people here, and the reason for his presence. It began with "I've Got You Under My Skin," and ended with "From Here To Eternity." In between, it played "That's Life," "My Way," and "The Lady Is A Tramp." Cain had a perverse sense of humor, and though no one could share his little joke, sometimes he just cracked himself up.

He entered the back bedroom and pulled the plantation shutters closed, and then called the dogs to come. To avoid the prying ears of the Secret Service should they be listening, he took the dogs into the bathroom and began running water in the shower. The dogs had no idea what he wanted, but they were so happy not to be in the kennel that they followed wherever he went.

Cain sat on the toilet, looked at Oscar, and patted his palms on his lap. Oscar dutifully placed his front paws on Cain's thighs and began trying to lick his face. With a light pop on the muzzle, he gave him a gentle rebuke, generating a quick whimper. Reaching inside the sweater, he retrieved the first of the two black pouches and laid it on the counter by the sink. He rubbed Oscar's ears and gently pushed him to the floor. Making the same motions to Felix, he assumed the position previously occupied by Oscar. Cain reached in and pulled out the second pouch. He stood up, which caused Felix to hop down. Opening the door, he let both dogs back into the bedroom and closed the door again.

The pouches were the bi-fold variety, and were sealed with Velcro rather than snaps or zippers. He opened the first one and removed a small black pistol that held five bullets in its butt well magazine. It was a Kel-Tec .32 automatic. At only three quarters of an inch thick, and weighing a mere twelve ounces, it fit easily in the palm of a man's hand.

It fit the hand of a woman even better. Most women's purse guns were .22s or .25s, which have small bullets and very little stopping power. For years, the .22 has been a traditional favorite of Mafia hit men because it's relatively quiet and doesn't leave a big mess. Cain couldn't afford to chance the smaller weapon. When one's plan is to kill a president and his wife with only three shots, a .22 might not guarantee death. The .32 caliber round packs a bigger punch. At point-blank range, it was perfect for the mission.

From the second pouch, he removed an identical weapon and a two-inch long silencer that had been specially machined to fit it. The first three rounds of this pistol's magazine contained blank cartridges, and were followed by two .32 caliber steel jacketed, hollow point bullets.

Cain placed the silenced weapon in the right pouch pocket of the Barbour jacket and put the un-silenced pistol in the left one. He draped the jacket over the back of a chair in the bedroom, pulled the novel and shaving kit from his bag, and tossed the novel on the bed. Then he went to the wet bar and grabbed a fresh bottle of gin.

Taking the shaving kit and the bottle with him, he entered the bathroom. He emptied about three drinks' worth down the sink and ran some water to wash it down. Looking through the shaving kit, he removed a small bottle labeled "Visine Eye Drops," and placed it in his right front pocket. He turned off the shower that had been running for several minutes and returned to the bedroom. There, he took a fresh shirt from the overnight bag and a heather-colored cotton sweater and put them both on. He placed some ice cubes in a glass and poured it full of plain water, with a small splash of gin for aroma.

Making his way to the front porch of the cabin, he pulled up a comfortable bent-hickory rocker to sit in. Placing the gin bottle and glass on the table, he removed the novel from under his arm, kicked back in the rocker, and placed his feet up on the porch railing.

Moments later, Oscar and Felix came out on the porch and lay at his feet. He opened the book and pretended to scan its pages. To the Secret Service agents making their rounds in the distance, he aroused no suspicion. When they looked at the man on the porch, they saw what he wanted them to see—Luke Reilly, trusted advisor to the president, enjoying a well-deserved drink and some quiet time. As the chair rocked slowly, he reached down and rubbed Oscar's head.

Pete Wilson passed by on his way to Aspen, and stole a brief glance at the scene on the front porch of Walnut. Though few people in the White House cared much for Luke Reilly, Pete was inclined to cut him a little slack. After all, a man who loved dogs couldn't be all bad.

Chapter Thirty-Six

A TIME TO DIE

"There ain't no way to hide your lyin' eyes."

The Eagles

Cain's watch read eight o'clock. It was time. He closed his book, stretched, and went back into his cabin. He removed the CD from his jacket pocket and tossed it in the briefcase. Oscar and Felix were lying together on the floor, snoring in unison. He looked over the room to make sure he'd left nothing he needed. He put on the Barbour jacket, picked up the briefcase and walked over to the Aspen Cottage.

As he entered the doorway, he was greeted by Allan Tinsley, the agent on duty. "Good evening Mr. Reilly. Havin' a pleasant stay?"

"It's been great so far," Cain said. "Are the Nortons in the lounge yet?"

"No sir. They're still in their own bedrooms." Agent Tinsley looked embarrassed, as though he'd divulged a state secret. Cain shrugged his shoulders, signaling it was no secret they were giving each other some space. Tinsley continued, "They said to make yourself comfortable, and they'd join you in about twenty minutes."

"Thank you...I will."

At the end of the foyer, Cain paused and looked into the dining room. The table was set for four. Earlier, Cain had heard Kelli tell her mother she wanted to have dinner in her room. Either she'd changed

386

her mind, or her mother had changed it for her. He turned to the right and went down the hall.

Entering the lounge, he placed his briefcase on the coffee table, opened it, and retrieved the CD. As he walked to the stereo in the bookshelves, he removed his jacket and laid it across the chair near the door. The CD changer held six discs. He put the Frank Sinatra CD in the number two position, set to follow "James Taylor's Greatest Hits." Cain picked up the remote control, pressed the Play button, and put the remote in the left front pocket of his trousers.

There was an ice bucket on the bar, so he filled three glasses. He looked around to ensure no one had entered the room. Removing the Visine bottle from his pocket, he squeezed six drops of the clear liquid into one glass, and four drops into the other. He moved the spiked glasses to the left side of the tray, and moved his own glass to the right. He prepared a double Scotch on the rocks for the president, and a vodka tonic for Mallory. He poured himself a gin and tonic, drew the outside blinds, and walked over to the fireplace. The logs were burning slowly, so he grabbed a poker and moved them until the fire crackled and roared.

Mallory entered the lounge to the strains of James Taylor's "You've Got A Friend." She wasn't sure why, but Luke had been working very hard to please her lately. She was having second thoughts about letting him go, so she decided to butter him up a bit. "What an appropriate song, Luke," she said. "You've been a great friend to Will and me. We would've had a tough time becoming president without you."

The word *we* wasn't lost on Cain. Smiling like the true friend she believed him to be, he said, "Thanks Mallory. It's been my privilege."

Will Norton entered the room with a nod and a wave, and said, "Evenin', Luke."

"Good evening, Mr. President."

"You can knock off the 'Mr. President' crap up here, Luke. Let your hair down and relax a little."

"Thanks, Will," Cain said. He handed them their glasses. "I took the liberty of making us all a drink."

"Wonderful," Mallory said. "I could certainly use one."

The president pointed to an empty chair. "Have a seat, Luke."

Cain waited for Mallory to sit down first. She chose to sit on the sofa, near the lamp on the end table. Cain took a seat in a plaid wingback chair next to her.

The president plopped down in a deep, maroon leather chair on the opposite side of the coffee table from his wife, propped his feet on the table, and looked at Luke. "So how bad have I screwed the pooch this time?" he asked. "Do the people want my head as bad as that bastard independent counsel and the Republicans do...or can we salvage this thing before it goes as far as impeachment?"

"Will...I won't sugarcoat it," Cain answered, in his best impression of his brother. "You're on damned thin ice in the heartland, but you're okay where it counts, in DC, New York, and LA. The situation isn't unsalvageable, but it's going to take every nickel's worth of political capital you have to head off an impeachment. You're about to suit up for the Super Bowl of political dogfights, and nothing you've been through before even comes close."

Cain knew that, for security reasons, there are no locks on the internal doors of Camp David. The Secret Service, however, respects a closed-door meeting. As he handed Mallory the latest polling data from Luke's briefcase, he said, "Do you mind if I close the door, Mallory? I'd prefer Kelli not hear our conversation, if she should pass by."

"Go ahead," she said, thinking, *he must really have some troubling news.*

As he was walking to the door, he heard the sound of a helicopter approaching. The president heard it too.

"Oh, that reminds me," the president said. "I forgot to tell you...I invited your brother, the general, to join us for dinner. We've gotta get people in this town talkin' about something else. It might be time to put on the Commander-in-Chief hat again. Saddam Hussein's still refusing to comply with the United Nations inspectors. His latest violation of the cease-fire agreement might offer us the chance to make a swift strike on Iraq. We kill two birds with one cruise missile, so to speak."

The president paused a moment to enjoy his little joke, then continued, "Luke, I think it's what we ought to do. We restore my presidential image a bit, and we distract the attention of Congress and the people for a while from this other mess. Mark won't like the idea one bit, and he won't go along with it just to save my ass, so I'm dependin' on you to take him aside tonight and persuade him it's in the best interest of the country to inflict a little damage on Mr. Hussein."

The surprise news of Mark's imminent arrival had caused Cain's hand to freeze on the doorknob. He had followed what Will said even while his mind was evaluating the unintended modifications to his plan. His original plan was unworkable with more than the three of them in the room. His mind racing quickly, he said, "Will...before I approach Mark with your idea, the *three of us* have some things to discuss that I'd rather he not hear. Would you please ask the Secret Service to keep him in the game room...or maybe the foyer, for just a bit?"

"No problem," he said as he picked up the phone and rang the foyer security station. Agent Tinsley answered on the first ring, and before he could say his name the president barked, "Who's this?"

"Agent Tinsley, Mr. President," he replied.

"Tinsley...General Reilly's on the helo settin' down outside right now. Please see that he gets a drink and anything else he needs. Ask him to make himself comfortable in the game room until I call for him. We shouldn't be more than...he paused as Cain flashed a quick one and five with his fingers...fifteen minutes or so."

"Will do, sir!" Tinsley responded.

In three large sips, the president tossed back the drink Cain had made him and rose from his chair to fix another. Mallory studied the report and absentmindedly swirled the ice cubes in her empty glass. Having difficulty concentrating on it, she placed her glass on the end table, rubbed her eyes, and leaned closer to the lamplight.

Turning to retake his seat, Cain saw the president momentarily lose his balance. Norton shook his head as though trying to clear it, and plopped down hard in his leather chair. "Damn!" he said. "I must've downed that scotch too quick."

Mallory glanced up from her reading to hear what he'd said, and the room began spinning violently. "What'd you say?" she asked, in words that slurred.

They looked at each other in growing confusion, and then tried to focus on Luke. The narcotic overwhelmed Mallory, and her head crashed backward onto the sofa. Will gripped the arms of his chair, trying to stand, but couldn't move. He stared helplessly at Luke, and sank deeper into his chair. The president's eyes rolled back, and his head cocked to one side.

Reaching into his pocket, Cain pressed the number two button on the remote, and Frank Sinatra's soothing voice crooned. "I've got yoooou under my skin...I've got yoooou deep in the heart of me." The track had been recently altered, and a conversation had been superimposed over the song. Now accompanying the music was a conversation between the president, the first lady, and Luke Reilly that had been taped three weeks earlier in a private meeting at the White House. The topic had been the same...the sex scandal involving the president and the young female intern. At the present volume, the conversation could be heard through the door. This would keep the Secret Service at a respectful distance, convinced there was still a meeting going on behind the closed lounge door.

The knockout drops were strong enough to keep Will and Mallory asleep for hours. It was of little consequence, though—in minutes, both would be dead.

To pull off the assassination of the century, Cain had to set the stage to corroborate the account of their deaths that he would later give the Secret Service. The president's news about Mark's impending arrival forced him to accelerate his timetable. He walked quickly across the room and moved the chair that held his jacket to a position blocking the door, wedging the back tightly under the doorknob. Reaching into the pouch pockets of the jacket, he retrieved both pistols and the silencer.

By this time, the recorded conversation had escalated into a full-blown argument, with angry accusations and swearing from both the first lady and the president. Cain allowed himself a split second of self-congratulation: he'd done a beautiful job of editing and re-recording. The music remained at a level volume, while the volume of the argument escalated enough to cause everyone in the foyer to stop talking and turn their heads toward the shouting down the hall. Although disturbing to hear, he knew the well-trained agents wouldn't interfere.

Cain moved back to the sofa and placed the un-silenced weapon into Mallory's limp hand, pressing hard on her fingers so the gun would have her complete fingerprints. He laid her hand, still holding the pistol, in her lap. Grasping the silencer in his left hand, he began threading it onto the end of the other Kel-Tec .32. In the lulls between shouts on the tape, he thought he heard greetings being exchanged in the foyer. No doubt Mark had arrived. Just a few finishing touches, and the stage would be set. When everything was perfectly staged, he would kill both Will and Mallory, making it appear to be a murder-suicide. His four-step plan would take only seconds to complete.

Step one required him to kneel slightly behind the first lady. From there he would fire two rounds into the president's chest with the silenced pistol. The first would be a heart shot; the second would be higher and to the left, piercing his right lung. Cain would then pick up the spent shell casings and place them in the potted plant on the coffee table. Pushed deep into the dirt and covered over, they would never be found even when the plant was discarded. Step two was to place the silenced pistol to the first lady's right temple and pull the trigger. To avoid powder burns and blood on his own hands, he had donned Luke's gloves from the pockets of his jacket.

Step three called for placing the un-silenced Kel-Tec in Mallory's lifeless hand and, while holding it, firing the three blank cartridges. Two quick shots, and one more after a momentary delay. Just before firing the third shot, he would scream "Mallory, Noooooooo!" Then he would let the pistol fall to the floor, run to the door, and toss his gloves on top of his jacket. The three un-muffled shots would bring every guard in the camp running to the lounge.

As the Secret Service came in a hurry, he'd perform the final step, hitting track three on the remote to kill the taped argument and switch to the next CD. Mallory would have powder burns and residue on her right hand, and *Luke* would be the only one alive in the room to give testimony about what had happened.

393

The entire drill had been rehearsed no less than thirty times. Every move had been perfected, and Cain had no concerns. The country would awaken Saturday morning to the news of the tragic murder-suicide of the president and his wife. At any other moment in history, or with any other first couple, it would have seemed preposterous. With the Nortons, it would be only too believable. For weeks the press had been speculating about how angry and hurt Mallory was with her philandering husband. It certainly wasn't news that he'd cheated on her with other women, but, this time, he'd humiliated her *in the Oval Office* while she was working under the same roof. The public would understand she'd been pushed past her limits. Wives all over the country would empathize with her, and believe that she'd been pushed past *any* woman's limits.

The scenario would play equally well with Washington's political elites. They knew precisely how mad she really was, and how ill-tempered she could be when her plans were stymied. His actions denied her the presidency. The country had never before been willing to elect a woman to the White House, but after the co-presidency she had engineered, she was sure they'd been warming to the idea. In her mind, she was qualified, the country would've accepted her, and she would've cruised to victory for eight years of her own. But her oversexed husband had thrown a monkey wrench into her plans. It seemed Congress didn't have the stomach to convict him in impeachment proceedings, but it was apparent that the average citizen had worn weary of the Nortons' moral bankruptcy.

Will's coat tails were sheared, and could no longer carry her to the presidency. She would have to seek other elective office to prove herself outside of her husband's shadow. Four years of a six-year senate term would now be required to pave the way. It had all been so well orchestrated…if her husband could've just kept his fly zipped up.

No, there would be no problem with the public, press…or Washington insiders believing she'd had more than she could stand.

★ ★ ★

As Mark entered the foyer of the Aspen cottage, the volume of the argument down the hall began to rise. "Trouble in paradise?" he asked Agent Tinsley.

"You know how they can be, General," Tinsley responded. "They're passionate people."

"How right you are, son," the general said with a wink and a grin. "I believe *passion* is at the root of their present disagreement."

Agent Tinsley laughed briefly, and then stifled it. Though the general's sarcasm was funny, he felt unprofessional laughing at his boss getting an ass-chewing from his wife.

Kelli emerged through the kitchen's swinging door with a Coke in one hand and a bag of potato chips in the other. She was on her way back to her room when she stopped and began listening intently. Mark noticed, and approached her to distract her attention from the shouting match down the hall. There was no need for her to hear the venom in her mother's voice, or the feeble excuses her father was trying to sell her. "Good evening, Kelli," Mark said. "How are things at school?"

Placing her finger to her lips, she said "Shhhhh! Please, General Reilly, I really need to hear this!"

As a former Marine general, he was unaccustomed to being silenced by *anyone*, let alone a seventeen-year-old girl. "They'll work it out, sweetheart," he said as he placed his hand on her shoulder. "This isn't the first time your parents have had this argument."

"I KNOW!" she said with a puzzled look on her face. "They had *this* one three weeks ago."

Missing her point completely, he said, "Well, Kelli, I'm sure they've been over this territory several times in the past few weeks."

Raising her voice even louder, she said, "General, you don't understand what I'm saying! This very argument happened in our living quarters *three weeks ago.* I was there. That's not them talking now: That's a *recording!*"

The realization of what she was saying finally sank in. A recording of an argument behind closed doors at Camp David set off alarm bells in Mark's head, and a sick feeling in his stomach. Something was, indeed, wrong in paradise, and though unsure of what…he knew it couldn't be good. Adrenaline kicked in, and he bolted down the corridor toward the door. Kelli was just a few steps behind him.

Agent Tinsley had paid them little attention until Kelli began shouting about a recording in the lounge. As he saw them both take off in full stride, he jumped up to see what the commotion was about.

In the process he turned the table over, sending its contents tumbling to the ground. The phone made a clanging sound on impact.

At about the time the table hit the floor, Agent Wilson entered the foyer from the kitchen where he'd been getting some coffee. He dropped his coffee mug and pulled his 9mm Beretta from its shoulder holster as he hurried after the others. He made it into the corridor just in time to see General Reilly slam through the door, followed immediately by Kelli and then Agent Tinsley. He heard crashing glass as a lamp fell from a table inside the lounge and shattered on the hardwood floor.

Just as Kelli and the general screamed "No!" a loud shot rang out, and Wilson saw the back of Agent Tinsley's head splatter across the hallway wall. Wilson reached the doorway with his Beretta fully extended. What he saw made his blood run cold.

Unaware the door was about to burst open, Cain could hear people talking loudly in the foyer. He was ready. His stage play would be believed. It was now time for people to die, and it would only take seconds to accomplish. He moved between the sofa arm and the end table and knelt on one knee, directly behind the first lady. He was about to pull the trigger of his silenced pistol and send the first bullet into the president's heart when the door of the lounge burst open…followed by people shouting, "No!"

Cain was startled by the crashing door as it splintered from its frame and was flung against the wall. From the corner of his left eye he saw a figure lunging at him through the air. He quickly turned the weapon from the president to a position across his body and pulled the trigger. There was a spit and a thump. The man's forehead spewed blood, but the momentum of his dive kept him falling forward. His body crashed into Cain, throwing him across the table and knocking the lamp and glasses to the floor.

Cain rolled with the blow and rose to one knee at the base of the sofa, aiming his pistol toward the second threat moving his way. The teenaged girl lunged at him too, but he was able to move to his right and deflect her feeble assault. She crashed in a sprawling heap at his feet.

The third person through the door posed the most imminent threat. Agent Tinsley aimed his Beretta from a combat crouch and fired a single round at Cain. The noise was deafening, and the bullet grazed his ear just as his Kel Tec spit out two more rounds. Tinsley's head exploded, sending him reeling into the hallway…his body slamming into the wall and falling hard to the floor.

With his left hand, Cain grabbed the trembling girl by the hair. He sprang to his feet, pulling her in front of himself as a shield, the silenced pistol pressed against her right temple. The final threat, Agent Pete Wilson, now stood fifteen feet away, aiming his Beretta directly at Cain's head.

"Put it down or she's dead, Wilson!" Cain snarled.

Believing he was talking to Luke Reilly, and trying to control his shock, he said, "Mr. Reilly…You don't really want to do this!"

"Put it down…Now!" Cain repeated, but more controlled than before.

Wilson had no intention of complying. He could see the slumped body of the president in his leather chair. He could only see the top of Mrs. Norton's head. He assumed they were both dead. The entire detail had failed to protect his president and first lady. *He* was not going to fail their daughter.

"Mr. Reilly…*please* put down the gun," Wilson said. "You know you won't leave this room alive if you harm this little girl." Kelli's eyes were filled with terror, but Agent Wilson paid no attention to them. His eyes were glued to her captor's, quickly assessing the situation.

Every president receives weekly threats from crazies. The FBI, CIA and Secret Service keep long lists of people they keep an eye on when threats come in. Luke Reilly had never given anyone reason to place him on such a list, yet here he stood, not ten feet away, posing more danger than all the watch lists combined.

Wilson was trying to determine if Luke was on drugs, or had suffered some sort of massive nervous breakdown. He didn't take his eyes from those of his adversary…and for the first time he saw in them something he'd never before seen. The eyes of the man standing in front of him were not those of a crazy man. They were the eyes of a killer.

His grandmother used to say that the eyes were the window to the soul. If the man holding the gun to Kelli Norton's head ever had a soul, he'd lost it long ago.

Mark lay flat on his back, just behind Cain's feet. The rising bullet had entered at an angle and glanced off the steel plate in his head. He'd blacked out briefly, and his vision was momentarily gone. For the second time in his life he was hearing people talk—but was unable to see them. He flashed back to the hospital in Japan.

Whose voices were they? The Navy doctor...Lucias Hammond...Nurse Goodbody?

No...These voices were different. Their tone was harsh...the words bitter.

Just as three decades before, the lights returned, ever so slowly. Mark looked up and couldn't believe his eyes. His brother, Luke, was holding a gun on the president's daughter. *He has to be out of his mind,* Mark thought.

Mark could hear Pete Wilson trying to make Luke drop the gun, but they were in a volatile stalemate. Blinking away the blood trickling into his eye, Mark tried to think what to do. He was in no condition to fight. He wasn't certain he had the strength to even rise from the floor. That's when he realized there was only one way he could incapacitate his brother. The answer was literally inches in front of his face.

In one quick motion, Mark rolled to his side and, with all his might, clamped his teeth around his brother's Achilles tendon. His brother's blood gushed into his eyes and mouth as his teeth dug deeply into the soft flesh and muscle.

Cain screamed in agony as Mark's teeth cut sharply into the back of his ankle. Excruciating pain shot up his spine, causing him to black out for a second. His leg buckled...instantly crippled.

The momentary blackout was all that was needed. Kelli broke free as Cain screamed in pain and loosened his grip. She spun to her left, creating an opening for Agent Wilson. Cain's eyes opened just in time to see the muzzle flash from the Beretta, but he never heard the noise made by the bullets that smashed into his chest, lifting him off his feet and vaulting him over Mark's prone body. Mark's teeth were still clamped tight, imbedded deep in his brother's leg. The force of the impacting bullets nearly wrenched Mark's neck from his shoulders.

Agent Wilson was over the body as soon as it hit the ground. Cain's right hand, still holding his pistol, began to twitch.

Wilson put one more shot into the man's forehead. Unlike the movies, this villain wasn't going to rise up from apparent death and make one last valiant attempt to kill. There would be no more mistakes this evening. The president's guards had made enough mistakes for one night.

Within minutes, there were more people in the room than had ever been in the Aspen's lounge at one time. Secret Service agents and Camp David medical staff were tending to the president and Mrs.

Norton, and removing them from the scene. Agent Wilson was being questioned by Special Agent Atherton. A Navy corpsman attached to the Marine security detail was tending the general's head wound.

Mark sat in the plaid chair that only minutes before had held his brother. Other than the fact that he felt like he'd been hit with a sledgehammer, the wound wasn't too serious. It required only cleaning, a few stitches to close it, and a good-sized bandage. The physical pain was nothing compared to how he felt inside. He ached for Luke, and couldn't imagine what would cause him to snap as he had. As if looking for answers, he stared at his brother's lifeless body, and could still make no sense of it.

From his immediate family, he was the only one left. Matt had been dead more than thirty years. Both his parents were gone. Now he'd lost Luke. He continued staring at the body, unable to shake the feeling that something looked out of place. Something about the head...*or the neck.*

And then he saw it...barely visible above the collar of Luke's shirt, there was an old scar protruding from beneath it, extending up his neck.

That's what's wrong, Mark thought. *Luke doesn't have a scar on his neck.*

Like some form of déjà vu, Mark knew he'd seen the scar before...*but where?*

It had been a long time ago, and he'd only seen it once. For a moment, that was all he could remember. Then his eyes widened as the recollection hit him like a Mack truck.

Matthew!

His heart began pounding. That, combined with the realization that three decades of grief was based on a massive lie, made him violently ill. He stood and bolted for the bathroom down the hall as the Secret Service agents watched in stunned empathy. The man had just been a party to killing his own brother. It was enough to make anyone throw up.

In the bathroom, Mark wiped his face with a wet towel and let the water continue to run. He tasted his brother's blood in his mouth, and tried to rinse it away. He could still feel the impact of the bullets try to tear his brother from the grip of his teeth. As awful as it was, he couldn't afford to indulge his grief. *If Matthew was lying dead on the floor, wherein hell was Luke?*

He sat on the toilet and pulled a secure cell phone from his coat pocket with shaking hands. He dialed the third number from the autodial memory. He let it ring more than a dozen times. There was no answer. Mark disconnected the call and dialed another memorized number. It was answered on the second ring.

The man who answered was the one he needed to speak with, and Mark knew he would do as he was asked. Without saying his own name Mark said, "Don't say a word until I tell you to. Now…Do you recognize my voice?"

The voice on the other end answered in the affirmative.

In a hushed tone, Mark continued, "This is what I want you to do." He gave detailed instructions that he was assured would be carried out to the letter.

"Call me when you leave there," Mark said, confident his orders had been clear. "We'll meet when I get back tonight."

He hung up the phone, turned off the water, and returned to the mayhem in the lounge.

★ ★ ★

Agent Atherton sat on the edge of the coffee table and propped his meaty forearms across his thighs, then leaned close to Mark's face and said, "General Reilly...do you have any idea why your brother Luke would turn on the president?"

"*Matthew*," Mark corrected as he stared at the body, now covered with a sheet.

"Excuse me, sir," the agent said. "I'm talking about your brother. *Luke*."

"*Matthew,*" he repeated sternly.

Agent Atherton thought the general must be in shock, and decided he'd save his questions for later. He stood up and began to walk away.

Pointing to the body on the floor, Mark said, "The man under the sheet isn't Luke Reilly."

His announcement caused Special Agent Atherton to stop in his tracks and turn around. "What did you say, General?"

"The man lying there on the floor is not my brother *Luke*." Mark let out a weary sigh. "He's my brother *Matthew*. Luke, Matthew and I were brothers. Triplets."

Everyone in the room stopped talking, and all eyes were instantly on the general.

"Open his shirt," Mark said. "You'll find a scar on his neck that runs to his shoulder. It stops there, begins again on his upper bicep, then runs down his arm. Matthew showed me that scar the last time I saw him—*in Vietnam*—two weeks before we were told he'd been killed in action." He glanced up to see Atherton's astonishment. "Send two Secret Service agents to Luke's townhouse in Georgetown," Mark said. "Tell them to go quickly, but discreetly. I suspect they'll find Luke there, dead."

The agent's eyes widened, but he managed to keep from gasping.

"And...Agent Atherton," Mark added, his voice stronger now, "none of what happened here tonight leaves Camp David. I want to speak to every person here that's seen or heard about this before anyone returns to Washington. Assemble them all in the chapel ASAP."

Attempting to reestablish his authority, Atherton said, "Excuse *me*, sir...but this is a Secret Service matter."

The general's eyes turned to fire. "Like hell it is!" he shouted. "This is a matter of national security—and *I* am the national security advisor to the president of the United States! The Secret Service shit in their mess kit BIG TIME tonight...so don't go trying to play turf games with me, Agent Atherton. I guarantee that's a battle you'll lose!"

Atherton snapped his fingers in the direction of an agent, who immediately dialed the phone to carry out Mark's orders. Then he, too, stood looking at the dead assassin. He'd never heard of Matthew Reilly. He'd always thought the Reilly brothers were twins. Whistling softly, he said, "Triplets…Well, I'll be damned!"

Mark said a silent prayer to God that Matthew wouldn't be.

Mark was on the phone again when Atherton came in and interrupted. "General Reilly, sir? We've just heard from the agents that went to Luke's townhouse. Your brother isn't there, and his Jaguar is missing from his parking space." He took a deep breath before continuing. When he did, it was with deep sorrow. "We found a suicide note on his computer screen, sir. We suspect your other brother, perhaps with the help of additional conspirators, killed him to assume his identity."

Hank Atherton couldn't fathom the emotions that must be going on in the general's heart. Even so, he seemed to take the news as if he had expected it.

"Find him…as quickly as you can, and without raising alarms," Mark ordered.

A Marine helicopter was approaching the helipad to return Mark to Washington. Before the whirring rotor blades got close enough to drown out conversation, he gave Agent Atherton more instructions. "Take Matthew's body to the morgue at Andrews Air Force Base. Tag the body as a John Doe, and mark the file CLASSIFIED to the hilt. This didn't happen on a whim," he continued. "You find out how this went down. Keep the FBI and the CIA out of this." Mark's anger boiled to the surface, prompting his final words to Agent Atherton: "I'll personally see to it that anyone who speaks of tonight to anyone besides me or the director of the Secret Service will wind up in a maximum security federal prison."

Atherton believed his every word. He nodded and said, "Understood, sir!"

With General Reilly on board, the flashing red light on the belly of the banking chopper disappeared over the trees. Atherton got busy before the helicopter was out of sight.

Chapter Thirty-Seven

RECOMPENSE

"Where have all the soldiers gone?...Gone to graveyards...every one.
When will they ever learn?...When will they ever learn?"

The Kingston Trio

Washington DC - November 1998

The grinding hoist stopped as the casket reached the bottom of the burial vault. The two undertakers wasted no time detaching the straps, sealing the lid, and dismantling the hoist. If they worked for a commercial mortuary, they would've remained at the gravesite to console the family. They didn't. They worked for the government. So, without ceremony, they went about their business of closing the grave. Besides...the only man in attendance, the one rendering a salute, didn't look like the kind who required handholding.

This wasn't a normal funeral. It was clandestine business, and the sooner it was finished...the better.

Mark's salute was for the brother he'd once known and loved, not for the assassin that lay in the unmarked grave. He pictured Matthew as he had looked the last time he'd seen him.

In his mind's eye, he would forever be twenty.

Mark needed to believe that Matt had lost his mind in Vietnam. To believe otherwise would mean he had truly been evil. God would be merciful to the insane…but upon the evil He would pour out His wrath.

In a lifetime, most men lose their brother only once. Matthew had been taken from him twice. Mark had missed the funeral in '67, when the Marines laid Matt to rest with honors that rightfully belonged to another man. Today's funeral was more appropriate…an anonymous burial for a shadow figure who'd tossed his honor aside.

Mark had grown tired of cemeteries. Through the years he'd buried too many people he loved. Just two days ago, Luke's casket had been interred in Arlington. At the gravesite, the president and first lady had offered their condolences, as did all of the White House staff that attended. The Reilly triplets were no more.

Change was indeed in the air. Mark had informed the president he'd be submitting his resignation as national security advisor. The president indicated he would accept it, albeit with great reluctance. He offered his sincere thanks for all Mark had done…and, for once, Mark knew the sincerity was genuine.

Matthew was finally in the ground, but there was still unfinished business on the other side of the Potomac. Mark got in his car and drove back to Arlington.

He parked and walked to the freshly closed grave. The white headstone read "Luke Aaron Reilly." His thoughts shifted from his brothers to their father, John Francis. In the spring of 1947, John had given his boys Biblical names of character…names of men they could emulate…the authors of the Gospels. Matthew, the tax collector; Mark, the faithful companion…and Luke, the physician, the curer of ills.

In bitter hindsight, Mark knew his father had erred. Their lives more closely resembled other Biblical figures. Matthew chose the life of Cain, the murderer. Luke apparently had much in common with Judas. And Mark…well, Mark felt much like Job: tested through trials, pain, and incalculable loss.

For the first time in his life, he was using his power for personal reasons…using his position to circumvent the authorities. He'd always operated as though the world was black and white, with no shades of gray. People who could equivocate without recrimination had called him a Boy Scout. Mark had no such illusions about himself. He was no saint, but a flawed man, like every man since Adam in the Garden. At this moment, he felt like the odd man out…with both brothers having taken a piece of his soul with them when they left.

"Semper Fidelis," the motto of his beloved Corps, had been his own. In English it meant, "Always Faithful," and he loved its simplicity. He'd found it true from the South Carolina marshes of boot camp to every battlefield he'd ever shared with Marines: Vietnam…Beirut…Kuwait…Iraq. The Marines wore their honor like a crown. At times, it was all they had.

The sound of slamming car doors ended his pensiveness. Mark stood facing the river below, and did not turn around as the two men approached. He knew who they were. One was his trusted friend, Don Jansen. The other was dressed much like himself...the suit, the same color blue; the tie, a similar shade of red. The man's hands were shackled behind his back. Mark asked the sergeant major to remove the handcuffs. He unlocked them and walked away to give the men privacy.

Luke rubbed his wrists to restore circulation. Mark turned to face him. With righteous indignation, Luke roared, "What the hell is going on here?"

Mark calmly said, "Lower your voice, Luke. We're standing on sacred ground."

He complied, if grudgingly. "Why have I been treated like a prisoner, and held incommunicado for more than a week?"

"Because, brother, for all practical purposes...you're dead."

Mark stepped away from the headstone, and for the first time, Luke saw his name inscribed on it. Shock was an inadequate word to describe the look on his face. "The government faked my death?" he asked.

"The *government* had nothing to do with this," Mark replied. "If they had, you wouldn't be standing here right now."

He studied his brother carefully. They were both older, yet their features still appeared identical. Though it felt like staring into a mirror, he had no idea who the man before him really was. Years ago in Newport, Becky had pegged it right. She'd believed that for more than fifty years, the Reilly brothers had been identical strangers. Out of the blue, Mark asked, "*Why*, Luke?"

Confused, Luke replied, "Why *what*?"

"Why did you hire our brother to kill the president?"

His face betrayed neither surprise nor insult at the question. He simply said, "I didn't."

Mark contained his urge to explode. "*Don't* lie to me, Luke. I've got incontrovertible evidence that you did." Luke remained silent as Mark laid out what he knew.

Upon his return from the bloodbath at Camp David, Major McGuire had given him the FedEx package he'd received from Raoul, via Leon, that Friday afternoon. Though Luke hadn't been mentioned by name, it hadn't taken a rocket scientist to conclude he'd been the inside source, supplying information to the conspirators. Raoul had chronicled the many deaths for which Matthew had been responsible, laying out the details of the plan to kill the president as he spoke at John Kennedy's grave on the anniversary of his death.

Had Mark received the information before departing for Camp David, the Secret Service might have prevented the loss of life that took place there, and Matthew might well be alive. He wanted to believe that had been possible. Deep inside, however, he knew that it hadn't been.

Mark said, "The Secret Service now knows that the assassin, Cain, was our brother Matthew. They know he chose to assume *your* identity, not *mine*. Short of killing you, or me, there's no way he could've gotten to Camp David without your help. You were in this thing up to your neck, Luke. They know it, I know it…and so do you."

Luke remained silent for what seemed like a long time...then, he finally spoke. "I never hired anyone to kill the president," he said. "I was blackmailed into supplying information to set up someone else."

"Who?" Mark asked.

"The president's wife."

Mark's jaw dropped in disbelief. "Why would anyone involve you in a plot to kill Mallory Norton?"

"Because I could...and I'd have been ruined if I hadn't."

Now it was Luke's turn to tell Mark what he *didn't* know. Luke had been approached by a friend at the FBI, who'd informed him of a plot by an Indonesian business syndicate to assassinate the first lady. The syndicate feared a congressional investigation of their foreign campaign contributions in exchange for technology. They wanted to prevent her from testifying, should she be subpoenaed.

Like the little Vietnamese boy Mark had seen blown away on a trail years ago, Luke had tripped his own booby trap. He'd been so busy defusing landmines that could bring down the administration that he'd missed the only one of his own creation...the one where he'd diverted large sums of the foreign money to his own bank accounts. Apparently, someone had been smart enough to follow his trail.

At first, he thought he was on his way to prison, but then the agent offered him a way out. The FBI agent was Steve Driscoll...the former *Lieutenant* Steve Driscoll, Luke's bomber pilot and friend during the war. What Luke hadn't known about his old friend was that, for years, he'd been working both sides of the street. Driscoll was active duty

FBI, but he also ran his own consulting practice on the side. Luke had been ripe for recruiting, and was turned into one of Driscoll's private assets, just as he'd done years before to Leon Chandler...the computer hacker who'd found Luke's accounts.

Over the next few months, Luke had been drawn into a conspiracy he never sought. He was hurt and exhausted from years of working for the Nortons. The thought of eight more years with Mallory at the helm made him nauseous. He convinced himself he could save his reputation, avoid going to prison and, at the same time, save the country from her. As with the rationalizations of all desperate men...it made perfect sense.

Though they thought they knew what they were doing, neither Luke nor Agent Driscoll had ever been privy to the real plan. They had no idea that Cain planned to kill both the first lady *and* the president. The men from Jakaarta—who were paying the fees—wanted no one left to testify. Cain had apparently decided on his own to scrap Raoul's plan. He must've believed that her death would be questioned less under his scenario of apparent murder-suicide.

Luke hadn't known that *his* name was also on the list of targets. Apparently Cain had experienced an unfamiliar pang of conscience, or had simply been unwilling to kill him. The weapon he'd used to shoot him fired a tranquilizer dart instead of a bullet. Matthew may have thought that killing his identical brother would probably have felt like committing suicide and surviving to see the aftermath.

Mark held up his hand to interrupt. "What ever prompted you to steal the money?"

Luke's face winced in exasperation, and he blurted, "Because there's no retirement plan for fired White House staffers. Nothing. Nada. Zip! After all those years of busting my ass, the game was over for me. I'd discovered weeks before that Mallory wanted me gone. For a little while longer, she needed my skills, but as soon as she was through with me, she planned to let me go and ruin me on the way out the door. If I was through in Washington, I was going to need the money. I convinced myself I wanted it...and that I'd earned it."

Mark's face showed he didn't understand. The brother he thought he knew wouldn't have done that.

Luke's face was a study in burnout. "You tried to warn me off these folks, Mark. You told me I'd get burned if I remained on the team too long. You were right. The longer I was in the administration, the fewer inhibitions I had. Corruption just snuck up on me. I suppose I was like the proverbial frog, slowly dying in boiling water and refusing to jump from the pot. Like him, I was lulled into paralysis since I'd been sitting in the water from the time it was cold."

Mark listened in stunned fascination as his brother revealed even more. "Mark...we sold our souls to anyone and everyone who'd write a check—*including* the Chinese communists. With our help, they've advanced their capabilities to guide nuclear missiles by at least twenty years. Within three, they'll have hundreds aimed at anyone they choose, including us. We sold them what they couldn't build, or steal. The damage won't end with what's been done already, either. The Chinese will want more, and they'll get it because refusal means exposure of everyone who was involved."

Mark's emotions ranged from disgust to pity. One minute Luke's face showed contrition, and the next moment...righteous indignation. It was as though he'd been an integral part of the chicanery, all the while feeling he was an outside observer, helpless to prevent it.

Luke continued, "I'm sorry to have been a part of this, but one day your sons, and many like them, might die on a battlefield at the hands of technology we sold the Chinese. It was treason, Mark, and no one in the public or the press cared about anything but oral sex in the White House."

Mark could stand no more. Cutting him off, he said, "Dammit, Luke...People get the kind of politicians they deserve. If they tolerate tyrants, they'll get one. If they condone corruption, they'll be led by the corrupt. You've always believed it was your destiny to cure America's ills...and now you're whining because you laid down with dogs and got fleas. What you've never understood is that no one ever anointed you to cure a damn thing. God sent His only son to save the world, Luke...not you! Mallory Norton can plan and scheme all she wants. So can her husband. It doesn't matter one whit. God's plan for the world will unfold in His own good time, *without* any help from you."

The rebuke caused Luke's self-righteousness to fade. In short order it was replaced by resignation, and his face showed deep remorse. "I can't say enough how sorry I am, Mark," he said. "I never knew that Matthew was alive, or that he was a professional assassin. For thirty years, just like you, I believed he was killed in combat. I'd have never intentionally done anything to destroy our memory of him. I never meant for things to turn out this way."

No one ever does, Mark thought. Luke was no different than anyone else who got caught with his hand in the cookie jar. He didn't regret what he'd done—he regretted getting caught. Mark did believe, however, that Luke was sincerely remorseful about his actions unveiling Matthew as an assassin; stripping him of his legacy as an American hero. The boys had always been told, "Regrets are hard to live with, but remorse can kill you."

Luke's feeble apology had an all-too-familiar ring. It was the same worn-out excuse always offered by men who considered themselves the victim. Mark recalled the many times he'd heard an incompetent Marine snivel similar words after making a mistake that had cost another Marine his life. Never mind that the man lying dead on the ground couldn't hear the apology, and had no use for it if he could.

Men like Luke always believed they were too smart, too noble or their motives too pure for a mistake to be their fault. They always rationalized, "I can't be responsible...I really meant well." In so many words, this is what his own brother was saying now.

Mark said, "Luke...you are one naïve piece of work. You still think this whole affair is about you and your 'intentions.' Nothing could be further from the truth. You were just a fly on the back of the horse. You didn't orchestrate this plan. Your own brother used you as a pawn. He had an agenda all his own, and he played you like a cheap guitar."

The words struck Luke like a kick to the groin. It hurt to know that, Matthew—the brother who'd always held him in contempt for his weakness—had manipulated him once more. The realization caused bile to rise in his throat…and it burned.

At this moment, Mark truly pitied Luke. He'd always been a true believer, out to change the world. He was smarter than many, but in politics, the smart sometimes get burned by the shrewd. Like a moth, he toyed with the flame and lost. Like the third man on a match, he'd made the fatal mistake of letting it burn too long, and had been caught in Matthew's crosshairs, facilitating his own egotistical plans.

The price for Luke's naiveté wouldn't be his life, but rather a lifetime of knowing he'd been used by old friends…and close family. Despite his keen intelligence, he'd never seen it coming. This would be a sentence harder than life behind bars.

As if Mark had spoken the words out loud, Luke breathed a deep sigh…and his shoulders sagged.

Mark summoned Don Jansen to return. "Is he going to arrest me now?" Luke asked.

"No," Mark replied. "He isn't the law, Luke…this is my good friend, Sergeant Major Don Jansen. He saved my life in Vietnam. He saved yours last Friday night." Then Mark told Luke about his realization that, if it was Matthew on the floor at Camp David, then Luke must've been either killed or incapacitated in some way. So he called Jansen from the Aspen cottage bathroom and directed him to go to Luke's townhouse before Atherton's men arrived.

The sergeant major had arrived just in time: He passed the government cars as he was spiriting Luke away, unconscious, on the backseat of his own Jaguar. To make it appear that Luke had either killed himself in remorse, or been killed by others to keep him quiet, Jansen had left a suicide note on the screen of Luke's computer.

From there, Jansen drove him to his hunting cabin in Maryland, sedated him further, and placed him under lock and key. He drove Luke's car back to Washington, and in the early hours of Saturday morning, drove it into the Potomac. He then placed a cell phone call to the Metro Police to report seeing a car veering off the road into the river. After he returned to the cabin, he contacted the reporter from *The Washington Post* and was interviewed over the phone.

"Last Sunday morning, your Jaguar was pulled from the Potomac," Mark told Luke. "The door was open, and your body wasn't in the car. Your funeral was held on this very spot two days ago. The story of your suicide has been in the news for a week. *The government believes the story, too.* They think Cain killed you to assume your identity. It was probably a scenario he actually considered, and might have carried out...had he made it back from Camp David."

Luke opened his mouth to speak, but Mark put up a hand to stop him. "It's in the government's interest to believe you're dead. The security detail protecting the first family dropped the ball last week. The Nortons' friend and close advisor betrayed them and tried to have

419

them killed by his brother, the long-dead war hero. By the way—this dead war hero had been an international hit man for the past thirty years, and had managed to remain unidentified, all that time, by our nation's intelligence forces."

The sergeant major handed Luke the front page of the past week's Sunday paper, detailing his tragic death. The report pointed out the irony that the Norton administration had begun with the suicide of a trusted advisor, and was concluding with the suicide of another. Luke thought the story read like Greek tragedy.

Mark said, "Luke, everybody burns if this assassination attempt becomes public. With you in a grave in Arlington, and Matthew in an unmarked grave across the river, *the lid stays on*."

Luke looked up from the newspaper article and asked, "What am I to do now?"

"If you want to go on living, Luke, you better start trusting me."

★ ★ ★

Luke's mind sorted through scenarios...searching for an option, an ace in the hole to trump the cards fate had dealt him. There wasn't one. All the cards were already on the table. Any way you cut the deck, he had lost his right to live as Luke Reilly. In truth, his eyes had the shell-shocked look of someone who had seen his life flash before him, but wasn't yet dead. "Where do I go now, Mark? How will I live?"

"Matthew has provided for you, Luke."

"How? He's dead!"

"The warning of the assassination plot wasn't the only thing we received from Matthew's associate," Mark said. "In that same package, there were listings of Matthew's properties and financial holdings. Foreign banks mostly: numbers, access codes, everything. Matthew was a very wealthy man. You're going to donate two thirds of his substantial fortune to charity. That's the least he can do in exchange for the lifetime of pain he inflicted on the world. The remaining third will afford you a handsome retirement. Invest it wisely."

Luke had no idea how much money Mark was talking about, but it seemed to be an appropriate disposition of Matthew's fortune.

"If you don't want Matthew's enemies tracking you down and putting a bullet in your head, I suggest you spend some of the money on plastic surgery, liquidate the rest, and then find the place of your choice to live—outside the U.S., of course." Mark reached in his coat pocket for one of Matthew's passports, which had been included in the package from Raoul. The name on the document was Paul Peterson. He asked Luke, "Do you remember the Bible story of Saul of Tarsus?"

"What about him?"

"Saul was a ruthless enforcer, more violent, but not unlike the role you played for the Nortons. He was a Jew, and he defended his faith by persecuting the Christians who threatened it. He hunted and imprisoned them. He was a misguided sinner, but God had use for a man of such passion, so He changed his heart. With the change in

421

heart, He changed his name to Paul. In essence, God forgave Saul's past, made him a new man, and gave him the mission to *change the world.*"

Mark held his brother by both shoulders, and looked into his eyes. "God wasn't through with Saul, and I doubt He's through with you, either. You've always relied on your own abilities to change the world, yet for all you've tried to do, you've made no lasting impact. If you still want to change it, *little brother*, it might be time to ask the God you used to know for some help." Mark removed the hand holding the passport from Luke's shoulder, and handed the document to him. "Here's your new identity. Your new name is Paul."

Thirty years ago, a passing remark made in a similar tone had so infuriated Luke that he lashed out at Mark, and they didn't speak for years. This time his words seemed comforting. "That's a big leap of faith for me," he said. "I haven't spoken to God since Vietnam."

"You didn't speak to *me* for a long time, either," Mark said, "and yet *we* were able to become friends again. Will you trust me?"

He smiled and answered, "No sweat, Mark."

The words came without warning, and they stung like a slap to the face. No matter how much Mark had hated that phrase before, today it seemed appropriate. Even though he associated the words with tough times in his past, those words had always preceded the job getting done.

Mark nodded in concurrence and returned his brother's smile. "Luke," he said, "I want you to go with Sergeant Major Jansen. He'll take you out of the country. He's my friend, and you can trust him.

Do *whatever he says*, and he'll keep you alive. Until you've changed your appearance, he'll be the conduit through which we'll communicate."

Luke asked, "What are *you* going to do?"

"Next Friday, President Norton will receive my resignation. Within the month, I'll announce my intentions to run for Hiram Smith's senate seat. To win it, I may need your help. Can I count on that...*Paul*?"

"How can I help you if I'm in exile?"

Mark smiled. "When the time is right, we'll talk. I believe someone with your experience getting candidates elected should be listened to. Don't you agree?"

Luke couldn't remember the last time either of his brothers had asked for his help. He felt as though he'd finally been given the respect he always craved from his siblings. It was obvious that Mark had taken actions, at great personal risk, to save him from a life in prison. He'd been given a new name, and a new life to go with it. Luke would do whatever he could to help his brother. Where he felt burned out and defeated only moments before, he once again felt the spark of passion in his soul. Luke's broad grin returned, and they embraced.

Mark said, "Be safe...We'll talk soon."

Don Jansen and Luke got into the gray government car and drove away. Mark watched them until they were out of sight.

★ ★ ★

He crossed the cemetery to the site of Matthew's original grave. Standing tall in the sunlight was the stone that bore his name...the stone that, for thirty years, had hidden the true identity of the Marine buried here.

This was another wrong that demanded recompense. Before submitting his resignation, Mark would ensure that Lance Corporal James Ashcroft would receive the honors at Arlington that had been improperly bestowed upon his partner, Sergeant Matthew Reilly. The identity on the white marker would be corrected, and would guard over the Marine who had *really* died for his country. The cross carved by his name on the Vietnam Memorial Wall would be modified into a diamond, indicating his change of status from missing in action to confirmed dead. No longer would his family bear the pain of uncertainty, shared universally by the families whose loved ones never came home.

Mark would make sure that Jim Ashcroft's family would never learn the actual circumstances of his death. Matt and Jim would simply trade places, forever. Matthew would assume the role of MIA, and Ash would become one of the 58,178 heroes whose names are carved on The Wall. All the Ashcroft family needed to know was that their son, and brother, had died at the hands of his enemy while defending his position. There was no lie in that statement.

In the past, God had given Mark many occasions to question His mercy. Today wasn't one of them. Even as he was helping his brother avoid prison, God had permitted Mark to honor his officer's oath.

Upon graduation from the Academy, he'd taken an oath to "defend the Constitution against all enemies, foreign and domestic." For three decades, he had fought his country's enemies on foreign shores around the world. On his native soil, he had taken a bullet for the president of the United States, and his family. He helped bring about the death of one of the world's most formidable assassins, and in the process, been responsible for killing his own brother. His oath had been to *defend* the Constitution...not to ensure that justice was done *after* its defense.

Like most Vietnam veterans, Mark felt he'd been shabbily treated afterwards. It left a bitter taste in his mouth to this day. America's termination of the Gulf War, stopping short of total victory, had brought back the same bad taste. What he'd just done for Luke left no sweeter flavor, but as he had learned to live with the disappointments of war, he would learn to live with this one, too.

Will Norton and his wife had nearly destroyed the Reilly triplets. In Mark's mind, Luke's flight from justice was equitable compensation.

He returned to his Corvette, opened the door, and slid into the driver's seat. He absentmindedly touched the stitches in his head, and winced in pain. A flood of images flowed through his mind...from childhood, through wars, to this very cemetery. The Reilly boys had been through a lot over the last half of the twentieth century.

425

Mark had learned two truths in thirty years of service to his country. The first was the observation made by Tip O'Neill, the former Speaker of the House, that "All politics is local." The other was that soldiers don't fight for lofty ideals, philosophies, or even countries. They fight for the people they love, and frequently that means the man on their left and the man on their right. *If all politics is local...then all war is ultimately personal.*

Matthew had sold his soul to the shadow figures who play God, determining who lives and dies. Luke sold his honor to the politicians who manipulate the masses for personal gain. And what of himself? Well...he had leapt from the pedestal of his black-and-white world and waded through several shades of gray to save his remaining brother.

He had one final obligation to fulfill from this place. On Matthew's behalf, he said a prayer, asking Lance Corporal James Ashcroft for his forgiveness. He said another one asking God to watch over the country he loved.

In the end, faith and love were the only things he could hold onto. It was time to go home to his children and shower them with both.

Turning the ignition key, the Corvette's engine roared to life. Revving it twice, Mark smiled to himself and thought...*even God has to love the sound of a Vette.*

His prayers hitched a ride on the engine's roar, echoed across the river, and floated to the heavens on the crisp autumn breeze.

★ ★ ★

About the Author

Robert Sutter graduated from Tulane University in New Orleans, and served as a captain in the United States Marine Corps.

He has been a professional salesman and sales trainer for the past twenty-five years.

A native of Atlanta, Robert lives there with his wife Laura, and their three children.

Odd Man Out is his first novel.

Robert Sutter

Author's Notes

Odd Man Out is a work of fiction. It draws heavily on real events that took place in the last half of the twentieth century, but the story is a fabrication of the author's imagination. Every conscious effort has been made to attribute no dialogue or quotes to real people who actually lived during this period, or who participated in actual events, unless those comments are documented in speeches, the media, or have become a part of the public record.

For this reason, the names of the members of the first family of the United States have been changed in this novel. Although many events surrounding the presidential term between 1993 and 1998 are integral to this story, all dialogue of the first family in this novel is *fictitious*. In *no way* should their dialogue be considered factual statements attributed to, or made by the real president, first lady, or their daughter. For dramatic purposes, *Odd Man Out* refers to these characters as, Will, Mallory, and Kelli Norton.

A scenario is painted here, as well, that suggests that Dr. Martin Luther King may have been killed by someone other than James Earl Ray, who confessed to the murder, was sentenced to prison based on that confession, and then subsequently recanted. Ray maintained his innocence, and pressed for a trial until April 23rd, 1998, when he died in prison of liver failure. The King family, as well as many of Dr. King's friends, believed there had been a conspiracy against him, and that Ray had been used as a pawn.

In November 1999 a wrongful death civil suit, *King v. Jowers*, was brought by Dr. King's family. After a four-week trial, the jury returned a verdict finding that James Jowers and "others, including government agencies" participated in a conspiracy to assassinate Dr. King. Among the "others" alleged to have been a part of the conspiracy was a mysterious person known only as "Raoul." In June of 2000, the United States Department of Justice issued a report regarding the King family's allegations. They investigated the allegations for a year and a half, and citing many inconsistencies in the statements and testimony of the accused parties, including James Earl Ray, issued their conclusion that none of the allegations were credible. The report recommended no further investigation "unless, and until reliable substantiating facts are presented." The author used this trial and report as the foundation for creating an alternative assassination scenario. Creative license was taken to develop the character of the fictional assassin known as, *Cain*. No offense was intended to the King family.

The chapter depicting the evacuation of the Saigon embassy is a relatively factual account, with the exception of the presence of Mark Reilly, a fictional character. Major James Kean, Ambassador Graham Martin, and Master Sergeant Valdez are real. Their story was chronicled by both *MSNBC* and T*he History Channel*, and is the source of the account contained here.

The account of Oliver North's presentation at the U.S. Naval Academy was drawn from Robert Timberg's book *The Nightingale's Song*. (Simon & Shuster, 1995.)

Reference was made to "The Best and The Brightest" when referring to the people in and around the administration of John F. Kennedy. This term was coined in the book of the same name by David Halberstam. (New York: Random House, 1972.f)

The Walk to Emmaus is a registered program of The Upper Room Ministries, Nashville Tennessee.

The description of the ceremonial flag folding at military funerals comes from an Internet account attributed to the 21st TSC Chaplain, United States Army.

Robert J. Sutter

Acknowledgements

Over the years I've heard people referred to as "self-made men." To me it seems a ludicrous term, because every successful person I've ever known received help, in ways large and small, throughout their lives. My father used to say, "Self-made men have short memories." My friend, Eddie Smith says, "If you see a turtle sittin' on a fencepost…it didn't get there by itself."

Like most others, this book would not have been possible without the help of many friends and associates. I would be remiss if I didn't acknowledge them and offer my sincere thanks.

First and foremost I thank GOD…through whom all things are possible.

I want to thank my wife, Laura, and my children, Preston, Mitchell, and Emily…from whom I stole time to write this book. My in-laws, Jim and Emily Mitchell, were also very encouraging. My brother Lloyd, my sisters Ellen Kappel and Hannah Martin, and the rest of my rather large family have always given me their support.

My brother, Corporal Richard F. Sutter, USMC, deserves a special thank you I hope he'll hear. In the summer of 1967, just a couple of weeks short of coming home, he gave his all for his family, his Corps, and his country, in a valley near Khe Sanh. Semper Fidelis…Richard.

Lifelong friends, Jim and Robin Sander, and Chip Parker offered much encouragement while writing this story.

Rick Lovell, of Rick Lovell Illustrations in Alpharetta Georgia, did a marvelous job designing the book's cover, and my photograph is courtesy of Deb and David Clymer. Arlene Robinson, my editor, provided outstanding advice, service, and encouragement. I also want to thank everyone who proofread, or provided technical advice to make this story better. They include the following:

Parke Ellis of New Orleans, Jim Lyons and Jim Pociask of Alpharetta Georgia, Mike Tripp of Barrington, Rhode Island, Coletta Kemper and Joel Wood of Washington, DC.

Special thanks go to two friends, Tom Pritchard of Atlanta and Mike Zak of Boston, who kept me honest and true to the story by pointing out places where it needed to be tightened, or where it needed to be expanded.

Finally, I want to thank Meredith Reddy, my son's high school English teacher. Her enthusiasm for reading an unpublished manuscript reminded me that, even in an age dominated by visual images, ideas expressed in the written word are still very powerful.

Semper Fi to you all.

Printed in the United States
910700001B